"I found the novel both engrossing and moving. I was quite sorry to finish it and found myself thinking about the events and relationships for a long while afterwards. I also enjoyed the descriptions of Spain, which were very atmospheric. But for what it's worth, I thought it gave real insight into what it is like living around Asperger's – I could certainly relate to the emotions and long-term impact on family life." - Jackie Harvey, mother of a child with Asperger's traits.

"A heartfelt and emotionally authentic moving novel written with love. By reading it, you can understand that we all see the world in different ways." - Margarita Sainz, farmer.

"I really enjoyed the very simple and natural way that Sofia Lake describes Isabel's feelings and emotions in the book. She manages to describe the character with great sensitivity, allowing the reader to empathise with Isabel's anguish, which creates this continual feeling of not knowing or understanding the rules by which she is meant to express her emotions, and her superhuman efforts to try to overcome these difficulties. This is a beautifully written novel which brings us a little closer to understanding of Asperger's Syndrome." - Beatriz Walter, clinical psychologist.

"A book of great emotional impact about Asperger's syndrome, which is unknown to so many people. An exciting, humane and moving story written in simple language, which grips you from the beginning to the end." - Juan Manuel Bustamante, solicitor.

"Sofia Lake paints the life journey of Isabelle in stark and raw colours. The intertwined threads of family, hereditary and environment, sometimes overlooked by other writers, are ever-present in this book and give a deeper understanding of Asperger's Syndrome." - Marita Cunniffe, special needs co-ordinator

"One's heart cannot fail to go out to Isabel through her often bewildering experiences as she grows. It makes for an interesting and sympathetic exploration of the effects on the individual with Asperger's traits." - Wendy England, mother of two children on the autistic spectrum.

A CONSTANT FEELING OF NOT KNOWING

Sofía Lake

authorHOUSE®

AuthorHouse™ UK
1663 Liberty Drive
Bloomington, IN 47403 USA
www.authorhouse.co.uk
Phone: 0800.197.4150

This is a work of fiction. All of the characters, names, incidents, organisations, and dialogue in this novel are either the products of the author's imagination or are used fictitiously.

Published by AuthorHouse   07/29/2015

ISBN: 978-1-4969-9297-0 (sc)
ISBN: 978-1-4969-9296-3 (hc)
ISBN: 978-1-4969-9298-7 (e)

Print information available on the last page.

This book is printed on acid-free paper.

There is no fear in love;
but perfect love casts out fear,
because fear involves torment.
But he who fears has not been made perfect in love.

—1 John 4:18

For John, my three children and Anita

TABLE OF CONTENTS

PART III: ISABEL

INTRODUCTION

In this novel, there are two different characters and the setting is Spain. The main character is Isabel, who manifests a different way of thinking based on rigid visual and rational thinking, leaving her in a position of not knowing, and where the internal and external environmental fear constantly collide. In her internal fight against loneliness and isolation, she will suffer delays in processing information, with an inability to get in touch with her own feelings and a great difficulty verbalising emotions, making it very hard to connect with people and social situations. Fear can easily become terror and the systemic bodily response will then be more like a deep panic; but there is the will and determination to conquer her surroundings, and an internal trust which matures and develops within the constant feeling of not knowing.

The second character is about her father, Roberto Grimaldi, and his emotions and poor empathy dictating the environment and dynamics of the family. His personality contrasts in a secondary way to Isabel's. The constant feeling of not knowing is obvious in both characters, but it is the willingness to connect and the determination of the younger character that establishes the clear difference between the two.

This work is fiction and, like any other novel, it is based on imagination, knowledge, personal experiences, and knowledge of others. All of the characters, names, incidents, organisations and dialogue either are a product of my imagination or are used fictitiously. It is structured in three parts: "Growing up with Dad", "Finding Myself" and "Isabel".

PART I
GROWING UP WITH DAD

Chapter One

MY FAMILY

"Alex, I'm going to shoot you," said Dad.

I instantly froze in place and raised my eyes to see where my brother was standing. My chest filled up with tight pressure, and my breathing became fast and difficult.

"No, Dad, don't do it!" I implored, standing just two metres behind my father.

My plea alerted Miss Spencer's, Mum's and Mr Garcia's attention, but before anybody could intervene, Dad shot his rifle twice towards Alex's left backside as he was crossing in front of him from the pine trees, without any time to hide.

Seven days earlier

The sun was setting and it was time to return home. I walked in silence all the way back from the park, holding on tightly to the side handle of the pushchair where my younger sister Beatriz was sitting. Miss Spencer, our nanny, was taking us back home and I knew that my future was inevitable. It was 13 September 1971 and school was starting the next day.

Beatriz was a smiley and chubby toddler who had just turned two a month ago. Her eyes were dark brown, and most of the time, she was a placid little girl. Her ears, though not large, were noticeable, sticking out through her short silky black hair and giving her a special look of being alert and ready for adventure. My father disliked the look of them and I could not understand why, as they were similar to his. Beatriz's tummy was still babyish, protruding through her little white dress while she was sitting and nearly reaching the metallic bar that she was holding on to with her two little hands. Her dangling feet in their navy blue shoes looked miniscule compared to her robust and sausage-like legs. Beatriz was a happy baby and Miss Spencer was always taking great care of her. I could not help feeling slightly jealous of how fortunate Beatriz was, being allowed to stay home and play while I had to go to school the following day.

I was already feeling incredibly tense and a sense of anguish was starting to overwhelm me, but I could not avoid gasping when the three of us turned the corner into our street. The sun was shining at the end of the road, just above my eye level, like a ball on fire. It was quite difficult to look straight ahead at it, as the brightness was hurting my eyes; the glare reflecting in my glasses was making the light even more intense. My eyes could only fix on the sea, which was lying right underneath the sunset. It was absolutely breathtaking. The seawater looked like real silver, reflecting the path that the sun had laid down on its way to the end of the ocean, moments before disappearing behind the line that separated the sky from the water. Colours of red, pink, orange and yellows painted the whole sky just above the sun, with hardly any clouds visible on the horizon. It was beautiful.

Miss Spencer was especially quiet. She had started working for our family just before Beatriz was born and she originally came from Gibraltar. I could not tell if she was a happy person or not, but she was in control of all of us. In my opinion, Miss Spencer was also afraid of my father, but it was useful and comforting having her around to tell me exactly what to do. She was a robust person, not very tall but large without being fat. Her curly black hair fell just above her shoulders. She liked using mascara and normally included a light green eye shadow that clashed with the black of her eyes. Miss Spencer's tone of voice was always soothing, but somehow this also irritated my father, who on many occasions had exasperated Miss Spencer by commanding her to speak louder whenever he thought he could not hear her properly.

Miss Spencer was patient, but she could also have a temper, threatening my brothers and sisters that she would leave the house when we were disobedient. I did not want Miss Spencer ever to leave, but she had sometimes nearly done so, going out the door with her luggage in hand. My body always felt rigid in terror whenever Miss Spencer did this and I did not know how to stop it from happening.

Our home was on the tenth floor of the last block of flats at the end of the road, just overlooking the Atlantic Ocean. We lived in Cádiz, in the south of Spain, where the weather was pleasant most of the time; but being so exposed to the sea also meant that incredibly stormy weather with strong winds and gales was very much a part of our lives, especially in wintertime.

"Good evening, Ramón," said Miss Spencer to the doorman.

"Good evening," replied Ramón, not raising his eyes from the newspaper he was reading.

Ramón's job was to check on people coming and going from the block of flats where we lived, making sure nobody unwelcome was allowed in. He also collected the rubbish from all floors and deposited it outside for the council to collect early every morning, well before the rush hour. Ramón also made sure the maintenance of the building was in good shape, replacing anything needed and keeping an eye on empty properties during the holidays. He lived in an apartment on the ground floor and he was married to Macarena. He had a dry personality and was short on words, hardly ever smiling. He was bald and looked about fifty years old, with a thin build, narrow face and a well-defined protruding nose. He also wore glasses like me.

I let go of the pushchair and raced to the lift button, pushing it hard to make the lift come to the ground floor. I stood there frozen, observing the orange light and listening carefully to the noises of the chains activating and manipulating the lifts, trying to guess which of the two would arrive first. Finally the right lift door fully lit up and I could see the standing platform steadily descending top to bottom through the obscure lift window. I always enjoyed calling and waiting for the lift and liked competing with my two brothers every time we returned home together. I opened the lift door, pulling hard at its vertical metallic handle, allowing Miss Spencer to get in with the pushchair as I squeezed tightly in at the side.

The flat where we lived had two doors, one that everybody used, which went straight to the kitchen, and an opposite one that was only used by my father.

"Oh, you're back from the park, Miss Spencer! Did the children have a good time?" asked Mum.

"Yes, Mrs Grimaldi," Miss Spencer replied. "The girls seemed to enjoy it and it was a lovely afternoon. By the way, may I ask what the children are having for dinner this evening?"

"I went to the fish market this morning, so they can have the lemon sole with some chips. They'll eat in the kitchen. Mr Grimaldi and I will eat after them in the dining room."

My mother was knitting in the sitting room, sitting in her armchair just under the big bay window. She always sat in the chair backing to the door entering the room from the kitchen and her beautiful short dark hair always appeared first as you came in. It was well combed, with her head always showing from the edge of the backrest. Mum was very tall for a woman, and she was definitely taller than all her friends were. She wasn't particularly slim, but her legs were long and well proportioned. Mum liked wearing dresses of delicate materials with matching shoes, and she could have the most beautiful shining smile in the world, which we mostly saw when Dad wasn't around.

There was also a second armchair where my father normally sat, on the opposite side of the window, across the coffee table in the middle. A large sofa lay across the window between the two, with the television standing in front of the three pieces of furniture. The sitting room was connected to the dining room, which led to the kitchen at the end of the flat, next to Miss Spencer's bedroom and bathroom.

"Hello, Mum," I said, entering the sitting room.

"Hi, Isabel. How are you? Are you ready to go to school tomorrow?" Mum replied, still concentrating on her knitting needles. Mum was skilled at sewing, knitting and doing crochet. Most of the time when I talked to her, she was occupied with something; and if not knitting, she would be reading the newspaper, a book or doing a crossword. It was difficult, for one reason or another, to get her full attention.

"Yes," I answered, looking down at the floor as I walked to my bedroom.

"I'll be taking you to school tomorrow morning. You are a big girl, and I'm sure you're not going to cry, are you?" Mum said, stretching out her arms to admire her piece of knitted wool.

"No, I won't," I replied.

Tears flooded my eyes, and a constricted sense of torment tightened my chest as I walked down the corridor to my bedroom. I entered my room and sat on my bed, staring at Beatriz's white wooden cot covered in teddy bear stickers and dressed with delicate white cotton bed linen.

I could hear my two elder sisters arguing in their bedroom, which was opposite mine. My eldest sister, María, was six years older than I was, and she was quite an argumentative and demanding child with a restless personality. She wasn't very tall for her age and she suffered from asthma. María loved playing the guitar. She would often sing at the same time and would always try to reach all of the highest notes, making a real effort to emphasise each word with great precision. The whole experience was often unbearable, causing great distress for Teresa, who shared the room with her. The difference in age between the two was only sixteen months, but in terms of personality, they were completely different. Teresa was always kind and understanding with me, with a gentle manner that matched her thin shape. She had a graceful demeanour and a beautiful face.

I was sitting quietly and mesmerised when Miss Spencer came into the room.

"Isabel, I'm running a bath. Please stop the water when it's ready and get in. Today you don't need to wash your hair. Try not to take too long because your sisters are coming after you. In the meantime, I'll feed Beatriz while you are washing, but come to the kitchen as soon as you finish and have your dinner, please. And don't forget to let your sisters know when you are done so they can take turns having their baths too."

"Where are my pyjamas?" I asked her. Miss Spencer knew how to organise all of us. She took care of Beatriz and somehow orchestrated everyone else in taking turns bathing and having dinner, which she always managed to cook for us. She did all this while she also prepared a different two-course dinner for my parents, who normally ate in the dining room, which also had to be set. My parents usually waited in the sitting room until Miss Spencer called to them that dinner was ready.

"I've already left a clean pair in the bathroom for you. Everything you need is there."

My two brothers, Jaime and Alex, were at the end of their meal when I finally arrived in the kitchen after my bath. They were quarrelling and competing to finish first in order to leave the table as soon as possible, to make the most of the remaining playtime before bed. Beatriz, sitting in her high chair, was watching them with great amusement and now and again, she tried to join in, babbling in her own language, throwing in happy noises along the way; it was clearly great fun for her. Jaime finished his piece of fruit first and attempted to leave the table, but Miss Spencer made him stay until Alex was finished.

"Jaime, remember to ask if you may leave the table before you attempt to stand up. It is rude not to wait for the person who is sharing a meal with you or to leave before that person is also finished, unless there is a good reason for it."

"But that person happens to be my stupid brother, who is incredibly slow."

"It doesn't matter who he is. You need to wait until he also finishes his dessert before both of you can leave the table."

Alex looked at Jaime triumphantly with a half smile, while Jaime dropped his shoulders in exasperation. Jamie was the older of the two, and there was a difference of three years between him and me. His thin physiognomy made him a cute little boy with a handsome face and dark eyes and hair. Jaime was very attached to my mum but was always very quiet and frightened around Dad, who always expected him to behave like a real man, as he was the eldest son.

Alex, on the other hand, was a big boy for his age. According to Mum, he was born incredibly large, which caused him a broken clavicle at birth. He was a strong boy who was about to turn six at the end of September, with a big head compared to his body. Alex's nature was noble but also incredibly stubborn. He was generally slow at doing things and according to Mum, he did not start talking properly until he was nearly five, for he had problems constructing full sentences and took some time to express what he had to say.

Alex had spent the last summer term being home schooled by Mum and was waiting to get into year one in the St Benedict's Boys School, the same school Jaime already attended. Alex was eighteen months older than I was and was left-handed. He and Jaime had spent the first two mixed preschool years in the school where my sisters currently were, St Mary's Catholic School, but things had not worked out very well for Alex. He could not concentrate too long on tasks and his teacher forced him to use his right hand by tying the left one to the back of his chair. Alex was kept in detention most of the time and therefore felt unhappy in that school. As a result, he was falling behind in his reading and writing. It was Teresa, who collected him every day from his classroom to take him home, who warned Mum about this. Mum took Alex out of the school before the end of the academic year and she had been tutoring him at home since then.

"May we leave the table?" both boys said at the same time, when Alex had finally finished his meal.

"Yes, of course. Mind you, there's school tomorrow and I want lights out by nine o'clock. You can play for a little bit, but when I go round to your bedroom, I would like you to go to sleep at once. And don't forget to brush your teeth."

"Okay, Miss," they answered, leaving the kitchen.

Miss Spencer was clearing the table and I could see that my supper was already in my usual place. I started cutting the fish, but for some reason, I did not feel particularly hungry today. Although having said that, it was my intention to eat it all, so as not to cause any concerns to anyone. Miss Spencer took Beatriz in her arms and walked with her towards the kitchen door.

"Isabel, I'm putting your sister to sleep, as it is getting quite late for her now. I will hopefully be back before you need your dessert, but if I get delayed, please help yourself and get some fruit or yogurt from the fridge."

"I will, Miss," I replied.

It was relaxing not having people around me, and I could smell my parents' dinner slowly cooking and gurgling on the stove. An overwhelming feeling of worry tightened my throat as I thought about what was ahead, as I did not know what to expect from school tomorrow. I liked being at home and always felt anxious every time I had to go anywhere. When I left the house, it was because I felt I had to, not wanting to cause controversy or tension around me. I could not understand things around me very well and being unnoticed was the best way to manage my surroundings. Today I had a strong desire to hide under the sitting room table and be invisible.

A loud shout from my father came from the sitting room, abruptly interrupting my thoughts.

"Stop crossing in front of me! I'm trying to watch the news and you are all disturbing my peace!"

I finished eating and as Miss Spencer was not back yet, I cleared my plates and cutlery, rinsing them under the tap and placing them inside the dishwasher. I crossed the dining room and sitting room, where my father was watching the news and my mother was still knitting, both waiting for their dinner to be served. I softly said good night to them as I crouched on all fours on the floor so as not to interrupt my father's line of vision as he watched television. Once I got close enough to the door leading to the corridor where our bedrooms were, I stood up, opened the door, left the sitting room and went straight down the corridor to brush my teeth before going to bed.

Beatriz had just fallen asleep and looked angelic with her little lips slightly apart, lying on her side with her right cheek on the pillow. Miss Spencer led María and Teresa to the kitchen, and I could hear her warn them not to cross the sitting room and to go out of the main front door of the flat, and come back inside the house again through the door next to the kitchen. It seemed that Miss Spencer had anticipated the need to avoid my father's anger, as the keys for both doors were in her hands, ready to be used.

I tried to get as comfortable as I could in bed; I liked sleeping on top of my pillow cuddling it tight against my body with my blankets covering my back up to my neck. Somehow, I couldn't fall asleep and stared at the light coming into my room underneath the door. I heard my sisters entering their bedroom too, and then I heard Miss Spencer after a while, polishing all our shoes for school tomorrow. The muffled sound of the telly eventually subsided and my parents made their way to their room, switching off the light from the bathroom outside my bedroom. My parents' master bedroom had a small adjacent study and an en suite bathroom. It lay between my brothers' room and our bedroom.

Hours passed as I tossed and turned in my bed. The small gaps through the window blinds allowed the rhythmic light from the nearby lighthouse to partially light up the ceiling of my bedroom every few seconds. It was a quite an entertaining feature that I particularly liked during the night, giving me a comforting sense that things were calm and under control in the sea next to us. Beatriz's heavy breathing filled the silence of the night.

Chapter Two

FIRST DAY AT SCHOOL

I sprang out of bed as soon as I heard Miss Spencer waking my sisters up next door. Beatriz was wide awake too, sitting up in her cot and looking at me as soon as she heard me moving. She was happy to see me, giving me a smile full of baby teeth. Miss Spencer slowly opened the door, and at once we were both standing and looking at her.

"You're both up! That's great. Isabel, breakfast is ready in the kitchen. I'll lay your uniform out on your bed and you can get dressed after your hot chocolate and toast."

My stomach felt full of butterflies and tears came to my eyes. I could hardly speak and was unable to greet Miss Spencer. I was feeling incredibly frightened about going to school. I put on my dressing gown and slippers and slowly walked towards the kitchen.

I could see light under my mother's door and realised that Mum was already getting dressed. My father was normally out of the house by this time in the morning and my mother was normally up by ten, but today she was taking me to school for the first time. Jaime and Alex had just arrived in the kitchen when I got there, and I could hear Maria and Teresa coming along behind me. Miss Spencer had lined up five mugs of hot chocolate and five plates with one piece of toast on each, along with olive oil, on the kitchen table. I drank my hot chocolate in one go, picked up my toast and walked back to my bedroom while eating it. My brothers were already arguing in the kitchen.

In the corridor outside of our room, I met Mum, who was ready to go.

"Good morning, Isabel. I'll be walking you to school this morning, and once I leave you there, I'll drive your brothers to school. Today is Alex's first day in Jaime's school."

"I'll be ready soon," I answered as I walked past her.

Miss Spencer appeared round the corner, holding Beatriz in her arms. She had just finished laying our uniforms and clothes on top of our beds for the four of us, and she was taking Beatriz to have something to eat too. I felt tense and moved stiffly. My hands were cold and I was almost shivering in fear. One by one, I held up each piece of my uniform and examined it. The first thing I put on, once I had taken off my pyjamas, was a pair of navy blue socks, as they were easy. I then took the beige short-sleeved front-pleated blouse with a round neck and held it in front of me, trying to work out where the buttons had to face, realising that they were backwards. I put it on and did the first button up behind my neck, but I could not reach any further to get the others.

I walked across my bedroom and into the corridor, where I luckily found Teresa, who was trying to get into the bathroom while Jamie and Alex were brushing their teeth. They were refusing to let her in and Teresa was knocking at the bathroom door with impatience.

"Teresa, can you help me with these buttons, please? I can't reach that well."

"Turn around," she said.

Teresa did them up with great speed and continued shouting at my brothers to open the door. The uniform dress was sleeveless and had two small front pockets close to the front edge, just above knee level, which was the length of the uniform. Looking at the clothing from some distance, it gave a sensation of being grey with superimposed bits of black. I felt like wearing the navy blue cardigan on top because I was frozen with worry, despite it being a warm day.

I went to the bathroom, where María and Teresa were combing their hair and brushing their teeth; my brothers were already gone. I had a pair of brand-new shoes waiting for me in the bathroom; they seemed so neat and perfect that I didn't want to spoil them. My sisters' uniforms were different to mine and consisted of beige long-sleeved blouses buttoned up the front, with sleeveless navy blue dresses pleated downwards from below the chest. They both wore navy blue ties and cardigans. Their socks were beige and up to the knees.

In contrast to us, Jaime and Alex did not wear uniforms in their school, just normal clothes. That was not all! Girls also had to wear light cotton pinafores at school at all times to protect their uniforms. Mine was beige and fastened by one single button at the back of the neck, and my sisters' were light blue, buttoned at the front, top to bottom, with belts from the same material.

I quickly combed my hair, using a clip to keep my fringe out of my face, and then I brushed my teeth.

I was holding my mother's hand tightly as we walked to school, feeling quite nauseated. María and Teresa were walking slightly ahead of us. Our school was opposite our flat, and from the sitting and dining room windows, we had a full view of the playground, but to get to the main entrance, we had to walk around it for about five minutes, as our flat was facing the side of it. There was a strong scent of seaweed in the air, as sometimes happened when the tide was low. It was bearable but sour and bitter. The sun was out and the day promised to be bright and clear, with hardly any clouds at all.

We reached the school without my saying a word along the way. Lots of mothers and girls between the ages of four and seventeen were gathering at the entrance. All I could think of was Miss Spencer and Beatriz. I tried to go through and remember every single detail about my house and my room, my toys and everything that was nice in it. I wished I could run back home and hide under a table, blocking my ears and not having to come out ever again. I had a tight knot in the back of my throat; I couldn't speak.

The doors opened soon after we arrived and a nun stood in the doorway, greeting everyone with a smile. I could only see a restricted fringe of black hair under her veil. She was of medium height, had glasses and was dressed in a light grey habit. Mum told me she was the headmistress, although I didn't know what that meant. My two sisters quickly said goodbye and disappeared into the multitude, knowing where they had to go. I was familiar with the entrance hall and the church, but I had never been allowed to walk any further inside, as I was not a student in the school. Also, the only boys that were allowed in the school were the students in the first two years, as Jaime and Alex had once been. No other boys or brothers were welcomed inside, because it was a girls' religious school. The only exceptions were the girls' fathers, as long as they were married to the mothers. Having said that, all dads normally went to work and mums usually stayed home with their children.

Mum seemed to know where we had to go and she walked slightly ahead of me. We went through a long, wide corridor leading up to a large staircase. Mum stopped at the foot of the staircase, turned right and pointed to one of the two doors.

"Isabel, that will be your classroom."

A sudden surge of adrenaline ran through my body, making me look up and tighten my grip on my mother's hand as hard as I could. My class door was dark brown wood and had a double door which closed in the middle with a glass panel on top that allowed light to penetrate through it, but this made it impossible to guess what was beyond it, as it was all obscure. Mum turned around and continued walking towards a corridor to the left of the staircase, which was also very long, and eventually led us to a massive transparent double glass door which opened onto the playground. Only mothers with reception children were in the courtyard.

The first part of the courtyard was covered with a roof and we had to go down about twenty steps, where we found two different options. If we went to the left, there stood the open playground, which included an area with swings and another one with fields of sandy soil. The other option was to go ahead, up five steps, into a large porch with multiple columns, which seemed to me an area to play on rainy days. This was where we all gathered to wait. Boys were separated from girls, but we all stood next to our mothers.

The headmistress appeared after a while, descending the stairs leading to the courtyard. She went directly to pull the rope of a large green bell that was hanging from a small arch next to the five steps leading to the porch.

Dong, dong, dong … The bell rang, and it had a powerful and deep sound that reverberated throughout the whole school and part of the neighbourhood. I was glad that Mum and I were not too close to it. I wasn't sure what that sound meant, but it was rather ominous and intimidating. Shortly afterwards four teachers appeared at the top of the stairs. Two of them remained, smiling at the crowd, and the other two descended to the porch, leading all the reception boys to the far end of the porch, where a different door gave access to two additional classrooms, which I could just manage to glimpse from where I was standing.

"It is time for all parents to leave their children with their teachers," the headmistress announced.

The second-year reception girls moved quickly towards their teacher and half of the group of parents started walking towards the stairs. My heart sank to my feet when my mother let go of my hand. My chest tightened so much that my eyes quickly filled up with tears. I wanted to be strong for Mum and looked down at the ground so she wouldn't see.

"Isabel, I have to go now. Try to enjoy your first day at school and I will meet you at home soon. Goodbye, my darling."

My throat was sealed and no words could come out. I was left feeling frozen to the spot in which I was standing.

"Good morning, girls. My name is Miss Cecilia, but you can call me 'Miss', and I am your teacher. Please gather round and line up so we can all go to our classroom together for registration. I am looking forward to getting to know all of you."

Miss Cecilia had a soothing voice similar to Miss Spencer's. Fear overwhelmed me and I couldn't move or look up at my teacher. The group of girls started moving and eventually formed a line. Some of the girls started crying, asking to go with their mums, but Miss Cecilia comforted them and rearranged the line into pairs of students holding hands, supporting each other. There was one little girl left out who was sobbing inconsolably and I still hadn't moved from where my mother had left me. Miss Cecilia held the other girl's hand while she continued to cry and came to where I was standing, reaching for my right hand too, inviting me to move along her side. My extremities were cold and my body felt rigid, but I reluctantly started moving, my gaze remaining fixed on the ground.

Miss Cecilia had long, thin legs and she wearing a red summer skirt with red sandals. Her hand was warm but not very comforting because it felt rather tense. All the way to our classroom, the three of us led the way at the front of the queue. The corridor was deserted by now and the only thing I could hear was the noise of our shoes on the floor tiles. I thought about home, Miss Spencer and Beatriz, realising how much I was missing them right now.

"Girls, this is the first year girls' reception class and this is where we will be learning but also having fun," Miss Cecilia exclaimed, opening the door of the classroom and standing at the entrance. "Come on in. Take a desk and sit wherever you like."

Thirty-eight girls slowly marched in two by two, while the little girl and I stood by Miss Cecilia. I still had my head down, observing the flash of legs passing in front of me. Miss Cecilia let my hand go and gently invited the other little girl, who at this moment was no longer crying, to enter the room, leaving me behind. Everybody was inside by now, except for me. I felt petrified, unable to move or speak. Miss Cecilia turned round and came to fetch me as soon as the other little girl was sitting at her desk.

"What's your name?" she asked, kneeling on the floor and coming down to my eye level.

I couldn't raise my eyes or answer. Anguish was overwhelming me and I could not avoid crying, still looking down at the floor. I didn't want to look at anybody, and I felt completely abandoned and alone. Everything seemed unfamiliar and alien to me. Miss Cecilia held my hand and tried to make me move forward, but I dropped her hand and stood where I was. My sobs gradually grew louder, as I couldn't control them.

"Hey, everything is fine. I know you miss your mum, but you will be home soon. Come into the classroom and I will give you a glass of water. I think you need it. There are many friends waiting to meet you. Maybe you can help me with the register. I need to give each of you a sticker with your name on it so I can learn all the names quickly. I'm going to read you all a story and we will be cutting, and gluing and also doing some colouring."

Miss Cecilia realised how upset I was and tried to get me in, but I did not move and was rigid; my feet started dragging across the floor. I immediately turned around and started screaming, pushing Miss Cecilia in the opposite direction with a violent reaction.

"Noooo! Nooo! Please! I don't want to go in! Please, please!"

Miss Cecilia stopped pushing me. "That's fine. I will leave the door open. You just come in whenever you feel ready."

Miss Cecilia went inside and sat at her desk. I did not want anybody to look at me and I continued sobbing, trying to control my emotions. I could hear Miss Cecilia calling out the name of each girl in the class.

After a while, there was a different noise in the room, as if the tables were being dragged into different positions. I was cold, I was frightened and I felt lost. Time passed and I still could not stop crying, although at least now I could do it in silence.

Suddenly, a siren went off loudly in all the corridors. My heart missed a beat and started racing even faster. The noise was unbearable and prolonged; I had to cover my ears with my hands. I crouched and sat on the floor, burying my head between my knees. When the noise had subsided, a large number of students filled the corridors, moving towards the fields. The girls in my class lined up at the door, waiting for the older students to go through before they were allowed to leave the class.

"Isabel, there's no reason to be afraid," Miss Cecilia said as she approached me. "It's break time now. You can all go to the field and play on the swings. You will have a much longer break than the older students will. When Mother Petunia rings the bell in the field, it will be time for the older students to go back inside. The second time you hear the bell, it will be time for all of you to return to the class; but don't worry, I will come to get you all. I won't leave you alone."

I didn't understand what she meant regarding the bells or Mother Petunia and I was feeling completely overwhelmed.

"Isa, Isa! A familiar voice rose among the crowd. "Why are you crouching on the floor? I'll wait for you in the playground."

"Teresa, is Isabel your sister?" Miss Cecilia asked.

"Yes, Miss."

"Isabel has been crying and does not want to come into the classroom."

"Oh, Isa! Everything will be fine! May I take her with me, Miss?" Teresa asked.

"You can wait for her in the playground. She will go with the rest of the class," Miss Cecilia said.

"Isa, I'll be waiting for you. Don't take too long!"

I didn't move from my position but managed to look at Teresa with my eyes full of tears. Seeing her triggered even more emotions, and I was unable to control it. My class left once the crowd coming down the stairs had diffused along the corridor. I still couldn't move and therefore was left behind. The peace and tranquillity was soothing and relaxing. I could hear my heart beating and concentrating on my breathing helped me to control my sobbing.

Miss Cecilia appeared again, pulling me up from the floor and holding my face tightly between her hands. She cleaned my tears and my nose with a tissue. This was the first time I had seen her face properly. My teacher had short ginger hair with brown eyes and her face was full of freckles. I thought her appearance was unusual. She was wearing a short-sleeved white blouse but the colour of her red skirt and shoes clashed with the colour of her hair. Miss Cecilia was not angry with me. She had a big smile.

"Isabel, give me your hand. May I call you Isa? Your sister is waiting for you outside and she will be worried if she doesn't see you. Come along with me and we will stop by the toilet just in case you need to go."

I reluctantly started walking along the corridor leading to the fields with Miss Cecilia, who attempted to enter the toilets on our way to the playground. I resisted the idea and therefore we both continued walking. I saw Teresa impatiently looking through the window with her face against it, waiting for me to arrive.

Teresa took care of me during playtime and I followed her round without talking. She introduced me to her friends, who all said hello to me. The bell rang for the older students to leave, and I couldn't help but start crying again. I was struggling to catch my breath while sobbing and Teresa looked at me with great compassion.

"Isa, why are you so frightened? Miss Cecilia is really nice and will take care of you. My classroom is upstairs on the second floor and I'll come to collect you as soon as the morning is finished to take you home for lunch."

"Please, Teresa, don't go! Don't leave me alone!" I implored, holding and pulling on Teresa's uniform.

Teresa paused to have a closer look at me. "I have to go or I'll be late." With difficulty, she broke free of my tight grip, turning around as she was leaving. I looked down at the ground and continued crying in silence.

The second bell rang again after a while and all the younger children disappeared. I wasn't sure what I had to do, but I slowly walked in the direction where the last girl I saw had gone.

Miss Cecilia walked us back to the classroom again and I tensed up, avoiding going inside, but this time she closed the door behind her. I managed to calm down again and stood leaning against the wall next to the door of my class. Miss Petunia approached me after some time.

"Hello, Isabel. I know your sisters – María and Teresa – and I also know your Mum quite well, in addition to your brothers, Jaime and Alex."

I looked at her but said nothing.

"It is quite tiring standing here in the corridor. Would you like to sit over there with me? At least we will be more comfortable," she said, pointing to a small sofa with two chairs next to it, placed in the area at the bottom of the staircase.

I agreed to go with her and we both sat on the sofa.

"Why don't you want to go into class, Isabel? There are lots of girls the same age as you who still don't know many people at school, and I am sure that they are willing to be your friends."

"I'm scared," I said.

"But scared of what?" she asked.

"I don't know," I concluded.

Miss Petunia kept trying to talk to me, but I was mesmerised by the short but rhythmic corridor bells that kept talking from one corridor to another in a code, as if they were having a conversation. I knew it was a code because Dad also had a special whistle at home similar to the one he used to command war ships. He would call to us all in exclusive ways, consisting of a combination of short and long whistles. He sometimes liked lining us up as if we were in the military, practising and recognising each others' codes. This experience was always worrying and frightening for me, as I could never remember the sound of my own code while trying to memorise those of the others. My tactic was to be alert and attend any call, hiding from my father just in case it wasn't mine, pretending to recognise it straight away. I didn't hear any of Miss Petunia's conversation, but when the bells finished ringing, she stood up.

"Nice meeting you, Isabel. I am afraid I have to leave you. Did you hear those bells ringing? Each nun in the school has a code, and it seems that they are calling me from the main entrance."

I looked at her in disbelief, as I couldn't work out how she knew where she had been called from. Everything seemed so confusing today.

When lunchtime came, not all the girls were taken home; some of them stayed to have school dinner. Teresa collected me and took me home, as we both finished at the same time. María had to stay behind; she had a shorter lunch break because she was one of the older students. María was a young child for her age group, but because she was very clever in reception years and could read ahead of her age, so she was put one academic year above her age group. The government was also changing the education system and had added one extra year to primary education, which Teresa had to do but María didn't. Therefore, despite my two sisters being close together in age, they had three academic years difference between the two of them.

When we got home, Mum had not arrived yet. She was still collecting Jaime and Alex from their school. Miss Spencer greeted us and asked us about our morning at school when we arrived, but I was disappointed that Mum was not home and continued walking straight to my bedroom, where I took a big breath and sighed. I could hear the muffled sound of Patricia setting the dining room table for lunch.

Patricia was the housemaid and she was in her early twenties. She was quite talkative and always told us many stories about her family or her plans over the weekend. It was entertaining to listen to her, but I felt sorry that her family was poor compared to ours. Mum sometimes gave them food from the supermarket when her father was not earning any money. She was short, with long black hair tied up in a ponytail and had small dark beady eyes, which always gave her an intense look. Patricia was second in command after Miss Spencer and she was still learning how things worked in our family, as my parents had only recently employed her. I liked Patricia and particularly loved the way she made our beds every day. The linen was always well stretched and tightened so every time I went to bed, nothing fell apart during the night. I profoundly disliked it if my bed linen was not in order while trying to sleep; it gave me a feeling of chaos around me.

"Food is ready and on the table!" Mum shouted.

I had missed Mum arriving home but left my room as soon as I heard her voice.

"Wash your hands, please," she commanded.

I quickly washed my hands in the bathroom and went to the dining room. In the middle of the room was a large oval mahogany table that had belonged to my father's grandparents. It was covered with a white linen tablecloth. Patricia had set the table perfectly, with two plates for each person, one for each course, and the relevant cutlery and glasses. There also was a bread basket in the middle and a large jar of iced water, which Patricia had left next to the bread after filling all our glasses. The salt was close to the right end, where my father normally sat; he liked his food really salty, always adding extra salt before even tasting it. A beautiful chandelier with three rows of glass hung from the ceiling over the centre of the table, occupying most of the roof. This chandelier was paired with a similar one next door in the sitting room. They were a spectacular feature of both rooms as soon as you entered them. They had been inherited from grandparents, although I cannot remember exactly whose.

My mother always sat in the middle of the front of the table and my place was between my parents. María always sat to the right of my father, Teresa alongside her, opposite Mum, and then Jaime. Alex would sit on the left side of the table, opposite Dad and Beatriz, who was allowed to sit with us at lunch, always seated to the left side of Mum. Beatriz had a special mat under her plate to protect the tablecloth from any mess; she still used a bib and had only one course for lunch instead of two.

The doorbell rang at the kitchen end of the flat and María entered the dining room shortly afterwards.

"Hello, María," Mum said. "We're about to start. Good timing!"

María disappeared for a few seconds and left her books in her bedroom. She came back and sat in the empty space next to my father. My parents usually ate together later on, when my Dad returned from work to have lunch, and we only had family meals during the weekends. Patricia, wearing her maid's uniform, went round the table holding a serving dish with lentils and chorizo, and one by one, we all helped ourselves from our right-hand sides, where she positioned herself. We were never forced to eat more than we wanted, but the rule was that however little or much we put on our plate, we had to finish it. I was not feeling particularly hungry, so I only took one spoonful from the serving dish that day.

"How was school today, children?" Mum asked, looking at all of us.

"There are two new girls in my class, and my science teacher seems very strict," Teresa replied, repeating what she had already mentioned to Miss Spencer on arrival.

"You're lucky. I already have homework. And I particularly hated chemistry," María told us with a frown in her expression.

I wasn't sure if she was angry, disappointed or relieved that she'd mentioned it.

"I played football with my friends," said Alex. "And I saw Jaime in the playground."

"Do you like your teacher?" Mum asked him.

"He gave me a sweet and allows me to write with my left hand. He's nice," Alex replied.

"I would like to play hockey, Mum," Jaime said. And can I bring my roller skates this afternoon, please? I want to skate in the playground with my friends."

"Yes, you can. But only for half an hour; I would like you to bring Alex home after school," Mum answered.

"But why can't he come back with his friends like I do?" Jaime implored.

"Because it's his first day at school and he doesn't know anyone yet," Mum answered. "Besides, Alex is still young. Maybe he will be able to do it in six months' time."

Beatriz was making a big mess of her food and lentils were splashing in every direction from her plate, although she was still managing to eat quite a lot of them. Mum came close to her and tidied things up for her. It was quite sweet to watch her.

"Isabel, how was school for you?" she asked.

"Fine," I said, staring at my food.

The bell from the other side of the house rang, silencing everyone for a minute.

"It's Dad," Alex said.

We were having our second course, veal steak with fried chips, when Dad entered the sitting room.

"I want you all to greet your father, please," Mum whispered.

"Hello, Dad!" we all said at once.

Dad didn't answer and seemed absorbed in his own thoughts. We continued eating in silence and Mum nervously joined him in the next room. My father seemed aggravated by issues at work and kept talking to Mum in a low voice.

Dad finally approached the table. He shone in his white summer navy uniform with golden buttons and three gold rings, two thick and a thin one in the middle, around the sleeves of his jacket and on his shoulders. His hair was thick and very short but also almost white. It was a family trait to go prematurely grey. His younger brother, Uncle Alberto, was also grey.

"Jaime, your hair is too long," Dad commanded. "You need a haircut. Next time you won't be allowed to sit at the table unless it is properly short and combed. Understood? Maria and Teresa, stop talking while I am speaking!"

The reply was total silence.

Dad took his place at the table and placed his napkin on his lap, tidying up his place, rearranging the glass and cutlery until it was equidistant and straight.

"May I leave the table?" we all courteously asked him one by one as we left the dining room, leaving our napkins folded and the chairs correctly tucked in.

Patricia lifted Beatriz from her chair and took her to Miss Spencer in the kitchen area to get ready for her nap. I was the last one to leave, as it took me a long time to peel my orange using a knife and fork. I cut the orange into eighths and then one by one I dissected the skin off each piece. It was the only way not to stain my hands with the juice, and my parents greatly approved of my doing this because it looked smart and well mannered.

As I left, I heard Dad telling Mum that Beatriz needed her bat ears mended. He ordered Mum to tape them to the side of the head for several months so they could grow straight. My heart tightened, but I walked away.

Maria, Teresa, Jaime, and Alex left together to have a one-hour English lesson with a private tutor before school started again at 3.30 p.m. I left the house at 3 p.m. with Miss Spencer, who had left Beatriz in her cot having a nap. A paralysing terror was controlling my body again. I was not able to articulate my thoughts and a constricting anxiety extinguished any tears attempting to emerge in my eyes. I was close to not being able to move at all. School finally ended at 5.30 p.m.

Chapter Three

THE PICNIC

The days at school passed slowly and my fear became even more difficult to control. Teresa struggled to leave me in my class, making her late for her lessons on a daily basis. I felt like crying all the time, although I was fighting hard not to show it. My sleep had become worse than ever. I cried myself to sleep at night and couldn't stop thinking how lucky animals were, like the pets at home or the animals in the wild or free out in the sea. They were fed, watered and taken care of by their owners, parents or their packs. Their fear was a survival tool and what constituted an actual threat, or didn't, was clear to them.

I, on the other hand, was facing an unknown threat which I was supposed to overcome. Adults were frightening and becoming one of them required a long process of working out millions of unknown fears. The prospect was simply terrifying. I was feeling alone and helpless. I really didn't know what I had to do or what was expected of me; I was completely lost.

On Friday evening, Mum told me before I went to bed that we were going out for a picnic the following morning, to the pine forest close to where we lived. My Dad and Miss Spencer were coming and apparently Mr García, Alex's teacher, had also been invited. Mr García was the head of infants in my brothers' school and had been to our flat several times, talking to my parents while Alex was being home-schooled before the summer.

It was nice to know that it was the beginning of the weekend and therefore there was no school; but even so, I had a restless night with broken sleep, waking up several times. The nightmare was always the same one: I was in our summer house in the north of Spain, standing on the sandy path leading from our house to the main street. I am not sure if in the dream I was trying to reach home or to go in the opposite direction, but there always was an unexpected ogre that kept appearing just outside the gate of my house that chased me and was trying to kill me. This ogre was large, with brown hair that covered his face and he had huge teeth. In the dream, I was desperately trying to run as fast as I could, but there always was a delay in starting to run; my legs were ordered to run and move but they were incredibly slow to do so. I was like a steam train leaving the station, with the wheels initially slipping away on the tracks and gradually gaining grip and the necessary speed. My legs were the same, and they did not seem able to run on time. What always woke me up was the overwhelming anguished panic that I wasn't able to flee on time and that the ogre was catching up to me, although the ogre never actually attacked me.

Morning came and it felt nice not having Miss Spenser wake me. Beatriz was still sleeping, but I could hear movement and people doing things in the house. I quietly left my bedroom and went to have breakfast in the kitchen. Miss Spencer and Mum were busy preparing lunch and packing things in picnic bags. They had been cooking since they got up and there were numerous plastic containers of different sizes displayed on the kitchen table. The food smelt good but too rich to try at breakfast time.

"Good morning," I said.

"Oh, hello, Isabel. It's a lovely day to go for a picnic today. Is Beatriz awake?" Mum asked me.

"No, she's still asleep," I replied.

"Here's your breakfast." Miss Spencer had left me a clear space on the table where my usual hot chocolate and piece of toast were.

"Thank you," I said.

Mum continued to organise the food and said, "We'll be leaving in one hour. Make sure you wear comfortable clothes today, maybe a pair of trousers and trainers. There will be plenty of trees to climb and enough sand to play with too."

"Mrs Grimaldi, I'll get Isabel her clothes because I am sure Beatriz must be awake by now and she also needs to get ready," Miss Spencer said to Mum.

"That's true," Mum answered. "Why don't you go ahead with the girls and I will finish this. It's almost ready anyway."

I always wanted to go in the car with Mum and asked to on every occasion. But Mum seemed to prefer that I travel with Dad, and today she told me that Mr García had to be collected at the school. Miss Spencer and Beatriz, with all the bags, were also going in her car. Miss Spencer had intervened today before she left the kitchen, without waiting for me to agree or disagree, and helped Mum see that there was actually space for me in the car. Mum usually seemed to give an automatic no as an answer, without thinking.

"Whatever you think best, Miss Spencer. But we need to get going; otherwise, we will never leave," said Mum.

It was a warm and sunny day in October, with a typically intense and colourful low autumn light that made the remaining colours in the countryside more intense. We were in the pine forest just outside the city. Some of the forest was very sandy because it was quite close to the sea, but the deeper you walked into it, the more firm and harder the ground became around the trees. The sand converted into clay and chalk, initially orange and then red. It was a great place to play hide-and-seek.

The adults and Beatriz stayed in an open space large enough to set out a table, some chairs and a blanket on the ground. All of us scattered around in different directions, exploring the area and looking for interesting trees to climb or bushes to hide in. There were plenty of fallen pine cones on the ground, which I started gathering until there was no more space in my pockets and hands to collect anymore.

I could suddenly hear noises coming from where my parents were. They were shooting noises. I dropped all my pinecones and ran back to my family. Dad had brought his hunting rifle with him. He had three or four of them, but they normally stayed in our country house, El Cortijo, where we often spent the weekends or winter holidays. This gun normally only shot pellets, and it was good enough to bring home hares, rabbits and partridges; but I also knew that Dad had even bigger bullets, the size of a thumb, which could shoot larger animals.

Dad liked hunting and always encouraged my brothers to go with him, despite Mum's disapproval. She especially disapproved of him hunting with Alex, as he was only six. He liked taking Marco, our German shepherd dog, and Polo, the large mastiff, with him. Both dogs, although not hunting animals, could detect their prey, which sometimes just turned out to be big rats, from long distances, sprinting off when least expected and chasing the creatures from more than one kilometre away and easily giving away their location to my father.

But today was different. We were having a picnic and we were away from El Cortijo, where acres of land surrounded the house. My siblings instinctively returned one by one to the open space. Alex was the last one to appear between two tall pine trees ahead and to the right of my father's line of vision.

"Alex, I'm going to shoot you …," Dad said.

I instantly froze in my place and raised my eyes to see where Alex was standing. My chest filled up with tight pressure and my breathing became fast and difficult.

"No, Dad, don't do it!" I implored, standing just two metres behind my father.

My plea alerted Miss Spencer, Mum and Mr García, but before anybody could intervene, Dad shot twice at Alex's left backside as he was crossing in front of him from the pine trees, with no time to escape.

"Aagh! Aagh!" Alex yelled, holding his backside with both hands, limping and trying to move out of range. "That really hurt, Daddy!" He was clearly trying to contain his tears.

"Are you out of your mind, Roberto?" Mum asked, sounding very alarmed, but she was also trying hard not to disrespect my father.

Miss Spencer shot up from her chair at once and ran towards Alex, mumbling between her teeth in absolute despair. "Who does he think he is? For God's sake, he is only a child! I wish I could shoot him back in return to see how funny it was for him …" Miss Spencer was furious.

"Alex likes his biscuits. His backside is quite padded enough to take it. Don't worry. It was just a joke." Dad plainly thought that it was funny and didn't have any sense of remorse.

By this stage, Alex was in tears. Miss Spencer came up next to him and gently looked inside his trousers to assess the injury. Luckily, Alex was far enough away that the pellets had not penetrated his skin, but two rather large red marks had already emerged on his bottom.

"Come with me, my little angel, and I'll put some ice on it," Miss Spencer told Alex, holding him by both elbows and helping him move forward.

Mum did not move, and if she felt angry, it never showed. Instead, she pretended that nothing had happened and continued talking to Mr García.

"He means well but is sometimes a difficult man," she said to Mr García, who clearly did not know what to think or where to look and therefore kept quiet.

My siblings did not move for a while and Teresa asked from where she was standing if Alex was all right. Miss Spencer told all of us to continue playing, as lunch was going to be ready soon. She sat Alex next to her and Beatriz, and gave him a drink. He looked to be in pain and was plainly unsettled. Once she had comforted him, Miss Spencer walked with great determination over to where my father was standing and without giving him a chance to say anything, Miss Spencer took hold of the rifle.

"That is enough shooting for today, Mr Grimaldi," Miss Spencer said with a stern look. "There are no animals around here, unless you prefer to go fishing instead. The beach is that way if that's the case." Miss Spencer briefly pointed ahead towards the beach while she walked straight to where the cars were parked. She opened the boot of the SEAT 1500, which she also sometimes used to drive and therefore had the keys, dropped the rifle in and locked it. I knew that she was not expecting anyone to challenge her, but Mum's eyes glared at her as she waited tensely for my father's reaction; however, in an incredibly dismissive way, he acted as if nothing had happened.

From then on, the afternoon continued with no further incidents, but I was feeling so shocked and worried that I couldn't function for the rest of the day. Now and again, I couldn't control my shivering and I didn't speak until the day was over. I preferred not to join in with any of the adventures and games that my brothers and sisters were playing. All I could think of was why Dad shot Alex. Why would anyone do something like that if the gun's purpose was to hunt hares and birds? Human beings were not supposed to be hunted, not even as a joke. How was Dad able to take the risk of missing his target and maybe hitting Alex somewhere else, like his head or between his ribs? Even a shot into a joint would have caused enormous swelling.

I hardly moved from where I was standing, in the zone behind my father's back, for the rest of the day's picnic. I managed to entertain myself looking for ant nests, observing what they were doing and how they worked together, and also collecting stones and pebbles; but overall, I was emotionally overwhelmed and unable to understand how I felt or why. I wouldn't and couldn't talk; my own emotions were tying my throat in knots.

I could not understand Dad or even predict his actions. He didn't seem to fit in no matter what the situation.

Chapter Four

THE STORM

I saw Mum crying again this morning. I saw her tears when she first left her room this morning to have breakfast, as my bedroom and hers were opposite and at a slight angle, so when both doors were ajar, things could be observed inadvertently without one of the interested parties being aware of it. It wasn't the first time it had happened, but I didn't know how to stop Mum's crying. Dad made her cry and it made me feel completely lost and helpless because I was unable to make everything right for her. I felt responsible for Mum and wanted to take care of her. I didn't want to cause her any worries about me or any concerns. I wished to grow strong and older as soon as I possibly could, so that I could become her support and never a burden, and I meant this because sometimes I had the feeling that we were all too much for Mum. I loved her dearly and I didn't want to see her upset by anything. Any sacrifices I had to make would be for her.

Mum was scared of Dad and I was terrified of him too. Mum always wanted us to make things perfect for Dad and was constantly telling us what to say and when to say it in order to reassure Dad that we liked him. This made me anxious because even when we thought that we were doing nothing wrong, we still had to behave differently in front of him. I didn't know what was expected of me in front of Dad and felt very confused; I just tried not to make him angry and to be unnoticed. Mum was always tense when he was present and, in a way, was trying to push us to one side to keep us out of his way.

There was nothing more important to Mum than Dad. He was always the first one to say something, to be listened to, to be attended to, to choose anything or to be served, always getting the best pieces of fruit, those with no scratches, marks or bruises. His wishes were commands and he easily felt disrespected by anything or anyone. Mum always had to tell him what to say to us or to most anyone, reminding him what certain situations or people meant and organising what he had to do or wear every day because he was completely absent-minded.

Dad also had an unpredictable temper. One night he ripped Alex's and Jaime's reading lamps off the wall because they wouldn't turn the light out to sleep. The house was left with no electrical power for a while. The cables were still hanging in the morning, but Miss Spencer taped the ends to stop sparks coming through them. He regularly beat María, Teresa and my brothers' backsides with his slippers whenever he thought they were disobedient or too noisy, especially at night. Things were very frightening for me and I always tried to behave the best I could, observing what was going on. Dad had never hit me, but it worried me that one day he could do it. He also liked to tell me that if I was not good enough, he would give me away to a gipsy to take me away.

It was November and the weather had taken a turn for the worse. I was sick in bed with yet another episode of tonsillitis, but I considered myself incredibly lucky as it would have been scary going outside on a day like today. School was a torment for me, and nothing had changed apart from the fact that I automatically stayed standing outside my classroom all day, feeling nervous and having the feeling of an imminent threat about to happen. I knew by now when the bells and sirens were going to go off and I could understand what they meant, despite their being so incredibly loud. The fear was very much still there, but it only became terror if somebody tried to get me inside the classroom or if I saw Teresa in the corridor; when that happened, anguish overwhelmed me and I couldn't control my tears as I tried to hold on to her.

The wind was howling and whistling through the gaps in my bedroom window. I could hear the sea thumping the rocks with tremendous force, and the waves splashing water over the road by the seaside. The tides were quite extreme at this time of the year. The noise of the elements had triggered my imagination in a vivid way, and it was easy to paint a picture in my head of what the ocean was looking like right now. The curtains in my bedroom now and again gently blew at the peak of the whistling, but the rattling noise of the wind through the blinds, the horizontal rain against the glass and the occasional slamming of doors left opened in the house were frightening to hear. María, Teresa, Alex and Jaime were all at school, and I prayed to Jesus that the weather would change and the rain would stop by the time they had to return home.

Mum wasn't home. She had gone shopping that morning, but before leaving, she came to my room to see how I was, promising to get me a treat for being so good while I was ill.

Patricia was also home and had already been round to see me when she was making the beds and cleaning the bedrooms. She noticed the intensity of the gale blowing in my bedroom, which was on the corner facing the open ocean, and suggested closing the shutters and blinds as an extra protective layer between the two windows, which helped. Miss Spencer was with Beatriz, who wasn't going to be able to go out for a walk today. Miss Spencer normally did the cooking in the house, as well as being our nanny, so I assumed she was probably cooking right now.

Ana and Carmen were also in the house today. Ana was the woman who did the ironing for the family. She came three days a week, but most of the time, she had left by the time we were back from school, so we normally only saw her at lunchtime.

Carmen was a gentle, quiet old woman with glasses and white hair that was always well combed. She did any sewing that was required and made most of our dresses from material that Mum had bought from the shops. Carmen was particularly fond of Beatriz and I couldn't blame her for it; she was just so cute.

Thump! I suddenly heard the main door close. It was too early for Dad to be back; it must be Mum, I hoped. "Mum, is that you?" I shouted from my bed.

"Yes, it is. What a terrible day! I'll be coming to see you in a minute, Isa. I need to ask Patricia and Miss Spencer to take all the shopping to the kitchen." Mum passed by and entered her bedroom, leaving her handbag and coat, returning immediately to the kitchen area and trying to get Patricia's and Miss Spencer's attention.

I waited for about twenty minutes before my beautiful mother finally appeared. She was the best mother in the world, I thought. It was difficult, though, to get her attention because she was always busy and preoccupied. My heart felt full of joy to see her.

"I'm feeling better, Mum," I said. "Can I get up after lunch and watch a little bit of telly this afternoon?"

"Of course, but if your temperature rises in the afternoon, you need to come back and stay in bed. Miss Spencer will tell you when to check it." Mum sat at the end of my bed and smiled at me. "I have spoken to Dr Toledano, the one in Seville, about your tonsillitis. He's the surgeon who operated on Jaime's adenoids and Alex's tonsils and adenoids three months ago. Dr Toledano is going to take your tonsils out so you don't get infections in your throat anymore. He doesn't normally operate on children under five but realises that you need this done; and I have told him that you are a very good girl who never cries."

Mum paused and looked at me, but I didn't change my expression, as I did not comprehend what tonsils or adenoids were. Somebody in Seville was going to stop me from having throat infections and I was expected to be good. I wasn't sure if that was good or bad; therefore, I said nothing.

"I nearly forgot, Isa. Here's your treat!" Mum exclaimed, handing me a book. "I hope you like it."

"Thank you!" I replied, looking at its cover.

Fear overwhelmed me, knowing that I would have to leave the house and go somewhere unknown in Seville, but Mum left the room before I had the time to find any more words. I didn't remember Jaime or Alex going to Seville with Mum, nor could I recall any of them mentioning tonsils or adenoids. After a few minutes, I opened the book and found different paper dolls with many different dresses and shoes that could easily be detached from the book. The clothes were interchangeable and easily clipped to the dolls, but when I had tried all the possible combinations for the different dolls, I piled them together on top of the book and left everything by my side table. I sighed, lay down on my back and stared at the ceiling.

Teresa and María arrived from school and both came into my room.

"How are you feeling, Isa?" María asked.

"I'm fine. I'd like to get out of bed," I answered.

"It was really scary getting to the end of our street. It was almost impossible to walk against the wind. I had to hold on to María because at some point I started going backwards," Teresa explained excitedly.

"Yes, it was really strange and Teresa made me laugh when I saw her face and she wasn't moving at all," María explained. I had to reach for her hand and hold tight to the door handle of a parked car at the same time, until the strength of the wind had passed. It's almost impossible to get past the corner of our building by the seaside."

"People coming from the corner into our street were being forced to run by the wind," said Teresa in an amusing way. "It's hilarious to watch because they behaved like puppets. There was a man who left a shoe behind and struggled to get it back; he couldn't return to where the shoe was, despite being so close to it."

They both made me laugh and I felt happy to see them, but we soon heard Patricia calling them for lunch.

"Bye, Isa," María said.

"We'll have peace and quiet for once because Mum has gone to collect Jaime and Alex and they're not back yet," Teresa explained with a smile full of satisfaction. "Bye."

After about twenty minutes, Patricia appeared through the door, although I could have guessed it was her with my lunch as soon as I recognised the rattling noise of the glass, cutlery and plate on the tray as she walked down the corridor.

"Here you are, Isa! I bring you soup and a French omelette today. Miss Spencer says to eat only what you feel like and nothing else; and to take your temperature. Here's the thermometer." She handed me the instrument as soon as she had rested the tray on my lap. "What would you like for dessert? I'll bring it to you in a little while and you can tell me your temperature then."

"Patricia, thank you, but I'll only have the soup; this is too much food for me. But I will have some orange juice if Miss Spencer wouldn't mind making me some. I don't think I have a temperature, but my throat is still too sore to swallow anything lumpy," I explained.

"I will be delighted to make it for you! Don't you worry about the omelette. I will keep it for my lunch later on; I love omelettes. I think we should have asked you what you wanted to eat before we brought anything to you anyway. Put the thermometer on and I will be back when your sisters are on the second course."

Patricia left my room happily carrying the plate with the omelette with her. I put the thermometer under my left arm and started eating the soup with my right hand. I wasn't particularly hungry but tried to eat as much as I could, and once the soup was finished, I read my temperature, which was 36.8 °C. Patricia finally returned, bringing me the orange juice, which seemed very appetising. I drank it all in one go and noticed that it slightly stung my throat, but it felt very refreshing.

"I forgot to bring you the vitamins for your eyes. Here you are. What's your temperature?" Patricia asked.

"It's 36.8," I said as I took a spoonful from the bitter syrup I took every day to make my eyes stronger. "Patricia, I would like to get up and watch telly this afternoon," I said with an inquisitive look.

"I'm sure you will be allowed when everyone has gone back to school again and your parents are having a nap," she replied.

When Patricia left, I kept thinking about my vitamins. Dad was worried that my eyes had to become stronger, and I always had to have these vitamins several times during the year ever since I could remember. I had terrible German measles when I was three months old and since then, I had developed a strong squint in my eyes. I had therefore needed to wear glasses since the age of one. Thinking about this, I started feeling sleepy and slowly fell into a light sleep, but I suddenly heard the thump of the main door opening, which gave me a fright, and my mother crying and screaming, cursing herself as she tried to run along the corridor towards her bedroom. My brothers came into the house behind her, but they went straight to the dining room to get some lunch.

"I've done it again!" Mum screamed as she ran in. "I am stupid, and there is no solution for someone like me! What a horrible mess! I want to die!"

"Mrs Grimaldi, don't worry, please!" Miss Spencer said reassuringly. I'll give you a hand. It's not the first time, and you know everything will be washed and cleaned in the end. Come on, Mrs Grimaldi, lean on me and I will help you to get to the toilet. That's it. We're nearly there."

The odour gradually spread and became overpowering. Mum had done a big poo again. She claimed that she had needed laxatives to be able to go to the toilet since she was an adolescent but was always obsessed with her alternating constipation and diarrhoea, not being able to control how to get to the toilet on time; defecating anywhere at any time, often when least expected. These accidents were frequent with Mum and we all knew about them. They made me feel sick and were very embarrassing, especially when they happened in the middle of the street or when driving in the car. We all knew not to say anything about the episodes and all of us acted as if we didn't mind; we just assumed Mum couldn't avoid acting like this and we all accepted it.

I was finally allowed to get up and leave my bedroom, where I had been for the last three days. I still felt a little weak and dizzy at times, but I enjoyed seeing Beatriz for a while and listening to the conversation of the rest of the women in the house. The telly was black and white and only had two channels on it, but I was lucky to put it on when the *Tom and Jerry* cartoons were showing. I was also looking forward to seeing *The Circus*, which normally took place every day of the week for half an hour, from 6.00 to 6.30 p.m., but just before it started, I developed a terrible headache and my temperature rose again.

"Isa, you look pale and feel hot. I'm going to give you an aspirin and you need to go back to bed. I'll come see you later," Miss Spencer told me, holding my head while resting her hand on my forehead.

I stood up, went to bed without arguing or even talking and fell asleep as soon as I lay down. By the time I woke up, it was dinnertime and everybody was home. I felt refreshed and a bit stronger, although slightly dopey after so many hours of sleep.

"Teresa, are you there?" I asked.

"Isa, you're awake!" she answered, poking her head through the door. "I was beginning to wonder if you were ever going to wake up at all. You must have felt exhausted to sleep like that."

I smiled at her but said nothing. Her face looked very serious to me.

"Were you worried about me?" I finally asked her.

"Something bad has happened, Isa. Do you know Luisa Barrero in year four? She has two sisters, one in year six and another one in two," she said.

"No," I said, moving my head from side to side.

"The three of them were walking to school together after lunch, although Luisa was slightly behind the other two," Teresa explained. "Something really horrible happened, and she died!" Teresa covered her face as she said it but then continued to talk. "A building crane in the main avenue collapsed on top of her because of the strong wind, and now she's dead. All three of them could have been killed, but the other two are fine. Everyone at school was shocked and many girls and teachers cried. It's very, very sad!"

There was silence between us and a sense of panic overwhelmed me as I absorbed the news. Was it really possible to die on your way to school? Could a child die at school? I questioned myself. I supposed any child could, and I remembered how I had been praying to Jesus in the morning so my siblings would return home safely. How could anyone control danger? Danger was everywhere! I thought of needing to be extra alert and vigilant, especially outside my house. I didn't want to die. I was frightened thinking of Luisa at the very moment the crane fell on top of her. Did she feel scared and lonely but unable to talk just before closing her eyes? I wondered …

I didn't notice that Teresa had left me, and for the rest of the day, I kept very quiet, trying to control my fear. I didn't sleep very well that night. The storm and strong winds had finally stopped, but I knew there was a thick fog instead. The lighthouse was failing to illuminate my room, which only occurred if there was fog as opposed to mist, and I could hear the intermittent warning foghorn coming from the lighthouse instead, simulating the noise of a real cargo ship from a distance. I could picture the ocean as being calm but at the same time could sense a feeling of warning and vigilance all around me.

Chapter Five

THE OPERATION

Three weeks had passed since I had the episode of tonsillitis and time spent at school was a heavy and arduous burden. I occasionally received a brief smile from Miss Cecilia, but we both continued with our mutual unspoken agreement of my staying outside the classroom and her getting on with her lesson. School made me feel unhappy and isolated. My levels of anxiety were very high, with a deep sense of a possible unexpected and imminent not knowing what was happening at any time.

Once I was back in the house at the end of the day, Mum said, "Isabel, we're going to Seville tomorrow to visit Dr Toledano. Do you remember when I told you about him?" She obviously wasn't expecting a reply, for she continued immediately. "He's going to take your tonsils out to stop your throat infections from happening so often."

I looked at her without knowing what to say. "Is there school tomorrow?" I asked instead.

"Yes, there is, but I have already informed Miss Cecilia that you are going to be missing school for a week."

I felt a kind of relief inside me when I heard the news about school, but somehow it sounded alarming that the doctor needed one whole week to sort my throat out; I still did not know what to think.

"Does it take one week to fix my throat?" I finally asked my mother.

"I suppose, all in all, yes. We need to travel to Seville and after that we will visit the doctor. Then you need to recover for two or three days at Grandmother's house and we'll see the doctor again to make sure everything is fine, and after that, we will return to Cádiz," she explained, counting the days on the fingers of her hand while smiling at me. "It will pass quickly, and you will be home and back to school before you realise it."

I looked her straight in the eyes for a few seconds but did not say anything at all, trying to find a reassurance in her voice, which somehow I couldn't find. Different completely unconnected feelings whirled inside me, tying my chest up in a big knot, and from then on, I remained completely silent.

The following morning came soon enough and I was awake early, although I stayed in bed waiting for Miss Spencer to open my door. I heard my siblings getting ready for school and preferred not to say goodbye to them because I knew that my fear could make me cry. Beatriz was breathing heavily and observing her always awoke in me a deep affection and a smile. Her peace and unawareness of danger were comforting to see. I was amazed that Beatriz could sleep through the racket of Jaime and Alex in the bathroom next door to us, brushing their teeth and getting their shoes. I would have thought she was deeply asleep, but as soon as Miss Spencer gently opened the door of our room, Beatriz opened her eyes as if she had been waiting for her to come in. She was so cute!

"Good morning, girls!" Miss Spencer greeted us. "It's a beautiful day today." She walked straight to the window to open the blinds and shutters, and immediately the light came through with great intensity. The sky was completely clear, without a single cloud, and the sea kept really still, with a gentle rocking of small waves by the seashore, coming and going in a rhythmic way.

I rubbed my eyes and asked Miss Spencer, "What shall I wear today? I'm going to Seville. Miss Spencer, I would like to get dressed before having breakfast."

"You should wear something comfortable, Isabel. Why don't you come to the wardrobe and choose it yourself? Come on! Get up and come close to me. We will choose your clothes together."

I stood up at once and went to the front of the wardrobe. I examined my clothes for a few seconds, but I was finding it difficult to concentrate on any of them at all because in reality, I didn't mind very much what I wore. I was preoccupied thinking about what would happen in Seville and how a doctor could take my tonsils out. I wasn't concentrating on anything in particular or hearing the people around me; I was in my own world, floating in a cloud and watching things happening as if they were completely distant from me. If I ever answered any questions, I was completely unaware of it. Before I realised it, I was fully dressed and standing by the door next to my mother. We were ready to go.

❧

Mum placed the luggage in the boot of the car and took the white SEAT 1500 out of our garage, which was behind our block of flats. There was space for two cars in the garage, but Dad had already driven to work with the silver SIMCA 1200. Mum was an experienced and confident driver and she made me feel safe inside the car. We crossed the brand-new bridge that crossed the Bay of Cádiz. Apparently, it was the biggest bridge ever built in Spain and you had to pay to use it, but Mum thought it would make our journey shorter.

Cádiz was surrounded by seawater except for a miniscule tongue of land, where there was only room for a dual carriage motorway, joining it to the mainland. This enormous bridge bypassed the effort of having to drive all around the bay, crossing different villages along the way, and could open up in the middle, allowing large battleships to enter the bay for repairs.

Dad always commented about how strategically important Cádiz was for the Spanish Navy – but not only that: the city also possessed a large cargo port. Cádiz was the first stop in Europe from Africa and the last stop in Europe before the Canary Islands and crossing the Atlantic Ocean towards America. It was quite impressive observing the gigantic cranes working on massive cargo ships to the left of the bridge, loading and unloading containers on the shore close to the city but also building new ships on the opposite shore from it. The inner part of the bay to the right of the bridge was the area where the battleships were moored in the naval shipyard for repairs. There were fishermen all along the bridge on both sides, trying their luck fishing, and the rest of the silver water underneath us was painted with different sizes of sailing boats and the two typical steamboats, which constantly took passengers to and from both sides of the bay; they always met in the middle.

Mum also chose to drive on the private motorway, which led us all the way to Seville. It had two toll positions for which she had to pay. The motorway, although also new, was slightly older than the bridge. There were no motorways in Spain as far as I knew apart, from the 150-kilometre Cádiz-Seville Motorway and the 10-kilometre stretch of land between Cádiz and the first town outside Cádiz along the bay, San Fernando. I knew well because every time we had to travel to our summer house in the north of Spain, I could only see country lane roads and plenty of mountains to drive across, suffering and overtaking every lorry on each of them.

Mum abruptly interrupted my thoughts. "Isabel, why are you always so quiet? What are you thinking about?"

"I don't know," I replied, tensing up.

"You are like a little clam. You hardly ever talk. I'd like you to tell me something about anything you like. How is school going?"

"Fine," I answered, getting increasingly worried that I was going to have to tell something, although I didn't know what.

"Miss Cecilia has said to me that you cry at the door of your classroom if she ever tries to make you enter it and that you stay outside the room every day. I would like you to get inside your classroom and to sit with all the other girls. What stops you from doing so?"

"I'm very scared," I said.

"But you shouldn't be!" she exclaimed. "Miss Cecilia is very nice and nobody is going to hurt you …"

I was sitting in the back seat behind Mum and she couldn't see how my eyes flooded with silent tears. I couldn't explain to anyone how I felt because I couldn't find the words for it. I felt completely lost at school, I couldn't work out what I had to do, and worst of all, I didn't know what was expected of me. I had no sense of direction or my role inside that building. Everything people said or did was alien to me, and it was so frightening. The only safe place was to stand alone outside my classroom.

We continued the rest of the journey without any further conversation, for which I was grateful. I managed to relax, feeling the warmth of the sun on my face through the window and enjoying the rich countryside around us.

We finally arrived in Seville and Mum drove straight to the private clinic, where Dr Toledano was expecting us. I noticed that Mum left the luggage in the boot.

A smiley nurse greeted us at the door. She was wearing a white nursing uniform with plain trousers and a top. "Good morning, Mrs Grimaldi!"

"Good morning to you," Mum replied.

"We are expecting you. Perfect timing! Everything's ready. Please come in away from the waiting area and into the next room, where you can settle for a few minutes before one of us comes to see you. You can take your jackets off and leave them in the room because we are not expecting any more patients this morning. Dr Toledano is already inside waiting for Isabel whenever she's ready."

I instinctively tightened my grip on my mother's hand when I heard those words. Me? Being ready for what? I wondered. Mum and I sat on the big sofa, and she helped me take my coat off and did the same with hers. She also had me take my shoes off. It was very much like a sitting room area, with two armchairs and a sofa, a coffee table with a jar full of artificial flowers and a single large window with thick beige curtains hanging on each side. There also were three or four landscape pictures scattered around the walls of the room, but before I had the chance to look at any of them properly, a different nurse walked into the room via a second door that I had failed to notice, close to the far corner of the room from where I was sitting.

"Hello, Isabel," she said, the first time anyone had acknowledged me since we had arrived. The nurse continued walking towards me, trying to distract me with her conversation from something she was carrying in her right hand. "Please lie down on your tummy. You can hug Mummy if you want to."

I looked at Mum and she nodded her head, holding my shoulders and starting to turn my body to lie down on my front on top of the sofa. I understood that I only adopted this position whenever I was receiving an injection in my buttock, and I knew that I was probably going to have an injection at any moment. I was terrified of needles and every time I needed one, I wanted to know in advance in order to prepare myself for it. I always complied without resistance, but I needed time to control my terror and nervousness around it. Today, however, I could foresee that the injection was only the beginning of something else, and without much time to do anything else, my dress was pulled up and my underwear slightly pulled down by my mother and the nurse. I couldn't avoid feeling distressed and incredibly tense, which forced me to tighten the muscles in my buttocks as hard as I could, making the prick of the needle through my skin and the injection itself incredibly painful. The fear I was feeling made me completely mute and motionless.

The nurse said something to Mum and left the room, while my mother gently covered me again and pulled my dress down. I stayed in that position waiting for things to happen and finish as soon as possible; there was complete silence between us. I heard the same nurse entering the room once more, but this time she didn't say anything until she was by my side and holding my shoulders.

"Isabel, you need to come with me now. I will walk you to the next room, where Dr Toledano is waiting to see you. Your mum will stay here until you are ready to go," the nurse said as she lifted me up from the sofa and we both walked towards the new room.

I didn't want to leave Mum, but I knew she wanted me to be obedient, so I did it for her. I wanted to look at her before I left, but I felt so rigid and frightened that I couldn't possibly turn around. Instead, I stiffly walked along next to the nurse without saying a word. Bright lights were illuminating the room and it smelt of medicines. The nurse who had initially greeted us was also there, and she took my hand as soon as I entered the room; the other nurse closed the door behind us.

Everything was white and there was a black chair with a large and strange group of lights and a big articulated lamp hanging from the ceiling. There also was a cabinet full of multiple metallic drawers to the side, next to one of the walls. The first drawer was fully opened, with different instruments laid out which I didn't recognise.

The receptionist/nurse, still holding my hand, sat on the chair and showed me how the chair was magic and could easily go up and down by pulling a lever with her foot.

"Come on, Isabel!" she invited me, clapping her hands onto her thighs. "Sit on my lap and I will hold you and show you how to go up and down together."

I held my arms up with my back to her, waiting for the nurse to pull me up on to her lap, which she did. As soon as I sat on the hard surface of her lap, I felt the bruising and pain of my backside where the injection had just gone in. She briefly showed me how the chair went up and down but afterwards said,

"Isabel, cross your arms in front of you and I will hold you like this." The nurse showed me how and held me tightly by my forearms and close to the elbows so I could not move.

Doctor Toledano finally came into the room. He had dark hair and a moustache, and he was wearing a white coat over his normal clothes.

"Hello, Isabel," he said without looking at me. "Your Mum says that you are a very good girl. I would like you to listen carefully to what I say and not to move. It is really important. This will not take long."

At the same time, he sat on a stool opposite us and placed a white plastic bucket on the floor between my dangling legs and him. He also reached for a headlight, which he placed on his head with an adjustable strap.

"Tina, get the mouth opener and the injections ready," he ordered the second nurse.

The doctor took hold of an object with two parallel metallic bars, which he put in my mouth and immediately pulled apart, forcing and fixing my mouth wide open. His headlight suddenly blinded my eyes, but Dr Toledano bent slightly, focusing it into my mouth, also adjusting the articulated ceiling lamp and flashing it towards me.

"Well done, Isabel. I need you to stay really still now. You will feel a prick on each side of your mouth, but there is nothing to be worried about. They will last one second each," he explained. Tina passed him two syringes, which he injected in each side of my mouth. I immediately flinched, tensed up and tried to complain of pain as soon as I felt it.

"Keep still, keep still!" the receptionist/nurse whispered, pressing my arms even harder.

The doctor then took a pair of forceps and slowly grabbed one of my tonsils, snapping it out of my mouth in one movement, repeating the action again and attacking the second tonsil too. An overwhelming and utter terror took control of my whole body, overriding any pain I could have felt. Blood poured out of my mouth and through my nose like a torrent, and the bucket in front of me filled up with it. The nurses around me were holding me tightly, and I could not move or run away. The device keeping my mouth opened was not removed until the doctor was satisfied that there was no further bleeding. I tried to kick the doctor, but my slippery shoeless feet were not making too much of an impact on him. Any attempts to cry or shout were muffled and suffocated by the gargling noise of the blood in my throat and my inability to articulate any noise with my mouth wide opened.

By the time the ordeal was finished, my will to fight had subsided. I had managed to distance myself from my own terror, like witnessing it from outside my body, not having anything to do with me. I had lost my eye contact and my bodily connection with the world. I had stopped feeling even firm touch around me. The world around me meant nothing to me. Still, I couldn't stop sobbing in anguish all the way back to my grandmother's house in Seville.

"Here we are, Isabel," Mum announced.

It was an enormous, beautiful detached wooden house with three floors. Aunt Lucía and Uncle Tomás, who was one of Mum's brothers, lived next door. They had eight children; only three of them were girls. The two houses were linked by the garden. Uncle Tomás decided to live close to his mother when she was widowed, but although the houses were physically close to each other, none had anything to do with the others. The garden was beautifully kept up and was full of flowers.

There was a large central balcony, which was the main feature of the front of the house. I liked my grandmother's house because everything was so modern and luxurious. I had never seen a house more beautiful than this one!

Matilde opened the door after my mother rang the bell. She was the maid.

"Good morning, Mrs Grimaldi."

"Good morning," Mum replied. "Is Isabel's room ready?"

"Yes, Mrs Grimaldi. The second room in the right corridor of the first floor is ready for her."

"Thank you. Can you ask the chauffeur to park my car inside the garage, please? I left it by the main entrance door. These are the keys," Mum said, reaching out one hand holding the car keys.

"Atanasio is in the garage. I will let him know. I don't think he realises you have arrived, Mrs Grimaldi," replied Matilde.

Grandmother's garage was underground and could be opened with a remote control. It could fit several cars, and it led off the lower ground floor of the house.

Antonia, the cook, also came to the reception hall. She could make the best cakes in the world.

"Poor little girl!" she said. "She is in a bad way."

Mum did not answer and continued walking with me inside the house. All the floors were marble and beautiful large chandeliers hung from the ceiling in the main entrance hall and the stairs. Expensive carpets partially covered the huge entrance and the massive stairs to the first floor, and there were antiques, valuable paintings and ornaments all over the house. Lighting, central heating, air conditioning, electric shutters, and reflective glass French windows worked to perfection everywhere in the house. All of the equipment in the kitchen and bathrooms was well designed and the latest technology. Rooms were incredibly generous in size, with solid doors and large fitted wardrobes everywhere. It was an amazing house.

Uncle Tomás and Grandmother always had the latest things brought from the United States; even my cousins had toys that nobody else had in Spain. Uncle Tomás had multiple businesses, including exports of shoes and leather goods and therefore he constantly travelled within Europe, parts of Asia and the United States. He was lucky enough to combine this with holiday trips round the world, taking Aunt Lucía and Grandmother with him.

Mum settled me in bed and shortly afterwards, my grandmother appeared.

"Hello, Graciela. How did it go?" Grandmother Isabel greeted Mum.

"She only cried at the end but is very upset now. Dr Toledano was happy with the operation," Mum summarised.

"It will soon pass. It is better not to give her too much attention. She will probably fall asleep soon. She looks exhausted." Grandmother stared at me as she spoke, but she wasn't really talking to me. "Come and have some lunch before you leave. Everything is ready. Matilde is already calling us to the dining room. Antonia knew you were coming today and has cooked your favourite food."

Grandmother was hard and strict but fair, and my parents had named me after her. Mum always said that Grandmother was widowed very young. Her parents were wealthy and Grandfather was also rich. I didn't think she was particularly warm with me and could never tell what she was thinking. It seemed as though she didn't like children around her, expecting exemplary behaviour all the time. Grandmother was always perfectly dressed in vivid colours, and her hair was always beautifully done and donned with coordinated jewellery. She rarely smiled and was impatient; deep down, I thought she dearly missed her husband and felt alone.

I lay in bed, still gasping for air and occasionally sobbing. My saliva was still stained with blood and I worried that my grandmother would get angry if I got my bed linens dirty. I waited and waited, calming myself down. I didn't feel like having any company and didn't wish to talk to anyone, but my mouth started to get dry and thirsty. Mum finally made her way up the stairs again.

"Isabel, how are you feeling? Do you need anything?" she asked, coming close to me.

"I would like some water, please. There's blood in my mouth and I'm afraid the bed linen is dirty," I replied.

"Don't worry about it. It's not fresh blood and it's normal to spit a little blood now and again after the operation. I'll bring you some water and some handkerchiefs to clean your mouth if you need to." Mum rang the bell from my bedroom and after a couple of minutes Matilde entered my room.

"Matilde, could you please bring Isabel a jar of fresh water with a glass and some handkerchiefs?"

"Yes, indeed, Mrs Grimaldi. It won't take me long," she answered.

"Isabel …" Mum hesitated. "I'll be leaving again soon. You know I can't leave your father alone; he needs me. Your brothers and sisters are also in Cádiz with Miss Spencer. I have many things I have to take care of and I need to get back. Grandmother will take care of you and I will phone every day. I'll be back by the end of the week and will take you to Dr Toledano again. If things go well and he is happy, we will go home together on Friday."

As I looked at Mum, a rush of anxiety overwhelmed me, but I couldn't say anything. Matilde walked in with a triumphant smile, having found enough handkerchiefs, and holding a tray with a jar of water and a glass. She placed everything on my side table.

"Is there anything else you need, Mrs Grimaldi?" she asked.

"Thank you, Matilde. That is all," Mum replied.

Matilde left the room and Mum looked at me in silence. I was no longer looking at her. She kissed my head and left.

The week passed slowly. I didn't know my grandmother very well and I felt unsafe without my mother's protection. The best place I could be was in bed. Aunt Lucía briefly visited me and so did Aunt Mónica, Mum's sister who was married to the son of the marquis of Montoro, who had eight children. Aunt Mónica had such an aristocratic accent that I could never be sure what she meant. She brought me colouring books and a pencil case. Grandmother visited me twice a day for an hour, telling me about Mum's news and knitting in silence most of the time. She also bought me some books with big pictures, as I still couldn't read. None of my cousins came to see me, though; I suppose they were all at school. But finally the person I was waiting for arrived – Mum!

I was taken home to Cádiz on the same day that we visited Dr Toledano to make sure he was satisfied with my recovery. It was an incredible relief to be back home again and despite not having done much for a week, I somehow felt drained and tired. Beatriz's face lit up with joy when she saw me; I thought she had missed me and that made me happy. I spent the weekend at home still recovering and I was grateful that I was not required to go anywhere. It was reassuring touching my toys and things and making sure everything remained the same as when I left.

Time flew and before I realised it, it was Sunday evening and I was getting ready to go to bed. I couldn't believe school had not been on my mind for nearly a week. Miss Spencer was putting Beatriz and me to bed, making sure everything was ready for the morning. Thinking about it made me unsettled and my nerves started overwhelming me. My head started throbbing and my heart began to pound. I was desperately trying to stop my tears from welling up, but it was too late to hide them. I was discovered while wiping my runny nose with my sleeve, and I looked down at my feet, closing my eyes.

"Isabel! My darling! Why aren't you even able to tell me that you are bleeding?" Miss Spencer said, clearly alarmed.

I opened my eyes and saw blood dripping on the floor. My sleeve was also heavily stained with red and it became apparent to me that my nose and mouth were full of blood too. I couldn't understand what was happening! Terror possessed me as soon as I realised that Mum was calling Dr Toledano on a Sunday evening and Miss Spencer was looking increasingly worried around me, trying to contain my haemorrhage. Dr Toledano advised Mum to attend his clinic in Seville early in the morning and to go to A&E in the local hospital if the bleeding did not stop. Miss Spencer spent the night next to me in my bedroom making sure the bleeding did not return. I worried, thinking what Dr Toledano could do to me again and wondering if I could actually die. My fear left me without words and I spent an extremely restless night with Miss Spencer sitting on my bed.

Mum drove me to Seville the following morning, but this time I sat on Miss Spencer's lap in the car. She held me tightly in her arms for the whole journey, which felt so comforting.

Chapter Six

INSIDE MY CLASSROOM

The Christmas holidays were over. I had remained in good health since my last visit to Dr Toledano, after my spontaneous bleeding episode. I had developed a late infection in the intervention site, which was treated with antibiotics. I had also just finished the course of iron tablets the doctor had given me; he was concerned that, considering everything, I had maybe lost too much blood for my weight and needed the tablets to make me strong again. Dad had taken the opportunity to treat me with some extra vitamins too because he didn't trust the iron to be enough for my deficits.

"Hello, Isa!" Teresa exclaimed, coming down the stairs at school, holding two large candles.

As I looked at her, my heart lit up with happiness, but I said nothing. I instinctively started moving to where she was on the stairs, starting to feel anxious that she was going to leave me again.

"My teacher has asked me to take these candles to the chapel."

I smiled and continued looking at her, ready to hold on to her uniform.

"Would you like to come with me to my classroom when I return? We're having a Spanish lesson and Mrs López always complains when I'm late because I stay extra time with you. I tell her that I don't like leaving you crying and the last time she said to bring you with me to class if necessary. Would you like to come with me? You already know some of my friends," Teresa coaxed.

"Are you sure it will be all right if I go? I don't want to be here alone," I replied.

"It will be more than fine. That is what she said to me."

"I will wait for you here, then."

Teresa and I entered in the middle of her Spanish class. Mrs López, who was explaining something to the group, suddenly stopped talking and everybody looked at the door.

"Mrs López, this is my sister Isabel. She was standing outside her class and I didn't want to leave her alone. Can she stay with me?"

"Of course. Let her in and share your desk with her. Ask her to keep quiet and let's get on with the lesson," Mrs López said.

"Thank you, Mrs López," Teresa replied.

"Isa, here's a piece of paper and a pencil. Doodle something until the lesson is finished, but please keep really quiet," she said to me.

I couldn't understand any of what Mrs López was saying and noticed that some of the girls were trying to look at me while concentrating on the lesson. Some of them were smiling at me.

I drew a house with one door, two windows and a big chimney full of smoke. The house had a big garden with one tree and some flowers. I also drew the outline of some mountains in the background, like the ones in the north of Spain and a bright and shiny sun. I didn't like it when people drew a smiley face on the sun; it wasn't supposed to smile at anyone. The sun could also kill you in a dessert or in the middle of the sea with no drinking water. I thought of adding a couple of clouds and a group of Vs in the far distance, simulating birds flying. I had practised this drawing many times at home, and in fact, it was the only kind of drawing I could do, apart from a single sailing boat on the sea with a Spanish flag on it.

My drawings were incredibly basic. People and animals had single lines as bodies and single lines as limbs; I could never do a chunky body no matter how hard I tried.

"Look, Teresa! Do you like it? It's the best house I've done so far!" I said this abruptly in a rather loud voice, pushing the piece of paper close to Teresa's face so she could see it.

"Shh!" Teresa immediately replied, staring at me with her finger to her mouth.

Mrs López stopped talking and forty girls turned their eyes on me at once in complete silence.

"It's beautiful, Isa. But if you want to continue staying with me, you must keep quiet; I mean no noises at all and no talking," Teresa told me assertively.

"Teresa," Mrs López said with a big smile. "I think it's time for Isabel to go back to her class. Do you mind accompanying her? I am sure Miss Cecilia must be wondering where she is."

"Yes, Mrs López," Teresa replied, pulling my hand and encouraging me to stand up.

"I like your classroom better than mine, Teresa," I said.

"Yes, but you are too young to have lessons here every day, Isa. I will take you back to Miss Cecilia."

Tears flooded my eyes again when Teresa left me, and I had the feeling Miss Cecilia hadn't even noticed my absence; but if she had, I couldn't tell.

Miss Cecilia opened the classroom door and spoke to me.

"Isabel, I would like you enter the classroom please."

"No!" I said, shaking my head.

"Come on. Give me your hand and let's go in," Miss Cecilia told me, reaching out for my hand and pulling at it.

"No! Please!" I screamed, resisting.

"Look, Isabel," Miss Cecilia said, kneeling down on one knee in front of me. "If you don't come in, I will take you to

Mrs Sánchez's year-two reception class next door. Maybe you will like that classroom better."

"No, no, please don't do it! Don't take me to any classroom! I want to stay where I am!" I exclaimed, starting to cry.

"You can't stay in the corridor any longer. Either you come inside or I will take you next door," Miss Cecilia told me, standing up and keeping her eyes on my face.

"I am scared! I can't go in!" I tried to explain, not controlling my tears.

"That's fine, then. Come with me and I'll take you next door. If you prefer that classroom instead, you can stay there."

Miss Cecilia took me by the arm and dragged me along the corridor until we reached the class next door. I screamed and shouted as if my life depended on it, resisting any walking and pulling in the opposite direction. Mrs Sánchez opened her door when she heard all the noise outside and Miss Cecilia managed to get me inside the room. By this time, I was on the floor and was pulled all the way in while I kicked and screamed in panic. Mrs Sánchez held me by the arm and Miss Cecilia took the opportunity to leave, closing the classroom door behind her. I quickly stood up and tried to run away, but Mrs Sánchez managed to turn the lock, which was placed high up in the door frame, out of any child's reach. I cried and screamed, punching and kicking the door and begging for the door to be opened, but Mrs Sánchez ignored me, going back to her desk to continue her lesson.

I was completely terrified. All the girls were staring at me in silence with their eyes wide open, giving me a sense of deep humiliation that they had all witnessed the event like in a theatrical play. It was incredibly difficult to conquer my anguish and my sobbing was making me gasp. The situation was helpless. I gradually surrendered, sliding my back against the door and crouching on the floor, covering my head with my hands. I was lost and wanted to die.

Some time passed, feeling like an eternity to me. There was a knock on the door and Miss Cecilia tried to open it but couldn't. Mrs Sánchez immediately stood up and unlocked the door, but I was still sitting against it. Miss Cecilia gently pushed it forwards, probably realising that I was blocking it, leaving a gap big enough for her to step inside the room.

"Would you like to come with me, Isabel?" she asked me, crouching on the floor next to me.

She was so close that I felt her unpleasant hair brushing my head. I nodded my head, still buried between my hands, but did not speak and she helped me up. We both walked outside to the corridor.

"Isabel, I would like you to enter my classroom. If you refuse, I will bring you back to Mrs Sánchez again," Miss Cecilia threatened while I was still crying in silence and looking down the floor. "Will you come with me?"

I nodded yes for a second time, still not making any eye contact, and reluctantly walked into my classroom, dragging my feet across the floor without looking at anyone. All the girls were sitting around the carpeted floor, waiting for Miss Cecilia. I sat at the closest desk to the door and covered my face, remaining there for the rest of the day.

My first year of school was a real struggle for me. It took me several weeks, until Easter, to join in any activity. As time passed, I remained at the same desk, not talking and hardly looking at anyone, not knowing how to do things. Distress overwhelmed me every time Miss Cecilia encouraged me to do an activity. I wasn't trying to be difficult or rebellious; I just didn't know what I had to do. If the girls in my class were cutting out shapes from pieces of paper, my anxiety would stop me from knowing which scissors I had to use, where I could find them or where I could find the paper with the shapes. I was terrified of doing something wrong and I knew my cutting wasn't perfect. I worried that Miss Cecilia might get angry with me when she realised I didn't know any letters and that I couldn't write, read, draw well, cut out shapes or sing. I wasn't aware of what anybody else could do compared to me.

It took me a long time to understand the dynamic of the class and how to stop feeling threatened. Miss Cecilia gave me a green grade card at the end of the year. Blue was the best and the red one meant having to repeat the year. I was relieved that the summer holidays had arrived and that school was over. Mum told me that it had been agreed that I would stay with Miss Cecilia during year-two reception, although a new group of girls were going to join me. Depending how my reading and writing got on, I would then be able to return to my old class in year one. I liked Miss Cecilia!

Chapter Seven

THE CAR JOURNEY

I was finding it very difficult to sleep. The suitcases were ready and the luggage was packed in both cars inside the garage. We were leaving early in the morning for the north of Spain, where we would be spending the summer holidays. All our bicycles were in Laredo, in our summer house in the county of Santander. I was looking forward to riding my bicycle again because now that I was five, I had stopped using stabilisers. My sisters and cousins had taught me how to ride during the Easter holidays in El Cortijo, but I wasn't sure if I would still remember how to do it. The noise of the cars driving by the seaside was keeping me awake because the windows were slightly opened and the shutters not fully closed; the light and the noise of the engines were difficult to ignore. The night was also far too warm to be able to sleep.

It had been fun to go to the beach every day since we were on school holidays. I still couldn't swim very well, but my doggy paddle style helped me to float for a few seconds when jumping waves. I liked getting in up to waist level and particularly loved ducking under the bigger waves; the deeper you went under, the less power you felt when the waves broke up on you. One day I would be able to go deeper beyond the breaking barrier. It seemed safer over there because the waves were still forming and when floating, your body went up and down gently, with no stress. The only thing to watch for was the sea current, making sure it didn't take you in.

It was 6.00 in the morning and we had already been travelling for an hour. Mum was driving the SEAT 1500 and Miss Spencer was accompanying her, with Beatriz and Jaime inside the car as well. Mum had suggested to Dad that Jamie, being the oldest son, was better in her car just in case there was a puncture and she needed any male support. Alex, Teresa, and I were travelling with Dad in the SIMCA 1200. María was spending the summer learning English in Dublin and had already left. Dad normally got confused with directions when driving, so we were following Mum's car the best we could.

"How much longer to get to Laredo, Dad?" Alex kept asking every now and again.

"Look, Alex! Stop asking me that; it takes eighteen hours to get there and we have only been travelling for one," Dad replied with slight exasperation in his voice. "We'll be stopping to get some petrol before lunch and will try to get something to eat just outside Madrid, in Aranjuez."

"How much longer to get some petrol, Dad?" Alex asked.

"I said *silence!*" Dad shouted. "I don't want to hear you asking me 'how much longer' anymore. Next time you wish to talk, you need to ask for permission to do so, and I will let you know if you can talk or not."

Alex didn't move a muscle and continued to stand still in the middle of the two front seats with his arms holding on to each of them. He liked to have a full view of the windscreen.

The traffic became heavier as the day went on and the number of lorries also increased. Mum's driving was sleek and smart. Dad was getting increasingly agitated, as she was managing to get several cars ahead every time she overtook a lorry.

"Where's your mother? Can you see her?" he asked occasionally.

"She's three cars ahead, after the lorry in front of us," I replied at one point.

Dad was constantly checking to see if he could overtake the lorry or not, and it was easy for me to see where Mum was because I was sitting behind the driver's seat. He would look to see if there was anything coming, but he didn't always judge it right. It was frightening facing cars or lorries coming in the opposite direction, close to a head-on collision, some of them using their flashing lights and honks in protest against Dad. Others had to pull over out of his way to give him the space every time he judged the overtaking short. I normally gave a general prayer to Jesus at the beginning of every journey to ask for protection, and from then on tried to control and ignore the nervousness that my own fear brought on me. But Dad didn't really have the patience to drive in traffic; he was restless and always thought that drivers did things on purpose to block him, not really understanding what the honking and flashing lights were about. Anybody else's manoeuvres were a direct threat against him. He always expected others to recognise his intentions when driving but failed to realise that maybe another driver had already initiated his movement well before him, especially if coming from behind.

"Don't, Dad! There might be a car coming round the bend," I suggested at one point, feeling panicky.

"Don't tell me what I have to do!" he snapped. "Understood? If I lose your mother, I'll get lost crossing Madrid. I'm the one here with a driving license!"

"Mum always waits for you, Dad," Teresa said. "Even when she gets ahead, she realises that you haven't had time to overtake and she waits for you to catch up with her."

It was difficult to overtake the lorry because we were getting close to the mountains separating Andalucía from Castile and the road was becoming narrower and with more curves. The sun was hot and we all felt sticky inside the car, even with some of the windows slightly opened. At some point, the lorry in front of us didn't seem to have the strength to go up the hill. It was heavily loaded and the road was rather steep. The lorry went slower and slower until the vehicle came to a halt and we all stopped behind him. My heart started racing because I could sense danger and looking at the load, which was watermelons, I just hoped that they were well secured and that they wouldn't fall backwards on top of us.

The lorry's wheels suddenly started rolling backwards despite the driver's best efforts to brake. We could do little as the vehicle got closer and closer. We were all ready for the crash, but the driver, at the very last minute, pushed the accelerator with a roar and managed to first stop and then get going again. There was a thick black cloud of smoke all around our car. Traffic had stopped in both directions, giving some space to the large lorry and Dad took the opportunity to overtake it, clearing its rear just in case it went backwards again.

Once we crossed Madrid, the traffic became more fluid. Dad got completely lost and Mum was waiting for him on the road exiting towards Burgos. The centre of Spain was a six-hundred-metre-high plateau, so it was fairly flat driving until we passed Burgos and entered Cantabria. The landscape was constantly changing from the dry and arid Castile to the green north of Spain, with high mountains leading to the beautiful coves along the coast and with villages of stone houses in every valley, as opposed to large but concentrated distant towns painted in white around the main sources of water in the south. The heat had been unbearable, but the further north we went, the better the temperature became. I couldn't wait to arrive! I was exhausted after such a long day and so much tension.

"Dad, I need a toilet break and some water," I said as soon as I spotted the petrol gauge with a red light. Dad clearly didn't realise that he was running out of petrol.

"Toilet?" he asked. "It might be a good idea, actually. We need some petrol. You know, children, this is my homeland. One can breathe better here."

"Dad, when will be arriving?" Alex asked once more, not listening to what Dad was saying.

"We're nearly there now – three more hours, I reckon."

Alex and Teresa had been chatting all the way, guessing which major town was next, competing to be the one to see more red cars first or playing games like "I spy with my little eye". They had both taken turns getting a little sleep and Alex had been questioning Dad about everything he saw and thought interesting. Alex couldn't pronounce words correctly and Dad always corrected him, making him vocalise them, losing his patience when Alex got stuck in the middle of a sentence or spoke too slowly.

"Children, there's the sea! Can you see it?" Dad exclaimed with a sense of relief. "The route we've been following from Madrid was the route used in the fifteenth century to take merchandise from all over Castile to the Port of Laredo. Laredo was the main port of Castile and merino wool from Spanish sheep was sold all over Europe, taken by boats to France, the Netherlands, and Great Britain. Kings and queens used Laredo as a departure point to visit other European countries, such as Katherine of Aragon when she got engaged to Prince Arthur, who was the eldest brother of the future Henry VIII, marrying both bothers after Arthur's death and becoming queen. Charles I of Spain, who also was Charles V of Germany disembarked in Laredo when he first arrived in Spain to claim his throne. He did it in the middle of a storm and when he put his foot on land, he said, 'I am saved.' That is why Laredo's beach is called Salvé, which means 'I am saved'. Part of the Gran Armada fleet departed from Laredo. In those days, Laredo and the villages around it had important shipyards making boats for the navy or to travel to America. Spain was commercially very important, but we were constantly battling against the British, who were also trying to intercept the gold coming from America, which was used to pay the army in the crusades against the Muslims; and the French were always changing sides, telling us that they were going to help us but somehow changing alliances ..."

As Dad went on and on explaining all this, I became mesmerised by the view. It was a beautiful summer evening and we were facing the Bay of Laredo. The Santoña Mountain formed one end of the bay and at the other was the Port of Laredo in a large C shape leaning to the left, separated by a long five-kilometre beach. The waters within the bay were protected, making the beach safe despite being in the Bay of Biscay, but the tides were incredibly extreme. People had to walk five hundred to seven hundred metres to reach the water at low tide. This made the beach spectacular, with an immense feeling of space and wildness. One particularity of this beach was the dunes. They were large and mobile, so every year they looked completely different and sometimes it was noticeable that they had shifted their position from the previous year. The sand was clean, white and incredibly fine, with not a single rock or stone in it; there were plenty of shells instead. Mountains surrounded the whole beach – La Atalaya beyond the Port of Laredo and Santoña at the front – but the spectacular sunset was always north-west, behind Montehano Mountain. It was a beautiful site, with small fishing boats starting to come out of the harbour with their lights on and sailing boats returning to the marina at the end of the day.

"We've arrived children! Is everybody awake?" Dad said, pulling on the handbrake.

"Where's Mum?" Alex asked.

Teresa looked at Dad. "She was well ahead of us," my sister said. "Do you think she had a breakdown?"

"I don't know. Mum will arrive soon. Help me with the luggage."

Dad opened the house, which smelt of having been closed for a long time. Teresa opened the windows and after we had been through the house, making our first contact with it, we realised that all our clothes were in Mum's car. There was no food in the fridge and Dad did not attempt to get any either, hoping that Mum would organise it as soon as she arrived. There was no telephone or television in the house either.

I went to check on the bicycles, which were in a hut by the kitchen door at the back of the house under the fig tree, but Dad told me it was too late to get any of them out. I went to my bedroom and realised that the beds were not made. I recognised objects and toys that were left from the previous summer, but after a long time, Mum had still not arrived. I was starting to get hungry.

Dad's temper changed for no apparent reason.

"I want all of you in bed now!" he shouted unexpectedly.

"I don't have my pyjamas," Alex answered. "And I want to see Mum."

"It doesn't matter, Alex," Teresa said, trying to reassure him. "Come with me and I'll put you to bed. She will be arriving soon. Isa, you will have to sleep in your underwear tonight. Go to bed, cover yourself up with the blanket that is already there and I'll come see you later."

"I don't have my toothbrush," I said.

"It doesn't matter if you don't brush your teeth tonight. You can do it tomorrow," she replied.

"Good night," I said.

I heard Alex crying because he was hungry. Teresa was with him in his bedroom. Mum was a good driver and couldn't be lost, I thought. I was sure the car had broken down. She had money and Miss Spencer was with her. I was sure I'd see her in the morning. I was so exhausted that I immediately felt asleep.

Miss Spencer walked into my room in the middle of the night with Beatriz asleep in her arms. She gently put her in her bed and turned to me to see if I was awake.

"What happened?" I asked. "You took a long time."

"We had a puncture in Los Tornos, the highest peak before descending to the coast, and the spare tyre was also punctured. So Mum had to get a lift from a passing car and go to the closest garage to have the wheel fixed. She returned after a while by taxi, but it was so late that we had to stop to have something to eat. We saw you guys passing by and waved to you, but your Dad didn't see us."

"He got very angry and sent us to bed," I explained. "Good night."

Summer was passing quickly. Our house had five bedrooms and was detached, with our own garden. It was about a twenty-minute walk from the beach where Miss Spencer took us walking every morning as long as it was not raining. My father loved the beach too, but Dad was only with us for three weeks in July and after that he always had to leave because of work. Mum didn't like the beach very much, so she hardly ever accompanied us. Both my parents' families were originally from the north of Spain and the majority of them spent every summer in Laredo. Every time we went to the beach, we met a large number of cousins and second cousins. Grandmother Isabel had just bought herself a five-bedroom flat with a view of the beach in Laredo and therefore was spending her summers close to my mum and Uncle Tomás. Her four sisters spent six weeks of the summer in the local hotel and they always met on the beach too. Grandmother Isabel liked swimming in the water every day of the summer regardless of the weather. Her house outside Oviedo was no longer occupied by anyone; that was where Mum used to spend her summer holidays as a child.

Dad always found it difficult to interact with his family and despite his two brothers being in Laredo during the holidays, he did not seem to get along with them.

"Your mother disrespects me!" Dad said to Mum. "Your family always forces me to be there. Why don't we go spend the day on the meadows on the slope of the Atalaya Mountain? After all, they all talk at the same time and nobody keeps quiet when I talk. Your brother- in-law calls me 'Roberto' and 'my friend', as if he knows me. I am certainly not his friend and I'm not sure where he is getting that familiarity from; he also pats me in the back and hits me because he thinks I am not listening to him. And your younger brother Pedro is always laughing at me about his jokes. If he ever asks you again, 'Graciela, my sister, are you sure you are smart enough for the occasion?' I will hit him. Who does he think he is?"

"Roberto, please. It's only a joke," Mum tried to reassure Dad. "You know how he likes teasing people. He says that because I am normally elegantly dressed. Nobody is disrespecting you at all. Quite the contrary. Aunt Lucía and my brother Tomás were commenting the other day how knowledgeable you are. My mother was also impressed when I told them that you are writing a book about the Castilian navy in medieval and Renaissance Times and writing an article about the Battle of La Rochelle against Napoleon's troops in the north of Spain. You have even been invited as a speaker to the University of La Magdalena in Santander. The navy will make sure all this gets published, Roberto."

Holidays in the north of Spain were a time for coming in contact with nature. When Dad was around, we never stopped going on excursions: climbing mountains, going to the river or swimming in the sea, reaching hidden spots and coves only by descending steep and complicated cliffs by holding on to rocks or jumping from one to another. Miss Spencer only joined us on these excursions if Beatriz was coming with us. I always worried because I sometimes found it dangerous and some of the places we got to were physically hard work. I had to concentrate a lot. Dad always went ahead at his own pace and never looked back.

But what I really enjoyed in Laredo was the sense of freedom and independence. We all rode our bicycles and moved freely, visiting our cousins, playing in different houses and going from one place to another, as we were so many. There was hardly any traffic on the sandy unpaved roads where we lived and we only had to let Miss Spencer know where we were. The only rule to follow was to have lunch, snacks and dinner at home, never in anybody else's house.

Dad soon had to leave us. His current war ship in the navy was part of General Franco's holiday escort. Mum told us that Franco was capturing whales off the north-west coast of Spain. Apparently, Dad was one of the best officers in finding where the whales were located and thanks to him, Franco had been able to kill two whales. Things were much quieter and more relaxed when he was not around. I was scared of Dad.

"Mum, why are you crying?" I heard Jamie asking Mum as I entered the kitchen to have breakfast one morning.

Miss Spencer was trying to reason with Mum. "Mrs Grimaldi, this happened two days ago, when they sent you the letter. Maybe you should ring and speak with María to have a better feeling of the situation now and decide what to do."

Jamie and Alex were sitting by the kitchen table not eating, and I was standing by the door, the three of us waiting to find out what was going on. Mum was with her back to us, facing the stove and holding an open envelope with one hand and a letter in the other one. She was sobbing but not talking to us.

"Your sister María has broken her leg in Ireland and is in hospital," she finally said. "Apparently, she dared the oldest boy of the family to jump off the garage roof. He did not have the courage to do it, but she did and broke her leg. I'm not sure what to do now. She is alone in hospital." Visibly upset, Mum left the kitchen.

Mum didn't take a flight to Dublin because she said that it was too expensive and her duty was to stay with Dad, who couldn't take time off work. Mum also argued that María was returning home a week later anyway. I couldn't imagine how life was in Ireland at all. María, although she was only eleven, always thought she had the best English of all of us. I couldn't say, because I didn't speak it – I just hoped that her English was good enough for the hospital and the situation she was in when she broke her leg.

Dad came back to Laredo at the end of the summer and we all drove to Cádiz. We stopped in Madrid to collect María, who had just arrived from Ireland, so we had to spend one night in a hotel. This made the journey better, I thought. María was using crutches to walk and her right leg was in plaster.

Chapter Eight

El Cortijo

Second year reception with Miss Cecilia was very easy compared to the previous year. I was familiar with the class and knew where everything was. Miss Cecilia was always asking me to help her with the new girls and I showed them what they had to do. Letters and numbers were fun to learn and my reading and writing were coming along in leaps and bounds. I hadn't cried once since we started the year and I always came into the class. My fear was much more under control, but I still didn't feel comfortable at school. I was constantly alert to figures of authority around me because I couldn't understand what they wanted from me when they approached me.

The playground, though, was not such an easy place for me. Reception children had to stay in the swings area, but we were not allowed on the big swings since a girl one year older than María had an accident two years ago. The swings were still there, but nobody could go on it. It had a large metallic frame with an enormous piece of wood where numerous children could sit at once, facing forwards or in horse-riding position, holding on to metallic holders. The piece of wood would move backwards and forwards, but the children would move sideways if sitting facing forwards. This particular girl fell off the edge and when the large piece of wood returned, it hit her in the back with everyone else on top. It broke her spine and she was now in a wheelchair.

My favourite swing was the one with a big pole supporting a cone-shaped red metallic frame which had a double circle in the base. Girls sat on the bar in the bottom circle while they held on to the top circle with one hand. All the girls used their legs at the same time to spin the frame clockwise and when the swing got enough speed, they lifted their legs off the ground but remained sitting, and one girl put a stone on the ground while everyone else tried to catch it off the floor at great speed, repeating the process all over again. The person who got the stone more times during break time won.

I particularly liked the feeling of spinning with the wind in my face and all noises suddenly becoming very distant. The playground was overcrowded and spinning around, gave me a sense of travelling in the space with the clouds, the sun and the sky moving around me, or watching the scenery in a sequence of successive but independent images like in an old film. I joined in and went for the stone just enough times to keep me in the game, and therefore in the swing, but what I really enjoyed was the spinning. I tended to follow groups of girls and watch what they did, but most of the time I was on my own. The place where I felt safest was in my classroom with Miss Cecilia and anything unexpected from the adults at school made me apprehensive.

It was the Easter holidays and Dad was going to take us all to El Cortijo in the SEAT 1500. Mum was already in Seville visiting Grandmother Isabel and she was going to join us there. Miss Spencer was sitting in the front with Dad, although she was clearly not very happy about that. Dad had already shouted at her and said to her that it was the only way we could all fit in the back seat together. We all knew that when we had to get in the car with Dad, we only had the few seconds it took him to sit down and start the engine to all get in and find our seats; he never waited or even checked if we were all in with the doors closed. All of us at one time or another had ended up being dragged forward by the moving car.

Travelling with Dad made me anxious, trying to anticipate his unpredictability. I was on María's lap and Beatriz was on Teresa's lap, with my two brothers in between. Miss Spencer was getting progressively more nervous with Dad's commanding orders every time there was anything to do or to pay on the motorway. Dad had forgotten his wallet, but luckily Miss Spencer had hers. We left the house half an hour earlier than expected because Dad was getting so agitated and couldn't wait any longer. He was the only one who was ready.

"Miss Spencer, speak aloud! I can't hear you!"

"But Mr Grimaldi, the tone of my voice is soft and I can't talk any louder than this," she tried to explain.

"I said louder! Didn't you listen to what I just said?" he insisted, without hearing what she was saying.

Tension was building and we were all quiet in the car. Dad had occasionally been swerving behind the wheel and I was getting scared. He was agitated, but suddenly the car came to a halt unexpectedly. Dad thought it must be the battery, as the engine wouldn't even turn over when he turned the key.

"I want everyone out of the car except Isabel and Beatriz! Come on!" Dad ordered. "Actually, thinking about it, Miss Spencer you stay inside the car too and sit at the wheel. We will all push the car for you, and when I give you the order, put the first gear in and try to accelerate. That should start the car."

"But, Mr Grimaldi, I've never done this before. I would rather push the car and you do it instead. You won't like it if I get it wrong," Miss Spencer replied, looking flushed and uneasy.

Beatriz had started crying. She was clearly sensing the tension in the environment and things were not working well so far. They all tried to push the car with Dad inside, but they did not have enough strength. The luggage and the three of us inside were making the car heavy.

Dad exited the car angrily, slamming the door behind him. Beatriz started crying again, and I therefore hugged her and started singing to her; this made her happy again.

"Miss Spencer, get inside the damn car at once!"

Miss Spencer replied the best she could without losing her temper. "I can't do what you are asking me to do. And for God's sake, stop shouting."

"Speak up! I can't hear what you're saying. Get inside the car!"

Rage was starting to take control of Miss Spencer and she stepped inside the car gritting her teeth. Her hands were visibly shaking and her movements were abrupt, changing her right hand from the wheel to the gearstick and back to the wheel again. The car had started moving when Dad started pushing.

"Take off the handbrake, damn it!" Dad screamed from the outside.

"Oh, yes, of course!" Miss Spencer said.

The car gathered some speed and Dad couldn't keep pushing, but somehow Miss Spencer couldn't work out the gear in which she had to put the car.

"Put in first gear and accelerate!" Dad kept repeating all, his voice becoming more distant.

"I can't do it! I can't do it! I don't know how to do it," Miss Spencer kept saying.

Beatriz was getting upset again hearing Miss Spencer's tone of voice. The car finally came to a stop and Dad opened the door, asking Miss Spencer to step outside.

"Children, push with me and I will also push, keeping the door open. When I say stop, I'll get in the car and start the engine," Dad explained to us.

So they did, and this time it worked. Dad asked all my siblings to get inside the car again, but he got out to talk to Miss Spencer, leaving the engine running.

"You have deliberately disobeyed me, not doing what I asked you to do," Dad said to Miss Spencer. "Therefore, I am leaving you behind on the motorway and you can find you own way home. Goodbye!"

We all heard it. Miss Spencer was speechless for a few seconds, but as Dad was climbing back inside the car, María opened her door and stepped outside again.

"If you're leaving Miss Spencer behind, we'll stay with her." María said this assertively, and Teresa and Jaime got out of the car as well.

"You are disobedient and disrespectful," Dad said as Alex also climbed out of the car.

"Alex, get in the car!" Dad screamed.

Alex immediately got inside and Beatriz started crying again. My head was telling me to stay with Beatriz, who needed looking after, but my heart wanted to stay with Miss Spencer. Dad finally drove away with the three of us. I couldn't trust Dad's driving and I felt terrified.

"Mum wouldn't have allowed you to leave Miss Spencer, and my brother and sisters behind," Alex said to Dad.

Not a single word was spoken again, but Dad was visibly angry, restless and offended.

Miss Spencer arrived by taxi to El Cortijo two hours after us. She walked into the house and told Mum that the taxi driver was waiting for someone to pay his fees and that she was resigning from her position straight away. She and Mum went into a room to talk. Miss Spencer didn't leave, but Mum came out of the room with tears in her eyes, asking us not to cause her any more problems. Seeing Mum like this made me feel helpless and sad. I was determined to become stronger and stronger for Mum, but I couldn't avoid feeling incredibly lonely. I couldn't know how anyone else felt; it was as if nothing had happened. I had difficulty working out if any of my siblings was at least worried. Nobody talked about it and Mum always tried to convince us that Dad loved us.

Easter fell in the month of April this year and the weather was already incredibly hot. We had managed to convince Mum to order Federico, the caretaker, to fill up the swimming pool. This was great news for all of us. The water for the swimming pool usually came from the well closer to the house, and it was freezing cold. Even in the hottest days of the summer, we did not manage to stay in the water for more than one hour in the morning and one hour in the afternoon; that was why Mum was always reluctant to have the pool ready unless the weather was boiling hot.

My cousins Francisco and Andrés were also spending the holiday with us; they were two of Uncle Tomás' sons. Francisco was the same age as Jaime and Andrés was the same age as Alex. There were two other families living within the premises of El Cortijo. The manager's family lived in the house by the main entrance. They had two children. The oldest was a girl between my age and Beatriz's, and the boy was still a baby. They were always away on weekends and school holidays and we hardly saw them.

The caretaker's family lived in the house further up in the first courtyard and they only took holidays in the summer. The oldest son was called Julio and he was slightly older than María was. The daughter was called Lola, and she was between Jaime's and Alex's ages. For some reason, Dad didn't like Julio and Lola to enter our house, but they were allowed to play with us in the private garden or on the land. They could also use the pool in the summer and swim with us as long as Dad was not using the swimming pool. Miss Spencer and Lola's mum, also called Lola, had an understanding, knowing when Julio and Lola had to disappear for a while. But not being inside the house had never been a problem because we used to spend the whole day outside and only came in to eat or sleep. Lola, the mother, cleaned our house and made the beds too. We also spent the evenings playing in the first courtyard until it was time to go to bed.

The complex consisted of three square courtyards connected by arches. Everything was painted white. The first courtyard contained our house and the manager's house as well as the stables. Previous owners had owned many horses, but we only had a brown mare, which was pregnant at the time. The rest of the stables were used as a warehouse to store olives when they were harvested from the trees in spring and autumn. If they were to be sold to be consumed, they were green, but for olive oil processing, they became black in the trees by the time they were collected.

The second courtyard had a large warehouse normally used to store corn when it was harvested during spring, but it also had a large garage with chains and heavy machinery to repair tractors and equipment for farming. The third courtyard had multiple apartments, which were currently empty. Labourers harvesting olives used to spend several months there with their families in the olden days, using these houses to accommodate them. Nowadays the third courtyard was only used to park tractors in, keeping them well hidden rather than outside the walls of the property. There also was a tall and beautiful tower separating the second and third courtyard, which was a large pigeon house.

"Miss Spencer, when can we go in the swimming pool?" Alex and Andrés asked Miss Spencer.

"I think we can all go now. Take your swimming trunks and let the others know. I will open the gate when all of you are there. No one can get inside the water until I say so," she replied.

"We're allowed to swim! We can go to the pool now!" both shouted in the house as they ran towards the pool.

I heard the news and hurried to be there as soon as possible. The garden of our house had twenty-seven old palm trees. They were much taller than the house and the noise of the leaves waving and rubbing against each other in the breeze or the wind could be scary, especially if I found myself alone in the garden. I always tried to avoid it if I could. There also was a tennis court at the bottom of the garden, which Mum and Dad sometimes used. The whole garden was too big for me; it had several paths to walk, some statues, and plenty of fruit trees. There were beautiful flowers with big areas of thick grass and one single water fountain opposite the garden door to the house.

Everyone was waiting, and Lola and Julio were also coming. We all raced to get changed as soon as possible and then sat by the edge of the pool with our feet in the water. Miss Spencer was helping Beatriz, now three and a half, get changed.

"You can get in now, children!" Miss Spencer announced.

We all jumped into the water at once, splashing in different directions. The older children were in the deep end, and Alex and I were in the shallow end, as we didn't know how to swim yet. It was refreshing and good fun. Lola was also in the water, and Beatriz had just got in at the deep end using an inflatable plastic ring as an aid. María and Teresa were looking after her while Miss Spencer went in the changing room.

Suddenly I saw a long grey water snake appeared over the side in the deep end of the pool, sliding into the water. It was over one metre long and bigger than anything I had ever seen before in the countryside.

"There's a snake! There's a snake in the water!" I screamed as soon as I saw it. "Get out of the water!"

They all reacted to the word 'snake' quickly, although they didn't know where it was. Everyone but Beatriz was out. The snake swam towards her.

"Miss Spencer! Miss Spencer! The snake is going to get Beatriz!" I shouted even louder.

"I'm in the middle of getting changed. I can't come out!" Miss Spencer said in the distance. "Ask Julio to go in with a stick to frighten it and to get her out!"

"Julio! Julio! The snake!" Everyone else called for him too. He was changing behind one of the palm trees.

It was too late to rescue Beatriz. The snake was next to her and Beatriz was crying, clearly not knowing what to do. The snake swam around her.

Splash! Julio jumped in right next to it and Beatriz, carrying a stick in his hand. The snake got frightened and swam towards the deep end, hiding in the hole leading to the drain. Julio took Beatriz to safety with Miss Spencer, who was now wearing her swimming costume. My brothers and cousins were all by the edge, on top of where the snake was hiding.

"Julio, it's right there!" Jaime kept saying, pointing with his finger. "We can still see it. It's trying to escape, but the drain is closed, holding the water in. It's in the hole. Over there!"

"Yes, over there! We can see it!" the others began to chime in.

Julio was fourteen years old and a very strong swimmer. He asked for diving goggles and María handed him a pair. He put them on and dived all the way down, pushing his stick inside the hole as hard as he could. After several attempts, he partially pierced the snake's body, causing it to curl around it. Julio came out of the swimming pool with his right arm raised in the air, holding the snake alive, fighting to free itself, but before it could do so, Julio threw the snake in the air and over the white garden wall at the top part of the pool.

"I'm hoping that it lands close enough to the stream running behind the wall. It'll swim away!" Julio said to all of us with a big smile on his face. "It was big, wasn't it? Don't worry – it was a water snake. It doesn't bite and isn't poisonous."

The tension broke and everybody went into the pool again, laughing and playing. I was shaking all over. I'd thought the snake was going to bite Beatriz. I felt helpless. I could have jumped in to get Beatriz but didn't know how to swim. She could have died.

I got in the water again and spent the afternoon learning to swim under the water. I had just turned six that week and I was determined to train myself to swim. I kept throwing a stone to the shallow bottom and fetching it, throwing the stone deeper and deeper as I got more confidence with each stage. It was helpful using diving goggles to see where I was. I liked staying under the water. It was all silent, and it was funny hearing bubbles around and distant voices from the others. My body felt very light inside the water.

Before I realised it, Dad was joining us for a swim. Lola and Julio were no longer there and Mum was standing outside the gate with Grandmother Isabel. They were going for a walk and were saying hello to all of us. Miss Spencer had taken Beatriz out of the swimming pool and was drying and changing her.

"Children, come over here with me. Let's play some fun games and exercise," Dad announced.

We all looked at each other and came out of the pool, walking towards Dad, who was in the deep end.

"What are we going to do?" Alex asked him.

"I've tied this piece of string between these two poles. I would like all of you to jump one by one over the string, diving into the water. You need to run in the grass, get up some speed and jump from the edge of the pool, which is smooth, going over the string. Easy!"

We all stood still and quiet. Nobody moved. The string was as high as my chest; there was no way I could jump that high. Alex and Jaime probably couldn't do it either. The edge of the pool was smooth but incredibly slippery when it was wet, which was exactly the case right now.

"Uncle Roberto, neither Andrés nor I are very sporty. We are much shorter than the others and we don't like doing things like that," Francisco explained to Dad. "We were about to stop swimming because we're feeling cold. The water is freezing. Come on, Andrés. Miss Spencer said we all had to get changed for lunch. Let's go!" Francisco gently encouraged his brother to move along towards the changing room.

"That's fine, Francisco, but all of you have to stay until you do it," Dad said, looking at all of us, clearly meaning what he said.

"Dad, it's too high for the younger ones to jump," María said to Dad.

"Do you think so? Maybe ... I'll lower it for Alex and Isa. Come on – get going!" Dad said, waving his hand.

Jaime started walking backwards, trying to hide in the group with tears in his eyes.

Teresa spoke. "I'm not jumping that, Dad! I'm not sporty and am not interested. It is too high and slippery by the edge."

"You will all jump because I say so!" Dad said, raising his voice.

"I can't dive or swim very well," Alex said.

"It doesn't matter. Just jump over the rope and land in the water whichever way you want to. But jump!" Dad began to shout at us.

"Dad, it's really easy! I'll do it for all of them several times over," María volunteered in an attempt to defuse the situation.

"But if Teresa doesn't do it, then Jamie won't do it either. I want Jaime to jump because he is the oldest boy," Dad told us.

"It is high for me, and it is high for everyone else, Dad," María told him.

"You are girls, and he's a boy."

"But boy or not, I am a head taller and stronger than he is." And without giving him a chance to say anything else, María took a run and did a big jump over the piece of string, diving in the pool.

"Fantastic! That's how I would like you to do it. Teresa, hold this pole here, and I'll do the jump."

Teresa took Dad's position and he easily jumped too. The string barely reached his knee level. I could only think about how I was going to manage in the deep end and secretly figured a plan by which, if I had to do it, I would try to reach the bottom floor of the pool as I had just been practising. I would then push hard with my feet, giving myself enough speed to emerge quickly to the surface. I would aim at coming back close enough to the border so I could hold on to the edge with my hands. I didn't really care if I went over, under or through the piece of string; but I was also worried about stepping on the wet edge of the pool. I knew I could easily slip. María interrupted my thoughts.

"Come on, Jaime," urged María. "Dive in the water now, without the piece of string. Dad's not looking; he's swimming towards the ladder." Jamie quickly came forward and dived in.

"Well done, Jaime! You did it!" María and Teresa screamed together.

Dad turned around and exclaimed, "Brave boy! I knew you could it. You just needed to be encouraged."

"Mr Grimaldi!" Miss Spencer interrupted. "The children are shivering and cold. It is time for them to have a shower and something to eat."

"Fair enough! You can go, children. I will stay here swimming a few lengths."

Jaime looked at Teresa and María with great relief, and we all quickly left.

El Cortijo was great. We could do so many things every day. We had divided ourselves into two teams, one led by Julio and the other one by María; basically, it was boys against girls. We spent several days building two tree houses, one for each team, by the stream of water running along our land. We used branches of eucalyptus taken from the trees by the main path leading into the building. We were planning to organise a picnic so we could discuss strategies on how best to attack the boys' fortresses, either the one built by the stream or the one made with plastic boxes used to collect olives. We built fortifications with these boxes every evening in the main courtyard. Boys had to capture girls, and vice versa, and at the same time, we tried to free our teammates. They were fun evenings of hiding and running under the light of the stars and the moon, which were stunningly bright in the countryside outside of the city lights.

We also made plans for activities for each day, so it was decided that riding Lucy, the mare, was something we needed to do since we still hadn't done so. We asked Mum for permission and she agreed. We asked Federico if he could have Lucy ready for us the next morning.

Federico was a solidly built man with strong hands. He had been working on farms and in the countryside since he was a child and had been employed by my grandfather, now dead, to work at El Cortijo. He wore a flat black cap and always had a lit cigarette in his mouth. He never stopped working.

"Federico, we would like to ride Lucy in the morning, but we can't do it without your help. Can you take the reins of the horse for us and walk us to the bridge and back?" María asked him.

"Of course I can! But your dad also wants to ride Lucy in the morning. Maybe you can do it in the afternoon. Lucy will need a rest after your dad rides her."

Federico had an incredibly strong southern accent, and the fact that he didn't have any front teeth made it difficult to understand him.

None of us knew how to ride; we just sat on top of Lucy, not even reaching to put our feet in the stirrups, which were left gently dangling by the side of the horse. Federico had the patience of a saint and took all of us one by one, walking next to Lucy to the bridge and back. The mare was used to us and was gentle natured, never overreacting to anything we did or said. We never rode any faster than a walk.

The following morning I saw Dad leaving the stable with Lucy. It was obvious that she was heavily pregnant. I couldn't understand who Lucy's husband was because there were no other horses around as far as I knew. Maybe God sent the baby horse to her and horses weren't supposed to have fathers. Lucy was restless and she wouldn't keep still. Dad looked heavy on top of her, and he was forcing her to twist and turn to his command. He occasionally dug the heels of his boots into her sides, and I could see that she already had two scratches. Lucy was violently moving her head up and down, and could not keep up with the commands. Dad finally guided her under the main arch of the entrance, beginning to trot, but he rapidly decided to gallop in the open space. Somehow Lucy was resisting it, but Dad continued digging his heels into her on and on, without any hesitation. Lucy's gallop became nothing more than a fast trot, but the digging didn't stop. Lucy couldn't manage it!

My mind was fixed on Lucy, not being able to do anything else. I was waiting for Dad to return and wanting to see how the mare was. Eventually, Lucy and Dad returned and I could guess that she was frightened and distressed, constantly panting, her mouth foaming. The two wounds on her sides were bleeding and she looked exhausted.

Marco and Polo, the two dogs, had announced Dad's arrival five minutes in advance, and they were restless, running up and down in circles, expecting Dad to dismount. Mum came out of the house, as did Miss Spencer, with Beatriz behind her.

"Roberto, the little one would like a ride on the horse. Would you mind taking her?" Mum asked Dad, who was still in the saddle.

"Yes, of course!" he replied.

My heart missed a beat and my body instantly froze. I thought it was dangerous. Why couldn't Mum see it?

Dad turned around, making Lucy face the way out again, and Miss Spencer approached the horse from the left, lifting Beatriz up with her legs opened, ready to sit in front of Dad. Beatriz seemed to enjoy it, but Lucy was still agitated. Dad was pulling the reins too tightly on her. Once Dad was finished, Miss Spencer helped Beatriz down from the horse, but as she walked behind Lucy towards the house, Dad dug his heels into the mare once again. Lucy whinnied, stepping backwards briefly and standing on Beatriz's foot.

Beatriz screamed shrilly, making me cover my ears with both hands.

"For God's sake, the man is insane!" I heard Miss Spencer saying.

She took Beatriz inside the house, holding her in her arms.

"What happened?" Mum asked Dad.

"I'm not sure. Maybe Lucy kicked her. She's very unsettled today."

Mum ran inside the house and I followed her, feeling almost nauseated with tension and fear. Beatriz had a big red mark covering her whole foot, which looked swollen as well. Miss Spencer put lots of ice on it, trying to calm Beatriz down.

"What happened?" Mum asked Miss Spencer.

"The horse stood on her foot; that's what happened," Miss Spencer answered. "Today wasn't the right day for the little girl to ride. Did you see the state of Lucy? She is about to give birth and looks exhausted and terrified by your husband. Did you see the wounds on her sides? I hope God can forgive me, but he is an animal, Mrs Grimaldi!"

"Miss Spencer, please! Mum said, plainly annoyed. "I think you're exaggerating. Beatriz had a pleasant ride with her father. It has been an unfortunate accident; Lucy was nervous today for some reason. That's why Mr Grimaldi had to hold her tighter. The horse will have a rest now. Why does everything have to be a problem?"

I didn't know what to think. I shivered and walked away. I didn't know where to go, but I was standing in the entrance hall and saw Dad walking from the stable across the courtyard. The dogs were circling him with their heads down, waiting for his approval, but as Dad got close to the door, he suddenly kicked both dogs hard to move them away from his side. Both dogs yelped in pain.

I opened the garden door and went outside, waiting at the swimming pool gate until it was time to swim again. I came to the conclusion that I didn't wish to ride Lucy ever again – or her future foal. I was disturbed and frightened by what I had just witnessed.

All I could think of was the sound of the water when sitting at the bottom of the pool. I loved swimming under the water and during the ten days that had passed, I could see that I had really improved. I could swim the width of the pool stopping for breath only once, so I supposed I could also swim the same on the surface. I could also fetch my stone from anywhere in the deep end and safely get back to the edge. I wanted to show Mum my achievements, but most of all, I wanted to try out breaststroke swimming on the surface before she saw me so I could definitely say that I could swim.

I think Mum was most impressed, for she promised to give me one hundred pesetas for my swimming. Alex also managed to do a full width doggy paddle close to the border just in case he had to stop, and Mum promised to give him some money as well. We were both very pleased with ourselves.

María and Teresa couldn't ride Lucy in the afternoon because Federico said she was still tired, so they postponed it until the following morning instead.

"Mum! Mum!" Alex came running, looking for Mum, who was sitting knitting in the garden. "Jaime and the cousins are stuck in the big mulberry tree by the main entrance. I couldn't quite manage to climb it with them, but now they can't get down!"

"Thanks, Alex. Go fetch Federico and ask him to bring a ladder. Tell him that I am sending you," Mum said, standing up.

"Dear, let me deal with this. I will show them how to get down; it will be a learning experience," Dad told Mum, also standing up and leaving the book he was reading on top of his chair.

Beatriz and I decided to join Mum and Dad. We were on the swings nearby, trying to jump off to see who could get further. María and Teresa were practising on the basketball hoop that was on one side of the tennis court; they clearly didn't realise what was going on.

Alex appeared again, running. "I told him, Mum."

"Go back, Alex, and ask him to bring a rope from the garage too," Dad said to Alex, not giving him a chance to rest.

We were all gathering underneath the large tree, which gave refreshing shade to the whole front of the house.

"How did you manage to climb up there, boys?" Dad asked, not waiting for a reply. "I will show you how we do it in the navy. I will pass a rope over this branch here and you can just hold on to it with both hands and feet and slowly allow yourselves to come down." He pointed at the branch with his finger. "We will see how strong you are. If you descend too fast on the rope, you can burn your hands, so be careful. You need to slowly carry your own weight down with your own strength."

"Roberto, they are far too young to do what you are proposing. I think the ladder is a better idea," Mum protested.

"You are always protecting them too much and contradicting me in front of everyone!" Dad responded, raising his voice.

Federico arrived with the rope and the ladder, and María and Teresa turned up as well, having realised that everyone else had disappeared from the garden.

"Federico, please go up the ladder and put the rope over this branch here, making a tight knot. The boys will use the rope to get down," Dad directed.

"Uncle Roberto," Francisco said to Dad, "Andrés and I will be using the ladder. It is far too dangerous to use the rope. We won't be able to reach out for it, yet alone use it. We are too crammed in the tree to stretch out and reach out for anything. We don't want to do it."

"I don't want to do it either," Jaime agreed.

"Jaime, you will do whatever I tell you to do," Dad said angrily.

"Roberto, don't make a scene of this, please," Mum pleaded.

"And you stop undermining me," Dad whispered to her.

"Let them use the ladder and I will go up the tree and use the rope. It sounds like fun!" María joined in, clearly trying to diffuse the situation.

"Shut up! I'm the man of this house – and you have to obey me. Understood?" Dad shouted at everyone.

"Francisco and Andrés, get down using the ladder, please," he told my cousins. "Federico, when they do so, take the ladder back to the garage. Jaime will use the rope. He doesn't need it."

I could see that Mum was uncomfortable and tense; I knew we were all worried about Jaime.

Mum tried once more while my two cousins were coming down the ladder. "You're making things difficult for everybody."

"Take it away, Federico," Dad ordered the caretaker, ignoring Mum.

Federico disappeared with the ladder in hand, clearly talking to himself on his way out and shaking his head from side to side in disapproval.

"Come on, Jaime! Reach out and grab the rope," Dad called.

"I don't want to do it, Dad. I'm scared!" Jaime said.

"Scared? What you are is a coward!" Dad sternly told Jaime.

"For God's sake, Roberto! Don't talk to him like that!" Mum intervened.

"Like what? You are making him weak! Don't you realise that? You overprotect him all the time. He needs to grow into a man," Dad argued.

"He is not nine yet and you always ask him to do things that are far too hard for him," Mum replied with tears in her eyes.

"Are you trying to challenge my authority, Graciela? If he doesn't do it, he is not coming into *my house* to eat or sleep until I say so," Dad said to Mum without any hesitation.

Mum started crying and Jaime looked at her.

"I will do it, Mum – don't worry!" Jaime finally said, looking scared.

Jaime was about three and half metres high in the tree, and he reached out to grab the rope with one hand, almost losing his footing in the tree. He obviously didn't know how to get both hands on the rope without falling off, so he jumped from the tree, grabbing the rope with both feet and hands at once. Dad moved forward and held the rope steady from underneath, stopping its swinging; but before the rope was under control, Jaime couldn't hold his body any longer and descended the full height quickly, sliding along the rope and giving out a loud cry of pain.

"My hands! I'm burning my hands!" he cried with tears in his eyes.

Jaime got to the bottom and walked away, still crying.

"You didn't follow my full instructions, Jaime. I told you that if you were not careful, you could burn your hands ..."

Chapter Nine

ELENA

Lucy the mare delivered a foal during the summer. His name was Tristán and Mum said he was beautiful. His hair was light grey like the typical Spanish horses. I was glad that Lucy couldn't be ridden for a while, until Tristán was bigger and stronger. I hadn't seen them together yet but couldn't wait to do so.

Mum and Dad had been away on holiday during the month of July. They went to Asia and visited parts of Thailand, China and Japan. We stayed with Miss Spencer in Laredo, but at the end of the month, we were very much looking forward to seeing them again, especially Mum. They brought us all sorts of presents and electronic gadgets that we had never seen before. Alex and Jaime had remote control cars with no cables attached to them. Dad had a calculator which could do instant sums, multiplications and divisions just by pressing a button. Each of the girls received a kimono. I had never seen one before and they were beautiful. I couldn't imagine Japanese people dressed in them all the time. I didn't think they were very practical.

We were in Cádiz again and school started the next day. We had been very busy since we returned from Laredo, organising books and uniforms for school. Beatriz was starting in reception and I would be wearing the same uniform as my older sisters because I was moving into year one. I was feeling unsettled about this because I had a new classroom and teacher, Miss Carmen. Mum had told me that I would be reunited with the girls I met in year one reception, but to be honest, I couldn't remember who they were.

Mum also told us that she was expecting a new baby. I wondered how she knew, for it was impossible to see anything different in her. Dad and my brothers were hoping for the baby to be a boy. María and Teresa preferred another sister. I couldn't imagine what it would be like having another younger sibling. It broke the structure of being in twos sharing the bedrooms and I was finding it difficult to cope with the idea that in the spring, there would be somebody else in the family. I didn't really mind if it was a boy or a girl. I was more worried about the disruption. Beatriz lived in her own little world and I wondered if she realised what was going to happen; she didn't say anything about it.

Mum and Dad were also talking about buying a sailing boat. Dad loved the sea and had a small fishing boat before I was born, but what he really liked was sailing, Mum said. It might be happening in the future, after the birth of our new brother or sister. Dad used to practice diving before having so many children, and we had plenty of souvenirs displayed in the glass cabinet in El Cortijo's entrance hall, such as Phoenician amphorae and objects found in the bottom of the sea in Cádiz. Mum was trying to convince Dad to take on an activity now that she was pregnant because she felt she wasn't going to be able to accompany him to do as many things as usual. Dad would get anxious if he was not doing things, so he decided to take a course on flying small airplanes. There were far too many things happening at once for my liking.

❦

Mum was taking Beatriz and me to school the first day. I felt like a real grown-up compared to Beatriz, who looked so young. Miss Cecilia was Beatriz's teacher, and I had already told her in great detail what it was like being in her class, what she had to do and what she should expect. Beatriz didn't seem to be bothered about starting school at all. I, however, was very worried. I couldn't sleep the night before, and today I was so scared that I could hardly talk; I was trying to hold back my tears the best I could.

My new classroom was the first one along the corridor leading to the courtyard after the large stairs, and Mum had accompanied me to the door on her way to the courtyard, where she would have to leave Beatriz.

"Isabel, this is the year one classroom and your new teacher is Miss Carmen. She's by the window. Can you see her?" Mum moved her head in the direction of the window when she mentioned Miss Carmen, and I followed that direction, finding an adult by the window.

Miss Carmen was certainly shorter than Miss Cecilia and she was wearing a short-sleeved summer dress with colourful flowers. She had long dark hair tied in a ponytail and had black eyes. I realised she moved around fast, which made me quite unsettled.

"Isabel please, do come inside the classroom," Mum pleaded. "Miss Carmen, this is Isabel. Where is she sitting?"

"Good morning, Mrs Grimaldi. Yes, please come in. She can sit anywhere she likes," Miss Carmen replied, sounding jolly.

Mum gently pushed me forward and I walked in slowly, dragging my feet on the floor. I managed to cross the frame of the door and sit in the first desk closest to the exit. Mum said goodbye and took Beatriz with her. I was so scared that I didn't even turn around to look at her. I stayed in my seat until Miss Carmen said goodbye to all the parents and closed the door. She asked us to turn around in our seats for registration. Looking around me, I didn't recognise anybody from two years ago. Miss Carmen had been in the school for several years, and I could not remember seeing her at school either.

Anguish was overwhelming me and I was trying my best to control it.

Beatriz didn't seem to have any problems with Miss Cecilia. She clearly liked going to school every day. I was in charge of taking and collecting her because Teresa had a different timetable now. I had also started English lessons before afternoon school with my brothers, so Miss Spencer was taking Beatriz to school after lunch.

I didn't like school at all. Miss Carmen lost her temper all the time and kept shouting at us. This worried me because it terrified me to ask her anything, but if I didn't, her reaction was even worse for not asking. We were no longer using pencils and it was difficult to write with a pen without making any mistakes. Miss Carmen was a nervous person and she had a few girls that she liked a lot; I was not one of them. I didn't understand what she explained to us or comprehend what she was teaching. I felt completely lost and didn't talk to anyone unless it was necessary.

"Now, children, following on the topic about Africa, I would like you to draw an animal that you could find in Africa. You can copy it from a picture or do it from memory, but I would like it to be big, occupying the whole page," Miss Carmen told us.

That was our task for the morning before lunchtime, and the whole class managed to do it, except me. I was completely blocked, not able to connect between Africa and its animals, because in my mind, "following on the topic of Africa" had nothing to do with drawing an animal. I couldn't think of an animal and I couldn't draw one either. I knew Miss Carmen was going to be angry and the fear of it was blocking me even more.

"Isabel, haven't you paid any attention to the topic of Africa? What animals did I say you can find in Africa?" she asked me in an irritated voice.

In my mind, when she mentioned animals, Miss Carmen was not talking about Africa; it was independent. Therefore, the topic of Africa, the way I understood it, didn't have anything to do with any animals. I couldn't make the connection. I couldn't answer and I kept quiet, not looking at her.

"Isabel! I am not having this. You will go home for lunch, but when you are back, I want you to do this project in the afternoon. You will stay in detention until you finish it if necessary," Miss Carmen said to me in a stern voice.

My whole body was shaking and I could hardly eat when I got home.

"What animals do you find in Africa?" I finally asked my sisters during lunch, interrupting the conversation.

They didn't seem to know what I was talking about, and they started taking turns suggesting animals, such as lions, giraffes, elephants, zebras, tigers and monkeys.

"Oh, that is Africa, then?" I said with surprise, as if I knew it all along.

"Those are the animals in Africa," Teresa replied, looking at me curiously.

"I need a picture," I said.

"Of Africa or an animal?" María asked me, not waiting for an answer. "Look in one of the magazines. There are all sorts of pictures there."

I returned to school with the picture of an elephant in my pocket. Miss Carmen pointed to my desk as soon as I arrived, and I sat there most of the afternoon staring at the picture, not being able to draw. I was almost in tears trying to work out in my head how to copy the elephant onto the paper, with a chunky body and bigger than it appeared in the picture. I wanted to do it the best I could, but I couldn't even get started.

"Isabel, what's wrong with you? Can't you draw an elephant? Just draw whichever animal you can – but draw something. You're not going home until you do it," she threatened me.

I couldn't hold back my tears any longer; I was very frightened. I drew a circle for a head, a horizontal line for a body and four single lines as legs. I included an eye in the circle with a big ear, and I also drew a long line simulating a trunk from the face. It came out small and to one side of the paper. It looked ridiculous.

"Well, you can draw after all and you also know the animals in Africa," Miss Carmen said to me, raising her voice and calling everybody's attention. "Saying you couldn't do it was lying to me."

By now, I could feel all the girls looking at me, although I was still fixed on my paper.

"I would like you to go to face the corner of the room, look at the statue of Jesus in that corner and have a little prayer asking for his forgiveness. He always forgives you if you repent, and so will I, but don't lie to me again," Miss Carmen told me.

I felt so stiff inside my body that I found it difficult to walk towards the corner. I was confused and could not understand what was happening or why it was happening. I wanted to be better and I didn't know how to. I had done something wrong and didn't know what. I was lost.

As time passed, the situation at school was not improving at all. If anything, it was reversing back to how it was when I first started in Reception. Miss Carmen talked in a language that I couldn't understand. Working out numbers was not a problem, but other mathematical concepts, such as Venn diagrams, were a complete mystery to me. Miss Carmen was out of her mind, asking us to directly question the verbs in sentences written on the blackboard when looking for the main noun in them, saying things like, "Verb, what is the main noun?" I couldn't understand what she meant. I always had a terrible fear of not doing things correctly and homework caused me a great deal of anxiety because I didn't know what I had to do, mostly due to my lack of understanding during the lessons. My marks were average or below.

I was almost in tears at home and had to ask Mum or Teresa for help, but Mum was already busy with Alex. He demanded constant attention and supervision because he wasn't able to concentrate for long. He had dyslexia, needing help with his writing and reading. For some reason, Alex could not understand what numbers were, and the concept of any kind of sums was a real battle for him. Mum knew what everyone had for homework and what tests were happening. María always memorised everything and liked Mum to listen to her repeating the lessons back. Mum also kept an eye on Jaime and Teresa, making sure that they did their homework too. Beatriz was learning to read and she spent as long as she could reading aloud to Carmen while she was doing the sewing. Her reading was really coming along and she was ahead of her age already. She truly enjoyed reading.

We all knew that it was better not to ask Dad for help. He only gave you one chance to understand things. He talked like an adult and used methods, especially in maths, which were far too advanced. If he could, he would give you extra explanations and information to learn on top of what you had. It was better to stay away from his teaching, however, María liked to show off in front of him, but Dad was not really interested in hearing María; if anything, it was my impression that María irritated Dad, but she was the only one who tried hard to get his attention.

The house was quite busy most days. Teresa had joined the local basketball club, and Alex and Jaime were taking judo lessons. Dad was doing his flying course in the afternoons, so my older siblings often took the opportunity to bring their friends home after school. The best place to be was in my bedroom.

Mum was looking extremely pregnant now, but she didn't seem happy for some reason. I knew that she cried, and I was trying my hardest not to cause her any problems. Asking for her help was something I tried to avoid at all costs, but it was painful because my situation at school was desperate.

I couldn't find the words to say how I felt. I was absolutely trapped and sometimes thought I could die. I spent the evenings in my bedroom trying to understand how to do my homework. I looked in the books to learn, but it took me an excessive amount of time and the majority of the time, anguish was getting the best of me. I was crying for hours, but I was determined to learn the best I could.

Thump! I heard the main door closing; I knew it was Dad and I walked to the sitting room.

"Hello, Roberto! How did you get on today?" Mum asked him, trying to sound interested.

"There was a strong breeze, but I managed to do a real landing for the first time. The airplane did three jumps on the runway before I managed to stay firmly on the ground," Dad explained, rubbing the back of his head; I wasn't sure if he was embarrassed or pleased with his achievement.

"I am glad I wasn't there to watch it. It would have been too stressful for me seeing the jumps," Mum said to him with a smile.

I sat on the sofa listening to both of them but not intending to say anything in particular. Beatriz came in from the kitchen, already wearing her pyjamas.

"Dad, I did a picture for you at school," she said, giving it to Dad.

"Beatriz, where is your dressing gown? You need to wear it on top of your pyjamas. It is disrespectful walking around the house in pyjamas and you can catch a cold," Dad scolded in return.

"Miss Spencer, where is Beatriz's dressing gown?" Mum interrupted before the situation got any worse.

Miss Spencer quickly appeared carrying the dressing gown in her hand and Beatriz stretched her arm while Miss Spencer helped her put it on.

"Thanks, Miss Spencer," Mum said.

"Let me see what you have done, Beatriz," Dad said, holding the picture in front of him.

Beatriz looked at Dad with a smile and waited for his reply.

"I can see what you've been trying to do here, but the boat is disproportionate compared to the sea ... and the people are not well done at all."

"The tall man with the cap is you, Dad!" Beatriz exclaimed.

"Thanks, my little one, but it is badly done. It you want to draw a boat, you have to do it like this." He immediately started drawing on a piece of paper. "This is a real boat." Dad suddenly stopped drawing and went straight to the bureau that was standing against the wall. He opened a small drawer and removed some Sellotape, which he immediately used on Beatriz, placing two large pieces on her ears, fixing them down against her head. "You look better like this, Beatriz. We need to correct your bat ears," Dad told her. "I don't like seeing your ears sticking out all the time."

Beatriz had tears in her eyes but didn't say anything.

"Roberto, why do need to talk to the children like that? Don't you see that you are making her cry?" Mum intervened disapprovingly.

Miss Spencer's face was angry and flushed, and she held Beatriz's hand and walked away without saying anything; but when she closed the door of the sitting room behind her, she made a strong noise as a sign of protest.

Dad tore Beatriz's picture into pieces and threw it in the bin.

I felt incredibly sorry for Beatriz, but I knew that it was never advisable to show anything to Dad. I never gave him anything we did at school, either for Christmas or for Father's Day. I sometimes passed something I did at school to Mum so she could show it to Dad if she wanted to, but I knew she never did.

Dad was obsessed with order and perfection. The sitting room and his bedroom had to be tidy all the time; he hardly ever entered our bedrooms unless he needed to hit someone with his slipper. He always threw away the newspaper once he had read it, it never occurring to him that somebody else might like to read it. Books were always tidy, and unnecessary papers were thrown away. He had a ritual of stretching out the tasselled edges of the carpets in the sitting room every day, and if someone disturbed them, we were asked to put them straight again. Dad also rearranged the cutlery around his plate when eating at the table, making sure everything was equidistant and parallel, not tolerating any stains in the tablecloth around the area where he was eating. He always ate his food in order when eating and didn't tolerate any deformity in anything presented to him. His uniform was always immaculate, with his medals and pins absolutely straight and parallel. I had noticed that Dad was wearing three thick golden rings in his uniform now.

Dad also had other peculiarities. He had a fixed way of seeing things and reading history books was his passion; but if he ever disagreed with whatever was written in a book, he would simply tear the controversial pages out of the book with great indignation. So it wasn't uncommon to find books in our house with missing pages. His personal belongings in his bathroom and wardrobe were also in impeccable order.

Spring had arrived and the Easter holidays were over. Mum had told us that she was going to have the baby soon. Her doctor was in Seville, where she had had all of us. This meant that Mum would be leaving us soon to spend some time at Grandmother's house and Miss Spencer would be looking after us in Cádiz while Mum was giving birth.

Dad was restless without Mum around. He continued working but knew that the birth was imminent and as soon as he was told the news, he would leave to meet Mum. Dad did not get along with Grandmother Isabel; he always felt undermined by her assertive and sometimes arrogant way of talking to everybody. Grandmother didn't like weak people and certainly didn't have time for emotional attention; she could be a difficult person.

Mum finally had a baby girl. Miss Spencer announced it with a big smile on her face as soon as she opened the door. It was lunchtime, and Beatriz and I had just finished the morning session at school.

"Really?" I smiled back at Miss Spencer.

"I like having a little sister to look after," Beatriz said, doing joyful little jumps.

I felt happy; it was good news. "Is Mum all right?" I asked.

"She is very well indeed," Miss Spencer said, reaching out and touching my face.

I immediately stepped back and started walking to my bedroom to leave my books. I disliked people touching me unless they had a firm touch. It was an automatic reaction, but I don't think Miss Spencer has ever noticed it.

We were all pleased about the news. Lunchtime was full of smiles and jokes. My brothers were disappointed at not having another boy in the family, but the feeling of joy and happiness was contagious. We were all wondering what she was going to be called. Dad had mentioned that if the baby was a girl, he wanted her to have a medieval Castilian name, such as Jimena. There was much laughter proposing possible names.

Elena arrived home a month later. She was a beautiful baby. Everything was perfect and miniscule in her, and at the same time, everything she did was mesmerising and funny to watch. Elena slept in a cradle next to Mum's bed because she was breastfeeding her, but Mum said that Elena would share the bedroom with Beatriz and me after the summer holidays, sleeping in Beatriz's old cot. I couldn't wait for that to happen.

I learnt how to change Elena's nappies, which were held by a couple of big pins on each side. The house was quickly full of baby stuff and there were cloths and gauzes drying out everywhere because that was what Mum and Miss Spencer used as nappies. Patricia had quite a lot of washing to do.

Chapter Ten

THE KINGDOM OF CASTILE

It was the end of the summer again, and I was eight years old. Elena was seventeen months old. She ate normal food now and was allowed to sit at the main table with us. Mum breastfed her for three months, until Dad got agitated over the last summer holidays at not having Mum's attention to go on excursions with him all the time.

This summer was somehow less stressful because Miss Spencer was taking full care of Elena so we could all follow Dad on his adventures. Teresa had been learning English in Ireland, but this year she went alone; María could have a full summer holiday to herself after three years of learning English. María seemed quite grown up now that she was fourteen. She had a big group of friends in Laredo and went to discos at the tennis club. This had been causing controversy with Dad over what time she had to return home and Dad disapproved of anyone whose parents were not wealthy enough. María never went out at night because she was still young, but rather than playing with all the children and cousins, she was joining teen groups, and some of my elder cousins were doing the same too. This was clearly stressing Mum out because of Dad.

I was in year three at school now, and I liked my new teacher, Mother Cristina. I was glad that after two consecutive years, I didn't have to see Miss Carmen every day. Mother Cristina was serious and rather old, but she never shouted and always treated everyone the same. She had no favourites, or if she did, I was not able to see it. I felt comfortable around her and I could understand the lessons well. Mother Cristina always made sure that everybody understood everything and always encouraged us to ask about anything that did not make any sense, even if it seemed to be the most ridiculous thing on Earth. She left silent gaps for people to come forward, and eventually girls did ask questions.

Mother Cristina also had a habit of explaining things in small blocks of information and every time she finished teaching us something, she randomly asked one of us to repeat what we had just heard. I was asking questions in class and was understanding the lessons; she didn't get offended if we got it wrong and she didn't think it was our fault. Having said that, I never came close to her; I looked and talked to her from a distance.

Homework was still not an easy task for me, though. Mum and Dad kept telling me that I ought to read more, but I disliked it; it caused me great anxiety. I was trying to be the best I could at school and I now did all the work by myself, not having to ask Mum for help at all. I was good with numbers but found it difficult to translate solving problems into numbers.

A girl in my class was excellent at it. Her name was Ana and her dad was also in the navy. When she explained to me in her own words the numbers which she had chosen, I could see why she did so for the problem in question, but it was not easy to do. I used to ask her at break time because I knew I would understand her; the connection was slowly coming. Then I would redo everything at home. I couldn't understand any theoretical lessons, science or other subjects like history or geography. Therefore, I memorised the books from page one to the end, one by one. I knew exactly which facts were in each particular numbered page. Not only that, but I kept repeating them throughout the year so I could deliver the information during the final summer tests. I was becoming a human machine full of facts, but I couldn't get order and structure in the information. I had started doing this last year, but the anguish was overwhelming me; this year I was in better control of myself. I was also surviving at school because I could now understand the unwritten social rules of what was expected from me, and I couldn't break them. I was strict and rigid about them.

"Come on, children! Are you all ready? Dad is going to take us in his new sailing boat. Make sure that you bring your swimming stuff and a change of clothes," Mum told us, plainly feeling energetic this morning.

"Why do we need swimming trunks if we're going sailing?" Alex asked. "Are we going to get wet?"

"We will sail across the bay, but it is such a beautiful day that I am sure Dad will put the anchor down so we can all have a swim," Mum told Alex.

"That will be fun!" Jaime exclaimed, listening to the conversation.

We arrived at the marina and saw the boat moored in the distance. It looked beautiful and elegant, all in white and with a design on the bow that gave it the impression of being able to break the water as it sailed through. It had several buoys hanging from the sides acting as defences when the boat drifted from side to side with the movement of the water coming too close to the other boats on each side. There was a general clinking noise coming from loose lines hanging around the masts of the boats; the noise was welcoming, like happy ringing bells. We all ran to the floating pontoon, which gave access to the boat. It was moored with the stern facing us, and we could see the words *Kingdom of Castile* across the back. The boat had two rear moorings and two front ones; all of them well secured to the pontoon.

"How do we get in, Dad?" Alex asked, watching the large gap between the edge of the pontoon and the boat.

Dad was nervous and tense. "Let me get through!" he said, not listening to Alex and pushing him and me aside without giving us the chance to move. Dad had the bag with the towels in his hands and threw it into the boat.

"Careful, Roberto!" Mum yelled from a distance, as she wasn't quite close to the boat yet. "There's no need to throw them like that! Something may fall in the water!"

But Dad was not listening and he continued to throw two more bags in the air, one with food inside, which partially collapsed on the landing, scattering Tupperware all around, and the second one with the spare clothes, which hit the edge of the boat on the way down. Some of the clothes fell into the water, as did the car keys.

"Roberto, the keys! I told you! Why do you have to be so impatient?" Mum cried, sounding truly upset.

Dad didn't say anything, standing on one of the rear moorings and drawing the boat closer to us. When it was the right time, he got hold of the rear rail and put one foot in the boat, pulling himself upwards and stepping inside the boat. María, Teresa and Jaime did the same while Dad got out a boathook and rescued the clothes from the water. Alex and I couldn't get in because standing on the moorings didn't make the boat come any closer. Mum helped us, pulling and holding the boat close enough to give us time to grab the rail. Mum also got in.

By then, Dad had already changed into his swimming trunks and without saying anything to anybody, he jumped into the water, which was oily and dirty. He was wearing diving goggles and he kept disappearing for long intervals before surfacing again.

"Roberto, the water looks dark and isn't clean. The chances of finding the keys at that depth are slim. Please give up and come back on board. We will telephone Miss Spencer when we get back. She can bring the spare keys from home. Don't worry. Leave it!"

The boat was like a small house. It had a large bed at the front where two people could sleep, a small shower with a toilet, a sitting room in the middle, a kitchen, a small area with a desk where Dad had maps and the radio, and two more beds at the back. Dad said that if necessary, two people could sleep on each sofa seat on each side of the sitting room table. Everything smelt new. It was great fun going in and out of the cabin using the hatch in the bow and walking by the sides of the boat. The stern of the boat was like an empty bath, with a large metallic wheel connected to the rudder and two sideways seats which you could open. Dad was using them to store ropes, life buoys, waterproof clothes and other instruments such as handgrips and a foldable boathook. The boat had a single mast with the sprit in a right angle, which was tied up and fixed to the floor so it didn't swing side to side when moored in the harbour.

We were all excited. It was a great adventure! None of us had been in a sailing boat before. Dad started the engine, and we all came outside the cabin to see what was happening. All of us were there except Elena, who was at home with Miss Spencer.

"Graciela, you hold the wheel. If you want to go right, turn left and if you want to go left, then turn right," Dad briefly explained to Mum.

"What do we do, Dad?" María asked.

"I'll jump to the pontoon again and loosen the moorings, starting with the front ones. María and Teresa, you stay at each side of the stern ready to receive the ropes; make sure they don't fall in the water. Graciela, as soon as I get inside the boat again, gently move the gear forward; that will give you enough speed to manoeuvre the boat out of the mooring space and out into the marina. Jaime and Alex, stay at the bow and be ready to receive the front moorings. When I tell you,

you need to get all the buoys inside the boat, but wait until Mum completely clears the other boats. Isabel, get hold of the boathook and stay vigilant; if you see Mum getting too close to other boats or to the rocks ahead of us, lean the rubber end of the boathook against the other boats or the rocks and push as hard as you can to separate our boat from them. That will help Mum."

"And what do I do, Dad?" asked Beatriz.

"I think it's better if you stay next to Mum and help Teresa and María with the moorings, but I need some space to get on board again."

Dad counted to three and we were off. Mum was able to control the speed of the boat well, so everything was smoothly done. I briefly pushed one of the neighbouring boats away, but it was not a real threat, I did it more to see how it felt than anything else.

We sailed by engine to the bay of Cádiz and Dad put the anchor down. It was all so exciting. We were ready to swim. Dad tied a rope ladder to the stern of the boat, which was the lowest part of the boat, therefore enabling us to get back inside after we went in the water. He also made plenty of knots in a large rope and threw it in the water, tying it up to one of the poles of the rail; it was for us to hold on to, just in case the current started to drift us away. He also threw two floaters attached to ropes which were tied to the boat; one of them was for Beatriz.

It was such fun! We all jumped from the boat splashing in the water. Mum and Dad also swam with us. It was a different feeling to anything else I had ever experienced before in the water. We were so deep in the middle of the sea that it was difficult to believe. The coast of Cádiz was far in the distance. I had a feeling of great freedom. The current was subtle, but when making a star in the water facing the sky, I could feel myself drifting slightly away. This gave us an idea and we all swam to the front of the boat and lined up, making stars on our backs while facing the sky and waiting for the sea to carry us to the other end of the boat. I also swam around the boat and it was actually even more impressive and bigger when you saw it floating in the water next to you.

After lunch, Dad was not talking to anyone, but eventually he said,

"Graciela, I am a sailor and would like to do proper sailing. A boat like this should never use the engine unless in an emergency or for manoeuvring in the marina."

"Roberto, the children have never sailed before and Beatriz is quite young," Mum answered. "Perhaps save it for another occasion when they are not here, or at least not all of them. You need more adults."

"No!" he said. "They will learn! They can be my crew and eventually compete in regattas."

Dad stood up and went inside the cabin, opening the hatch at the bow after a few seconds. María and Teresa were sunbathing and had a real fright when the hatch fully opened and Dad's head appeared through it.

"Jaime, Alex!" he called. "Help me get these two sails out."

My brothers joined María and Teresa, who were already there. The four of them pulled the two large sails, which Dad fed them through the hatch of the cabin. There was so much sail at the bow that it was difficult to see who was who; only feet, hands or arms were occasionally seen.

"Roberto, this wasn't the plan and all this should have been prepared when we were moored in the marina. I am starting to feel seasick with the movement of the boat. Can we get going, please?"

Dad ignored what Mum was saying and we had to wait a good hour until Dad was ready. Mum told Beatriz and me to stay with her because the bow was too crowded. Dad managed to get the front sail attached to the mast and it was ready to be hoisted. My brothers and sisters were working hard while receiving instructions from Dad and the sails were heavy to handle. They all moved to the middle part of the boat and started doing the same with the second sail, but this one was attached to the mast and the sprit. The sails started flapping with the wind, making strong noises, and Dad ordered everyone to the stern of the boat. He was moving up and down the boat quickly and with no shoes on; he just went wherever he had to go but didn't warn anybody and just pushed passed people. This was making me scared.

Dad pulled the lines tightly around the mast. The sails had two long ropes attached to each side at the bottom. One fed to port side and the other one to starboard. Dad rolled them up around the winches on each side of the boat – two in the middle of the boat and two others in the rear third – and he gave one rope to each of my siblings, positioning my bothers at the front and my sisters at the back.

"I'm going to pull the anchor up!" Dad announced. "Graciela, the boat will start drifting with the current. The wind's blowing south-west, so you need to govern the boat, pointing north-west and following the compass right on top of the wheel. When I say so, Teresa and Alex from the port side will start loosening their ropes, feeding them gently to María and Jaime, who will be pulling as fast and hard as they can from the starboard side."

"What is port and starboard side, Dad?" Alex asked him. "I don't understand!"

"Port is left side, when the boat is facing forward, and starboard is the right side," Dad answered, already crouching and activating the engine, which was bringing the anchor on board. "María and Jaime, the sails will start pulling hard against the wind so be ready to pull hard; if it gets too tight, don't let the ropes go, but don't get your hands burnt either. If it gets to that, bite the ropes in the snappers next to you and wait for me to help you."

Mum proposed to raise the rear sail first and the front one later. She was standing up by the wheel, trying to smooth the actions.

"This is how we do it in the navy, dear. These are my sailors," Dad replied, enjoying the moment.

Dad stood at the bow, facing all of us. I wasn't sure what was coming next, but I felt a tense expectation.

"On my command, one, two, three! Jaime and Teresa, pull faster than that! Pull, pull!"

Dad quickly moved to Jaime's position, pushing him away so abruptly that he nearly lost his balance. "Go help María. I'll take over here," Dad said.

Dad pulled quickly, leaning backwards with half of his body over the rail. The sails were violently shaken by the wind, making loud noises on top of the reverberating flapping, and the four winches in use were rapidly clicking like a chain on a bicycle when moved backwards – the ones on the left letting the sails go and the ones on the right bringing both sails up and to the right side of the boat. It was thrilling but intimidating. If any of our fingers ever got caught in the ropes working at that speed, any of us could have easily had an accident.

"Dad looks like he could fall in the water, Mum," I said.

"I hope he does and we finish with all this," Mum answered. "What a man!"

I couldn't understand why Mum wanted Dad to fall in the water; surely that would only make things worse. Dad would have been lost by the time we had all worked out how to haul down the sails, put the engine on and turn around to rescue him. I felt we were not in control of anything at all.

Both sails were hoisted and Dad used a handgrip on the winches to further tighten the ropes to the maximum, finally biting them in the snappers and tying them up in the rope holders. He showed us how to tie up the ropes quickly, without the need for a knot. He also made sure the ropes on the port side were secured and adjusted the sprit, moving it to the right and tightening it after that, making sure both sails were parallel to each other. The boat immediately heeled over with the wind.

I wasn't expecting that. I didn't know sailing boats did this and it was scary. I was sitting on the up side and I was so frightened that I didn't feel it was safe moving from where I was.

"Isabel and Beatriz, stay where you are and hold on tight. The boat won't capsize. It is meant to be like this," Mum said.

The breeze was in our faces and the boat started gaining speed, jumping gently over the waves, which occasionally splashed over the boat. The taste of salt was strong because the seawater was constantly spraying over us. I looked backwards and saw the wake left behind marking our path in the water.

"This is fun!" María and Teresa agreed.

"Do you like it, children?" Dad asked.

"Yes, we do!" both girls answered.

Everyone else remained quiet.

"María, let's go to the bow to lie down there!" Teresa said to María.

They both did and my brothers eventually joined them. We could see them going up and down as the boat jumped over the waves and they thought it was funny. Dad changed course and we had to repeat the same manoeuvre, this time Alex and Teresa having to pull fast and hard. Dad assisted Alex too. The front sail was bigger and more difficult to handle than the rear one. The sprit was adjusted to the left this time and the boat heeled over to the other side instead.

"Dad, what happens if a sailboat capsizes?" I asked.

"It is rare for them to do so if they're big boats like this one. The wind has to be incredibly strong, like in a gale. This boat is designed to spontaneously recover its neutral position provided all the sails are down," he explained to me. "If that did happen, it would be better to cut off all the ropes with a knife and the boat would do the rest, but if you did that, you would be losing your sails forever." After a brief pause, he said, "My emergency knife is in the first drawer of the desk inside the cabin."

The wind was increasing and getting stronger. Mum was following directions according to Dad's orders. I was planning in my head what I would do if we capsized. If I was trapped inside the cabin or the rear part of the boat, I would stay there and breathe the air naturally left inside the air chamber. I would try to find a rope, floater or something I could use as an aid to float and I would come outside to the open air. I hadn't seen any life vests in Dad's boat so far.

We headed towards the marina at the end of the day. Mum was looking pale, not feeling very well, and we were all exhausted. The sails were hauled down, but the one in the main mast got stuck and wouldn't lower down. Dad was getting angry and frustrated with it.

"Graciela, start the engine, please! And, Jaime, come here! I want you to climb up the mast. I will tie you to this rope and help you pull yourself up. I want you to get to the top and untangle the sail. One of the ends must have come loose and might be blocking the other ones in the carrier channel."

"I'm frightened of doing it, Dad. It's all slippery and the boat is moving side to side with the waves," Jaime said, his voice quivering.

"Do as I tell you, Jaime! Don't start!" Dad shouted at Jaime.

"I'll do it, Dad. I don't mind doing it," Alex intervened.

"Fine, then – any of you!" Dad answered.

Alex was pulled up, but it was clearly very slippery. He was constantly losing his footing, dangling in the air. Mum was tensing up about this. I was worried about Alex falling down and couldn't wait for this adventure to finish. Alex was struggling to loosen the trapped end in the channel and had to remain where he was while the boat reached the marina and we initiated the mooring manoeuvre. Dad didn't explain very well what we had to do, and everything was quite chaotic towards the end. Mum somewhat figured out reversing into the mooring space, but I realised that she nearly scratched a neighbouring boat. I quickly stood up and reached for the boathook, pushing the boat away, but I had to run to the other side to do the same when our boat drifted to the opposite side.

"Children, quickly get the buoys out around the boat!" Dad shouted at us. He ran and jumped to the pontoon with one of the rear moorings in hand.

He tied it securely and asked Jaime to throw him the second rear one. The boat bow continued to drift side to side, despite Mum stopping the engine.

"María! Teresa! Pass me the moorings from the bow of the boat," Dad asked.

They both did, but Teresa dropped hers in the water, so she had to pull it back and throw it again to Dad in the pontoon. Alex was still tied up in the mast.

"Dad, please get me down," Alex said, crying. "I have managed to loosen the end."

Alex was frightened and had hit his body several times against the mast while the boat was moving so much. He had been calling out for help, but nobody had heard him in the middle of the commotion. He was brought down, but we still had to wash the sails with fresh water to get rid of the salt. Mum took the opportunity to go to the clubhouse to ring home in order to ask Miss Spencer to bring the spare car keys. We dried the sails, allowing them to flap in the wind, and we then folded them around the mast and sprit, using covers to protect them. They were in position and available to be used again soon.

Chapter Eleven

SAILING

Dad had become obsessed with sailing and we had been going out to sea every weekend, Saturday and Sunday. We were getting quicker around the boat and we could all understand what to do now, but none of us had Dad's strength. Sailing still frightened me. Beatriz was no longer coming with us because she was too young. She would be allowed to join us on good days with little wind or if we ever went swimming again. I wished I could find a way of saying no to it as well.

Dad had a new sail called a spinnaker. It was huge and light sailing material, much like silk but stronger, which was hoisted last above the other ones. It was light blue and looked like an air balloon. I have to say, it was beautiful when it was out, and it made the boat easily identifiable from the distance. The downside of it was that it could easily become tangled and ripped off in strong winds, but it made the boat go fast.

Dad didn't mind what kind of day we had sailing. He liked sailing and wanted all of us to be good at it. I panicked if it got to the point that we could touch the water with our hands when the boat heeled over. That was too much wind for me. It was also getting to the point that I was so frightened that I chose not to move from one particular point, waiting for the day to be over. Dad was constantly being demanding and getting angry, shouting and pushing us around. I really thought an accident could happen soon and preferred not to be there. I didn't feel safe with Dad at all. María had been missing some days because of homework, Teresa loved it, Jaime seemed to like it – although Dad was constantly being horrible to him – and Alex always thought it was an adventure and followed Dad around, totally unaware of any danger. Mum seemed to want to please Dad as much as possible taking care of the wheel; it was her duty to do what Dad wanted.

"We'll get the spinnaker out, children!" Dad shouted one day.

"There is a blasting wind, Roberto. Are you sure about this?" Mum insisted.

"I am positive, Graciela. If we ever find ourselves in a middle of a race, the weather can abruptly change. I want to train the children to handle the spinnaker, even if we hoist it and have to haul it down suddenly. They have to be ready for everything and to get used to both strong and soft winds with it."

We all got the spinnaker out through the hatch and got it ready to be hoisted.

"On three, children!" Dad commanded. "Pull! Now!"

We all did our best, but the sail was trying to become tangled in the blasts of wind.

"Teresa, don't let the sail go so fast. Keep the tension on starboard and wait for Jaime to ask for it on portside. Jaime, pull!" Dad said.

The wind shook the sail in every direction. "Alex, come with me to the bow and we will help the sail to stay inside the rail," Dad said, and both of them moved ahead.

The spinnaker was almost up, but Jaime didn't have the strength to finish hoisting it.

"Let me help you, Jaime!" Dad told him, taking over.

Dad stood at the edge of the boat, pulling fast with half of his body hanging outside, as he normally did. Suddenly, the winch completely snapped and went flying in the air, and Dad fell backwards into the sea.

I stood up, shouting, "Dad! Dad!"

"Oh my God!" Mum exclaimed, holding on to the wheel, as the boat was sailing extremely fast.

"Isa, quickly throw him the large rope stored under the seat and tie it to the rail the best you can," Mum told me.

I quickly did it and saw how Dad had emerged from the water and had already started swimming, following us the best he could, but he was still far away from the rope.

"Children, lower all the sails at once!" Mum yelled.

We did so quickly and this managed to drastically decrease the speed of the boat, which instead started rocking heavily because the sea was quite choppy. The spinnaker was half in the water, as there was no one to receive it. We all gathered at the stern of the boat and Mum abandoned the wheel, waving at Dad and calling him.

"Can you reach us, Roberto, or shall I use the engine to turn around?" Mum asked nervously.

"You are hardly moving now. I'll reach you – don't worry," Dad shouted from the distance.

He swam and swam for about ten minutes and finally got hold of the rope, and by pulling it, he managed to reach the boat and raise himself up in the air, gripping the rail with his hands.

"How are you going to get on board?" Mum asked him, stepping backwards.

As she did so, the sprit, which had been left loose, swung heavily and hit Mum on the side of the head. Unconscious, Mum fell to the floor.

"Mum! Mum!" we all screamed.

Jaime tightened the sprit, and the four of us gathered around Mum. There was no blood anywhere and after a couple of minutes, Mum opened her eyes, looking very dizzy.

"I'm fine. Where's your Dad?" she asked.

We all turned around and realised that Dad had managed to climb up the boat using his own strength.

"Dad, thank goodness you managed to get back!" Teresa exclaimed. "Mum has been hit by the spirit."

"I know. I heard it." Dad sighed, sitting down to rest.

"Here's a towel, Dad," Teresa said.

That was the last time I went sailing with Mum and Dad, although they continued to spend weekends at sea, mostly with Teresa, Jaime and Alex. I instead tried to join the local sports centre, looking for something to occupy my time, making sure sailing wasn't an option for me anymore.

"Mum, I would like to do gymnastics," I said, trying to find an alternative to sailing. "I asked Teresa what other sports they do in the sport centre where she does basketball and my brothers do judo. She says that they do gymnastics, football and ballet. I don't really want to do ballet or football, but I may quite like doing gymnastics."

"Are you sure about this?" Mum replied, looking at me while she was knitting in her chair in the sitting room.

"Sure about what?" Teresa interrupted, entering the room.

"Isa would like to do gymnastics," Mum told her.

"Isa, it is a really high level, nothing like they do at school. I see people doing very difficult things in the air. You'll need intensive training for it. I don't think you can do it."

"I'd like to try it. I can stand with my legs in the air and roll on the floor," I replied.

Teresa smiled at me, though I wasn't sure what I had said that was so funny.

"I want to do it too," Beatriz joined in. "I'd like to do gymnastics with Isa."

Mum kept quiet for a few seconds. "What days do they do it, Teresa?" Mum asked eventually.

"They're always there when I do play basketball on Mondays and Fridays," Teresa answered.

"Well, I'll collect you with your sisters on Friday and will talk to the person in charge. Let's see if they will take you on. We'll ask for the price too," Mum said to Beatriz and me.

We smiled at each other, and I knew she was also feeling pleased with the decision.

Dad started joining regattas, but he didn't want Teresa to participate in them because he didn't think she had enough strength. Dad made an agreement with one of the sailors doing the compulsory military service where he worked and got extra adult help. Soon Dad started winning most of the regattas, getting plenty of cups and trophies in the region. He was getting ready to compete in the race going from Cádiz to Tangier, in North Africa, crossing the Strait of Gibraltar. That was a long stretch, and the Spanish Navy was hoping to escort them in case they met any difficulties. Dad was so excited about this particular race.

"I've just written an article for the navy, informing them about the currents in the Strait of Gibraltar," Dad told all of us. "Currents go in one direction on the Spanish shore and in the opposite one on the African shore. The middle area is determined by the tides and the month of the year, so it will go in one direction with low tides and in the opposite with high ones, depending on the Mediterranean and the Atlantic Ocean, the direction of the winds and the intensity of the tides. I know it all very well, and I'm going to get there first because the others will get caught in the currents."

"Who will be commanding the escort?" Mum asked.

"Captain Carlos Benavente," Dad replied.

"Is that Ana's dad?" I asked.

"Who's Ana?" Dad asked.

"Ana is one of Carlos and Nuria's daughters," Mum told Dad. "She's in Isabel's class. Their oldest son, Luis, is in Jaime's class."

"Oh, yes. I know who you mean now," Dad said.

Beatriz and I joined the gymnastics club. We were attending it three days a week. The coach was delighted to have us because he reckoned that the best age for starting the sport was Beatriz's age, six; but my age of eight was also good. We were the youngest in the group. I was shy around the coach and didn't talk to him unless he asked something. His name was Juan, and he was passionate about the sport. He was very strong but short, with curly brown hair and a moustache. Juan had been a gymnast when he was young, and he did coaching every day of the week. Mum said that he did it for free, although the federation gave him minimal wages. He had refused any payment from Mum.

The area where we trained was limited in resources. It was the old boxing ring corner of the pavilion. There was a trampoline, a vaulting horse, a beam, the rings, a pommel horse and a set of parallel bars for men that had little to do with the women's ones; having said that, all the girls trained on them, as there was nothing else to use. The equipment was cramped, and we had to take turns rotating the different pieces and folding them away. The floor we used was the one used for judo, and we had to wait until the judo lessons were over late in the evening to use it. It was old and bad quality, with gaps between some of the mats and permanent bumps scattered around. All this made the training tricky, having to use reinforcements on the ankles to avoid injuries, but also the bounce of the mats was dampened compared to what it should have been like.

The warm-up exercises usually took us about forty-five minutes to do and there was quite a lot of running involved around the pavilion and up and down the steps in the stands. Juan found Beatriz very funny and she hardly did any exercises. As soon as she got tired, she sat next to Juan and started talking to him. I didn't know anyone in the group and just copied and followed them around. They seemed good and experienced but talked very differently to what I was used to hearing at school or home. They all used swear words and had an incredibly thick southern accent.

Juan kept us rolling and rolling on the floor; initially it was on mats but not anymore. Now we rolled forwards and backwards on the hard floor, making sure we tucked the head well in, landing on the top of the back. I could do it well now, doing ten consecutive ones and standing up at the end with the impulse gained from the final speed. We were also working on handstands and cartwheels. Legs and arms had to be straight and tight; it was becoming easy to convert a handstand into a forward roll by tucking the head in. We were also doing straight jumps on the trampoline; it was a training tool and there was a team that only did trampolining. Juan was teaching us balance and control in the air as well as helping us get more strength in our backs. We aimed for high jumps, but we needed to always land on the same spot. It was all fun and we did it for three hours, three times a week. If we carried on improving, Juan would eventually ask us to get coaching every day of the week and Saturday mornings.

Gymnastics helped me to sleep better and time flew by when practicing it. I needed to keep alert and focused on what I did, helping me to forget all my worries and fears at school. Despite the physical demands, it was a place where I could relax and be myself. I liked the structure, the directions I got and the signals. It was different to anything else I had ever done, and although I realised that challenging gravity could cause me an injury, doing it under controlled steps was thrilling and rewarding. It required order and discipline, which was already causing me to readjust my academic work and homework. The training was demanding and I was trying to do all my homework during breaks at school and lunchtime. I also did an hour after training, but the rest was done in my spare time during weekends.

Dad was allowing me to use his study next to his bedroom to do my homework. It was a good place because it was between the bedroom and the en suite bathroom. I liked revising and repeating lessons aloud; it helped me to memorise things. Elena was now sharing the room with Beatriz and me; therefore, my bedroom was never a quiet place. Somehow, despite all my repeating aloud, Mum and Dad were even noisier than I was at times. I could sometimes hear their muffled voices in the distance, which could become heavy panting and rhythmic cries. It got to the point that I had to cover my ears because it disturbed my peace and concentration. Dad sometimes liked doing exercises in his bedroom to keep fit, but I doubted that Mum was doing them too. I didn't really know what they were doing.

Chapter Twelve

CHANGE OF TIDES

Mum and Dad had taken us out to have dinner in a restaurant in San Fernando. We were celebrating Dad's victory crossing the Strait of Gibraltar. He wasn't only the first to get there; he arrived in Tangier and was back to Cádiz over an hour ahead of the others.

"The wind was so strong that the race was nearly called off," he said. "They all took a different course to me, and some of them thought I had got confused and were trying to wave at me. What they didn't realise is that as soon as they turned around Cape Tariff in the south of Cádiz, they all followed the current in their favour. But that was the current closest to the shore, and it soon changed. I cut across it in the opposite direction and soon found the middle current in my favour, which helped me to sail across. We had to do two quick manoeuvres in a short space of time and I managed to maintain the spinnaker as long as possible only hauling it down after that. The boat's mast touched the water on two occasions but managed to keep steady. The boat was like a rocket, reaching Tangier faster than anybody else's did. All the others were dragged by the current closest to the shore and drifted too far out of the route, having to recover their way back against the wind. Four boats had to retire from the race, two were disqualified and two more broke their masts in the middle of the straits and had to be rescued …"

Dad went on and on in detail about everything that had happened. The waiter was hovering around trying to change some plates and start serving, but Dad was forgetting to eat.

"You're disturbing me, waiter!" he shouted. "What is it that you want?"

"Sorry, sir. I wasn't sure if you were all finished and were ready for the next course," the waiter answered nervously, at the same time topping up Dad's glass of wine, which was empty.

"I will let you know when you can come back – and don't pour any more wine. Who asked you to do that? What you're trying to make me do is to drink fast so I need to buy another bottle, aren't you? Go away! Who do you think you are?"

The waiter blushed and quickly disappeared. We were seated in the middle of the restaurant, and the people around us were staring.

"Roberto, please. Calm down. He's only trying to do his job," Mum said.

"He doesn't know how to do his job and he is bothering me. He's standing too close to me. It's difficult to know what he wants. And why is that couple over there looking at me? He was sticking his tongue out!" Dad said in distress.

"Roberto, he was licking his lips because he was eating."

"How do you know?" Dad answered, bringing his tone down.

Dad didn't wait for a reply and tried to recommence his story about the race. María was joking about something that had happened at school, telling Teresa and Alex about it. Her voice was quite loud and she was interfering with Dad's conversation. Jaime was also talking about motorbikes with Alex.

"*Silence, please!*" Dad shouted. "*You can only talk when I am finished!*"

Everyone kept quiet, including the people eating around us.

"María, elbows *off* the table!" he suddenly added, smacking María's right elbow hard with the handle of his knife.

"You're a beast, Dad. It is difficult to find any respect for you," María said with tears in her eyes, holding on to her right elbow with the other hand.

"Stand up from this table at once! You are going back home, walking. Dismissed!" Dad commanded.

"With pleasure!" María answered.

Teresa immediately stood up and said, "I'm going with her."

"Me too!" Jaime said, joining in.

Miss Spencer gently pulled at Alex's, Beatriz's and my arm, indicating to stay in our seats, so we didn't move.

"Fair enough! Go!" Dad said.

"Roberto, is this necessary? It's ten kilometres to Cádiz, down a dark country lane." Mum was almost crying, looking at the rest of us as if to say, *I hope you all realise how much I have to put up with,* but she was not really intervening or protecting my siblings.

My heart was racing and I was fixed on Dad. I was terrified of ever being told to leave like that. I realised that for my own sake, I had to learn quickly how buses and trains worked and where to find them, just in case Dad ever asked me to leave. I was glad that María wasn't alone, but I was worried about my siblings, not knowing how they were going to manage to get back home.

Miss Spencer was red in the face but said nothing; she knew very well that my brother and sisters did not have any money to get back home. She opened her purse under the table and without Dad noticing, she gave a one hundred pesetas note to Jamie, who kept it in the pocket of his trousers. No one else said a word for the rest of the meal except for Dad. We were not really listening and Mum was the only one engaging with him.

My siblings finally arrived home one hour after us. They did not seem upset in any way. If anything, there was a sense of camaraderie as they ignored my father on arrival and got ready to go to bed. I felt real terror for them, thinking that I would have not been able to cope as they did.

129

I had been making real progress in gymnastics, and I loved it. Coach Juan eventually invited me to train every day, although Beatriz was still attending three times a week. My days were passing quickly, but my schedule was incredibly tight. I had to take advantage of any available spare time to do homework during the day. My life consisted of going to school and attending my training straight after that. I didn't watch any television or have any time to play.

"Isa, you'd better go home early today," Juan told me unexpectedly one day.

"Oh, why is that? Am I not doing my exercises well?" I replied, completely focussed while still on top of the beam.

"Don't you realise that the place is half empty, and hear the noise of the people outside? General Franco has died," Juan told me.

"Has he really? How do you know?"

"People have been talking about it, and the military police that normally patrol the pavilion have confirmed it. It is not safe out there, and it's getting late."

It was 20 November 1975. I hadn't noticed any of this at all, but when I walked home, I realised that the streets were not safe. Young adults were shouting, writing on the walls and destroying things. The military police that usually patrolled the roads had disappeared. We were used to having them around us all the time, and that was the only reason that the streets were safe, with no robberies or assaults. I felt frightened all the way home, and from that day on, I chose to run to get to places every time I was unaccompanied in the streets.

The situation at school was tense among the students. Luckily, I never talked much, and I continued to avoid doing so. There were students in the class and around the school commenting about the imminent referendum that the provisional government of Adolfo Suárez was proposing to the nation: "Democracy, yes or no?" Some of the girls felt strongly about the idea that if they discovered any family voting yes to democracy, they would be considered traitors.

The school was full of families from the navy and the army, but my parents were full supporters of a parliamentary monarchy under the newly crowned King Juan Carlos I, rather than a military government led by him. It was better to pretend not to know anything.

A parliamentary monarchy was basically a constitutional monarchy, Dad told us. If it went ahead, it was going to be the first one in Europe, and what made it different from the rest, including the British one, was the fact that the people chose whether or not to have the king representing them. The king had no powers, all his possessions belonged to Spain, and he was not even able to dissolve the government if the situation arose. People could choose to discontinue the monarchy if the king ever abused his position or stopped representing people's needs in an adequate manner. The king's role was to be an ambassador for the country, with an honorific title of superior commander of the whole army, but he didn't have any power.

The situation was tense due to changes in politics, but I had several friends at school now and I occasionally played with them. I was also being invited to birthday parties, but I could never relax in anybody else's house. In addition, I was focused on studying and doing gymnastics, so I never really engaged with anything or anybody else. I was doing about three hours of homework a day and six each day of the weekend. Memorising facts and constantly going through everything I had learnt took time, but my grade cards were getting very good. My anxiety and obsession around studying was powerful and I felt that if I didn't have the gymnastics, I could possibly lose my mind. I couldn't avoid feeling tense at home. The situation was such that I couldn't remember the last time I actually played at home.

"Isa, why don't we play together? You haven't played with me for a long time," Beatriz complained, coming into the study, where I was revising, Elena following her.

"Sorry, Beatriz. I don't seem to have the time for it," I answered, feeling sorry for her.

"Isa, I want to play going fishing with you in an adventure like you used to play with Beatriz. You've never played with me," Elena told me.

I looked at both of them. They didn't realise my need to grow fast and to become independent to be able to help Mum out, becoming a strong support for her. They didn't understand how serious my studies were, that they were the key to my future. Despite all my studying, I knew that I could forget things, and I had an incredible fear of doing or getting things wrong. I thought that there were no second chances for me. I was feeling a permanent anguish inside my chest.

"You are right, both of you. Let's play! But I have to tell you both that although I'm only eight, I can't be an eight-year-old anymore. I have to become a grown-up as soon as I can to help Mum. I need to study, find a job and earn money so I stop depending on Mum and Dad. I don't want to be a heavy load and would also like to help you both if I can," I said to my sisters, meaning every word.

They looked at each other and then looked at me. "What do you mean, Isa?" Beatriz asked.

"I mean that this is the last time I will ever play with you at home," I answered.

They were speechless for a while, clearly not knowing what to say or understanding what made me reach that conclusion. I timed my playing for forty-five minutes and then left them together, enjoying each other's company. Beatriz was six and Elena was nearly three.

I missed being a child, being able to enjoy trivial things or waste time watching something funny on the telly. I sometimes cried at night because I found life hard, but my need to become perfect was the only way I could find to fit in and create a deep sense of structure in my head. I was coerced and trapped in my own routine, not being able to break through or contradict rules. The price for being perfect as well as invisible was incredibly high.

I frequently sorted out my secret drawer, which is where I kept my treasures. Doing this made me feel better. I liked collecting beautiful things like stickers of all kinds, cards with beautiful prints, glass marbles with bright colours and a few dolls, which I never played with. I had porcelain animal families which were small as well as beautiful. I liked anything that looked delicate. I was keeping all my things to pass them on to my future children, if I ever had any. I hoped they would be able to enjoy them. My decision involved making big sacrifices, and contemplating the treasures in my drawer helped me heal my pain.

Chapter Thirteen

CHRISTMAS HOLIDAYS

It was Christmas 1977. We always spent Christmas and New Year's Eve at Grandmother Isabel's house in Seville. This was what Grandmother expected and what Mum also liked, but it was always a source of unhappiness for my father.

My mother had inherited El Cortijo from her parents, as well as two other villas that were also in the county of Seville. These villas had smaller houses to live in but lay in richer land by the River Guadalquivir so we never lived in them, although the land was exploited for business purposes. My grandparents had ten of these large villas in the south of Spain and three other enormous houses, two in the north of Spain and a third one in Seville, where Grandmother Isabel was living now. They made their fortune trading coffee and tobacco from South America and with the sugar cane business in the Philippines.

Mum's brothers, Uncle Tomás and Uncle Pedro, as well as her sister, Aunt Mónica, also celebrated Christmas with Grandmother. We hardly ever saw Mum's eldest brother, Uncle Eduardo, who lived in the north of Spain. Great-Aunt Antonia, Grandmother's sister, who was a widower, also liked joining us. Uncle Tomás had just had another son, so he had now nine children. Uncle Pedro had seven and Aunty Mónica had ten. There would be thirty-three cousins between the ages of one and seventeen for Christmas Eve. Mum very much wished to attend, but Dad had been very angry about it. I heard them arguing in their bedroom, and Dad had been slamming doors in the house.

"I'm not going, and that is that! I would like the children to learn Christmas carols and to sing for us on Christmas Eve. We will stay in Cádiz and go to your mother's on New Year's Eve," Dad said. "Children, come here! All of you!"

I had been listening to the conversation and therefore was there right away. Jaime also arrived quickly.

"María! Teresa! Alex, Beatriz and Elena! Present yourselves to the high commander right now!" he shouted. "Please form a line in front of me." One by one, everyone arrived and lined up for him. "Listen carefully; it is Christmas Day in two days. I would like each of you to learn two carols by then, and you can each play an instrument as well. You are allowed to pair up or sing in a group if you wish, but each of you has to sing twice one way or the other. We are staying here for Christmas and will go to El Cortijo after that. You are dismissed!"

"Roberto, for God's sake!" Mum stood up from her chair with tears in her eyes and went to her bedroom.

We all looked at each other, not moving.

"That's a fantastic idea, Dad!" María exclaimed enthusiastically. "We've been learning carols at school and I can also play my guitar. Can we dance?" she asked.

"Of course you can, María," Dad answered, looking pleased to think that his idea had been positively supported.

We all gathered in Teresa and María's bedroom.

"It's fine for you, but Alex and I don't know many carols," Jaime said worriedly.

"I know two from school. If you want, I can sing them to you and the three of us can sing together. They're not very difficult," I explained to Jaime.

"I can sing the one I know from school alone and join your group for the second one," Beatriz said.

"What do I do?" Elena asked, looking at all of us.

"Sing with all of us too," I quickly said.

"But what shall we do about the instruments?" Jaime asked.

"I'll play the tambourine, but I'm not singing," Alex announced.

"Elena and Beatriz can also play the tambourine," Jaime decided. "And that will be our plan."

"I will sing both carols doing a solo and playing my guitar," María told us with a big smile on her face. "I would like Dad and Mum to listen to me."

Teresa didn't like that idea. "That will leave me having to sing alone twice. María, you could at least sing with me once."

"Okay, I'll sing with you, Teresa, but I will still be playing the guitar."

Teresa rolled her eyes to the ceiling and said, "If you must, so be it!"

It was Christmas Eve, and before lunchtime Mum told us that we were leaving as soon as possible for Seville. We all packed quickly and drove to El Cortijo; there had been a change of plans and we were spending Christmas Eve with our grandmother. Dad was not talking very much. I didn't think he was very happy about this.

There were three large tables laid out and prepared in Grandmother's house – one in the dining room for all the adults, a second one in the corridor from the sitting room to the dining room for the older grandchildren, and a third one in the entrance hall for the younger grandchildren. Everything was luxurious, with huge chandeliers above each table and linen tablecloths on all of them, silver cutlery with a delicate porcelain dinner service and fine cut glass, even for the small children. Men were wearing dinner suits and women were wearing evening dresses; male cousins were also wearing ties and blazers, and girls were as smartly dressed as possible.

The noise in the house was loud. All the small children had each been given a present before dinner, although the

Three Wise Men wouldn't arrive until 6 January to bring the rest of the presents to the children. I stopped believing in the Wise Men when I was seven; I'd heard someone at school say that they were our own parents. The older grandchildren had each received an envelope with a generous amount of money from Grandmother. With the excitement of the presents, it was difficult to keep the younger children under control. Miss Spencer was not particularly bothered because Beatriz and Elena were well behaved, but some of Uncle Tomás' children and Aunty Mónica's daughters and sons were loud and badly behaved. Their nannies were having a real struggle getting them to maintain good manners. It was funny to watch. This year was the first time I had ever received an envelope with money. I felt like a real grown-up.

Antonia, the cook, was in the kitchen, trying to have the entire meal ready at the same time, and Matilde, the maid, was rushing in and out of the kitchen to serve us consommé, prawns and king prawns, smoked salmon with condiments, roast turkey with vegetables and typical Christmas sweets and cakes, all cooked by Antonia.

I was at the table with the younger children and Miss Spencer and other nannies helped serve the food. The older children helped themselves from trays left in the middle of the table.

When we finished eating, Matilde and Antonia left to have dinner with their families, and Miss Spencer and her colleagues had some food in the kitchen. Some of my older cousins stayed in the sitting room with the adults, María and Teresa among them. Jaime also stayed, but everyone else from Alex's age downwards preferred to go to the lower ground rooms to play hide-and-seek. It was good fun, as there were so many of us. My cousins Enrique, Adolfo, Magdalena and Natalia – Aunty Mónica's children – were quite exquisite and tried to behave in a dignified manner. They were the grandchildren of the marquis of Montoro.

"Enrique, it's your turn to look for everyone," my cousin Andrés said.

"Okey, but if I get hold of anyone, please don't pull hard on my jacket or shirt. I don't want them stained or torn," he answered.

"Don't be an idiot. Playing is playing," Alex said to him.

"We certainly won't go on the floor with our dresses," Magdalena interrupted, talking about her and her sister. "Mum got our dresses from Paris especially for the occasion."

"Are you playing or not? Take off your clothes if they're so precious – but get on with it. Otherwise, go upstairs with the grown-ups," Margarita, Andrés's sister, who was my age, said in an irritated tone.

Teresa rushed into the room. "Isabel, Alex, Beatriz, Elena, we're leaving now! Dad's angry and upset. I'm not sure why. He suddenly stood up in the middle of the sitting room and said, 'This is unbearable! I'm leaving!' He's already in the car and if we aren't there within five minutes, he's leaving us behind. Quickly! Hurry up!"

"This isn't fair!" Alex said angrily. "It's always the same with him. We haven't even had the chance to start one game. What's the point of coming here if we always have to leave in a rush?" He continued protesting as he went up the stairs.

Mum had her usual face of bearing a heavy burden and Miss Spencer left the house putting on her coat as she rapidly walked through the garden; she was still chewing her dinner. It felt terrible and stressful having to leave Grandmother's house like this. It wasn't new to us, but we never had the time to say goodbye to anyone. Our extended family knew that Dad had a terrible temper and that he was unbearable in many ways. Mum, always had an excuse for him.

"Nobody was talking to me!" Dad said, infuriated. "Your brother-in-law speaks so softly that I couldn't hear him. How rude is that? I was trying to maintain a conversation with him, but people chose not to notice that I was talking, and all of them continued talking and ignoring me. I can't stand the noise; my head was going to explode … And did you see Pedro's wife? She is so boring. That woman hasn't got a brain. 'Roberto, the colour of your eyes matches my blouse.' What kind of comment is that? She keeps calling me Roberto as if she knows me. She's a stranger to me …" Dad went on and on the whole journey home. It was so disappointing.

Mum and Dad allowed us to invite some of our cousins to spend five days in El Cortijo. Francisco and Andrés were always willing to join us, but on this occasion, their younger sisters, Margarita and Verónica, came as well. Verónica was Beatriz's age. My cousin Margarita was my age but was always very attached to her mother, not wanting to go anywhere without her. It was unusual for her to want to come to El Cortijo with us. Mum also invited Aunt Mónica's younger daughters, Magdalena and Natalia. Magdalena was eleven months older than Natalia, and I was six months younger than she was. They were precious girls but sometimes rude, especially Natalia; even their casual clothes were so co-ordinated and perfect that I wondered how they were going to cope with the mud and the roughness of our games.

We decided to build tree houses by the stream running at the bottom of the path leading to the house, next to the bridge. Julio and Lola were also joining us, and as usual, María was leading the girls and Julio the boys. We were all well protected against the cold and damp weather of the winter. Mum had knitted all of us extra thick jumpers to be worn on top of our normal clothes; we sometimes slept in them as well, as the central heating wasn't great in the house.

"Let's jump over the stream!" María said to all of us.

It was certainly a nice width and I could see how inviting it was. We all started jumping towards one shore of the stream and later on to the other side. There was plenty of laughter because as people grew confident, the impulse they took for the jumps was getting more relaxed. Andrés nearly fell in the water, wetting his left shoe. Magdalena and Natalia were hesitant, but after some thought, they gathered some speed before the jump and both of them, holding hands together, were brave enough to do it.

"I'm not doing it!" Margarita said.

I tried to encourage her. "Come on, Marga. Take my hand and we'll jump together, or if you prefer, I will reach you from the other side and pull you across as you jump."

"Do you think I can do it?" She hesitated.

"Of course you can. Don't think too much about it," I said, holding her hand tightly. "One, two, three!"

We both jumped, and I made sure that I made a much longer jump than she did so I could pull her forward as I landed ahead of her. It was easy for me after all my training in gymnastics.

"That was scary, but I'm glad I did it," Margarita said.

Verónica was mesmerised as she watched everybody jumping, and she didn't seem to realise that as she positioned herself close to the border, she was holding Beatriz by her jumper in case her feet slipped away. Beatriz clearly wasn't aware of it and unexpectedly jumped forward, dragging Verónica with her. Beatriz made just a big enough jump to reach the shore, but Verónica, completely unprepared for the jump, fell in the middle of the stream. Beatriz lost her balance when Verónica didn't let her jumper go and she fell in the water too, sitting on her bottom. They both screamed but started laughing and we all joined in the laughter.

"The water is freezing!" Verónica said.

Beatriz turned to Verónica, looking slightly irritated. "You pulled me in with you. You should have let me go."

They both stood up. The water only reached their knees, but they were both completely soaked.

"Go back to the house to get changed," Teresa told them. "Tell Miss Spencer what happened; she'll give you different clothes. We'll be right here building the tree houses."

Julio had found a straight wooden plank between the trees and managed to put it across the stream. It was stable and secure, and we immediately started crossing the stream. It made it easier transporting branches across the stream to the place where we were building the two tree houses. Magdalena and Natalia were making comments about getting their hands dirty or getting mud on their trousers and beautiful shoes, but we all ignored them.

"Hello, children. What are you doing?" We all looked up to see Dad riding Tristán on the pathway.

"We're building tree houses," Jaime answered.

Dad slowly approached us on the horse, getting closer to the stream.

"How clever of you! Whose idea was it to use this piece of wood?" he asked.

"It was Julio's idea. He found it between the eucalyptuses," Alex answered.

"We'll come to the other side to meet you," Dad said, encouraging Tristán to get closer to the wood.

We all immediately stood up and turned around to see exactly what Dad meant by the word "we".

"Come on, Tristán! Get on the plank. Come on, come on!" Dad repeated, pricking Tristán's sides with his heels.

The horse didn't like it. It was narrow and he had to keep his legs too close together to do so. My heart started racing. I didn't think the wood would take Tristán's weight with Dad on top. He was going to break his legs. I didn't like Dad forcing the horse to do anything he didn't like. Dad started hitting Tristán with his whip, but he started going backwards, shaking his head up and down while whinnying and blowing hard.

"Please, Dad, don't do it!" I said, nearly in tears.

"It's better if you get off the horse and walk across it with him; but I tell you Dad, it's not secure enough. It moves because the ground is wet and the fitting points are getting loose. We've been going over it all morning," Teresa explained to Dad, exaggerating slightly.

Dad hesitated but clearly preferred not to dismount Tristán.

"Fair enough!" he said, turning around and finding his way back to the pathway leading to the house again. "I will be getting ready for a game of orienteering and treasure hunting. I would like all of you to play after lunch."

We all looked at each other and said nothing. I sighed, taking a big breath. I didn't like Dad's treasure hunting games; they were too long and boring, spoiling most of our playing time.

It was afternoon already and the day continued to be cold and grey with no rain. Dad organised everything from the top of the horse and when we were all lined up in front of him, he split us into two teams of mixed abilities. He also gave us two maps containing instructions on how to solve the first clue, which would lead us to more information on how to solve the second one. In all, there were four clues to solve. The team who found the treasure first and brought it to him would win.

"I'll be in the house waiting, but if you take too long, I will come and find you to see what the problem is. One more thing: each team will need a compass. Good luck!" Dad turned the horse around and slowly rode him back to the courtyard.

I was not looking forward to this. It normally took about three hours to complete one of Dad's treasure hunts, and it also involved an awful amount of walking. I was on a team with María, Teresa, Lola and my cousins Francisco and Andrés. All the others were with Julio. We managed to guess the first clue before the others, and we found a second map with more clues in the well that was over one kilometre away from the house. Julio's group was spying on us so they found out that they had to go to the well soon too. We all sat down to have a rest, drink some water from the well, and share some biscuits.

"I'd rather be playing something else than this … or even finishing the tree houses," Jaime said.

"It's hard work, with lots of walking across the land," my cousin Margarita complained.

"Can we tell Uncle Roberto that we don't want to play?" Magdalena asked.

"You might be able to, but I doubt very much that he will let his children go until we complete it," Jaime answered. "Dad will get offended."

"Come on. Let's do it together. At the end, we'll split the groups again so only one team receives the prize. The sooner we finish, the better for us," Julio said, standing up.

We all stood up and walked to the second well, over two kilometres north-east, and from there to the third well, closest to the house. That was one and a half kilometres away from the previous one. By this stage, all my cousins had headed back to the house, exhausted and hungry. My siblings and I knew we had to stay. Lola started complaining and Julio sent her back to her house too. We also knew that the arrival of all my cousins to the house was going to make my father curious, so we decided to split up and walk in the two remaining teams for the last quest, waiting for Dad's imminent arrival on Tristán. The last clue was directing us to the furthest edge of the villa from the back of the house.

"I can see that you've close to finding the treasure," Dad said to us. "You're nearly there!"

Nobody said anything and I certainly couldn't walk any faster. We still had to return to the house from where we were. My brothers suddenly saw a small shed giving shelter to an electrical pump that was buried in the ground; it was used for watering the olive trees in the spring and summer. They knew the treasure was hidden there and the two of them ran with Julio to get it. It was a bag of sweets and one hundred pesetas to be shared by the team whose last member was Beatriz.

For some reason, Mum always thought that we loved playing this game with Dad. We all knew that it made Mum happy, and we obliged her by playing it; but I couldn't comprehend what relief or satisfaction she obtained from it. She encouraged Dad to organise it too frequently. Mum seemed proud and happy with Dad.

Days were short in the month of December, but it felt that the sun had set even earlier today. The boys were all in one room and the girls in two, as we were so many. Miss Spencer allowed us to play for half an hour in the rooms before switching the lights off. Luckily, Mum and Dad's bedroom was in the opposite wing of the house.

The boys were playing a fighting game and were shouting and laughing. María and Teresa joined us in our room and a pillow fight commenced among all the girls. We were jumping from one bed to another, chasing people around and hitting anyone we could with the pillows. Margarita didn't like the fight very much and was scared of being hit. My cousin Natalia hit the younger girls with the same force as the older, aiming to hurt as much as possible, so soon Verónica and Beatriz were in tears. Teresa and María started protecting them, but Magdalena allied with her sister.

"You stupid cows, leave my sister alone!" Magdalena shouted angrily.

"Your sister is hurting Verónica and Beatriz. We've told her to stop doing it and she doesn't care. That's why we're hitting her back!" Teresa replied.

"I'll tell my mother as soon as I get back home. You are bigger than she is."

María joined in. "And so what. She is trying to make them cry. We will continue until she stops."

"You are horrible monsters!" Natalia finally stopped hitting, latching on to what she had just heard. "You have been deliberately hurting me, and I will tell my mother." Natalia screamed with false tears in her eyes.

Miss Spencer appeared at that moment and diffused the situation, sending everyone to bed. María and Teresa left our room and we went to bed. My bed was in an absolute state, completely undone. I disliked sleeping like this and despite my best efforts, I knew the bedding would be wrinkled and quite loose throughout the night.

The plumbing of the central heating was a distinctive feature all around the house, visible and running along the walls, quite close to the very high ceilings. The house was from the nineteenth century. Airlocks in the system sometimes caused thumping noises and the sound of the shaking pipes was quite loud. There were small explosions in them, blocking the water and allowing it to run at intervals. We were all used to it, but some of my cousins were frightened of it. Miss Spencer had to stop the central heating to solve the problem, but she warned us to wear jumpers to sleep because it was going to be cold in the night.

Another issue also bothered my cousins. The lizards! It wasn't uncommon to see small lizards crouching completely motionless in the middle of the ceiling or hiding behind the pipes. They came in every day when Lola opened the windows to clean the rooms. Because the house was old, there were small gaps in the window frames where they could easily get in and out. These lizards were not poisonous and liked to remain attached to the ceiling or the walls. They never dropped on top of anyone but occasionally moved their position. They were useful to have because they took care of any irritating mosquitos or flies in the room. Again, we were all used to them being part of the house, and Miss Spencer always told us to leave them alone and ignore them as if they were not there. My cousins were not used to living in the countryside at all.

The calmness of the night was relaxing. I could hear the hooting of the owls as they took turns talking in the distance. Overall, it was all very quiet; crickets in the warmer seasons usually made the nights spectacularly musical, but this wasn't the case during the winter.

I liked sleeping hugging my pillow tightly and all my blankets covering my back, also close to my neck. It was soothing and comforting, giving me a real sense of protection and security. The long pillow acted as a pole with two fixed points between my knees and my arms around it. My pressure on it was such that it would exhaust me, helping me to relax and sleep; but it was occasionally better and quite tender, the feeling of the gentle rocking of my body in bed instead. I felt safe in bed, and I had always slept this way since I was a toddler. Although I usually slept throughout the night, my major difficulty was falling asleep, but I had been noticing lately that I sometimes woke up in the middle of the night with a feeling of real palpitations, hot and sweaty but not remembering any particular dreams.

We spent the following day playing in the tree houses and in the garden. Taking advantage of the number of cousins who were there, we decided that playing baseball was a good idea. We used a tennis racket as a bat and from the tennis court, we hit the ball to any direction in the garden, although to have the best chance at winning, it had to go over the tennis court fence, avoiding the palm trees. It was good fun and Beatriz and I discovered that we were good at it; both of us had well coordinated and powerful strikes, much better than our own brothers and cousins, Francisco or Andrés. We became popular in the game and all the others wanted to have us on their teams. It was an excellent feeling. We could hear hunters in the distance and the occasional shots of rifles as we played. Hunting season was open and we saw Dad today, getting ready with his rifles too. Marco, the German shepherd, didn't stop barking. When we finished playing baseball, some of us went to the main courtyard and found Marco chained to the wall and quite agitated. Both dogs were normally free all day and night; they were only tied up for short and specific situations.

"Marco, what's the problem? Why are you tied up?" Alex ran to him and stroked his back. "Where's Polo?"

"Federico, do you know why Marco is here?" my cousin Andrés asked the caretaker, who happened to walk by through the courtyard.

"Mr Grimaldi tied him up and said to leave him like that until he came back. He has taken Polo with him," Federico answered.

"That's unusual. Dad always takes both dogs hunting. If anything, Polo is old now and can hardly walk," Jaime explained.

"But Dad isn't hunting anymore. I just saw him reading the newspaper in the sitting room when I went to get some water," I told everyone present.

"I'm going to ask him if we can free Marco!" Alex said, running back to the house.

We all waited in the courtyard next to Marco, but suddenly Verónica and Beatriz screamed.

"Polo! Polo! What's happened to you?" Beatriz exclaimed in distress.

"Oh, my God! I'm going to be sick!" Verónica said.

We all turned around and saw Polo, our huge mastiff, limping towards us with blood running down the left side of his head from a large wound just above the eyes. His mouth was open and his tongue was hanging out; he had his head down, and he was walking with difficulty, almost falling over. He managed to get through the main entrance into the courtyard.

The girls were screaming and shouting. Francisco and Andrés had horrified expressions on their faces.

"Dad shot him!" Jaime whispered next to me.

Terror ran through my body. It was such an unexpected sight and we were not ready for it. Marco wouldn't stop barking, trying to rip off his chain. Federico immediately came to the courtyard again when he heard all the noise and the screams. I froze and couldn't move from where I was. I really thought Dad was capable of anything.

Federico started muttering angry sentences between his teeth, looking very annoyed. He tied a rope to Polo's collar and took him out of the courtyard again, towards the countryside behind the house, but Polo was struggling to get away.

Dad eventually came out of the house with Alex behind him.

"Federico has taken Polo away. He is injured and bleeding from his head!" Verónica explained to Dad.

"Damn it! I thought I had put him down with my shot," he said. "He is ill and is a very old dog. It's time for him to die."

Dad went inside the house again to get his rifle and followed Federico behind the house. We all heard a shot and saw Dad returning home; he walked inside the house and closed the door behind him. Federico took longer to come back; he buried Polo but never told us where. When I finally managed to move again, I went to my bed and hugged my pillow. I didn't want to talk or play with anybody. I really wanted the holidays to be over.

It was the end of the holidays and my cousins had already left. Having so many cousins with us made Christmas holidays special and helped us stay away from Dad, who had been sporadically agitated. Uncle Tomás came to have coffee after lunch one day before New Year and collected everyone, included Magdalena and Natalia. I was not sure if the two girls had had a good time or not; we'd had plenty of arguments with them both. I knew my cousin Margarita was looking forward to seeing her mum again.

We had spent the New Year in El Cortijo and the Wise Men had also arrived, but school was starting again tomorrow. The luggage was packed and both cars were ready. The others, with the exception of Miss Spencer, Elena and me, were travelling with Mum and her car was in the second courtyard. They were all waiting.

Dad's car was by the main entrance at the front of the house and Elena was already inside. We had said goodbye to Julio, Lola and their parents, but Mum and Dad were still standing in the main entrance under the arch, having a conversation with Nicolás, the manager, who had just arrived before we left. His wife, Pamela, was also there. It was difficult to understand what they were talking about, but Dad's voice was becoming louder. He was clearly angry and distressed, and Mum looked tense. I was standing close to Miss Spencer while we were both waiting in the courtyard, not able to cross the arch without interrupting the conversation.

"You are a thief! I don't have anything else to talk to you about!" Dad pushed past Nicolás and Pamela, striding towards the car.

Mum was trying to apologise and to arrange to continue the conversation later over the phone when we arrived in Cádiz. I could see that Dad was not really waiting for Miss Spencer and me; I wasn't even sure if he had noticed that Elena was already inside his car. Dad's car was facing the property and he suddenly reversed with aggression, making a semicircle and backing into the main entrance, ready to accelerate and drive away.

"Mr Grimaldi, don't go! Wait for us! We are meant to go with you!" Miss Spencer shouted, waving her hands so Dad would see her in the rear-view mirror.

But Dad didn't seem to notice.

"*Roberto!*" Mum shouted loudly.

Dad braked at once, and Miss Spencer and I walked as fast as we could towards the car.

"Where's my son? Where's José? He was here a minute ago. He was playing by my side," Pamela said with alarm.

José was Pamela's toddler.

We all stopped and looked around the corner of the house. José was nowhere to be seen. Pamela nervously looked under the car and yelled, pulling José from underneath.

"Oh my God, José! My son! You've run him over! What kind of person are you? You are insane!" Pamela shrieked with fury.

Nicolás put his arm around Pamela and they both checked José over. The toddler was crying and was visibly injured in the head, face and the left foot.

"Pamela, is José all right? Do we need to take him to the doctor? How is he?" Mum asked, plainly concerned, but Pamela and Nicolás weren't allowing her or any of us close to José.

"Leave us alone and go! He is an animal!" Pamela screamed.

"Roberto, go, please," Mum told Dad. "Take Miss Spencer and Isabel with you. I will follow you soon."

We got in the car and Dad drove away.

"Did you hear what she called me? It's unbelievable!" he exclaimed. "What was that toddler doing there? It's all her own fault."

Nobody replied.

I was speechless and very frightened.

Mum arrived to Cádiz much later than Dad and as soon as she did, she called Nicolás straight away, asking how José was. Mum told Miss Spencer and me that José had been checked over by the doctor, and although he was bruised, nothing was broken. I felt relieved but with great tension inside my body, hardly being able to move and not being able to say in words how terrified I was.

Chapter Fourteen

María

I was eleven and therefore in fifth year, the last year in primary school before the three years of middle school. Elena was in first year reception by now, which seemed incredible to believe. María was in her last year of school but was only sixteen. She followed the old education system that my parents had also had when they were young; but from Teresa onwards we all had a different system. There were three academic years' difference between my older sisters, despite being only fourteen months apart; Teresa had a year extra added in the system and María was moved a year ahead in reception because her reading and writing were advanced for her age. Our school didn't have the last course before university, so María was taking the last year at my brothers' school, a mixed school.

María had changed a lot. She was starting university and would still be sixteen when she did so. She already had a boyfriend she had met in Laredo, but somehow her demands and behaviour were still those of a spoilt girl. María was always testing and pushing the boundaries as much as she could in order to obtain what she wanted. The atmosphere in the house was tense, so Mum and Dad were arguing most of the time. I couldn't understand my sister, how she was insisting in getting what she wanted, not caring about the consequences of her selfish attitude. Everything around the house was about trying to accommodate her needs, which seemed to be endless. I felt resentful and angry towards her, although I found it difficult to convey that. I was quite good in detecting what could cause a problem for Mum and I disliked the fact that María, despite knowing how Dad was, still insisted. On the other hand, Dad was finding it difficult to adapt to any changes in our routine and it was clear that anytime María wanted to go out, socialise or return home later than usual, it was causing great disruption in the family.

"I have been invited to spend New Year's with Antonio's family. They are planning to go skiing," María told us while we were having lunch with Mum and Dad.

"But who is Antonio?" Dad asked.

"Roberto, I have told you many times that María is going out with this boy called Antonio."

"Boyfriends mean nothing to me," he responded. "When he is in a position to marry you, he can come to talk to me and from then on, you can go to his house and visit his family, not before. I am certainly not interested in seeing him before that. Besides, what does he do? What does his father do?"

"He is at university in Bilbao. His parents are from the Basque Country ..."

"*Basque Country*? You mean the County of Biscay, which belongs to Spain!" Dad shouted before María had the chance to finish her sentence. "They are communists and separatists! What does his father do?" Dad insisted.

"The family works in the fishing industry," Mum intervened, hiding the fact that Antonio's father was the owner of a large fishing boat.

"María!" Dad said angrily. "You broke your leg again last summer because you went on his motorbike without asking for my permission. You had an accident and while he was fine, you ended up in hospital with a broken leg. Now you are planning to go skiing. Our family doesn't ski. You are not going anywhere with him. You are not married. Over my dead body!"

"Roberto, they'll be with his parents. They're not going to be alone. I think we need to be a little more open-minded about this. It's not like in our time, when we couldn't even dance together because it was a sin ..."

"Antonio is nobody to me," Dad answered. "You approve of all this happening? You're just going to encourage María to spend as much time as possible with him, aren't you? Again, over my dead body."

There was a real tense feeling around the table and none of us dared to say anything at all.

"You aren't my owner, Dad," María said. "Grandmother Isabel is giving me money for Christmas and I will have enough to pay for the plane ticket. If his family is inviting me, I'm going."

"Who the hell do you think you are? You are only sixteen and still under my care! Who do you think is paying for your food? You are living in my house – do you hear me?" Dad shouted.

"Not for long, Dad," María answered, looking straight in his eyes. "I'm going to live with Grandmother after the summer. She has more money than you and a much bigger house. You won't have to spend much money on me anymore. She can easily pay for anything I need."

Dad's agitation was overwhelming.

"*Stand up at once!*" Dad shouted, pulling María by the arm. "*Get out of this house!* You are not allowed to live in this house anymore until you apologise!" Dad was pushing María away from the table and out of the dining room; she was losing her balance and tripping over at times. "*I want you out of my sight!*"

"Roberto, please! Stop pushing her like that! Calm down!" Mum kept saying, holding her head between both her hands. "I can't take this any longer ... María, please don't give me any more problems. You are both upsetting me greatly." Mum had tears in her eyes.

Dad pushed María all the way through the sitting room as well and to the main entrance of the house, slamming the door closed after her.

"Out of this house now! Don't ever come back!" He finally returned to the table.

None of us moved or continued eating. My body was shaking; I couldn't hold my cutlery still so I hid my hands under the table. Dad was sitting on my right, and I could sense his anger and tension; he was too close to me. Mum was sitting on my left, and I was aware of her unease and sadness. I truly could not move; my fear was paralysing me.

Suddenly, the doorbell rang. Teresa immediately stood up and went to open it.

"Don't let her in!" Dad commanded, but Teresa ignored him.

María showed her face again and said,

"If you're throwing me out of *your* house, I'm taking *my* things. Mum bought them for me with *her* own money because you don't have enough for all of us," María said defiantly to Dad.

"*Out of this house!*" Dad screamed, punching the table. Plates and cutlery jumped in the air.

"I'm leaving with her too. I'm not coming back until she's allowed in," Teresa announced, and she accompanied María to pack their things.

"Roberto, this is my house too; it's not only yours. I will never tolerate you throwing any of my children out of the house," Mum said at last, tears running down her face.

"If that's the case, I will be the one leaving this house. There is nothing else to talk about." Dad stood up, slammed the door, and left the house.

Three days passed and Dad was still gone. Mum was devastated, crying all the time and asking us to behave and not to give her any problems. I didn't miss Dad, but Mum's anxiety was hard to ignore. We knew by now that Dad was living on the boat. Mum couldn't take it any longer and finally decided to go talk to him. If my parents were ever thinking of sending María to university in Cádiz, this had changed matters completely. By now, María and my parents had both agreed that she should live with Grandmother. I was finding it difficult to understand how a parent could ever throw a child out. Teenagers were vulnerable, and anyone who was underage should never be put in such a stressful position; we children didn't have any money and were not allowed to work to earn it. We were expected to go to school and be taken care off. The whole experience was very confusing. I felt anxious and my need to grow fast was imperative. Dad could easily leave any of us stranded.

Part II
Finding Myself

Chapter Fifteen

THE COMPETITION

Things had been calmer lately, but I was finding it difficult to cope with the tension at home. My routine was incredibly tight and I was trying to keep to myself as much as possible. Homework still concerned me but my memory was incredibly good; I rarely made a single mistake at school. My training was also going well and Juan had taken us to do gymnastic exhibitions around the county to promote the sport, as it was not well known among the public. I didn't have to do anything related to sailing now, which was a huge relief, but my training was becoming so important for me that I had even missed going to El Cortijo some weekends, staying in Cádiz with María and Miss Spencer. María was revising hard, getting ready for her pre-university exams.

I hardly ever said anything at home and found it difficult to express what I thought. My chest felt locked up most of the time. Mum was still helping Alex with his homework and he was managing to scrape through. Teresa and Jaime both needed extra tutoring in maths and physics. María absolutely despised chemistry, also needing help with extra tutoring.

Beatriz always came to me for any extra help at school. She was very bright but rigid in her thinking, and I could relate to that; I could easily explain things to her and she got a better understanding from me than she ever did from her teacher. It seemed to me that Beatriz tried to be anonymous in her class, not wanting any attention.

I disliked two particular things at home. Mum continued releasing her bowels in public at times, when least expected. It really unsettled me when she did it. And I couldn't understand how she was not able to get better control of herself. I tried to block it from my mind as if it never happened.

The second thing that was tormenting me was the fact that I now knew Mum and Dad occasionally had sex in their bedroom when I was in the study doing my homework. For over a year now, I had known everything about girls having periods every month and how mums got pregnant. My teammates kept referring to it all the time and I asked Mum what they meant. I thought the whole thing was disgusting. Some of the girls in the club even said that Juan touched us on our backsides during training. I would rather Juan touched me if he had to than my breaking a leg because he didn't. How was he expected to get hold of us when we were about to crash when learning a new exercise? We didn't have security belts or dips of foam available for training.

There was really nowhere else I could go to study where I could read aloud without disturbing anyone else. It made me anxious and vigilant having to try to finish my homework as soon as I possibly could, just in case Mum and Dad started making noises. There was no warning before I could hear them together, having to cover my ears. I felt absolutely trapped whenever this happened, not being able to get out of the room; I really didn't want to see them together. Mum sometimes entered the study when they had finished having sex, checking how I was. I really hated this happening; seeing her semi-naked and smelling of sex so close to me was sickening. I wished I could have my own room.

Juan, the coach, was talking about competing in Madrid before the summer in the national championships. I wasn't sure what he meant by it or if he was intending for everyone on the team to go. I had never competed before, but the team in general seemed to be reaching a good level. Juan was just back from Belgium, where two of our teammates had taken part in the European trampoline championship for the first time. Angela was ninth overall and there was a sense of tremendous achievement.

We had all been practicing mandatory and routines of exercises in the four different disciplines because it seemed that Juan was organising a show in Cádiz for everyone to see. The mayor of Cádiz was attending, as were many other authorities and politicians. I had tried to ask Juan what all this was about because I was getting confused and was not sure what to expect or what I had to do. He told me to carry on training and to repeat the exercises, when he told me to do so in front of everyone.

I wished we could have spare equipment to practice on; having only one piece of each made it difficult to train as much as I wanted to. We always had to take turns and the chances of immediately repeating what had just gone wrong were slim. I tried to take advantage of the twenty minutes of free playtime that we always got at the end of each session, when I could take the opportunity to constantly repeat the exercises that were causing me trouble; it was the best time to get a specific apparatus with no interference.

The beam was the hardest one for me. The tiniest hesitation in your body or your mind would come through, making you lose your balance. I was trying the best I could to block out my surroundings when I was on the beam, and I had noticed that provided I was on my own, I would not fall. For some reason, sensing people around me would almost certainly make me fall. There was not much room for hesitation. The floor and vault horse were more straightforward for me; I had learnt by now how to feel comfortable in the air. The main thing was to achieve enough height and to know where you were in space in relation to the ground. We all knew how to roll on the floor to avoid injury if the landing was incorrect. I was feeling slightly worried because I had just learnt accelerating backflips, which seemed to be coming along nicely, but somehow I still didn't have the feeling of having the correct height. I worried that I could fall short one day, hitting my head on the floor.

The parallel bars were quite fun. We used magnesium powder and hand guards to protect our hands and to improve our grips on the bars. It was important to have dry hands to eliminate any sweat as soon as possible because blisters could occur frequently. Last month the skin of my entire right palm completely came off in one movement when spinning around the bar. It was incredibly painful and it took almost two weeks to heal fully. I had managed to gain an excellent swing and movement between the bars, but it was incredibly off-putting every time I changed from the higher bar to the lower one rolling around my waist; most of the time, the lower bar came undone from the hook keeping it up collapsing to the lowest possible height. It always made a terrible noise and prevented me from doing any more exercises.

It was incredible to think how high we managed to jump in the air coming off any of the apparatuses; somehow the energy spent in the movement during the air diffused the impact on landing and made it hardly noticeable.

Mum said that the show was going to be too noisy and with too many people around for Dad to attend and that she didn't want to leave him alone. It seemed that everybody knew about the gymnastic exhibition, and students at school were asking if I was taking part in it. I was surprised because I had never mentioned it to anyone and couldn't quite work out how so many people knew about it – unless of course Teresa and María had been spreading rumours. María wanted to attend the event, and she was going with my friend Ana and her two older sisters.

"Ana, how do you know this is happening?" I questioned her.

"Mum told us because apparently it is advertised everywhere, even in the newspaper," Ana told me at school.

I was flabbergasted. Why hadn't I noticed it? I really didn't know how this exhibition was any different from any of the others; people never knew I attended those.

It was the day of the exhibition and Juan had told the team to be in the pavilion one hour early. The stands had been decorated and there were colourful banners on all the banisters. The judo floor had been moved to the centre of the pavilion, right in front of the special seats for the VIPs. Technicians were testing the sound and the loudspeakers. There were extra lights and cables everywhere. All the gymnastic equipment was nicely rearranged and prepared so as many people as possible could see it.

Juan had managed to get funding for new gymnastic suits, which were royal blue with a single thick white line running on each side from under each long sleeve to the hips. We were all changed and had been warming up for an hour while the stands were filling up with people. The noise was overwhelming, giving me a feeling of complete chaos around me. I had never been in the middle of so many people in my life. We had tried the equipment out and finally put our tracksuits on, sitting in a line formation on the floor and waiting for everyone else to be ready.

One by one, we all took turns on each apparatus. The floor exercises were accompanied by music. I could feel an incredible tension in my body and a stiffness which I normally didn't have. I was worried that I might not be able to obtain the correct height in my backflips, but I managed to cut out the noise. I didn't notice what anyone else was doing; I wasn't even aware of what score I – or anyone else – received. I just did everything as I usually did every day, but somehow I fell off the beam once because it felt different today, having been moved from the place where it normally stood.

People were clapping; there was music and occasionally somebody talking in the microphone. There were speeches from some of the authorities and photographers were everywhere. I wanted everything to finish as soon as possible once I had completed my exercises.

Prizes were given out: certificates, medals and trophies. When the names were called, the members of the team had to go up the central stand through the middle of everyone shouting, clapping, and trying to touch us.

"Isabel Grimaldi …!" the man shouted down the microphone.

"Isabel Grimaldi …!" he said again.

On the third occasion I was called, one of the VIPs shook my hand and said with a big smile on his face,

"Isabel, there is no need to keep bringing all your prizes with you every time you are called. Leave them by your seat and come here empty-handed. You are going to be called more times."

I didn't really know what was happening and why the prizes were being given out. Why was I being called two more times? It was all too much for me.

When all the prizes had been handed out, the man who had spoken to me in the stands walked down to the centre of the pavilion where we were, holding a huge silver metallic cup with a large pearl in the middle of it.

"Isabel Grimaldi!"

I looked at Juan, not knowing what was happening now, while a huge roar of applause came from the stands and everyone stood looking at me. I didn't move initially, but Juan came close to me and said,

"Come on, Isabel, collect the cup. It's yours!" He gently pushed me in the back and kept clapping like everyone else.

"We need to celebrate this, Isabel!" María exclaimed enthusiastically. "I have never seen so many trophies at once in all my life! You were the best by far compared to the others. We will stop by the bar next to our house and I will buy you a Coke. If I could, I would get you champagne, but I think Coke will do the job. I will fill the cup with Coca-Cola and you can drink it from the cup. That is how they celebrate it on the telly."

María did buy a bottle of Coke and tried to pour it inside my cup, but I stopped her.

"Thanks, María, but I don't really want to spoil the trophy. I don't want it to get damaged. It looks so shiny and new," I said, removing the cup from her reach.

"As you wish, but we could at least share this bottle," María replied.

"Thank you!" I said.

Dad made a real fuss when he saw my medals and cups. Everyone in the house came to have a closer look. Dad, without asking, took my two cups and put them on display next to his multiple trophies. I kept my medals and diplomas in my treasure drawer.

The following day, I overslept in the morning. I felt exhausted. The competition had left me completely drained. It had been a real effort to remain calm with all that noise and all those people; I wasn't sure that I enjoyed the experience. As soon as I entered the sitting room, María was there waiting to show me my picture in the newspaper. There was a full page talking about it.

> *Isabel Grimaldi, aged 11, was proclaimed regional champion in her category after coming first in parallel bars with a score of ten and also first in the floor exercises, second in the vault horse, and third in the beam ...*

I couldn't quite believe what I was reading!

"Mum, what happened yesterday? It was quite the exhibition for people to see, wasn't it?" I enquired Mum, who was sewing in her armchair.

"It was the regional championship," Mum said. "They gave you two gold medals, one silver and one bronze. But you got a ten on the parallel bars, and therefore they also gave you a special award, that smaller cup over there." She pointed to the cabinet. "The extra-large cup is for being the regional champion." Mum smiled at me.

"Really? I didn't know ...," I replied in amazement, rereading the words in the newspaper.

Juan was thrilled with the results of the championship. People congratulated me, but I never spoke of it or mentioned it to anybody. I didn't know how the others had done or what medals anyone else had received. I felt slightly embarrassed that I couldn't recall anyone's performance; I just continued training.

"Isabel, I will be taking you, Clara and Tamara to Madrid for the national championship," Juan told me. "I'm also taking everyone else over thirteen, but you three will only take part if they authorise it in Madrid. Because you're under thirteen, I'm not sure if they will. In any case, even if they don't allow us, I'm also putting you forward for the national pre-test for the under thirteens. If this is the case, you won't be doing the four apparatus disciplines. It will be tumbling instead, which is a series of accelerating exercises in a line on the floor. We need to get a different routine of these exercises ready, just in case."

We were spending five days in the capital. Madrid was a big city. I had never stopped there but always driven through on our way to Laredo. It was the first time I had ever been away from home. Everything seemed bigger and more modern than in Cádiz, and people had a completely different accent; they pronounced the *s*, whereas in the south, it was always omitted.

It was not new to me because half of my cousins were from Madrid. Juan had taken us all sightseeing to the centre of the city and we had travelled by underground. I had read about the underground, but it was a unique experience using it. People rushed in and out quickly. I didn't realise that trains left the stops in such a hurry; there was hardly any time to get in or out of the carriages. You needed to be alert; otherwise, the doors would close on you. I thought it was fascinating.

"Isabel, have you called your mum since we left Cádiz?" Juan asked me.

"No, why? I didn't know I had to call her," I answered in surprise.

"Apparently, your grandmother is planning to come and see you in the championship," he explained. "They need to know that you are doing tumbling in the pre-test, the address of the place and the time. It's also good to let your mother know that you are well."

"She told me to call if I needed anything or wanted to talk. I was just waiting to need something," I replied.

"Here's a phone box. Come with me!" Juan said to me. "Have you got any coins?"

"Yes, plenty," I answered.

When I called, Mum said that Grandmother Isabel was in Madrid visiting one of her sisters and that she might attend the championship. I wasn't sure if I was allowed to perform with the over thirteens, so I told Mum that I would prefer it if she did not attend. Grandmother's correctness and perfection scared me. I didn't want to make mistakes in front of her, and my world in gymnastics was very different to her way of life. I was concerned about her meeting my teammates; I thought that she might disapprove, not necessarily in front of me but later on to Mum. I preferred not to have any witnesses.

I gave Mum the address and timetable that Juan told me, confirming that I had been accepted in the pre-test. I told her that I was well and she asked me if I missed her. I said no. I never called again, for I didn't need anything.

The sports centre where the championship took place was enormous. There were several pavilions within the premises. The one for gymnastics was larger than the one we had in Cádiz and it was only for gymnastics. They had up to five different changing rooms with nice showers as well as plenty of apparatuses for training, different floors and ditches full of foam to land in soft areas. I was simply amazed with the facilities.

The pavilion was for all participants to use and to warm up in. We had practice sessions, morning and afternoon, for two days before the championship. It was unbelievable. We met different candidates from Barcelona, Bilbao, Madrid and some other cities around Spain; they were very confident and it wasn't the first time they were competing.

Juan allowed me to use the parallel bars to get a feel for what it was like using the real female apparatus rather than the one in Cádiz for men. It was so much easier to use; I could move from one bar to the other one with much less effort and the grip was thinner compared to the thick, bulky wooden bar I was used to. The bars were made of steel and were flexible; I noticed that they were taking the weight of my body when spinning around and that the flexion in the bars acted as a catapult, helping me to quickly move position or throwing me in the air really high when leaving the apparatus. I was used to the stiff rigidity of the bars in Cádiz and this was like a dream – so easy to use!

The floor mats were equally amazing. They had a material that gave your body a great spring. The speed and the height that you could obtain were incredible. We had nothing like this in Cádiz. The girls from Barcelona were looking at us with surprise; our standard of exercises was as high as or even better than theirs was.

"Why do you keep making remarks about the equipment?" one of them asked.

"Because in Cádiz things are very different to here. Our equipment is not designed to help us fly in the air," Tamara answered with a smile.

⚬⁓⚬

When the day of the competition arrived, we were anxious. I didn't fancy meeting my grandmother; I was finding it difficult to include her in the context of gymnastics. We arrived early and did our warm-up exercises. I had got so used to the spring in the new mats that I wondered if I was ever going to be able to use the mats in Cádiz again; they were truly awful.

Halfway through the warm-up, I realised that my grandmother was in the stands with two of my cousins and my aunt Sofia, my father's cousin. I got nervous when I saw them; I didn't wave hello and I immediately stopped doing my exercises. I think grandmother noticed that I had seen them. I sat on the bench, but after a while, I looked at them, waved and decided to say hello. Juan allowed me to go to the stands and I went to greet them.

"Isa, you stopped doing exercises. I love watching you. Please do some more," my cousin Sara told me.

"Why did you stop when you saw us?" Grandmother asked me.

"I felt embarrassed," I said.

"It's incredible how fast you can twist and jump in the air!" my aunt commented.

"I have to leave you now. We'll be starting soon," I said, walking down the stairs.

"Isabel, tell your coach you're coming with us to eat after the championship. My chauffeur will bring you back to the hotel," Grandmother told me. I nodded and continued walking down the steps.

I explained to Juan my Grandmother's plans as soon as I reached the benches. I would have preferred to stay with my colleagues and watch the whole competition. My teammates came from very humble backgrounds. Most of them had never left Cádiz before and never went anywhere on holidays. I deliberately left the word "chauffeur" unmentioned. Juan gave me the address of the hotel and agreed with the decision, but he never spoke to my grandmother and my grandmother never attempted to approach him or my team.

The pre-test was good. I was particularly worried about a front somersault I had to do at the beginning of one of the series, landing with my legs one after the other like scissors, and joining any other exercises in tumbling after that. Front somersaults were tricky for me because I couldn't see the floor until just milliseconds before the landing, so I had to rely on my awareness of where I was in space rather than looking where I was going. I had much better control doing back somersaults because the first thing to flick backwards was my head and from that moment on, I could do the whole movement without losing sight of where the floor was. My teammates thought front somersaults were the easiest instead.

Everything went well, but we didn't get any scoring for what we did, which was a shame because I thought we were better than the others were. Our performance was highly commended and considered an exhibition.

I couldn't see the performance of the over thirteens because Grandmother took me out, but I found out that we were fifth overall. It was a positive experience.

Chapter Sixteen

THE BALCONY

People now knew who I was at school, but I didn't really know most of the girls who said hello to me. It seemed as if I was perfect in every way and the fact that I was better than anyone at sports, made things even more perfect. But all this translated into deep respect rather than huge popularity. Girls were very much into clothes, shoes and gossiping about friendships, such as about who had been at whose birthday party and who had been left out. They were also beginning to worry about knowing the names of boys and who they were.

I instead liked playing with the elastic band, trying to catch it under my feet while jumping, making sure I ended up standing on it. It was a game well known at school and the level of difficulty gradually got higher. The height was increasingly more challenging too. I also liked playing hopscotch and skipping rope. I played with whoever was available; girls allowed me to join in as long as I was good enough at the game, and I was usually very good.

Occasionally groups of girls formed cliques and didn't let me play with them for a while. I knew that I just had to let it pass and after some time I would be allowed in again. Girls occasionally shared a secret or mystery together, thinking they were special for this reason. I didn't know about gossip, clothes, boys, mysteries or anything like that; all that was on my mind was having enough time to revise in order to make time for training. I had been thinking lately that competing was getting stressful. I was not sure I liked it. Some of the girls on the gymnastics team were getting unpleasant with their comments about me. I was starting to feel tense during training too and even if I tried to make nice comments about them, they tried to make me believe that I was showing off or putting them down. I really didn't understand.

Today I couldn't find anyone to play with and I hadn't been accepted in any of the different groups of girls, so I decided to go for a walk on the playground. I went up and down all the steps in the stands at the end of the playground. Standing at the top of them, I could see the sea right behind it. It was a sunny day and the water was still. I liked the smell of it. I had just realised that there was an empty space between the back of the stands and the wall of the school, full of wild vegetation and rubbish that the wind had probably accumulated with time. This place was a hidden area not visible from any part of the school. I decided to have a closer look at it.

It was difficult to walk about without the branches scratching me. There was stinging nettle everywhere, which I didn't want to touch. I started collecting rubbish in my hands with the idea of putting it in the bin afterwards, trying to cover the whole area. It was somewhat scary being in this place; it was a forgotten and hidden area. I wondered if there were any animals hidden in this place …

"Isabel Grimaldi, what are you doing there!" a voice called to me.

I looked up and saw one of the nuns observing me from the top of the stands. I didn't know her name.

"This is an absolutely restricted area. It is forbidden to be in here. You are in serious trouble; go immediately to the head of lower school's office. Now!" she shouted at me, pointing with her finger in the direction of the school building.

I started shivering and my heart was racing. I hadn't been aware that this area was restricted. It was the first time that I even knew it existed. I feared the worst; I didn't know what was going to happen to me. I walked as fast as I could, but the tension in my body was such that I had to fight my own stiffness in order to move. On my way to the head's office, I met Teresa by chance in the playground.

"Teresa, I'm lucky I've found you. I've been told to go to the head's office because I was playing in the area behind the stands. I don't know what's going to happen to me. I didn't know it was a forbidden area," I said, bursting into tears.

"Older girls use that area to smoke, Isa. There's always a nun patrolling there. I think you've been unlucky," Teresa explained. "I'll come with you. The head is your own teacher, Isabel, and she knows how good you are."

Teresa held my hand, but I couldn't stop shaking. We walked the rest of the journey together and Teresa knocked at the door of the office.

"May I come in, Mother Ana?" Teresa said, opening the door tentatively.

There were two other older girls in the office talking to Mother Ana.

"I don't want to see any of you repeating it again. You know your punishment now. You can go!" Mother Ana finished saying to the girls as they left the room. "What can I do for you, girls?" Mother Ana asked us with a big smile.

"Mother, Isabel was playing in the forbidden area today and has been caught and told to come to see you immediately. She didn't know it was forbidden and is very frightened because she thinks she is going to be heavily punished," Teresa explained.

I couldn't stop sobbing, but I was embarrassed to be seen crying.

"Isabel! But you are such a good girl. Were you on your own?" Mother Ana asked me.

"Yes, Mother," I answered, looking down at the floor.

"What were you doing there?" Mother Ana continued.

"I found it when I was walking in the stands. It is so wild that I wondered if there were any animals living in it, but I also was collecting some of the rubbish to throw it away. I have never been there before and didn't know it was a restricted area," I answered.

"Well, you know now," Mother Ana told me in a gentle voice. "There are no animals over there and you might hurt yourself playing there. From now on, play somewhere else and if you see anyone going in there, tell her to get out. I know you didn't know. Wipe your tears and you can go. I'll see you in class soon."

I felt incredibly relieved and thanked Teresa for accompanying me to the office.

It took me some time to relax again and I couldn't eat much at lunchtime at home. Mother Ana had given us some exercises to do in the afternoon session and told us that she needed to be away from the class for thirty minutes to attend a meeting.

"Girls, I don't want to hear anybody talking," Mother Ana said. "Everyone must stay quiet doing the exercises. I'm going to leave one of you in charge, sitting at my desk. That person has to make a note of anyone who talks or even whispers. You are not allowed to ask the time or ask for a pencil or even a rubber. I want absolute silence. Understood?"

"Yes, Mother," the whole class responded.

"That person is going to be … Isabel Grimaldi!" Everyone turned to look at me. "Isabel, come forward and sit at my desk to do your work facing the class. Please write down on this piece of paper the name of anyone who even slightly opens her lips."

Our teacher left and closed the door. I didn't like sitting facing the class at all, so I immediately opened my book and started doing my work. I wrote down the names of anyone who spoke or whispered, but overall everybody behaved well. I wasn't sure why Mother Ana wanted the list if everybody was completing her exercises.

"Well …," Mother Ana said, entering the classroom again. "I hope everybody completed the work and remained quiet. Did you make a list, Isabel?" she asked me, looking in my eyes.

"Here you are, Mother," I replied handing my piece of paper back to her and walking to my seat.

Mother Ana started naming the girls in the list one by one, ordering them to remain in detention after class. All the students stared at me with angry faces; I could feel tension in the environment around me.

I didn't know what happened to those girls on the list, but some girls in the class became hostile towards me from then on. Some of them were insulting me and pushing me in the playground, blocking my access if they could or trying to trip me over. I felt so bad that I was spending break time locked in the toilet. I was crying. I only did what the teacher asked me to do, but I didn't know she was going to punish people after that, rather than looking to see if everybody had completed the work.

Although I was trying my best not to cry in front of the other girls, they were so horrible that I couldn't control it any longer. I looked up and saw my friend Ana standing on one of the desks and shouting at the class. She was furious.

"Leave her alone at once! Aren't you all happy now that she is crying? How long are you going to carry on tormenting her? What wrong has Isabel ever done to you all? The teacher asked her to write the names and she had to obey. What do you think would have happened to all of us if that list were empty? We all would have been punished – and Isabel probably worse than that. She was testing her. Isabel wouldn't have been the only one to write names on that list. Think about it!"

I was grateful for her support, but I didn't know how to express it. The girls stopped treating me so badly, but I continued avoiding them for a long time; I was lost and didn't know whom to trust. I preferred to be alone rather than with anyone else, including Ana, who kept watching me from a distance.

"Isabel, my friend Nuria, Ana's mum, has told me that you have been having problems at school," Mum told me one day at home.

Mum was now personally looking after the lands in Seville after the manager had been sacked; therefore, it was difficult to know when she was going to be home or not. Mum was constantly traveling to Seville, either to visit her mother or to go to El Cortijo. She never told us when she was going and it was making me unsettled not knowing if Mum was going to be home when I came back from school.

I didn't know how to talk about what had happened at school and it was terrifying to think that I had done something wrong. I was feeling trapped and wasn't sure how to distinguish between right and wrong, especially when an adult was telling me that something was the right thing to do but it turned out to be wrong. I was angry and I didn't like my friend Ana knowing better than me if my mother was at home or not.

Mum used to like having coffee with her friends at the end of the morning before lunch, and Ana knew my mum and hers were together in the bar close to my house most days. Ana could hear my mum's plans when she was telling Nuria and the others. I never had the chance to stop by because I had to take advantage of the lunch break to do homework, but Mum never stopped to explain to any of us what her plans were. She just told Dad and Miss Spencer.

I didn't know how to talk to Mum about anything that worried me, I always denied to myself that I was worried. I pretended that nothing worried me. I was feeling alone and scared.

"It wasn't anything serious and that was a long time ago. Things are back to normal now," I answered Mum, hoping that she would not continue with the conversation.

It was summertime again. This was the last summer Jaime would spend in Ireland to learn English and this time Alex was accompanying him. My cousins Francisco and Andrés were going with my brothers; I was not sure how much English they were going to practise when they were all over there together. Jaime had become a real teenager now and was far more confident since he had been going to Ireland every summer. He didn't seem so dependent on Mum and did his own thing with his friends all the time; he also seemed confident around Dad.

Conversely, Alex had been bothering me a lot just before he went to Ireland. He was becoming very intrigued about women's bodies. He had been explaining to me how soon I would be getting hair in my private parts and how my body was going to change. He had also been giving me details of how his body was changing. Even his voice was starting to sound different – more like Jaime's. Alex was incredibly stubborn and once he fixed his mind on something, he didn't let it go. He had been asking me to show him my body because he had never seen a naked girl's body before. It was slightly embarrassing and I told him to leave me alone because I was neither interested in any of these changes nor curious to find out about boy's bodies. A body was just a body, the carrier of your intelligence and soul.

He got me out of bed once when everyone was asleep and I showed him what my body looked like, thinking that was going to be the end of it, but he had woken me up several more times ever since, trying to convince me again. Luckily, Miss Spencer had noticed him being awake late and hovering around my bedroom; she put a stop to it. I was glad that he was gone to Ireland now and hoped that he would forget it and leave me alone.

We were all in the north of Spain after my brothers left for Dublin. María was going to university to read history after the summer, and she would live in Seville with Grandmother Isabel. She was going out with her boyfriend, Antonio, all the time and Mum was hiding where she was from Dad most of the time. Teresa also had many friends and was in the tennis club frequently, starting to attend discos with all my older cousins.

Life was quiet in general because Dad didn't seem to do as many excursions with us now. He and Mum chose to go to places together in the afternoon instead. We went to the beach with Miss Spencer every day, and Beatriz, Elena and I met and played with the cousins our age. María and Teresa went to the beach with their own friends and stayed in a completely different place to us on the beach. My sisters had to be dead on time for lunch every day and this caused arguments with Dad because they were often late or because they hadn't had a shower and therefore were not allowed to sit at the table until they had done so.

"Miss Spencer, is the weather good for the beach today?" Beatriz liked to ask every morning.

The weather was not 100 per cent reliable in the north of Spain and it wasn't uncommon to have misty mornings that completely cleared up close to midday.

"Let me see," Miss Spencer said, opening the main door and looking at the sky. "Yes, it is!"

"I'll get changed into my swimming costume," Beatriz answered.

I could hear the conversation from the kitchen downstairs, where I was having my breakfast and talking to Patricia, who this year had come to Laredo with us instead of going on her own holiday. Patricia had never left Cádiz before and was delighted to find out what the north of Spain looked like. She had made many friends and she went out every Friday and Saturday. She couldn't believe her eyes when we drove through Spain; she was so happy and wrote long letters to her family, explaining how different things were over here.

"Isabel! Miss Spencer! Help me! I can't get out!" I heard a voice calling from upstairs.

"Patricia, I think I can hear Beatriz asking for help," I said, quickly standing up and walking towards the stairs. "Beatriz, is that you?" I asked in a loud voice.

"I can't get out! The bolt is stuck and I don't have the strength to shift it across. I have been trying for a long time now," Beatriz said, starting to cry from the other side of the door in Mum's bedroom.

"Don't worry. We'll get you out. But why did you get changed in there?" I asked.

"Teresa was in the bathroom and Elena was in our bedroom; I don't want her to see me when I'm changing," Beatriz answered.

Patricia had gone outside the house looking for Miss Spencer, and she called Mum and Dad, who were sitting outside in the garden under the apple tree.

"Beatriz, use both hands to try to slide the bolt while I pull the handle, closing the door tighter," Dad said. "Are you ready? One, two three!"

"I can't do it! It's too hard!" Beatriz replied, starting to panic.

"Don't cry! We'll try it again, but this time you go wrap a piece of clothing round your hand to get a better grip with your fingers. I'll pull the door inwards. Ready? One, two, three!" They tried again.

"It's not moving! I'm going to be trapped here forever!" Beatriz cried even louder.

I could see that Mum was beginning to worry, and she suggested to Dad that they break the door.

"That bolt is brand new. I fitted it yesterday. I don't want to break the door or the bolt. We should try something else," Dad responded.

"But what else can we do?" Mum asked.

"We'll put the long ladder across from Isabel's balcony to the window in our bedroom. Isabel! Where are you?" Dad immediately asked. "Oh, there you are! I want you go across the ladder and climb into my bedroom through the window. Do you think you can open the bolt? It's stiff because it's new."

"Yes, I think I can. I tried it yesterday," I answered, but before I could say anything else, he became tense and agitated, taking me to my bedroom.

"Get to the balcony and be ready! I'll go fetch the ladder," he told me, turning around quickly. "Beatriz, open the window wide open! Isabel is going to get into the room through the window. Open it up, please!"

"Roberto, this is dangerous. Think about it!" Mum pleaded.

"She's a gymnast, Graciela! She's used to heights and falls," Dad replied.

"Oh my God, this is not right!" Mum exclaimed, walking down the stairs towards the garden.

Miss Spencer was talking to Beatriz through the door, giving her instructions.

"Beatriz, we'll get you out one way or the other. Go to the window and open it up fully. Isabel or Dad will give you a ladder; just make sure it is well positioned on the window. Make sure the ladder goes well inside the room and hold it steady. Isabel is going to walk across it to get inside the room and open the door for you. Do you understand?" Miss Spencer asked.

"Yes! I know what I have to do," Beatriz answered, trying not to cry.

Miss Spencer came to the balcony with me, waiting for Dad. As soon as he came, she helped him place the ladder from the balcony and left Dad holding it.

"Dad, I'm still wearing my dressing gown and my shoes are uncomfortable. I would like to get changed into something else or at least change my slippers for something better," I told Dad.

"There's no time for that, Isa. Get on the ladder now and don't look down," Dad said.

I looked down the balcony and saw Mum looking worried, and Miss Spencer and Patricia were looking concerned at watching me up so high. I climbed up the balcony and got onto the ladder, crawling on my hands and knees and trying not to get my dressing gown tangled. It was difficult to walk with slippers. I looked ahead and saw Beatriz desperately trying to hold the ladder firmly, not looking down at all. I was just hoping that Beatriz and Dad were able to keep the ladder in position; if they slightly moved it, it could be enough to tilt it and for me to fall. I didn't think I could survive a fall from this height, even rolling on the ground as we did in gymnastics. I was scared!

I slowly advanced and managed to get into the room. The bolt was extremely stiff, but I pushed the door forward with my foot and at the same time tried to shift the bolt, managing to open it. Beatriz and I hugged each other, full of relief.

Miss Spencer took us to the beach, but I couldn't stop thinking of what had just happened at home. I felt shaken and distressed, but somehow I couldn't show it or express it with words. The beach was full because it was a weekend and the tide was high. I didn't feel like talking to anyone and went straight to the water. Miss Spencer trusted me, as I had become a very confident swimmer. I liked swimming under the waves and diving for as long as possible with my diving goggles. I didn't realise how long I spent in the water, but it was almost all morning. I never got to see any of my cousins, which was strange because they normally took turns in the water and I kept bumping into them one way or the other.

I looked up and took my diving goggles off, realising that I had drifted along the beach with the current and that I was far from where Miss Spencer normally placed all our things. I came out of the water and walked along the seashore towards the place where we usually sat on the beach. I went up to the dry sand and looked again, trying to find Miss Spencer. I tried searching from the sea upwards and from the entry of the beach downwards, but I couldn't find them. I was lost, feeling cold and wet. I felt like crying, but instead I decided to walk home barefoot and with no clothes.

"Dad, I got lost at the beach. I have been looking for Miss Spencer but I can't find her," I explained to Dad, who was sitting in the garden reading the newspaper.

I was scared and felt very lonely, but I couldn't express this to Dad.

"Don't worry. You're here now," Dad said, without raising his eyes from the newspaper.

"Miss Spencer may be worried and looking for me, but I can't find her," I insisted.

"She'll realise that you are nowhere to be found and come home. Don't worry," Dad answered, clearly not feeling alarmed.

I quickly changed into normal clothes and rode my bicycle to the beach. I locked the bicycle and started walking in a straight direction towards the sea. Soon enough, I saw Miss Spencer walking up towards me. She was crying.

"Isabel, I have been looking everywhere for you! I thought something had happened to you," Miss Spencer told me, hugging me tightly.

"I got lost and couldn't find you anywhere. I looked and looked again until I was so cold that I decided to walk home. I asked Dad to help me find you, but he said that you would eventually realise you couldn't find me and would come home soon enough. I am really, really sorry. I was so scared," I explained to Miss Spencer with tears in my eyes.

It had been a bad day. I really didn't feel like doing anything at all. I wanted to be home alone, not doing anything with anybody. Life seemed so dangerous.

Chapter Seventeen

MY BACK

I was halfway through middle school, which lasted three years, and my new teacher was called Mother Amalia. She was my form tutor in middle school but also taught us maths, triple sciences and religious studies (RE). She had had a very interesting life and had travelled around the world being a missionary in Asia and South America, so she had plenty of stories to tell us.

Mother Amalia was short, slightly overweight and had a strong personality. Her hair was white under her head veil. She was an excellent teacher full of knowledge, but we had to work hard with her. There was definitely a step up in homework.

There was no doubt now that I had become a machine full of facts in my head. I could remember things from previous years with great clarity and kept remembering facts explained in the class as well. Teachers normally took turns bringing students to the front of the room to quiz us, where we had to write things on the blackboard and answer in front of the whole class. Sometimes it was pure theory, but the teachers kept scoring the answers. This marking always counted, on top of the constant written tests they made us do.

Teachers liked asking me hard questions and I always worried that I would not be able to answer them. Occasionally they displayed the questions to be asked in advance and if a hard question landed on someone who didn't know the answer, they asked me to answer for the person so the student didn't get a bad mark and was given the chance of getting a slightly easier one. But if I got it wrong, it would be a bad mark for me. The girls in the class liked me saving them, but it was an incredible pressure on me. Having said that, though, I still hadn't got anything wrong.

Algebra, equations and chemistry were easy for me; something about electrons and atoms really triggered my mind. Mother Amalia had been asking me unusual questions in front of the blackboard about how many orbits each element of the periodic table had and how many electrons were distributed in each layer. I was not sure how I was able to work it out, but there was a clear formula in my head, and I wasn't sure if I had read it or if my mind had worked it out on its own. It was completely logical to me how the distribution of electrons, protons and neutrons in different atoms of matter could lose or gain extra particles or even collide, giving out different reactions and energy, forming molecules with different characteristics which were already predetermined according to the new distribution of electrons in the atoms. All these could also change by altering the atmospheric pressure or temperature of the environment, which could simply change the state of the matter. I could easily formulate substances in a mathematical way and equate reactions. Girls in the class were asking me to explain it to them, but I didn't know why I knew these things.

It was hard because people didn't realise that I remembered things in pure isolation and not related to one another. The information in my head was not in order; I couldn't take shortcuts. I remembered full pages of written information or pictures as well as graphs. I had to find in my head the exact page and the wording of the lines where the information lay, repeating back exactly what was written and finding it difficult to use my own words. My memorised knowledge was vast but very enclosed and rigid. It was not what I remembered; it was the amount of detail that I remembered associated with it. It was difficult to explain it and I felt that in a few years, I would not be able to cope with this lack of order in my mind. It was something that I couldn't express or put into words. It was stressful remembering things like this, but it was almost the only way that I had to express the exact words of what I was thinking to people.

Elena was growing up and was funny to watch. She was able to come close to Dad, and he didn't seem to mind it. He found anything she did hilarious and Elena was able to get away with things that we had never been able to do in front of Dad. She even climbed up on his lap and sat there. Elena was not a very good eater, but somehow it didn't matter. Rules were suddenly changed for her. Mum was the one who kept losing patience with her. It was as though Mum was so focused on Dad that she had run out of steam for the childish demands from Elena; she wanted all of us to behave like mature people and, most of all, not to cause her any problems that would make her upset.

I was getting to the point at which my studies were becoming a real priority over gymnastics after five years of intense training. I loved the sport, but I didn't like competing, and Juan had taken me as far as he could, considering that he was coaching all levels as well as girls and boys, with trampoline in each category. My body was reaching puberty now, and I was heavier. It was embarrassing noticing my breasts developing. People had noticed in the club too and the gymnastics suit was inevitably tight against my body. Mum gave me a bra to wear, but even so, it was noticeable.

I already knew all about getting periods, but the day it came, it was lunchtime after school and Mum was in Seville. Miss Spencer wasn't home that day either, because she had to go visit her mum in Gibraltar. Teresa stayed for lunch at school, so I had to tell Patricia, the maid. I was nervous because

I didn't expect to see so much blood, but she told me what to do and helped me out. It was worrying thinking that blood could seep through my uniform and people might notice it.

The house was incredibly quiet and peaceful without María and Dad. The navy had sent Dad to the Canary Islands for two months. He was taking measurements of all the islands, making updated maps and studying the water currents in the area. I was not sure which ship he was commanding. There was certainly very little tension in the house. We could all be ourselves, and my siblings were taking the opportunity to bring friends home.

My back had been causing me trouble over the last few months. Bending backwards was becoming difficult since I had become bigger and heavier. I could feel that my body was stronger and powerful but somehow slower in the air. Mum had taken me to a back specialist in Seville. He had ordered some X-rays for me. We were finding out the results today.

"Mrs Grimaldi ... Isabel! Please do come in," the nurse called, opening the door leading to the doctor's office.

Uncle Tomás had recommended Dr Fernández. All my cousins suffered from severe scoliosis, with one leg slightly shorter than the other and one hip also slightly raised compared to the other one. Uncle Tomás had passed it on to all his children. He had palsy in some of the nerves in his legs, and his gait and walking were peculiar, reminding me of a penguin. Funnily enough, Mum's walking reminded me of him too, although Mum looked straighter and taller. My cousin Gonzalo, the one after Verónica who was younger than Beatriz, had one of the bones protruding between his shoulders. It was a big lump and they were considering surgery to insert metal rods to straighten him up. His elder sister constantly wore an orthopaedic brace from neck to hips to support her entire spine, trying to avoid surgery.

"Good afternoon, Isabel. How are you today? May I see the X-rays, please?" Dr Fernández asked.

"Yes, of course," Mum replied handing him the big envelope with the X-rays.

"Let's have a look at this," he said, switching on the screen where the X-rays were displayed. "Humm ..." Dr Fernández stared at the films, not saying anything for a few minutes. "You have some degree of scoliosis at the bottom of the spine, which you shouldn't at your age. Your back is incredibly strong, though. But the constant pulling from your muscles when you do gymnastics is becoming too much and that is why it hurts. There are some movements you should never do, such as bending backwards; that is particularly bad for you. I will put you in a brace from your chest downwards to support the bottom of the spine, and when you take it off at night, you should do some exercises, but you have to wear it all the time. You need to stop doing gymnastics ..."

Mum continued asking questions, but I stopped listening from then onwards. I didn't want to stop doing gymnastics just like that. How was I going to tell Juan? I felt my body was very strong and I didn't want to wear an orthopaedic corset. I would lose my agility and ability to do any sports. It was devastating. Moreover, I didn't want people to see me wearing the corset under my clothes.

I didn't say a word until we arrived in Cádiz again. I started doing even more revision and kept to myself, pretending that everything was fine. Mum spoke to Juan, but I never had the chance to say goodbye to him.

After some months passed, it felt that my back was deteriorating fast. I was fully dependent on the corset to help me stand up, to the point at which removing it before having a bath caused me severe pain. My back was not able to support me anymore; I had lost all my strength. Dr Fernández had told Mum that I should stretch my back by hanging from a horizontal bar occasionally. Dad had installed one of these bars in the bathroom and several times a day I jumped up and hung from it; it reminded me of the days when I practiced on the parallel bars. The pain was becoming excruciating and I was so locked inside myself that I never thought of mentioning it. Pain was the least of my worries. Mum took me back to the doctor after three months, not because it hurt, as she never knew, but because I couldn't really stand up without the brace.

"Isabel, I have reviewed the new X-rays, and your back is slightly worse," Dr Fernández began trying to explain. "Some of the bones at the bottom of your spine are rotating and one of your hips is slightly elevated. I think that the orthopaedic brace has made you worse; your Mum has done the correct thing by bringing you back. But we can improve things so don't be too alarmed …"

"Are you planning to operate, Doctor?" Mum interrupted, looking worried.

"Nothing of the sort, Mrs Grimaldi. I have actually avoided surgery in her cousin Gonzalo; his case was very worrying and complex because his bones were so out of place that the spinal cord was at risk. Have you seen him recently? The lump in his back is gone." Dr Fernández told us this with what seemed to be great relief and satisfaction. "I am actually moving away from the traditional way of using corsets. I'm convinced that intense rehabilitation, back exercises and constant swimming can save many backs from surgery. Corsets destroy any muscle strength remaining in the backs. They can be dangerous things and I think that is what has happened to you."

I was heartened from listening to what the doctor was saying.

"I also think the corset has made me worse," I said.

"But, Isa, why haven't you told me before?" Mum asked me. "You know, she never says anything. The reason I brought her back is that one day she told me she could no longer hold her weight standing up and I got worried. I don't even know if it hurts. Does it hurt you, Isa?" Mum asked me with tears in her eyes.

"Yes, very much," I said.

"Here's the plan! Throw the corset in the bin and swim as much as you can," Dr Fernandez advised me.

"But, Doctor, we live in Cádiz and there are no indoor swimming pools in the entire city, not a single one," Mum explained to him in a worried voice.

"I'll swim in the sea, Mum. Can I join the gym again and do some of the exercises they do there? They really made my back strong before. I promise not to bend backwards. Maybe I can help Juan with the training and do some of the exercises ..." I said this with real hope that the doctor would agree with me.

"That's a great idea, Isabel, but I would like to see you again in three months to make sure everything is under control," the doctor said.

I felt hugely relieved when I left the doctor and I realised that I had been holding real anguish inside me about my back. I now had the chance to meet Juan again and say goodbye properly if I had to. I had put on weight during the time I was wearing the corset and I had quite a lot of catching up to do; I was incredibly weak for someone my age. All these thoughts were inside me, but once again I couldn't convey anything to my mother.

"Are you happy, Isabel?" Mum asked me in the car.

"Yes, very much," I answered.

"You act the same whether you are happy or not. I don't know when you are in pain or what goes through your mind. I have never seen you crying. You don't seem to laugh at home either. How can I know what you are thinking?"

"Everything is very serious at home. I never thought I was allowed to laugh," I explained to Mum. "I wouldn't know if you would like or dislike me laughing. It may be inappropriate when I laugh. I can't trust myself to laugh, because it may be the wrong time to do it."

"You can laugh anytime you like," Mum said with tears in her eyes.

"I don't think Dad will understand my laugh," I answered, looking away through the window and not talking again during the journey.

My back started to improve quickly and I recovered most of my strength. Despite having been off and wearing a corset, I could tell that my five years of training had not been in vain. My core abdominal muscles, legs and arms were still strong; my back muscles had been affected more. I was happy to be able to attend the gym again and I helped as much as possible, but I could actually witness with my own eyes that I had fallen behind on the team. I was big, I was heavy and I couldn't do the same training as the others.

It made me happy talking to the younger gymnasts; they seemed to know who I was and I could sense a tone of admiration. They had heard people talking about me, and they asked me for advice and wanted me to coach them in some of the exercises. This made me happy for a while. On the other hand, it made me sad to realise that I had to say goodbye to gymnastics and accept that I was never going to be good again.

On 23 February 1981, Juan unexpectedly sent us home early once again while I was in the gym. It was a feeling of déjà vu, as I had lived it before, when I was only eight years old.

"Everybody needs to go home as soon as possible. There has been a military coup d'etat and the army is trying to take control of the government. There will be no further training until the situation settles down." Juan explained this to all of us in a very calm voice.

Some parents were already in the gym collecting their children early.

Luckily, the army's attempt against the newborn democracy in Spain was stopped soon enough. Nobody missed a single day of school.

The weather improved and spring started earlier this year. I had started swimming as much as I could and finally stopped attending the gym. I knew that I was saying goodbye to Juan, but on the other hand, I was glad that I had been given the opportunity to finish attending the club when I felt ready for it.

"Juan, this is my last day. I won't be coming anymore. Thank you for letting me rejoin the gym and help you." I reached for his hand and shook it.

"Isabel, if you ever want to come back, you can always do so anytime you like," Juan said with a big smile on his face, holding my hand between his two hands.

Dad was concerned about my swimming and wanted to accompany me to the open pool in the sailing club where the *Kingdom of Castile* was moored. I noticed that Dad was slightly suspicious of leaving me alone and I thought that maybe he didn't approve of girls being on their own among strangers. On the other hand, I couldn't work out if Mum was using me to distract Dad into doing something without her and finding some time for herself.

"Isabel, you are a responsible girl and very good student; I think you will go far in life because whatever you decide to do, you will achieve it," Dad told me when I had just finished doing my lengths. "You have an outstanding will and determination."

I didn't understand why Dad was talking like this. I did what I was supposed to do. School set the level and the amount of work I had to do. I looked at Dad but said nothing.

There was a tall boy by the pool, looking at me from the distance. I recognised him. He also lived in our road and his parents were German, although they had been living in the city ever since I could remember. Dad also noticed him and I didn't think he liked him staring at me.

"Isa, I will sink you in the water and push you down with my foot to help you reach the bottom. But you need to hold your nose with your hand," Dad said, trying to interrupt the scene.

This pool was five metres deep and when trying to reach the floor in the deep end, one's ears would ache because of the pressure. It was a challenge to reach it. I agreed, although I didn't know exactly what Dad wanted me to do and why it was necessary to hold my nose. I sank myself to a height where he could reach me with his feet and waited. Dad aimed at my head with his feet leaning on my hand, making me stop holding my nose and with a second kick, he pushed me to the bottom of the pool.

"Did you reach it?" he asked with a smile when I surfaced.

"Yes, I did," I told him.

"Now you can do the same to me," Dad said, immediately sinking in front of me.

I aimed at his hand first and pushed him down to the bottom as hard as I could.

"Fair enough!" he said, surfacing. "I think we should go home now," he added, swimming towards the ladder.

I wasn't sure what he meant by 'fair enough'. I couldn't tell if he was pleased or displeased, but I followed him out of the water.

Dad didn't accompany me swimming anymore, and from then on, I started swimming in the sea. I preferred to be alone, and it was clear that Dad had lost any interest in my swimming.

"Isa, did you kick your father in the face, forcing him to stop holding his nose, the last time he went with you to the pool?" Mum unexpectedly asked me one day.

"The game was to help each other sink and reach the bottom of the pool," I replied, confused. "He did it first and removed my hand from my face by doing it. I thought it was part of the game. I didn't realise he did it by accident. He told me to repeat what he had done to me."

Chapter Eighteen

THE ROCK

The tide was still low but had already started to rise. The main line of rocks parallel to the sea coast was completely exposed and so was the main oasis of sand normally hidden by the water behind the rocks, where walking and swimming were free of any obstacles. This was an area that you needed to know well in order to identify it when it was covered by water, avoiding any possible accidental kick to any of the big stones surrounding it. It didn't make much difference to me, as I always swam deep, until I had reached enough depth to start swimming lengths across. I didn't mind knowing that there were huge rocks underneath; I knew that being deep enough, I would not accidentally encounter them.

Swimming gave me a real sense of freedom. Wearing goggles protected my eyes from getting any seawater in them, but the deep ocean was quite dark. I could occasionally see huge shadows resembling massive rocks overlapping each other and covering the bottom of the sea. I counted my strokes each way and constantly checked that I hadn't been swept away by the current; this was easy to do when catching my breath between strokes and facing a reference point at shore. The sound of my breathing and my heartbeat were my only companions for long periods of time. The strength in my arms was such that provided my rhythmic breathing was maintained, I could go on for long periods. It was an interesting experience being able to sweat and not being aware of it, but at the end of my swimming sessions, my face and body were as flushed and red as if I had been running, with the difference that I was not short of breath or feeling suffocated.

I didn't mind the waves getting bigger or stronger. Beyond the breaking barrier, the water was peaceful and accommodating. To be able to trust the sea, I was able to read its signs, but I never challenged them; the ocean was an enormous creature that could embrace you, allowing you to play, but equally, its abrupt movement and dangerous force could easily become a threat. By swimming, I was able to let my body go in complete harmony with the see-saw movement of the water; by allowing myself to float in the water, I was able to advance quickly, feeling my body sliding through the surface of the sea.

"Isa! Isa!" a voice called from the seashore.

I removed my goggles and looked ahead as I was coming out of the water, trying to identify where the voice was coming from.

"Hello, Ana!" I said, smiling at her. She was waving at me, standing behind the line of rocks.

"I rang your home and they told me you were here swimming. I spotted you from the window in my house; you are like a real fish, you know? How can you swim so fast for so long? I decided to come to the beach to meet you, hoping that we could play in the rocks when you were finished," Ana explained, looking jolly and full of energy.

"That's a good idea," I replied, thinking that it was probably the right time to do it and that it was going to be fun. "You know, Ana, I can't run for long because I always get short of breath, but this never happens to me when I swim. My arms never seem to give up on me as long as I keep catching my breath with the same rhythm all the time."

The tide was nearly up by now. The sea was just covering the line of rocks by the beach. Only the largest one on the far left was still visible. This particular rock was buried in the sand with an oblique orientation and a height of about three metres; therefore, it was used by the locals to dive in the water when big waves came crashing into the rock. I had never tried it but had always admired anyone doing it. It worried me not being able to calculate the depth correctly. Big waves on that rock had a particular see-saw motion that made them huge as they were approaching but also caused a vacuum effect after them, lowering the water level more than usual. Missing the dive could easily make you hit the ground with your head; I preferred not to try it.

Ana was also quite physical like me. If anything, she was too flexible, and her long legs sometimes seemed disjointed. But Ana was not afraid of taking risks.

"Come on, Isa! Let's swim and stay behind this rock in front of us. The waves are breaking over the rocks and covering them completely," Ana said while running into the water.

I knew at once what she meant by that, and I could see the logic in it. We positioned ourselves between waves, facing the rock with our feet touching the edge of the big stone, in a horizontal position. The first wave pushed us upwards, lifting us onto the rock until we managed to stand on it with hardly any effort. Subsequent waves followed each other, giving us time to situate ourselves facing the ocean. We both giggled as we watched how big volumes of water passed between our legs with not enough strength to push us down. The roaring noise of the waves was loud behind us where they were breaking off, just after the line of rocks on their way to the shore.

"Ana, be careful! Look at that wave coming. It seems bigger than the other ones!" I announced to my friend.

"Oh my God!" Ana exclaimed. "By the time it gets here, it will reach us above our waists. We're going to fall!"

"Dive in, Ana!" I shouted and both of us dived head first into the huge wave. It was so exciting.

"Let's do it again, Isabel!" Ana said as soon as she surfaced.

"I've noticed that we get one big wave every eight. You see? After the eighth one, there's a pause, with no waves for a little while, and then they start getting bigger and bigger again. That will give us enough time to get on top of the rock," I explained to Ana.

"If we get it wrong, we can get awful cuts," Ana told me, getting in position while waiting for the next wave. "The edges of the rock are very sharp indeed."

"We won't get it wrong. I'll swim around and wait to get on top of the rock with wave number eight. That should be fun," I announced.

The wave not only placed me on top of the rock; the force was so much stronger that I lost my balance and fell, rolling over the edge and closer to the beach, into the water again, scratching and cutting my legs and knees, which I didn't mind because I'd thought it was a possible outcome.

It was such a thrilling experience. Ana and I continued playing on and off the rock, using the waves to dive in or jump into the rocks. We truly had a good time together.

"Ana, are you going out this Saturday?" I asked Ana curiously while we were both drying out in the sand and having a rest.

"Yes," she answered. "I go out every Saturday with Emilia. Would you like to come with us? We met two boys in the park. We don't know who they are, but they looked nice at the time. I had a crush on one of them and Emilia on the other one. Our mums found out and were not very happy about it so we had to stop seeing them, but I also think they were kind of boring."

"Oh, I see." I was listening carefully, fascinated about the story.

"Do you know Pepe? He's Emilia's older brother, one year ahead of her."

"Yeah, I know who he is," I answered.

"We go out with him and his friends. They are all very clever, you know, and it is nice to be able to go in a group all together. Our mums allow us to go to the city centre with them and stay until eleven or midnight. Everybody our age goes out in the centre, having tapas and Cokes. I've seen my sisters around and they ignore me, pretending they don't know me. I know they're drinking beer instead of Coke. I've also seen Teresa and your brothers with their friends. Come with us! We normally walk there and return by bus so we keep one of the bus fares to spend," Ana explained to me.

"Yes, I'd like to go with all of you," I said, wanting to join in. "I've never really gone out before; I've always been too busy in the gym club."

"There will be a disco at our brother's school in two weeks. The students in the upper form are organising it to raise money for the end-of-year trip. We might have a chance of going. We are going to talk about it this weekend. Our parents shouldn't object to it," Ana told me, revealing her plot. "If our mothers talk to each other and realise that we are all together, they will agree, fixing a returning time. The boys will accompany us back home. They wouldn't mind." Ana smiled and opened both her hands, showing her palms and shrugging her shoulders.

I smiled back, fixing my eyes on her. The intensity of her blue eyes in contrast with the darkness of her hair and her tanned skin was quite striking. I thought Ana was a bright girl and for some reason, although we had never been close friends, we had always been friends from a distance.

Springtime passed quickly and the end of school was approaching. My new routine attending school and swimming during the weekends and at least two lunchtime breaks a week was now settled. I still used my spare time to revise, but in a more relaxed manner and going out on Saturdays was always appealing. There had been some weekends which my family spent in El Cortijo, but I was able to invite Ana and Emilia to come with me and that was quite fun too.

My trip to Dublin in July was already fixed. This was going to be my second summer doing it, and so I knew the school and the family I was staying with. The previous summer

I went with my brother Alex and my cousins Andrés and Margarita, but this year it would be different; I was going on my own. Alex and Andrés had finished their trips, and my cousin Margarita missed her mother too much last summer even to think about attempting going again. I knew it was an advantage to be learning my English alone, but I didn't like being by myself.

Dad was still sailing and competing in regattas often. Jaime and Alex were always going with him, but Dad was still being hard on Jaime, to the extent that he sometimes came home crying and Mum had to talk to Dad. Jaime had one more year to do at school and was looking forward to reading economics at Seville University and living in my grandmother's house with María, who was having the time of her life. Jaime had reached the point where he no longer wished to sail with Dad, and Mum was trying to cover his absences with millions of excuses.

He and Dad had recently attended a regatta in the south of Portugal, close to Lisbon. On their way back to Cádiz, they encountered an intense fog. Dad would always prefer to stay out at sea rather than mooring somewhere else, unless it was a real emergency. He was not comfortable in unfamiliar places, especially if he was acting like a normal civilian and not a naval officer, where, as soon as he walked in, everybody knew his rank and position, paying him full attention.

Dad was good at reading the stars and the hour according to the sun, positioning the *Kingdom of Castile* in the right place according to the shore, calculating knots of speed and winds. He used a compass, maps, a radio, and an ultrasound machine that could estimate depth to the seabed whenever he thought there was a shallow area; everything else he calculated manually. The blindness of the fog made him disorientated and before he realised it, the boat ran aground in a sandbank close to Villamoura in Portugal. He had obviously come too close to the coast.

The impact and sudden stopping of the boat threw everyone to the floor and my brother Jaime fell into the water. Dad thought that Jaime was a coward and that he was frightened and therefore had panicked and jumped into the water to abandon the boat. Dad humiliated Jaime in front of Alex and Miguel, the sailor who usually accompanied him. He was shouting and screaming, completely beside himself, and he was so angry that when he realised that they were by the seashore, he asked everyone to disembark and walked off by himself. Miguel and my brothers couldn't find him anywhere and when they eventually went into a place to have some food, they found him having a meal on his own. He refused to talk to any of them. Mum had to drive to Portugal to rescue them and help Dad organise getting the *Kingdom of Castile* repaired. I was not surprised that my brother had had enough; I was glad I didn't have anything to do with sailing anymore.

Chapter Nineteen

DUBLIN

"Goodbye, Isabel," my aunt Maribel said, kissing me twice on each cheek. "Poor little thing – I can see that you would rather stay than go to Dublin."

I looked at her and said nothing. I couldn't talk. I was anxious and feeling incredibly sad about leaving. It was the first time that I was going to be completely alone. I came close to my dad's brother, Uncle Alberto, and kissed him goodbye.

"Thank you for having me in your house here in Madrid and taking me to the airport," I politely said to both of them.

My cousin Laura was also present. She was my age and was very shy, but somehow I felt that she knew what I was feeling. I had had a great time with her in Madrid and especially enjoyed the swimming pool in her house.

"Isa, I will see you in Laredo in August when you come back," Laura said to me.

"Goodbye, Laura," I said, looking at her but failing to smile.

I turned around and walked through passport control without looking back again.

The plane was full of other students travelling in groups with teachers and I guessed that they were also going to Ireland to learn English. I was travelling on my own. I said goodbye to Mum and Dad in Seville when they took me to the airport to catch my plane to Madrid. I knew Mrs Murphy would be waiting for me at the airport in Dublin. Mr and Mrs Murphy lived at 71 Summerset Avenue in Rathfarham, south of Dublin. They had two boys and two girls; the youngest girl was my age but was completely spoilt. Her name was Heloise. She could be nice but also unbearable. Her sister, Karen, who was three years older, was incredibly nice. She was the one who did all the chores at home.

Things in Ireland were very different from Spain. The country was incredibly green, with a large number of parks and open spaces. There was fine natural grass growing everywhere and people were allowed to stand on it. In Spain, grass was always fenced up, and you could easily be punished with a fine if you were ever caught spoiling it. People lived in houses rather than flats, which made the whole scenery more pleasant, but consequently the population lived very spread out. Sometimes all the identical houses blurred into one monotonous mass. The weather was humid and the general lack of light was difficult to get used to. Light enhances the intensity and degree of colours, and when it's missing, things tend to look dull around you. It was rainy country. People stayed indoors from six o'clock at night on, and there were few children playing in the streets compared to Spain. It was indeed very different.

The Irish normally ate early, and the main meal was at about six in the evening, after relying on a sad sandwich at midday to keep you going. They didn't have the type of bread that you could get in Spain or France, and the choice of fillings for the sandwiches was incredibly bizarre, such as jam, bananas, peanut butter, dry lettuce, tomatoes with no dressing and so forth. The portions I always got in my main meal were fixed and rather small; I was not expected to help myself. I knew that I would not taste any kind of fish for the next four weeks and it was rare to see any fruit around the house, yet alone eat it.

The main vegetable in their diet was potato, which I knew I would eat on a daily basis as a jacket potato, roasted, mashed or fried. Salads usually came without any dressings, vegetables were served just boiled and with very little taste and they loved cakes and puddings, maybe too much. Olive oil was not used much; they cooked with butter instead. However, chocolates were amazing in Ireland. The selection was incredible and far more than anything you could ever find in Spain. People in Ireland ate a lot of chocolate.

Having said that, I felt hungry in Ireland, and despite eating everything they cooked for me, I felt deprived of food. Mum had always commented that we all put on weight in Ireland but I am convinced it was the diet heavily based on carbohydrates; and this was what made me feel hungry because I was not too keen on cakes, puddings or chocolates.

I was only allowed to have a bath once a week in Mr and Mrs Murphy's house and they did not have a shower. Baths were only for children in Spain because they required a large amount of water, but in Ireland saving water was not so important and I could see they had plenty of it. It worried me when my time of the month came in Ireland that I would not be able to have a shower every day.

Like the people in Spain, Irish people liked talking a lot and they liked playing tennis and golf as well. I could see on the telly that they also liked playing something called cricket, a type of baseball but far more boring, everybody wearing white and matches taking days and days, where it's impossible to work out the rules or what is actually happening. The Irish hardly kissed each other like in Spain and I guessed, they didn't like touching; you were just supposed to shake hands when offered. I had also noticed that they did not use their hands to express themselves and I had learnt to talk keeping my hands still when I was in Ireland.

As far as I could see, the Irish did not follow any kind of fashion like in Spain. They dressed in an odd way, wearing socks with sandals and they were not colour coordinated. They had incredibly pale skin generally, with a kind of whiteness that I had never seen before in Spain.

There were also some peculiar things that I found fascinating. For instance, drivers were on the right-hand side and they drove on the left side of the road. This was incredibly confusing, and I had to be careful when crossing the road because I always looked to the opposite side to where the car was actually coming from. When playing cards, they started dealing them from the left and the first player to start was always the one on the left; in Spain, it was quite the opposite. They liked using pepper in their meals, but it was interesting that the container for the pepper had several holes and the one for the salt, only one. In Spain, the salt container always has several holes. In Ireland, therefore it was a common mistake to pour pepper all over your meal when you were expecting salt.

I liked to know about things that were different so I could be prepared, knowing what to expect, and the challenge of finding different ways of thinking to my own one amazed me. I tried to be incredibly logical in what I did according to what I thought, and it felt like a challenge finding out that people from a different country could take specific ways of thinking for granted which were completely shocking outside of a very restricted culture. For example, the Irish did not feel any kind of inhibition about walking in bare feet in their houses, which is quite rude in itself if you really think about it. On the other hand, it is far more comfortable doing so in your own house, I find. Mr and Mrs Murphy had carpets in the whole house, including the bathroom and kitchen. I thought it was not hygienic, but if walking in bare feet was normal for them, then one could begin to understand that keeping your feet warm was important.

Shaking my hand, Mrs Murphy greeted me when she saw me. "Hello, Isabel. It's very nice to see you again. Did you have a good flight?"

"Nice to see you too. Yes, I had a good journey, thank you," I answered politely.

"I've come on my own today because Heloise is in Galway learning Irish until Wednesday of next week. Karen is at home, though, and dinner will ready by the time we get there. The boys have a summer job in a bakery and we hardly see them. They alternate nights and spend most of the day sleeping," Mrs Murphy explained, giving me a summary of what was going on while she was trying to maintain the conversation.

"My mother has given me a gift for you; I mustn't forget to give it to you as soon as we get to the house. She also sends her regards," I told Mrs Murphy.

"How are your mother and family? Is everyone okay?" Mrs Murphy asked me.

"They're all fine, thank you. María is doing very well at university and Teresa has just finished her second year at university, reading geography. Everyone else is still at school. My cousins are also doing well."

"Ah, I forgot to mention something important," said Mrs Murphy. "There was a bus strike announced, lasting for the whole month of July. Drivers are claiming a better salary. What this means is that busses are working every hour or so and with very random timetables. It's frustrating, and I think it's better if you walk to school for your English lessons. Do you know the way?"

"Yes, I do, Mrs Murphy. I do like walking and sometimes walked home from school last year," I replied.

I was wondering how I was going to get to the city centre or find the way to it. I certainly didn't want to spend my limited money on taxis. I had to find a way to go at least once during the four weeks that I was staying.

When I got to the house, I realised that I was not only sharing the room with Heloise but that we were also sharing a double bed; I wasn't sure I liked this. I quickly came downstairs as soon as I had unpacked my things, making sure I took the gifts my mother had given me for Mr and Mrs Murphy.

"Hello, Karen," I said walking into the kitchen. Karen was as gentle natured as always. It was really nice to see her again.

"Hello, Isabel," she said, shaking hands with me. "How is everyone at home?"

"They are all fine and asked me to pass on their regards," I said with a big smile.

"Heloise is not coming till Wednesday, but I can show you where the indoor swimming pool is," Karen told me, trying to be helpful. "Your Mum told us that you need to swim for your back."

"Thank you. That will be very useful. I'm not doing gymnastics anymore. I was confined to wearing a back brace during the winter but thank goodness I got rid of it. Now I have to swim instead. Maybe I can start tomorrow if you are free to take me this weekend," I said to Karen.

"Yes, I could take you after lunch. When are you starting English school?" she asked me.

"On Monday," I answered.

I wondered which level of English they would put me in this year. We were following the grades of Trinity College in Dublin. Last year I was in grade seven out of twelve. While I was thinking about this, Mr Murphy walked into the kitchen.

"Hello, Isabel. It's nice to see you again. How is everyone at home?" Mr Murphy asked me, shaking hands with me.

"Very well, thank you, Mr Murphy. They all send their regards."

"Did you have a good journey?" he asked.

"Yes, Mr Murphy. The plane was on time," I said.

I couldn't help feeling inhibited in front of Mr Murphy. He had a strong Irish accent and it was a struggle to understand him. He spoke rather fast, hardly vocalising the words. We always kept our conversations short.

Karen showed me where the swimming pool was and went swimming every other day. It wasn't that easy to swim there, as there wasn't a dedicated lane for swimmers and I soon started to avoid weekends, when it was full of families with young children. Karen stayed with me the first day, but I always went alone after that.

English lessons also started. It took me forty-five minutes to walk each way to and from the school. There was a group of Spanish students of mixed ages from ten to seventeen, the majority of them from Madrid and Barcelona. They all came through an organisation; I was the only one from the south of Spain and the only one who came independently. I was glad to have been graded in level ten, but I wasn't very happy when I was given three books to read over the four weeks I was staying. We always had a test at the end, which was written and oral, with an external examiner. The books I had to read this year were *The Little Prince*, written by Antoine de Saint-Exupéry; *Brave New World*, by Aldous Huxley, and *The Merchant of Venice*, by Shakespeare. The latter was written in Old English. I thought it was completely unfair and I profoundly disliked reading. It wasn't fun for me at all.

I was glad to have the room to myself, giving me time to adjust to Ireland again before Heloise's arrival. In addition to being afraid, I was in a state of alertness and vigilance in trying to do the right thing and trying to fit in. I was forcing myself to ask and find out about things; otherwise, I could have easily remained stuck in my bedroom all day. I was not sure if the way I asked things was adequate or polite enough and I couldn't determine whether I was expected to share chores in the house. Every time I asked Karen if I could help her, she said no. She could well be meaning yes. I wasn't sure.

My sleep had been much disrupted in the last month, but arriving in Dublin had not made much difference; I guessed I was still anxious. Sleeping while hugging my pillow was still comforting, but I had been realising for a while now that I had to be cautious because the rubbing of the pillow between my legs could occasionally bring on sexual arousal, making me agitated and causing me to experience an explosion of embarrassment and sexual images in my head. These images were fantasies of what I thought sexual contact might be or how it could feel having hardly any clothes on next to someone you truly fancied. It made me think about the level of trust someone needed to have in the other person to be able to reach this state of intimacy and privacy, not to mention how vulnerable one might feel. I would love to find someone special in my life in this way. I very much wanted to feel the love and the affection, but I wasn't sure about the touching.

Thinking about all this and having these feelings made me feel guilty. The wanting it to happen and the comforting feeling attached to it all was something that I knew adults would not like me to have. Mum had always transmitted to me the message that a woman never had sexual desires but was always available to her husband whenever he wanted. A woman denying giving herself to her husband made her a bad wife, pushing her husband to look for other women.

Somehow my thoughts were comforting and secretly I would never want to stop them, but I tried to, feeling guilty and ashamed because of it; deep down I liked having these thoughts of having a profound intimacy with someone really special who could reach and touch my soul. I was not sure if this possibility even existed. I wanted to feel love from the very bottom of my heart. The physical act of loving someone in a private and intimate way would become my tool to express my love for someone. I would find it difficult ever to find the words to express my love for someone if I ever fell in love, but I could imagine myself being able to transmit it in a profound and powerful way. I would like to reach and feel the person I loved without having to hide anything. If this way of feeling was not there, I should not give anyone physical access to me, even if that person was my husband. I was looking forward to creating a life in a completely shared love when the time was right for me, but I would also use the physical act of loving to embrace communication through love, and I would desire it. I couldn't see this like my mother would wish for me to see it. I was trying to hide it and repress it, but I would like to feel it and show it when I became master of my own self and was independent. I hoped God would forgive me if I had got it wrong.

Heloise had arrived from Galway. She had definitely put on weight compared to the previous year, but I couldn't say much about this because the same had happened to me. Heloise was my age and had quite a few friends. It was interesting going out with her after school if she allowed me to do so. She had a bicycle that I could never borrow. Heloise was always in command and was a spoilt bully with her friends and with me on occasions too.

"Isabel, this is my house and I have decided that since this is my bed and my room, you have to sleep on the floor," Heloise told me with a defiant look in her eyes.

"I really don't care where I sleep, Heloise. Thinking about it, I'm better off sleeping on the floor," I said, taking my pillow and the duvet and settling myself in a corner of the room away from the door. "You can have the bed. I'll have the duvet."

Before Heloise could say anything, I was ready to close my eyes. She was standing there mesmerised, clearly not expecting my reaction. She opened the wardrobe and helped herself to another rather thin and short blanket and also went to sleep. Two weeks had gone by with this arrangement and Mrs Murphy had never noticed it. Heloise eventually told me to share the bed again if I wanted to and I allowed her to have the duvet back.

Bath time once a week was quite precious, but going to the swimming pool on alternate days was giving me the opportunity to have a shower on a regular basis. Heloise was doing her best to make my life difficult. The previous year,

Alex and my cousin Andrés had always been teasing her and that was probably why Heloise thought it was her time for revenge. Every time I had a bath, I knew Heloise was going to try to break in to catch me naked. She had tried several times already, but I had always been ready for it and she had never succeeded. I was stronger than she was and was able to hold the door closed, but her attitude spoiled my bath time. I hated having to rush it and be alert, blocking the door with as many objects as I could find, just in case I had to leave the bath in a hurry to hold the door against her. Mrs Murphy never said anything to Heloise, so she could do and say whatever she pleased on most occasions.

Time was passing quickly in Ireland. I was alert and slightly anxious; I was able to cope, but I was feeling very lonely. I really didn't want to tell anyone about Heloise, but she was a real cow to me.

I had managed to go once to the city centre during the summer by joining a group of older students who were going together from the school. It was my chance to get some presents for my family. It took us two hours of walking, but the major problem was the way back home. We all dispersed at some point and I had to walk all the way home on my own, which was scary, as I wasn't sure I could remember my way very well. I finally managed to return safely home, but I was absolutely drenched by the rain; I was caught in the middle of a summer storm.

I liked going to the city centre and I admired the idea of shopping centres in Ireland. It was a concept of shopping that did not exist in Spain. There were also places for fast food, serving pizzas or burgers which were really good. In Spain, there were bars or restaurants, and we had the concept of tapas as fast food, but everything was homemade and completely different from one place to another, depending where you chose to eat.

My English exam had come two days before I returned home. I found *The Merchant of Venice* difficult to understand and comment on. Talking about books was something that I had never done at school before, but overall I was happy to have been able to achieve 77 per cent on my test.

Chapter Twenty

BREAKING BARRIERS

Ana was leaving Spain to live in Washington, DC, for three years and she was devastated because it felt like such a long time to her. She had never been abroad or even in a plane before, but her father had been promoted to vice admiral, becoming the Spanish naval attaché in the United States. Ana had been receiving intensive English lessons throughout the summer. She was feeling nervous about going. I knew it was not a permanent thing and that it would be useful for her because you learn many things when you are abroad. Ana was lucky to have this opportunity and to be able to live with her family at the same time.

As it happened, Emilia had also left Cádiz with all her family for good before the summer holidays. Her father had also been promoted, although he wasn't in the military forces, and they had moved to Mallorca. I knew I was never going to see Emilia again. Somehow, I couldn't feel that Emilia and Ana's almost simultaneous departures could have any consequences for me.

By now, Dad was a captain in the navy with four gold bars on his uniform. He had always been more senior than Ana's dad before, but somehow he had reached his limit before retirement. Very few were able to rise to admiral. Ana's dad had been one of them. I felt proud and happy for him and his family.

Dad instead had suddenly been made a Knight of the Holy Sepulchre. I had tried to ask him why or what it meant, but he got angry and didn't want to say much about it. I wasn't sure if he felt embarrassed, thinking that people would laugh about it if they found out, or if he was meant to keep it quiet. I really didn't know. Mum only said that he had to go to Barcelona and it was because he had noble surnames dating to medieval times. Mum and Grandmother Isabel were going on a trip to visit Israel and the Holy Land. Dad didn't wish to go, so grandmother was going instead.

I was fifteen now and things at school were slightly different. My Spanish literature teacher was Mrs López. I remembered her well from when I first entered her class when I was in reception. She still adored Teresa, calling her the 'Parisian girl' all the time; I think Mrs López meant that she was good-looking and fashionable, because Teresa was not really from Paris. Mrs López was strict and had high standards of teaching. I found doing comprehensions difficult, spending a large amount of time on them and not really understanding how to do them at all. Mrs López was struggling with me because I couldn't see what everyone else could. It created great anxiety in me to face any homework related to Spanish.

"Isabel, it's been nearly eight weeks since we started with this and you're still not getting it. What I am expecting of you is a full analysis of any text; obviously, poetry will be different from narrative text," Mrs López tried to explain to me with a meaningful positive energy around her. "The method is the same, although you will be looking for different things depending on the type of text. It's like describing this glass of water in front of me. You should talk about the definition, shape, colour, temperature, functionality of it and maybe possible hazards. So in an orderly manner, you can face any object and just develop each point fully in writing. It is the same doing a comprehension. I think you're getting stuck not knowing how to break the information down, but you are better than anyone else at knowing the use of the theory of grammar, vocabulary and the use of different tools like similes, metaphors, adverbs, verbal paraphrases, and so on. The deep meaning of the structure is very different from the superficial one and that is what I would like you to analyse. What is the author trying to communicate … and what is he not saying? If you are clever enough, you will be able to decipher his mood or how well educated the author is."

"Mrs Lopez, it would help me tremendously if you could break down for me a skeleton of what I should be looking for in a narrative text to start with, the same way you have just done with the glass of water. Once I practice on it, I can then do the same with poetry, journalism, biographies, and so on. I can see the logic in it all now and I know I can do it." I said this to Mrs López with great happiness in my heart. Being able to visualise the whole picture rather than just a part of it was as if a jigsaw puzzle had been completed in my head.

"I can certainly do that, but rather than following individual questions for each text doing a comprehension, I would like you to analyse the entire text, writing an essay about it and following the order in your head. I am sure it will so powerful and good the way you do it that it is going to be just amazing. You have so much potential, Isabel."

Mrs López couldn't be more proud of me. According to her, my comprehensions were thorough, long and good quality. I did so many of them and started to apply the method to other types of writing, enjoying my own analytical resources. It was fascinating how I couldn't see anything at all when reading text for the first time, but how deeply I could reach inside it once working on the task. This also helped me with the stressful way I remembered things. I was working hard to find skeletons in the narratives of what I memorised, which was particularly helpful in subjects such as history and biology, but I also found an improvement in memorising everything else. Deep down, what I was finding was a way of classifying information in a particular order and getting a structure in categories and subcategories. Remembering bullet points took the pressure off my mind; the main content of the idea stuck in my mind rather than the precise wording that came with it. It was an efficient and stress-free method of remembering things and it made me happy.

Thinking in this way was also making me realise that there were many things I was very good at ignoring when I wasn't sure what they were all about; people's reactions and sometimes situations surprised me. Trying to structure and rationalise behaviour and social interactions was also helping me to find the essence of what people intended to do. I could shuffle different possibilities and analyse the evidence around me, and this helped me to comprehend the true meaning of people around me; even if I got the understanding at a later stage, when everything had already happened and it was all over, it was still rewarding. I was feeling much more confident around people or even having an opinion about things that had happened around me. Things were suddenly becoming more manageable.

"Teresa, your friend Carmen is always at home with you. She's like your boyfriend," I said, half joking but also with some measure of resentment, as it was becoming impossible to talk to Teresa lately. She was spending a great amount of time not talking to anybody and confined in her room.

"Leave me alone. Are you stupid or what?" Teresa answered, slamming her bedroom door.

Teresa had changed since the summer holidays. She was kind of bitter and any attempts to approach her were in vain, which was making me anxious. I couldn't work out what was happening in the house, but Mum was depressed and crying about everything and nothing. Dad was angry, so we all instantly fled from his presence. I was choosing to stay in my room as much as possible, as it was the only safe place I could find in the house. I always thought that when Jaime left the house to study economics in Seville, things might get easier with Dad, but my father was such a stressful person to have around. Things had not changed at all. If anything, they were worse.

"Isabel, I need to talk to you," Mum announced one day, unexpectedly walking into my room without knocking.

I looked up at her interrupting my revision and waited, not saying anything while she stood next to me. Her face was serious and she spoke with a deep sense of aggravation in her tone.

"Teresa is pregnant. She's expecting a baby in late spring."

"Oh, I didn't know," I finally said after a moment of silence.

There was a storm of feelings invading me, as I did not understand the meaning of it or how it could have actually happened to Teresa. She was popular and had many friends, but I was not aware of her being in a formal relationship with anybody in particular, although to tell the truth, I didn't know many details about Teresa's social life. She had been trying to be particularly distant from my parents; I thought she found them controlling and repressive in many ways and they disagreed with almost any choice of friendship, clothes or anything that Teresa found attractive or interesting. It was my parents' avoidance that had probably made Teresa grow apart from her siblings and family. The fact that María and Jaime were living with Grandmother made her personality stick out like a thorn when trying to get any understanding from Mum and Dad.

"Teresa will be getting married before Christmas," Mum announced, acting and talking as if the problem were really hers and had nothing to do with Teresa.

"Who's the father of the baby?" I asked.

"Teresa got a boyfriend over the summer holidays. His name is Fernando, and he is in his last year at university and will become a civil engineer ..." Mum started crying, holding her face between her hands. "Your father is beside himself. He thinks Teresa is a whore, and to be honest, she is too attracted by men. You only have to see the way she likes dressing. She is too pretty and knows men feel attracted to her. She has humiliated the whole family. How are your Dad and I going to face our friends and relatives? It has been agreed and they will marry before people notice." And without waiting for me to say anything, she left the room to continue crying in her bedroom.

I felt frozen and did not know what to think. All this had been happening around me and I wasn't aware of it. It was unfair, and I hated my parents undermining Teresa. I was angry, frightened and worried about what could happen to Teresa, and the pain was tearing me up inside. Everything was too sudden and abrupt and I felt a real panic about losing Teresa. She really was my point of reference in the family and the thought of her leaving the house in trouble and unhappy made me ill. The idea of facing Dad's blind and unpredictable temper alone was making my body shake and shiver.

"Teresa?" I timidly said, knocking at her door. The music was loud and I wasn't sure if she'd heard me, so I knocked again. "Teresa."

"Leave me alone. Who is it?" Teresa shouted over the music.

"It's me, Isabel."

I waited for a couple of minutes and the volume of the music was turned down. Teresa opened the door a crack.

"What do you want, Isa?"

"I know you're expecting a baby. I want to know if you're okay. Is it true that you are getting married? I don't want you to leave the family," I struggled to say.

"There are many things you still don't understand. I don't want to get married, but in a way, I am forced to do so. I prefer not talk to anybody, but even if I marry, I will stay until the baby is born," Teresa told me, still not opening the door all the way or inviting me to come into her bedroom.

"Okay. I'm very happy to become an aunty. I'm sure he or she will be a beautiful baby."

"Please leave me alone now, Isa. I prefer not to talk about this," Teresa replied, closing the door.

I wished Teresa were allowed to stay in the house, bringing her baby up like another sibling in the family until she was ready to leave, but I knew that Teresa's baby had to be away from my father. He would never tolerate him or her around. Any imperfection, physical abnormality or chronic illness was a deep sign of weakness and humiliation for Dad.

Anxiety and fear were overwhelming me. I wasn't even sure if I was supposed to discuss this with anyone else at home or not, and I didn't know who knew about it. Mum was acting as if she were carrying the world's weight on her shoulders, with an unhappiness similar to what you would feel with the loss of a close relative. I was not sure what to do to help Teresa and she wasn't allowing anyone near her. I had managed to control my tears and sadness the best I could and had forced myself to focus on my studies, not allowing myself any kind of breaks; more like punishing my anguish instead and forcing myself to be as strong as possible.

Ironically, my grade cards became better than ever.

Chapter Twenty-One

TERESA

The atmosphere in the house was tense and unpleasant; my parents' attitude towards Teresa was making sure that she had all material necessities covered but also reminding her about the effort and support that they were making for her. It seemed that Teresa had to feel and pay for whatever negatives came along with having fallen pregnant. There was no sympathy. It was more important for everyone to know about the negativity and the impact of how Mum was feeling and how hard she was trying to support Teresa despite her sadness than anybody stopping to think about how Teresa could be feeling. In Dad's mind, she was still a whore. It was as if the subliminal message remained: "You're getting what you deserve; you're worth nothing."

None of us had ever said anything nasty to Teresa and my siblings and I were all very much looking forward to the birth of her baby. Nobody had ever questioned Teresa, but we couldn't reach her or comfort her in her own pain and disillusion. Teresa continued to attend university while her wedding and pregnancy were going ahead.

Miss Spencer was also angry and in a bad temper. It was better not to approach her. Somehow, it seemed to me that she was maybe in disagreement with my parents over how things were unfolding. I felt that maybe Miss Spencer was forced to act in Mum's name, but overall she had become most irritable.

Things got worse when Mum and Dad announced that my father was retiring from the navy in two years' time and that the plan was for all of us to go and live in El Cortijo. Miss Spencer was trying to qualify as a teacher, attending evening courses and combining it with working full time in our house, with the intention of changing her job when this happened, but Mum was also encouraging Miss Spencer to buy a property for herself and to get a mortgage. All these changes were too much for Miss Spencer and there were times when she was too stretched out or maybe thinking that she was no longer needed in the family, receiving very little acknowledgement from Mum's constant demands. It truly seemed that the only important matter was how Mum was feeling.

Alex was also spending most of the time in his bedroom when he was at home. He was particularly quiet and thoughtful. He had become more studious and responsible, getting much better marks at school too. Alex was in his last year of school and until now he had always wanted to join the navy like Dad. He had developed a passion for windsurfing over the last two years and was always at sea, either sailing with Dad or by himself. He was winning many regattas and we were all full of admiration last summer when we had the chance to appreciate how skilful he was. Training during wintertime in the south of Spain in the open sea with strong winds had made him a strong competitor in the summer regattas. Alex was able to flick the sail anywhere he wished to and to move the board forward, backwards or even sail standing on the edge of the board after having rotated it by ninety degrees. It was simply amazing to watch.

One day and without anyone expecting it, Alex announced that he was going to leave the family in the autumn after his last year at school and join a seminary to become a priest. He was abandoning everything to help the poor.

My friends Emilia and Ana had left, Teresa was getting married and leaving the family, and Alex was also planning to leave soon after Teresa. I preferred not even to think about the prospect of Miss Spencer leaving the family and all of us moving to live in El Cortijo in two years' time.

I would also have to do my last year at school in my brothers' school, as my two older sisters had before getting to university. It had got to the point in which I had stopped talking and was feeling nothing; my soul was torn apart.

"What do we have to do? Will we be okay?" Elena asked me when she and Beatriz walked into our bedroom.

"Are you going anywhere, Isabel? Are you staying with us?" Beatriz asked, giving me a penetrating stare.

"Beatriz, I'm going with you to Dublin this summer. Apart from that, I'm not going anywhere at the moment. We don't have to do anything, just stay together."

"Why is everybody so angry? We are going to be aunties. I've told all my friends at school!" Elena said, full of satisfaction. "God has sent a baby to Teresa, like the Virgin Mary."

"Isabel, do you know Teresa's future husband?" Beatriz asked me.

"No, I have no idea who he is. I'm sure we'll get to meet him soon enough," I replied.

"Is Teresa a prostitute?" Beatriz insisted, without taking her eyes off me.

"No, she is not! Teresa does not sleep around with men, but she has made a mistake," I answered, staring into Beatriz's eyes. "Have we ever made a mistake because we didn't know better or because we thought we knew but we didn't?"

"What's a prostitute?" Elena asked, but without waiting for a reply she continued. "I wore my uniform by mistake last Friday when it was Mufti Day."

Beatriz kept quiet, still looking at me and I think she was understanding.

"Elena, let's go. We're interrupting Isabel's homework," Beatriz said.

"Wait!" Elena insisted. "I want to ask her what she's going to wear to the wedding."

"I don't know yet, Elena. I am sure Mum will have something ready for us."

"But I want to look beautiful. Have you ever been to a wedding before, Isa?" Elena asked me.

"You will look beautiful because you are beautiful – and so is Beatriz. I went to our eldest cousin's wedding when I was staying at Aunt Mónica's house one summer. I didn't realise it was a wedding because nobody told me until we were inside the church and saw the bride coming in. In a way, I missed everything because it took me a long time to find out what it was all about. But I wouldn't like to miss anything at all this time," I explained to Elena, smiling at her, but somehow she was still looking confused.

Teresa's wedding was in Seville and the celebration was held in El Cortijo. We finally met Fernando and his immediate family, and as usual, the number of guests attending from our family, even immediate relatives, was numerous. I felt awkward not knowing the groom very well and, even more so, encountering my parent's friends, some of whom had students in the school. I had been avoiding talking to anyone at school about Teresa's wedding, and suddenly facing people I knew from Cádiz made me feel embarrassed. It was like having to acknowledge in front of them that Teresa was pregnant, although I knew very well that they were all aware of the fact.

Life continued after the wedding and Teresa was getting ready for the birth of her baby while still attending lessons at university. But there was still another surprise for all of us. Teresa was expecting twins. Mum didn't want to take any chances and had booked Teresa in with the private doctor who had delivered all of us in Seville.

It seemed that there was no time to feel comfortable and relaxed at home, because soon after Teresa's wedding, María, who was in her last year at university, announced that she also wished to get married. Mum was depressed, acting as if she felt incredibly tired all the time and letting us know that everything was too much for her. She couldn't face another wedding and was trying to convince María to delay hers for some time.

It was strange because normally Dad would have never allowed any of us to marry until we were independent and earning a salary. He didn't want any of us to depend on our husbands or wives. I guessed it was all too much for him even to protest. It felt that María's wedding was not necessary so soon after Teresa's, but I wondered how unsettling it felt for María to watch Teresa getting married when she was the oldest one. But María had grandmother's unconditional support, and we all knew how María was able to push the boundaries to the limit in order to get what she wanted.

María had started planning her wedding to be held in the early spring, after she finished university. Teresa's twins would be less than one year old by then. But how was María going to live? Her new boyfriend was still at university with her and neither of them had a job yet. I thought they were rushing things, and it was suicidal in my mind, planning all this without a permanent job. I couldn't understand anything at all.

Despite all this, Mum didn't lose the opportunity to punish Teresa with her insinuations and comments. She was still bitterly resentful.

"Teresa, your sister will have a proper wedding, not like yours. She will lawfully be entitled to wear a white dress, not having been with a man before. She knows not to flirt with them and is a lady ..."

Teresa was clearly trying to keep her fury inside her. "I'm very happy for her, Mum, if that is what you would like to think."

I couldn't believe how Mum could possibly say anything like this to Teresa. I felt like screaming in anger. Teresa went to her bedroom in response, and I followed her.

"Teresa, Mum's very cruel and I know that María slept with her first boyfriend many times. She used to talk to him on the phone in Mum's bedroom every day late in the evening, when I was still doing homework in Dad's study after my gym club. María was talking to him about how they had slept together and about missing it when they were apart. I didn't want to be nosy, but María knew very well that I was in the study and pretended I wasn't there. It was impossible not to hear it sooner or later." I'd never thought I was going to disclose this painful secret to anyone.

"Don't worry, Isa. I know it very well. I have been covering for María for many years and she has pushed things to the extreme. Somehow she always finds the way and things seem to work out for her. But there is nothing I can do apart from hearing Mum's hurtful words. We can't give María away; after all, she's not pregnant and deserves a nice wedding. But Mum intentionally tries to hurt me every time she can and I can say very little because they are supporting me, but they act as if they are doing me a favour all the time. I don't need to be humiliated." Teresa paused, looking at me.

I tried to encourage her. "Maybe when you have the twins and start living with Fernando, you'll be better."

"I'm not sure, Isa." She started to open her heart to me with real sadness. "I think I should have never married. Grandmother and Uncle Tomás have given me a substantial amount of money, but now Mum and Dad have decided to put it in Fernando's name because he is my husband. It's as if they have a better opinion of him than they do of me; he has nearly finished university and is a civil engineer. They seem to like him, but with me it's all different. I'm suddenly worth nothing; they probably think I seduced him. It's like I was a sinner, a whore."

"Please, Teresa, don't talk like that. You're going to make me cry."

I couldn't tell Teresa how Mum and Dad had both said on numerous occasions that she was a whore but that they had to help her because it was their duty as parents. It was as if they had to make sure that in front of people, they showed that they were good parents and Teresa was the bad daughter. I couldn't imagine Mum not loving Teresa, but she was making a great effort to show her depression as a measure of how much she loved Teresa rather than physically loving her. There was no real affection for her that I could appreciate. María loved Teresa, as did the rest of us. I was feeling torn by Teresa's suffering.

Teresa finally had her beautiful twins, a boy and a girl, during the month of May. She spent two weeks in Seville but finally returned home with Juan and Lucia. They were gorgeous. Teresa had stopped her studies and was looking after the babies the best she could, but the experience was overwhelming. The house was noisy but full of life. Mum made sure the babies had anything they needed, but she never looked after either of them directly, telling everyone else what ought to be done instead.

Miss Spencer had taken a job teaching in a primary school but was still living with us and trying to work extra hours in our house to pay for her mortgage. She had finally bought herself a flat in Seville, thinking that she would like to live there when we all moved to El Cortijo. Teresa didn't have enough hands to attend the babies and was soon exhausted. Miss Spencer could only help her sometimes, and it was obviously not enough. On occasions, Teresa was feeling resentful or slightly rejected, as if she were deliberately left to struggle. Mum just continued making everyone see that if anyone was taking the day-to-day care of those children, it was she. She was trying to trigger pity and admiration for herself.

Teresa and the twins finally went to live with Fernando in July. Fernando was still unemployed, but Grandmother had allowed them to borrow one of her houses in the north of Spain until they were in a better position to rent a property.

"Teresa, good luck. I hope everything goes well for you in Oviedo. I know you're going to be really busy." I managed to hold in my anguish, knowing that our relationship was probably going to be very different from now on. I felt I was losing my sister.

"Yes, I will, and it will be difficult to be away from everyone I know," Teresa said as she was going around kissing everybody goodbye at the airport.

"I bought you this soft doll with all my saved money. I will be thinking of you," I said to Teresa, handing her my gift.

"Isa, this is really expensive. You shouldn't have done it," Teresa said, kissing my cheek.

Teresa and her family finally departed.

Chapter Twenty-Two

THE VOYAGE

After many discussions and enquiries, Alex had agreed to go the university at the same time as joining the seminary. Mum and Dad were worried that if for any reason Alex changed his mind, he would end up stranded and not able to get a proper job; it made sense. After all, Alex was only eighteen and was choosing a very difficult path, which was fine if you had the full commitment for it and was what you really wanted in life, but it had its risks if you had no alternative route to follow if it did not work out. Alex was quite reluctant and the only thing in his mind was helping the poor; he found it difficult to envisage that his life could ever take an alternative path. It was hard to approach Alex at all; he was almost monopolised by Mum and Dad. I didn't really know what made him change his opinion from a career in the navy to becoming a priest – or even when he started thinking about it. I wondered if the chaos we had in the family lately had anything to do with it, but I wasn't sure.

Mum was encouraging Dad to go sailing this summer holiday in Laredo. Dad had taken it literally and although I don't think Mum had meant taking the *Kingdom of Castile* to the north of Spain, this was exactly what he was intending to do. Dad had been very stressed out and upset lately; he never mentioned Teresa and any news came through Mum.

"Roberto, there are not enough days in your holiday to take the boat north and bring it back. Why don't we just rent a sailing boat for two weeks when we're over there? It would be easier and cheaper," Mum argued, trying to convince Dad.

"Um, I hadn't thought about the number of days I needed for each voyage. It has been decided. I will take the boat by lorry across Spain and I will sail back with it!" Dad said with his eyes wide open and an expression of happiness that Mum could not resist.

"God help us, but if that is what you prefer, so be it. It is a dangerous journey and the sea starts getting rough towards the end of the summer. Please choose a competent crew. I won't allow you to just take Alex," Mum said, trying to make Dad plan ahead.

"What about Alex and Jaime?"

"Dad, Jaime's doing his military service this summer," I reminded him. "I'll help Mum bring the car to Cádiz with all of the luggage," I rapidly volunteered, making myself needed. I thought the whole idea of sailing the boat all the way to the south of Spain was absolutely dangerous and terrifying, as I knew very well that Dad was hardly going to make any stops and would sail through all weather conditions.

"Why don't you ask your two brothers? They both like sailing and may enjoy the experience. You need a minimum of four to take turns at night." Mum continued to plan for Dad, surely knowing that he would sail through the nights too, but Dad wasn't listening. His mind was somewhere else.

"Why don't you come with us, Graciela?" Dad suddenly said.

"Roberto, I am exhausted and have had enough this year. The last thing I want is to join you for that trip, hardly sleeping for days, getting wet and taking days to arrive. I have to close the house in Laredo and travel back with the rest of the family. I can't just drop everything to be with you," Mum replied, almost annoyed.

I thought the plan was dodgy. Dad had never got along with his brothers, and the three of them were equally socially shy and similar in many ways, although Dad's blind temper was the worst. One thing I was sure of was that my uncles were not competitive at all, and as far as I could see, their idea of sailing was making short trips in good weather, having picnics and swimming in different coves. It was very much about finding beautiful spots or sailing to nice places to enjoy nature. They owned a boat together. Dad, being the oldest of the three, was always bossy, not listening to them and trying to tell them what to do all the time. I could not imagine the three of them together for too long. I really didn't understand how Mum couldn't see this.

"Alex, would you like to sail the boat back from Laredo with Dad?" I asked Alex, who had been listening but not saying a word. The fact was that we were never asked about anything. We were told to do things instead.

"I would love to do it, especially before joining the seminary. One of the things I'm going to miss is sailing and this will bring me very happy memories," Alex answered with a tone of sadness in his voice.

Beatriz and I had returned from Dublin, and we were both enjoying the sunny weather in August and the good home food in the north of Spain. Heloise had behaved decently this year and she had been quite amenable and approachable. Maybe she felt slightly guilty about how she'd treated me the previous year. I never said anything to anyone and acted as if I were above her, not getting upset by anything, just being my own person. I rather felt that maybe this attitude bought back her respect, as she wasn't expecting it.

Beatriz's behaviour in Dublin was rather strange, though. It was the first time she had been away from home and although she was looking forward to it, everything changed soon after arrival. Beatriz struggled to fit in and was incredibly unsure about everything, wanting me to decide everything for her. It was as if she couldn't trust Mr and Mrs Murphy, excluding herself and disappearing all the time. There were days after school when Beatriz would just simply go out without saying anything to anyone, returning home well after dinner. I didn't know where she was and Mrs Murphy was not impressed. But Beatriz would not listen to anyone else, even me. The fact that she did not understand the routine of the family and the language made her suspicious about everything and everyone, making her feel rejected when there was no such rejection. She was incredibly insecure. My time with her in Dublin was stressful because of this and I was glad to be back in Spain. Beatriz had refused to go back to Ireland again and I had tried to explain the reasons to Mum, but Mum thought it was just immaturity.

It was nice to see Teresa and the twins again during the summer holiday. She was looking tired and had lost weight, but the twins were growing fast and were looking great. Fernando was struggling to find a proper job and was helping out with small projects, so their financial situation was still precarious. It seemed to me that Fernando was living as if they didn't have any money worries and with illusions of grandeur. He had even bought himself a brand-new car despite having little money. Teresa, on the other hand, was trying to economise as much as possible with her and the children. It was obvious that she was wearing old clothes and that she had not been to the hairdresser for a while.

Fernando was not much help with the children or with anything related with the house. Teresa did not have a happy marriage and I thought that she would have hoped that despite living not too far from Laredo, Mum would have gone to visit her during the holidays, but Mum's priority was always being with Dad. Mum never looked after the twins to give Teresa a break unless Miss Spencer or some other maid was physically looking after them. In my mother's eyes, others had to carry their own crosses. Her duty was to dedicate her full attention to Dad, hoping that everyone would appreciate how difficult she thought her life was and what a faithful and devoted wife she also was.

Dad had the *Kingdom of Castile* moored in Laredo's yacht club and sailing was an almost daily activity. Mum and Alex always went with Dad, and Alex was doing extra windsurfing whenever possible. However, there were not enough regattas available for Dad and they all were short distances. He was used to high-intensity sailing, and sailing just for pleasure, although initially appealing, had a limited attraction for him.

"Children, I insist that one of you should be able to swim across the bay in Laredo. This is something I did twice when I was young and I also swam across Cádiz's and Santander's Bays." Dad always repeated his achievement year after year, hoping that one of us would finally agree to do it. He had already grilled Alex and me about it and was starting to pressure Beatriz instead.

"Beatriz, I am not taking any more nos for an answer," Dad told Beatriz with a stern tone. "I have been waiting long enough. I'll arrange it this week, when the tide is ideal, and drop you by the lighthouse. You just need to swim to the harbour."

Beatriz opened her eyes wide and looked at him, not saying anything, likely trying to guess if he was serious about it and really meant it.

"I am not swimming anywhere, Dad. I don't want to do it," Beatriz said, not hesitating in her answer. "You can't force me."

"Oh, why not? I'm your father and this is my house; I pay for your food and clothes. I deserve your respect and I am the one who says what you should or shouldn't do. Do you understand? You are nobody in this house," Dad added, probably feeling offended and launching one of his usual attacks to repress people by abusing his authority.

"I won't do it. Take it any way you like it," Beatriz reiterated.

"You are going to do it because it is what I want ..."

"Dad, there's no need to get angry," I interrupted. "You know how much I enjoy swimming. I have always said no because I never felt ready for it, but I would like to do it. I think I could do the whole stretch without stopping once. What is the width of the bay, Dad?" I asked, trying to sound positive and make him interested in my point of view.

"It's about five kilometres, depending on the tides. It is actually very safe if you choose the right moment, Isabel, because the current won't sweep you away. It will push you towards the beach instead. Are you sure about this?" His anger was diffusing and his body language was becoming calmer.

"Yes, Dad. You know I can do it. I probably could have done it a couple of years ago, but I wasn't sure. I've been swimming one kilometre in training nearly every day, for several years now. When can it be organised?" I asked, thinking ahead.

"We need to time the tide from low to full, and if my calculations are correct, that will happen in the middle of next week between noon and six at night. It will be the perfect time to do it. I will accompany you from behind in a small boat. I can't use the *Kingdom of Castile* because I will easily overtake you with the engine on. It's better if I hire a small rowing boat from one of the fishermen in the harbour. Just give me a couple of days to organise it and we will plan it for Wednesday of next week."

Dad left the sitting room before I could say anything else, and Alex, Beatriz and I looked at each other without saying anything.

"If I ever have a family, I will make sure that everyone feels that the house and everything in it belongs to everyone – that no one is in possession of anything or anyone," I finally said, breaking the silence.

The fact was that Dad wasn't sure who or how to approach any of the fishermen in the village. He thought that by stating his surname, rank and title, people were going to immediately comply with his wishes. He didn't know how much to pay or how to negotiate a fee for it either. Therefore, Mum had to intervene to arrange the deal, always making sure that it looked like Dad was the one in charge.

Gonzalo, my cousin who was four years younger than I was, got excited when he heard the news. My father was so pleased that he had been mentioning it to any relatives or family friends that he had met in the street; there was general anticipation in the family. Gonzalo had been swimming regularly for several years now as well, almost every day and therefore he had managed to avoid surgery on his back. He was always curious to compare how much I was able to swim and for how long I could do it; it felt as if he knew he was not alone and that gave him reassurance. I wasn't sure if he felt admiration for me. I was never interested in timing myself; I just swam. The few people who ever saw me commented on how I could slide forward in the water making significant progression with each stroke. I was able to move big volumes of water. Any comparison with my cousin was not relevant because I always swam in the sea and he did it in swimming pools.

Mum had arranged for one of the fishermen to take us in his rowing boat and Gonzalo chose to accompany us on the adventure. On the way to the lighthouse, we passed close to a couple of large fishing boats and the crews greeted us, enquiring where we were heading. They were tidying their fishing nets before coming into the harbour. I looked straight at the lighthouse, enjoying the view and soaking all my senses with the feeling of the breeze, the taste of the salty water on my lips, the gentle sound of the water around us and the movement of the boat underneath my feet. My cousin kept the conversation going with my father while Manuel, the fisherman, kept rowing.

"Uncle Roberto, I'd like to swim next to Isa. May I jump in the water too?" Gonzalo asked as soon as we got close to the steps leading up to the lighthouse.

Dad did not seem to know what to say for a few seconds. "Yes, of course. You can do it together if you wish." He was plainly surprised to have such a forthcoming volunteer.

"Isa, do you mind if I swim with you?" Gonzalo asked me too.

"I don't mind at all, Gonzalo. It's better if you set the rhythm and I will follow your pace. It's very brave of you swimming with me, but if you get tired, let us know," I said, passing him a pair of googles and having a last look of the stunning view before I got into the water. There were natural caves by the edge of the mountain, making interesting passages in and out of the rock and helping the water flow around. The sound of the sea inside the caves was hypnotic and the place was deserted, with just a curious group of seagulls coming to greet us, flying around the boat.

I realised that my cousin's pace was rather slow as soon as we started swimming.

"Isa!" he exclaimed. "We can't even see the harbour from here. This is really far away!"

The lighthouse was round the mountain of Santoña, close to the open ocean, and it was impossible to visualise it from the beach. I knew that we had to swim about four hundred metres around the mountain, before we could attempt the crossing in a straight line. I soon started to overtake Gonzalo, as he was clearly not able to keep up the pace.

"Isabel," he said once we got the first view of the harbour in the distance, "I'm coming back inside the boat. I can't really do this. I need to learn how to swim in the sea. The water is too choppy for me and I can't breathe regularly. I'm swallowing water most of the time." Gonzalo made a signal to my father who helped him inside the boat.

"You're a very good swimmer, Gonzalo. One day soon, you will be able to do it." I put my googles back on and never stopped swimming again until we got to the harbour and my father asked me to stop.

I lost track of time. My body heated up with the physical exertion and therefore did not feel the cold. I unexpectedly swam through a bank of seaweed and I really had to control myself to remain calm. The light touch of it, especially over my head, stroking the back and sides of my body or dangling from any of my extremities was incredibly unpleasant. I felt like screaming. The seaweed then felt like sandpaper on my skin, with occasional electric shocks. I swam even faster, with the hope of getting through it as soon as possible. I blocked my mind, not allowing myself to feel anything or to overreact. I was determined to reach the harbour. I was on a mission! Nearby fish occasionally slipped away from my legs. I knew that this time of year, people could see dolphins, whales and small sharks just outside the Bay of Biscay. I prayed to God that the adventure would be finished as soon as possible.

It took me two hours total, including the time I spent with Gonzalo, and Dad was very proud indeed. He told relatives and friends about the achievement and people were amazed and impressed by it. I was just happy to have finished with the constant threat that had been hanging over us for years. It wasn't a goal that I would have ever chosen to do otherwise; I really could not see the point of it and felt that it was dangerous, but whatever fear I felt, I kept it to myself.

The summer holidays had ended. Dad had departed, sailing towards Cádiz two weeks earlier with Alex and his two brothers. Mum had driven the rest of the family and Miss Spencer back to Cádiz. It was difficult to say goodbye to Teresa once again and it was becoming obvious to me that her marriage was unsuccessful.

Dad had only got as far as Finisterre in the north-west of Spain when the weather turned for the worst. They encountered gales and stormy weather, but Dad did not want to stop. Uncles Alberto and Mario had an argument with Dad and both disembarked in Galicia, returning to Madrid by train. But Dad was determined to continue his adventure and hired a temporary sailor from the navy to accompany him and Alex. They suffered strong winds, lightning, thunder and heavy rain in the sea; still Dad would not moor anywhere. Mum was agitated and anxious, waiting for Dad's journey to finish, somehow expecting the worst; she made the decision to sell the boat as soon as Dad arrived in Cádiz.

Weather conditions improved slightly after Dad passed beyond Lisbon. He encountered days of fog, but luckily he did not end up in an accident this time. Alex and Dad finally arrived in Cádiz safely and as soon as Alex left the family to join the seminary, the *Kingdom of Castile* was sold.

PART III
ISABEL

Chapter Twenty-Three

BECOMING POPULAR

Changing to a co-educational school was a big deal after thirteen years in an all-girls school. The nuns had been getting on my nerves lately, forbidding us to do anything and everything with their rules and sense of guilt, so I was almost looking forward to the change. It was amazing how many little things one could take for granted but you only realised that they were missing when you didn't have them anymore. Walking into a building where I didn't know where anything was reminded me very much of my first day at school when I was only four. I could only recognise the main door; from then onwards, everything was alien to me. Not knowing who was who and the roles people had in the school, especially adults, was incredibly disconcerting. It was impossible to work out which year students were in and nobody wore a uniform. Even the priests were wearing normal clothes, although the older ones had clerical collars that at least gave me a clue as to who they were. I didn't know where my classroom was and I had never had male teachers before; everything felt very strange.

I had opted for pure scientific subjects for the International Baccalaureate, which were indeed the more difficult ones, including maths, physics, chemistry, biology, Spanish, English and philosophy. I generally felt very alert, trying to work out how things functioned around me and what was expected of me, trying also to decipher the dynamics of my tutor group. It initially worried me that I might not have a good enough academic level in this particular school because it was considered to be the best for preparing you for university in Cádiz. But soon I realised that the others didn't know as much as I did, and I was almost surprised to find out that they still had not covered some of the academic material that I had already gone through. Everything except philosophy, which I had never studied or read about before, was a repetition of what I had already studied at school. So things were pretty easy for me!

Teachers isolated me during tests and students clearly considered me some kind of genius. I really didn't know how best to handle the attention. There was another girl from my old school in my tutor group, but despite having covered the same academic material that I had, she didn't seem to remember things well and was only average in the group. I couldn't understand why.

My chemistry teacher was particularly delighted with my raising the level of the questions in each test with a section of university level questions that seemed designed to challenge the limit of my knowledge. I couldn't explain my clarity of mind for it. I just seemed to remember everything I had gone through at school in great detail. What limited my chemistry knowledge was not being able to reach the type of mathematical calculations that were used at university, but not the chemical concepts such as those related to atoms and electrical distribution of particles releasing energy.

People's admiration was something I had never encountered before – or at least noticed.

"Isabel, do you study at home? What I mean is, how many hours do you spend doing work at home?" one of my fellow students asked me one day.

"About five to six hours a day. I've done this for years. My routine does not change," I answered in an honest way.

"But you seem to know everything!"

"I have so much information in my head that I need to structure it, like creating a skeleton, where the information provides the flesh. That's all I do. I need to see the structure of what I know and what is already in my head; otherwise, I can't deliver it." As I tried to explain it to him, he looked totally disbelieving.

"I really don't understand what you're saying, but at least you're not denying that you actually do study a lot," he finally said. "By the way, we're organising groups to do revision together for the end-of- year exams before the national tests for university. Would you like to join us? It would be extremely valuable to have you in the groups," he added hopefully.

"Yes. Just let me know when and where. I would like to join the groups," I said with a big smile, thinking that it was probably going to be better joining other students than spending time alone revising, although I also knew it was going to slow me down.

Since Teresa left, I had been allowed to move into her bedroom. I had never had a bedroom to myself before. Beatriz and Elena were still sharing despite Alex and Jaime's room being empty. The real advantage for me with this change was having a desk of my own with all my books and my own space to study. I was glad not to have to use Dad's study anymore and not to have to listen to them having sex nearby. It was stressful, feeling trapped every time that it happened, without being able to leave the room in time. I could still hear them from Teresa's bedroom across the corridor, but the sounds were more muffled and distant and therefore more bearable. Mum and Dad always chose the time when everyone else was having dinner and watching telly before going to bed; my dinnertime varied according to the amount of work I had to do, so I rarely had dinner at the same time as everyone else.

Ana and Emilia had left two years ago and a great many things had happened, but I never felt any lack of friendship at all. The significant void was the huge gap left by Teresa's departure. I had no direct communication with her and the fear of having to face my day-to-day life without her reference or help left an empty feeling inside of me. During all this time, I had occasionally been going out with the group of boys that I used to know when my friends were here, but only when I felt as if I had to. I had also occasionally asked girls in my class if I could join them, but it had been more my asking them than them calling me to go out; and again, I had kept changing the groups of girls to go with.

I knew of Ana via Mum, but I was not in contact with her either. It seemed that I had been invited to go to Washington during the summer holidays to spend the month of July with Ana's family. I was quite looking forward to it! But since I had been in the new school, I had been busy revising and trying to work out how best to fit in.

I was going out every weekend with groups of girls and boys. There were discos once a month to raise money for the final year school trip to Mallorca, and it was convenient to do so, as it was a good place to get to know many people at once. It was good fun because I was able to be spontaneous with the rest of the students. I felt that people accepted and liked me; the fact that I had such good grades and was also involved in sports, parties and going out with everyone made me popular.

Everyone was anxious to make sure my marks stayed high, especially in chemistry, where the teacher had set up a personal challenge, hoping to find the limits of my knowledge. Every time we got the test results, my friends were all waiting to find out if I had managed to defeat the teacher's hopes. But I also laughed with them, danced or even drank small amounts of alcohol at times. I seemed invincible, but nobody realised the internal effort and improvisation according to rational thinking that I had to apply in order to maintain this degree of social awareness.

"Isa, how come you have never had a boyfriend?" Gloria, one of the girls in the non-science tutor group, suddenly asked me. "You are really admired and there are few people like you. You are incredibly intelligent, open and fun to be with. People like you a lot because you are also humble. You are good at sports and are taking part in everything. You are amazing and could have anyone you like because on top of everything, you are also good-looking. How come this has never happened?"

Obviously, Gloria was under the influence of a few drinks, as the party had been going on for a while, but she sounded serious as she said all these things about me.

"I never saw myself as you're describing me, Gloria, but thank you very much. I suppose I have never stopped to think about it and have never felt any need or attraction for anyone in particular. I am quite happy being friendly with everyone," I replied honestly.

"But don't you feel the need to share your thoughts and feelings with a particular person, even being able to feel special and intimate with that person?" Gloria insisted.

"I suppose that it will come with time, I am not actively seeking it as such. I need a university degree and a job with a regular salary; I am so focused on this target that anything else would interfere at the moment."

"But haven't you realised that there are some boys interested in you?" Gloria continued, getting more to the point of the conversation.

"In me? Who? Nobody has ever approached me," I answered with curiosity.

"You seem so comfortable and confident that boys don't know how to come close to you. Haven't you noticed Nacho? He is always hovering around you and doesn't allow the other boys to talk to you for too long. He always knows where you are and what you're doing. He is waiting for a signal from you to take a step forward."

"A signal? What signal?" I asked in amazement.

"Isabel, please. To let him know without telling him if you could be interested in him."

"I suppose he is nice, but what I am going to do talking to him all the time? I'd like to move around and talk to everyone," I replied.

"You are quite unique, you know? I'm only asking you to watch for Nacho. Maybe now that I've told you, you might start looking at him in a different way. He really cares for you and he is a nice person too," Gloria said, leaving her drink on the table and walking to the dance floor. "Let's dance. This is my favourite song."

Gloria's words played in my mind for the rest of the night. I had never thought of dating anyone; it wasn't something that was in my plans. My clear objective had always been to get qualified and be independent, earning a regular salary; once this was achieved, I could think of finding a partner or having a family. How could I give a person my full attention when my mind was somewhere else? But thinking about it, almost everyone already had a girlfriend or boyfriend and it seemed that you automatically fit in at any celebration if you arrived as a couple, especially at the discos. I didn't like the idea of letting somebody look after me, as that was my impression about my fellow girlfriends having boyfriends. Some of them behaved like fragile porcelain, with the boys by their sides for physical and moral support. Some girls were even asking permission of their boyfriends before doing anything, as if they had to get a special blessing from them. I was not sure I could behave like this; I wouldn't last a week if this was supposed to be having a boyfriend. I continued thinking while dancing.

Nacho was a nice guy and a friend, but so were so many others in the year. It was true that he was quite attentive to me. Since Gloria and I talked at the last party, he had been more charming than ever and I was more aware of him. Every time the group met in the city centre, Nacho was not too far from me, and the fact that I was allowing that was probably giving him some kind of signal, as Gloria said. The whole thing was making me anxious because I could foresee Nacho closing the distance until he wouldn't ever move from my side, unless I actually asked him to. I would have to ask him to stay away and to be more normal with me. This feeling was terrible because there was no way out; either he would eventually ask me out or I would have to tell him to give me some space, but both ways were uncomfortable situations. I was under terrible pressure.

"Isabel, will you be going to the next party at school?" Nacho asked me when we were all sitting outside the bar by the harbour.

"You know I always go. Why are you asking?"

"I'm only asking because Gloria isn't going," Nacho replied, clearly trying to be casual about it.

"I don't normally go just with Gloria. I go with whichever group of girls is going and we will all meet up at the party later on with you guys. That's how it's always done," I answered, fixing my eyes on his black eyes.

"Have you thought what to study at university yet? Will you be staying or going away to Madrid or Barcelona?" he asked me with great interest, holding his empty glass of beer between his two hands.

"I'm thinking of studying mechanical engineering. I'd like to specialise in the oil industry so I can design and dig oil wells all over the world. I would like to travel and move around." This was the first time I had ever spoken about what my plans for my future were.

"I see. What's so interesting about travelling?" Nacho asked me.

"I really like to see how people behave in different countries. We are all the same deep down but somehow we think we are different. I like appreciating how cultures are marked by their own environment, what constitutes normal behaviour in a particular place and what makes it inappropriate in a different one. I would like to appreciate the goodness of everyone around the world; I believe that will make me a more rounded and better person." I paused, staring at him. "My family is moving to live in Seville next September anyway."

"You will need to go to Madrid to study mechanical engineering, you know."

"Yes, I know. I don't think my parents will object. What are you planning to do next year?" I asked him with curiosity.

"I am definitely going to Madrid too, to study law and economics. My parents will give me a loan for the accommodation and I will have to work during holidays and weekends to save some money, but I am definitely going provided I get the marks I need," he explained, waiting for my reaction. "I suppose you don't need to worry about marks. Any university will be happy to have you. It's a nice position to be in."

"I'm not complaining. The reason I get good marks is because I seem to remember everything that has been taught at school in great detail, and as it happens, I have already covered everything we are studying this year in my last school." I smiled, trying to play down my ability to remember things.

"I think there's more to it than just that. You are also able to analyse things in a different way to other people."

We both stopped talking for a while, observing what a group of people were doing just in front of us at the door of the bar. There seemed to be a dispute about an opinion and they were raising their voices, getting carried away with the argument.

The evening was warm and looking ahead over the sea, you could clearly appreciate the bright stars and the moon on the horizon. There was a feeling of calmness in the environment, despite the argument.

"Isa, I really fancy you and would like to go out with you," Nacho suddenly said, pausing for a brief second. "I think you are aware of it." He stopped for a second time. "I know I will have to work hard to deserve you because there is something special about you which is very different from the other girls. I will take this challenge if you allow me to do so," Nacho finally finished saying as we both looked at the horizon.

I hesitated for a few seconds, as this conversation, although foreseen, was unexpected today. My heart started racing, and I was thinking that maybe by being honest, I could end up losing a friend, but I didn't have any other way of dealing with the situation.

"Nacho, I enjoy your company and I don't dislike you, but I would be lying if I said that I am in love with you. There is so much that I would like to do before committing myself to any relationship and I need to do and undo as I wish. Therefore, I need my own space too. I'm prepared to see how it goes and give it a go, but it feels too soon for me, so please don't expect anything adventurous with me, because I'm not ready for it. I don't see myself as being as special as you see me," I said, looking straight into his eyes.

"Really? I do understand and what you're saying is good enough for me. I am so happy!" Nacho smiled and blushed, showing all his perfect white teeth. He covered his face with his hands in disbelief and his curly black hair fell over the edge of his fingers. The whole situation was making me smile too. "Can I walk you home today and every day we go out from now on?"

"I normally go home on by my own, but I suppose it will be nicer if you accompany me," I said with some embarrassment. "Talking about which, it's getting late and it's time for me to go home now. Do you mind if we leave?"

Going out with Nacho gave a new dimension to my life. We were still very much with a large group of people, but it was nice to have that extra attention from someone; it was something that I had never experienced before. It was comforting knowing that Nacho was there for me and he certainly knew how to give me as much space as I needed.

Joy and happiness gradually grew within me, in a way that I had never felt before. Nacho was making me feel secure about myself and I was feeling more spontaneous among my peers.

"Would you like to dance with me to this song?" Nacho asked me one night.

"Don't be daft; you know I never dance slow songs with anyone," I replied in a dismissive way, probably sensing what was going to happen.

"Come on – don't be shy," he said, pulling my arm.

I could feel my own embarrassment and my heart beating fast inside my chest. I had never been so close to Nacho before and I didn't really know how to dance with him. He didn't say a word but just held both my arms, placing them around his neck and supported me by my waist. The music started and he gently moved from side to side, following the beat of the music, forcing my body to accompany him. It was rather easy and gradually I began to relax as the music went on, neither of us saying anything.

The song finished but Nacho didn't let go of my waist, waiting for the next one to begin. I could feel his desire to embrace me and I was feeling very unsure about myself. I had never been in a situation like this before, but before I could react to it, his hands moved towards the middle of my back, holding me tight in a big hug and dancing to the rhythm of the second song that had already started. His chin was resting over my right shoulder and our cheeks came in contact while both hearts faced each other, chest to chest together. My body gradually responded to the sustained comforting pressure of Nacho embracing me. I finally let go and became soothed by the experience, but I couldn't help feeling butterflies all in my stomach. I couldn't actually remember the last time anyone had ever hugged me in a meaningful way and I was feeling overwhelmed by it. My senses became very aware of Nacho's presence; I could smell his body, feel his curls brushing my face, his breathing around my neck and each of his ten fingers feeling the skin of my back. Nacho had me firmly trapped close to him and I honestly didn't wish to move either.

"The song is over, Nacho," I said when the music stopped, but he still wasn't moving. "I think I need a drink."

Nacho moved away, took my hand and we walked towards our table where the drinks were.

The party was over and since the slow dancing ended, I had spent most of the time talking to some of the girls. I felt nervous being alone with Nacho. I was trying to be as casual as possible, but my heart was still beating fast. I needed to think about what had just happened and why I was feeling so unsettled; I couldn't wait to go home.

"It was a good party," Nacho said as we walked home together. "I like dancing with you, Isa."

"Yes, it was nice, and it wasn't very difficult after all," I timidly replied, remembering him so physically close to me.

"From now on, I will ask you to dance at every party. I wouldn't miss it for anything in the world," Nacho said, reaching for my hand, his fingers between mine.

We were nearly at my door, but I couldn't find any more words to say. His hand felt very solid in mine. We walked in silence.

"Here we are," I said, letting his hand go. "I'll see you on Monday in class."

"Wait!" Nacho interrupted me as I was about to turn to go up the steps towards the entrance. "I would like to kiss you, Isa. May I?"

I immediately blushed and struggled to control my shaking. I didn't feel ready at all for this, although I supposed that when something like this happened, it was without much warning. I couldn't speak and I didn't know the right thing to do. Before I realised it, Nacho had taken a step forward and was holding me tightly in his arms once again.

"Isa, you need to trust me," he whispered in my ear, spending what seemed a long time holding me in a hug. "Stop shaking and relax. I love you so much."

My heart was beating out of control and I couldn't figure out how to calm it down; the expectation was too much. Nacho moved his head from my shoulder and found my lips, which he gently kissed. He held my face between his hands and smiled at me, almost leaning his nose on mine. "You are so beautiful! I am the luckiest man on earth."

And without waiting for any reaction, he went on to kiss me again, and this time the wetness of our lips made me open mine. I started kissing his lips too. I felt a tremendous urge to respond and my hands started moving and sliding across his back, feeling his body against mine with tenderness. His tongue finally made contact with mine and we embraced in a prolonged and deep kiss.

"Good night, Nacho," I said when we came apart, turning around and getting into the lift.

Full of excitement, I couldn't sleep that night. I couldn't quite believe what had just happened. I was still able to feel Nacho's closeness and his presence with me; I could vividly remember his smell and his kissing. I couldn't describe what I was feeling. I was confused and feeling overwhelmed.

Chapter Twenty-Four

ANA

I had never travelled out of Europe before and I was worried about changing planes at JFK in New York to get to Washington, DC, on my way to visit Ana. It was a thrilling experience visiting the United States and seeing Ana again after such a long time. Ana's parents had arranged for me to attend the summer school English lessons where Ana normally went to school.

My family had just moved to Seville and I was starting mechanical engineering studies at the Complutense University of Madrid in September. I had been awarded the best student of the year trophy at school, with top marks in everything and I had made many friends at school. It was sad that all of us were going in different directions after school, doing different things and I knew it was impossible to keep in contact with everyone. Nacho had been admitted to read law and economics in Madrid, but at the Autónoma University. It was nice to know that at least someone familiar was going to be in Madrid, but I had mixed feeling about the whole experience. I was going to miss Beatriz and Elena in particular, and I still wasn't sure about having a serious relationship with Nacho. I was feeling anxious about finding my way at university and being able to respond to the challenge, but I supposed all this was normal.

In the meantime, Teresa's marriage had failed and she was separated from Fernando. Teresa had moved back to Cádiz now that the flat had been left empty. Miss Spencer was no longer living with us and had managed to find a job as a teacher in a primary school in Seville. She was in regular contact with us, though. I felt sorry for my two younger sisters without Miss Spencer and with everyone else living away from home. Mum continued to be devoted to Dad, and probably Beatriz and Elena were going to find it hard living in the countryside. María was already expecting her first baby, Jaime was still at university living with Grandmother and Alex was in the seminary.

∽

"Hello Isa! How nice to see you again!" Ana said, running to greet me and hug me as soon as she saw me in the airport. "Did you have any problems changing planes in New York? Let me carry your suitcase for you."

Ana immediately took the luggage for me.

"I had a great trip. I was worried about the transit in New York, but it was easy and there was no delay. The plane to Washington was half empty," I said as we walked towards Ana's mum, who was waiting just a few steps behind Ana. "Hello, Mrs Benavente. It's nice to see you. Thank you for inviting me."

"Hello, Isa. Please call me Nuria. You are a real woman now. Look at you. You are so beautiful," Mrs Benavente said joyfully.

"Thank you, Nuria," I said with some difficulty. "Ana has also changed for the better, if that is at all possible."

Ana was a stunning girl: tall, slim, with long black hair and the most beautiful piercing blue eyes that I had ever seen.

"We have to show you everything," Mrs Benavente said. "We live outside Washington, DC, in a residential area in Maryland. We will come and visit Washington while you're here. You will see the Potomac River on our way home. It will take us about forty-five minutes to drive there. Everything is very spacious in this country; even the cars are too large for my liking and most of them are automatic."

"Mum, don't interfere. Let me talk to her, I haven't seen her for a long time," Ana protested.

Ana wanted to know everything that had happened these past two years – all the news and all the gossip. She was gesticulating as she talked and was in a euphoric state of excitement. From my point of view, my life in Spain was trivial and it was more the other way round. Her life in America was the novelty. I guessed that Ana had been missing Spain.

"How's your English, Ana?" I asked with curiosity.

"Oh, Isa. The first year here was terrible. I couldn't understand anything and couldn't communicate either. They thought I was stupid. It was very stressful. But now I understand and it's much easier."

The journey home continued with an exchange of news. Mrs Benavente was also asking questions and joining in the conversation, and they were both taking turns questioning me. I noticed that Ana deliberately avoided any questions about boys and I didn't ask her anything either. It was probably wiser to talk in private about this later on.

Ana's house was large, as you would expect in the United States. Everything seemed to be spacious and built in generous proportions, the gardens well looked after and wide streets in good condition. Overall, I was missing brick buildings and character in the town. Things were almost too new and prefabricated for my liking, but I couldn't say they were ugly. Ana's younger brother, Miguel, greeted me on arrival and so did Carlos Benavente, Ana's Dad.

"Hello, Isabel. It's so nice to see you. How's your father and your mum?" he asked in a most formal tone.

"They are both well and send their regards. Thank you for having me here. I was looking forward to coming and seeing Ana again in particular. My parents have moved to live in

Seville now and Dad has retired from the navy," I told Mr Benavente.

"So I hear," Mr Benavente replied. "They're in El Cortijo, aren't they? It's a beautiful place. Well, say hello to them from me next time you talk on the phone."

"I will, Mr Benavente."

"And please call me Carlos. You are one more member of the family," he told me, turning around and walking into the sitting room.

Everything was pleasant at Ana's house. We hardly saw her Dad, as he was always at work. I shared a room with Ana and my English lessons started two days after my arrival. Ana was doing extra maths, although she didn't need to as she had been accepted at Maryland University to study maths and computer programming.

I couldn't believe my bad luck. I had chosen English to improve my language, but the course was about English literature, so I needed to read again, but this time it was *Julius Caesar*, by Shakespeare. However, this course was deeper than the one I had done in Ireland and more like the comprehensions I used to do with Mrs López in my old school. I wasn't very impressed with the general knowledge of the students in my class and I was asked several times where Spain was and even if it was a state of Argentina. My teacher asked the students about the difference between 'connotations' and 'denotations', and I was the only one who knew the difference.

Time went by quickly. We'd go to the local swimming pool every afternoon after lessons and meet with some other Spanish families also living in the area, working for the Spanish government. Ana and I also rode bicycles around the residential area and there was very little sense of being in a busy town.

Mrs Benavente occasionally took us to the local shopping mall and she also took us to Washington, DC, to visit the Capitol, the obelisk and the National Mall, the Lincoln Memorial, the White House, Arlington National Cemetery and Georgetown. The list was immense but not only that – Mr and Mrs Benavente also had a week's holiday before I had to return to Spain and they drove us to Baltimore, where we were allowed in the US Naval Academy in Annapolis as guests. The family also drove via Virginia to Ocean City after Baltimore for a few days to visit a summer beach resort. The landscape and scenery were beautiful. Driving towards Ocean City, I was able to see lagoons and lakes of different sizes, and we drove over large bridges, longer than I had ever seen before, some of them so long that the first half was in a tunnel underwater and the second half was over the water. It was simply amazing to appreciate the advanced engineering work that this country had in place. Mr and Mrs Benavente were indeed generous with me and I was grateful for it. It was a unique experience.

"Isabel!" Mr Benavente suddenly said, catching my attention. "I had a call from the school in Maryland. They are impressed with your work and are asking if you are at all interested in pursuing your studies in the States. They'd have to do some tests to confirm any place in any college or university, but the offer is there. It would be for the following academic year, as September is already full and round the corner. It also depends on what you would like to study."

I wasn't expecting anything like this in the slightest; this news was a big surprise for me.

"But how it this possible? No one has ever mentioned anything to me at school. I'd like to discuss it with my parents," I said, feeling uncertain about the whole thing.

"You may have to prolong your time with us until you have finished the tests at least," Mr Benavente said to me. "But don't worry – that is not a problem for us at all."

"But my English is not that strong, although I get by, and I haven't revised anything for at least six weeks." I started worrying.

"They have obviously seen something in you. I don't think you need to revise. They just want to assess your knowledge as it is."

"Oh my God. Will Isa really be able to stay with us?" Ana joined in with great surprise.

"If there is a possibility of anything happening, it will be for next year. Isa will have accommodation in whichever university she accepts, but unfortunately we will be gone to Spain by then," Mr Benavente explained.

"But I'm starting university and maybe I could stay here and we could study together," Ana said in a clear attempt to convince her father.

"No, Ana, you are coming with us to continue your studies in Madrid," Mr Benavente said, closing the conversation.

Ana and I couldn't sleep. We were back in Maryland and I was doing all my tests the following day. My parents had agreed that I would run all the tests to see what the offers were. I was amazed that during all my years in Spain, nobody had ever offered me anything in particular apart from a "well done" in the girls' school and the award trophy for the best student in my last year. I certainly didn't get any special offers from any universities. I suppose it was because they were all free.

"Isa, there's something I've been meaning to tell you. I am madly in love with a boy who used to be in my school last year, but now he's at university getting a degree in biology. His name is Martin. You haven't met him because he's been on holiday, but my parents are worried about my staying in the States because of him," Ana started telling me, pausing and to see my reaction.

"How serious is the relationship for you, Ana?" I simply asked her.

"I love him and I can't stop seeing him. My mother suspects it and she is doing everything she can to split us up. If my father found out, he would send me back to Spain straight away; that is why I don't have any pictures of him and haven't even mentioned him so far. It would really help me if you stayed in the States," Ana finally confessed.

"Ana, I think it will be unlikely that they will offer me anything good and if they do, I would like to investigate how good the universities are. I couldn't stay without a scholarship which is an even more remote possibility, and lastly, the fact that I would have to do one year in Spain and then move to the United States is kind of hard. I doubt they will accept any credits from Spain and I will lose a year," I reasoned with Ana, trying to clarify my mind too.

"University degrees are about three years long in this country, while in Spain it will take you five years. Even if you had to do that, you would still finish earlier than expected," Ana said with a big smile.

"It's all very confusing at the moment, Ana. Let's take one step at a time. But tell me: am I going to meet Martin at all?" I asked, changing the conversation.

"Yes. He's organising a party with his friends on Friday. People from my school will also be there. Mum won't allow me to drive, as usual, but Martin will collect us both and also bring us back. Mum will be happy that you are here with me."

"But, Ana, don't tell me that you have a driving license already."

"Yes, I have had it for over a year now, but I could only drive with an adult next to me until I was eighteen, and now that I'm eighteen, my parents simply don't trust me, especially if I am going out at night," she replied with some resentment.

"I also have a driving license ... but only since the spring. But my parents are expecting me to drive one of the cars from Laredo back to Seville at the end of the summer holidays; they have done it for too long and they will be flying instead of driving now," I said to Ana, thinking that I had not mentioned Nacho to her at all since I had arrived at the beginning of the summer.

"Ana." I hesitated. "I also have a boyfriend ..."

"Have you! Why have you never mentioned him? What's his name?" Ana asked, sitting up in her bed at once and switching the light on. "Tell me all about him!"

"His name is Nacho and he was in the last year of school with me. He is also going to study in Madrid, at the Autónoma University, doing law and economics. He's nice, but I have only been going out with him for a few months. I really made a big group of friends in that school and going to Mallorca at the end of the year was really fun."

"Have you slept together yet?" Ana interjected before I could get any further in the conversation.

"Ana!" I blushed. "Life is not all about sex, you know. He's a good friend, a special friend, if you will, but I really have too many things to do yet before I seriously commit to any relationship. I think you should never agree to be sexually active until you have a regular salary and place of your own. It is irresponsible otherwise. Look what happened to my sister Teresa." I looked straight into Ana's eyes.

"Isa, please. Why do you always have to be so conscientious about everything in life? You can go on the pill or use condoms. It would be incredibly unlikely for you to get pregnant. You talk like a nun."

"It's not that, Ana," I tried to explain to her. "I'm not ready to have an intimate relationship with anybody yet. My mind is focused on other things. Maybe I'm not in love."

"Or maybe you're scared of ever being so physically close and intimate with anyone. But you guys do kiss and hug each other, don't you? Don't you feel an internal desire to go for more and become intimate with your clothes off?" Ana insisted. "It is a really powerful experience and your own sexual desire will lead you to have an orgasm. Martin really knows what he's doing and the way he touches me simply takes me to a different world."

"Ana, I'm getting embarrassed hearing what you're telling me. I'm not sure I want to know it in so much detail," I replied, trying to stop the conversation and feeling uncomfortable.

"Wait until you go back. Sooner or later, he will put pressure on you or will try to touch you in a different way and you will have to confront the reality," Ana said assertively.

"Thanks for your advice, Ana, but at the moment, it is not my priority. I will think of you if that ever happens to me, though."

"Good night, Isa. I am so excited about Friday that I can't get to sleep."

"Good night, Ana. I'm feeling anxious about the tests tomorrow."

I was glad the tests were over. They all consisted of short multiple-choice questions about maths, chemistry, physics, biology, English, geography and history; and overall they were easier than I thought, although detailed American history and geography were my weakest points. We were waiting for the results before I returned to Spain to join my family.

Ana and I were getting ready for the party where I was supposed to meet the famous Martin. Ana could hardly control herself and she was a bag of nerves, not having seen her boyfriend for at least a month. It worried me that she could have plans to disappear with him, with the word sex written all over her face. I didn't really know anyone and the thought of maybe returning home without Ana was going to become a problem for me.

"Ana, I hope you're not going to disappear all night with Martin. I mean, I don't mind if you do, but please make sure we come back together. I wouldn't like to face your parents without you; I am not a good liar," I told Ana.

"Don't worry. We'll be finished by the time we have to come back," she replied, obviously having thought about it.

I didn't want to tell Ana that I was worried about being left alone from the very beginning, but I supposed that I had to be brave and try to mix around as soon as possible. Ana was still not sure about what pair of shoes to wear, but she looked stunning in her red summer dress.

"Ana, the black sandals are the best ones. Don't think about it anymore, please. Your friend will be here soon."

"I think you're right. I am so excited about seeing Martin again that I can't think straight. I'm almost there now."

Mrs Benavente knocked at the door and came in, checking on our progress.

"You both look beautiful. Isa, that skirt with the flowers looks beautiful on you and the colours are stunning. I like the way you have done your hair up. It really suits you," she commented, looking surprised.

"It was Ana's idea, Nuria. Nothing to do with me," I answered, telling the truth.

"I am trying to modernise Isa a little bit. I'm glad you agree with me. She looks beautiful with her hair like that. What about me, Mum?" Ana asked with an inquisitive look, spinning around.

"You are always stunning and you know it. Now, Ana, don't make it too easy for that boyfriend of yours. I am delighted Isa is with you tonight," Mrs Benavente commented.

"You mean Martin. I like him, Mum, and you know it."

"Please don't do anything silly."

Those were the last words before we heard the bell ringing. I followed Ana, who left the room as if it were on fire. By the time I reached the bottom of the stairs and said good night to Mr and Mrs Benavente, my friend was already inside the car talking to Martin. But someone else was there as I approached the car. Ana and two young men got out of the car.

"Isa, this is Martin and this is David. I didn't know David was going to be here tonight but he's Martin's old friend who has just finished university, also in Maryland."

"Hello, Isabel. Ana has not stopped talking about you all year since she learned you were coming to the States. Very nice to meet you," Martin said, shaking my hand.

"Nice to meet you too, Martin, and hello, David. How are you?" I said, also shaking David's hand, although I didn't know which of them to talk to first.

Martin's attention instantly disappeared, turning quickly to Ana, but David's continued staring into my eyes, making me feel slightly embarrassed. He was blond with receding hair, reasonably tall and with beautiful big green eyes. His clothes were quite casual for a party, but his navy blue blazer gave him a formal touch, enhancing his slim build with broad shoulders.

"Ana said that you know Martin quite well. How long have you been friends?" I asked, trying to distract him from staring at me.

He finally spoke for the first time while I was opening the door and getting inside the car. I couldn't avoid noticing that David had a natural and spontaneous smile that was very attractive. "We've grown up together from elementary school to college. In fact, we were neighbours, although I am two years older than he is."

"So you have just finished university. Do you have a job? What are your plans now?" I asked, trying to make conversation but not sure if they were the right questions to ask, as I had just met him.

"Yes, I have been employed by British Petroleum and although I'm based in Washington, I am working on a project in the Gulf of Mexico. We are digging new oil wells there, and I'll be moving to Miami for six months until the design and the drilling goes ahead. I'm a mechanical engineer and have just been employed as a project manager. Of course, I will work with senior engineers above me."

I couldn't believe it. "Are you really? I am starting university in Madrid in September and that is exactly what I would like to become, an engineer specialising in oil extraction. It is so interesting meeting you!" I was delighted to meet David and had millions of questions to ask him. My interest and attention seemed to be making David feel happily curious, as if it was unexpected for him.

The car ride flew by in an instant and we arrived to the party too soon for my liking, as I hadn't quite finished my conversation with David and still wanted to know more about what he did and how he managed to get his job. Ana and Martin soon disappeared. I wasn't sure if the party was held at Martin's place, but the house and the garden were huge. The place was heaving with people I didn't know. I lost David quickly, as he immediately recognised familiar faces and friends and was dragged in the turbulent current of people moving from one group to another.

The summer night was warm and there was a band playing in the garden, which was nicely illuminated. I walked through the ground floor of the house towards the garden, following the noise of the music. There was an improvised dance floor just in front of the musicians and a bar on the other side of the garden. I ordered a beer and took a few nuts in my other hand, walking and inspecting the greenery around me. I was glad we had been invited to this party and thrilled to have met David too. I recognised a girl from the summer school, although she wasn't in my class; but I smiled at her and we both said hi.

"Hey, Isabel!" David called from the entrance of the garden, forcing me to turn around. "I was looking for you. There are so many people I have not seen for a long time … Sorry I left you behind; it wasn't very polite of me."

"Is this Martin's house?" I asked.

"His parents live here, but they're on vacation. My parents' house is just four doors up the street."

"The neighbours may not be very happy about this party."

"They have all been invited, and Martin has promised to stop the music at midnight and get everyone out by one in the morning. Let's see if that happens, although he is normally very good."

As the party continued, David hardly moved from my side all evening. We talked and talked, and he occasionally introduced me to some of his friends and neighbours. Although he had a shy personality, David was a pleasant companion. Neither of us wanted to dance and I thoroughly enjoyed his company because I hadn't seen Ana once since we arrived.

"David," I said later that night, "the music stopped at midnight and Ana's parents told us to be back by one. I really don't want to arrive at the house without Ana, but I'm not sure what her intentions are. Her parents will kill her if she doesn't show up tonight." I was feeling concerned.

"I'll leave Martin a note under the door of his bedroom and will walk you home. If we're lucky, by the time we get there, Martin and Ana will have followed us in the car," David said, standing up at once and walking towards the hall of the house.

The streets were almost empty and I could hear the insects hidden in the vegetation in the night. There was a gentle breeze, refreshing in the humidity of the night. Before I realised it, I had told David all about my tests and starting university. He then questioned me about my family and friends, wanting to know how life was in Spain.

"I don't have any brothers or sisters. You are lucky to have such a big family. Do you mind giving me your address and telephone number in Spain? I have never visited Spain before, but I may soon, especially now that I work for BP. I guess eventually I will have to go to London for some meetings," David casually said.

"Please do call if you come to Spain. It would be nice to see you there. But I'm afraid I don't have anywhere to live in Madrid yet. It's something I will have to sort out when I get back to Spain. If you give me your telephone number or address, I could call you instead or write to you with the details once I have them." The idea of seeing David in Madrid was appealing for some reason.

"When are you returning to Spain?"

"On Wednesday," I said.

"Do you mind if we go out again before you leave?" he timidly asked.

"I would love to. Maybe we can go out with Ana and Martin for dinner? It would be nice to say goodbye," I proposed, not sure if he was intending for us to go out alone. I didn't think it was appropriate doing so during my last days in the States.

"Yes, of course. That will be nice. May I ask you, Isabel, do you have a boyfriend in Spain?" David said, looking at me.

"Yes, I do." I paused, observing his expression. "Is that a problem? Does it change anything? I'm not sure why you're asking me this. Shouldn't I be asking you?" I asked, feeling confused.

"There's nothing wrong, Isabel. You are very beautiful, after all. I don't have a girlfriend at the moment; I guess I'm too busy," he immediately replied, almost apologetically.

"Anyway, I mean it. If you ever stop by in Madrid, it will be nice to see you there. I can introduce you to my friends and will show you my university too. We can do some sightseeing together. I don't know the city that well myself. I'm originally from Seville but have lived in Cádiz, which is in the south of Spain, most of my life," I answered, trying to make David more comfortable.

"You have a driving energy that is very positive, Isabel," David finally said as we got to Ana's house.

"Thank you, David. I'm not sure what's in your head, but what you are saying is nice. I think the evening has been so enjoyable. I'm glad I came to this party," I said in return and we both smiled.

Suddenly, Martin's car appeared round the corner. Ana was next to him. It was just after one.

"I'm glad you made it, Ana. I was getting worried that we were going to run into trouble with your parents," I said with great relief when I saw her.

"No worries. I always knew we were going to be on time. What have you guys been doing?" Ana inquired.

"We were at the party listening to the band in the garden and then we walked here hoping that you were going to be on time," I answered.

"And so did I!" Ana replied, kissing Martin good night.

"Can we meet again before Isabel's departure? It would be nice to repeat this, just the four of us," David suggested.

"Yes, sure," Martin replied. "I'll arrange it with Ana and will let you know."

"Bye, girls," Martin said, shaking my hand.

"Bye," I answered, wanting to shake David's hand too, but he kissed my cheek instead. "Bye, David," I said to him after the kiss.

The letter with the results arrived on Monday, two days before my departure. I had butterflies in my stomach opening it and my fingers moved in a clumsy way as I was trying to tear the envelope open while pulling the letter out at the same time.

Dear Miss Grimaldi,

We would like to inform you that after considering the results of your tests, having met with the University Studies Committee of Maryland High School, and having proposed your case to Maryland University, we are in a position to offer you a place at Maryland University. You will be accepted to enrol for the course in mechanical engineering, and the university will be contacting you soon confirming this decision.

Please note that the course is fully subscribed for the present academic year, starting in September 1985, and if interested in this offer, it will only apply beginning September 1986.

The committee would also like to inform you that due to the way this case has been put forward and the lack of background and communication with your previous high school in Spain, the process to activate and request a scholarship has been impossible on this occasion, as you are not officially a formal student at Maryland High School. The committee acknowledges your potential and assures you that it may also be worth applying for other universities in other states aside from Maryland.

We wish you all the best in the future, and we again congratulate you in receiving this offer, as it is unusual for a foreign student to get access to a university in the United States of America in such a rapid manner.

Yours sincerely,

T. M. Hopkins
Principal of Maryland High School

I was flabbergasted and thrilled with the news, although I knew well enough that the plan was to start my studies in Madrid. I supposed I didn't lose anything by trying to get a full scholarship from Spain. I wished the letter from the university would arrive soon so I could contact them to enquire. I wanted to visit the university before I left. Suddenly, I wanted to do many things at once, but I had very little time left.

Mr and Mrs Benavente congratulated me, and Ana was delighted as well, already making plans which included her staying in Maryland after her family left.

"Ana, if your boyfriend loves you so much, he should go and find you in Spain once you have finished your studies. Only then will I allow you to go with him. I don't want to hear you talking like this again," Mr Benavente said sternly.

They were amazed that I had managed to get the offer. The letter from the university also arrived and the dean wanted to meet me before I left; the visit would also include a tour of the university. Martin, Ana and David accompanied me that day. Everything that was happening to me was thrilling but maybe happening too fast for me. The university was enormous and had excellent facilities. The dean had an informal interview with me and encouraged me to apply for a full scholarship from Spain, telling me the documents required for it. He explained to me how there were very few places for gifted foreign students and how Maryland High School had been so impressed with me, adding that my tests had confirmed it. He also mentioned my outstanding results in chemistry.

I finally left Washington with a big sense of achievement; I had really enjoyed the time with Ana, and Mr and Mrs Benavente had been incredibly generous to me. Madrid was my next target.

Chapter Twenty-Five

MADRID

The summer holidays in the north of Spain flew by. After my return from the United States, I stayed one extra day in Madrid and managed to arrange accommodation for September. It wasn't that difficult because there were many adverts from students advertising shared flats and available rooms to rent in the university grounds. I visited four different apartments and chose the most conveniently located, also balancing the price. It was a flat to share among three and although I didn't know the extra person, I didn't think it was going to be too much of a problem changing accommodation if I didn't like it. My parents helped, paying for the deposit.

I also drove the family car from Laredo to Seville, and Beatriz came with me. Elena was lucky enough to take the plane with my parents. It was an interesting experience and although we did the journey in one day, taking us ten hours, it was far more relaxing not having my parents around. Spain was changing rapidly and it was noticeable in the amount of new motorways that had recently been built. Two-thirds of the journey could be done on good condition roads now, but there was still so much roadwork along the way that it could be dangerous, and there were many accidents.

My family, although amazed about my achievements, didn't act as if the possibility of my studying in the States was an option. Mum especially acted to put herself in control of the situation, making sure that I needed her financially. It was almost as if she were trying to convince herself that we had what we had because of her.

It was frightening starting a new life in Madrid and although Maryland was in the back of my mind, I still didn't know how to compare it with Madrid or any other possibility anywhere else in the States, as the principal of the high school had suggested. I was determined to apply for a scholarship and get all the paperwork done. I could always say no at the end if I liked Madrid and what it had to offer, but my parents were not aware that I was keeping this option open. I also had Ana in Maryland to give me her insight about the university.

I had been in occasional contact with Nacho in Cádiz over the summer, but I did not have time to see him before university, as there was very little time between arriving in Seville and having to leave again for Madrid.

El Cortijo had been renovated and it was incredible how good it looked now. The outside of the building was still the same, but the inside was modern and beautifully done, keeping the character of the house and the Andalusian style. The garden was immaculately kept and everything looked pristine and well looked after. Mum and Dad had also installed a new central heating system, and the pipes, although still remaining where they were, had been hidden beyond the ceilings of the rooms, as they had all been brought slightly down in height. Despite the change, they still looked high ceilings. The roof and wiring had also been renovated, alongside the new bathrooms, tiling on the floors and the redesign of a completely different kitchen and modification of two bedrooms. As usual, none of us had ever been asked our opinion. We did not even have a say as to the type of furniture or colour for our bedrooms. It did not matter to me too much, but Beatriz and Elena were still very aware that El Cortijo was not their home but my parents' house.

"I'm going to miss you so much when you go, Isa," Beatriz told me in El Cortijo.

"I know, Bea. Please come to see me as many times as you can. Try to enjoy El Cortijo and the swimming pool," I answered.

"This is like a golden cage," Beatriz complained. "We are not allowed too many friends now that Dad is retired; everything belongs to Dad, as he always reminds us; and we are too far away from Seville city centre to go out and come back. There's no public transport to get here and there's nobody around for miles."

"They will give you a car as soon as you're eighteen," I said encouragingly.

"But that will be in two years' time. What are we supposed to do until then? Elena is only eleven, but I would like to go out with my friends."

"Maybe you could stay at Grandmother's house at the weekends."

"I'm not sure," Beatriz told me. "Grandmother is too serious and very hard with me. Plus all our relatives are gossiping about the Grimaldis taking advantage of Grandmother's fortune and saying how she favours Mum's children. María lived with her since she was sixteen years old, until she married, and Jaime's still living with her while he is at university. Mum's not even considering him moving to El Cortijo. I have the feeling that I will not be as well accepted by Grandmother."

"You're right, but as you said, in two years, you will be allowed to drive. Maybe you should ask for it occasionally rather than staying in Grandmother's house every single weekend. If you remain in Seville for university, maybe Mum will agree to renting a flat for you and Elena, although she may disagree because Elena is still quite young. I think you have to wait and see how it goes; maybe Mum will get tired of driving Elena to school all the time by then."

Madrid was a large and lively city. The Complutense University was nearly seven hundred years old, one of the oldest in Europe, and was located inside the city, close to the Barrio de Salamanca and Moncloa. Most students, especially in the first two years, lived in residential halls, normally separated by sex, which were not far from the university. It was unusual for a first-year student to share accommodation, but I preferred it. I was slightly fed up with schools and boys separated from girls. I wished to live according to my own rules.

Nacho was living in a hall close to the Autónoma University, which was fifteen kilometres away by car and twenty minutes by public transport but more in the outskirts of the city. I had not seen him for almost eight weeks, although we had spoken a few times on the phone, and I was getting butterflies in my stomach thinking about seeing him again.

"Nacho! What a surprise! I thought we were meeting later on in the evening."

Nacho had found me in the cafeteria having lunch before the afternoon lectures, and before I could say anything else, he walked across the room and gave me an enormous hug, kissing my cheek and almost raising my feet from the ground. People around us stopped to see what was happening but continued eating.

"I couldn't wait any longer to see you again. I was starting to forget what you look like," Nacho whispered in my ear, kissing me again on my neck.

"I'm glad you came. I was getting anxious as the day went on, thinking that we were meeting today. Have you finished for today?" I asked him, trying to work out how much time we had together.

"Yes, they dismissed us quickly today to give us time to finalise our paperwork and accommodation. What time do you think you'll be finished? Can we escape now?" Nacho asked, holding my hands between his and kissing them.

"I only have one more lecture. I'm finishing early today too; if you wait for me here, I'll be back soon." I wished I could go now rather than going to class. There was so much I wanted to tell Nacho about the holidays. "I would like to show you my flat, and I would also like to see where you live."

"We can do that as soon as you finish here. Also, there's an initiation party at my university this evening. Maybe we can go together if you fancy it. But I am not moving from your sight today. I have been waiting too long."

"That sounds good to me. Our party is tomorrow, Friday; maybe we could also attend that one."

"Brilliant! And I could stay at your place overnight after the party, not having to return to my school," he said, challenging me with a look.

"We shall see. I would rather not upset people in the flat too soon. I'm not sure if we are supposed to bring boyfriends over. I hardly know them," I answered, feeling very uncomfortable with the idea of Nacho sleeping over. "But I will soon find out."

Nacho waited until my lecture was over and we went to my flat. I showed him around and we met up with the other two students living there, one of whom I had never seen before.

"Hi, I'm Daniel. You must be Isabel. Carmen told me about you. This is my second year in this flat and I'm in my second year of architecture. Sorry, I have taken the biggest room because my drawing table is enormous and I needed the space. I hope you don't mind." Daniel introduced himself in a charming way but looked quite camp.

"Hello, Daniel. This is Nacho, a friend of mine from the Autónoma. I'm in my first year of mechanical engineering and Nacho is starting law and economics. Don't worry about the room; you obviously need a bigger one. I am perfectly happy with mine. I only need my bed, my desk and my books." I shook Daniel's hand and Nacho did the same after me.

"Hi, Daniel. I'm her boyfriend. Please look after her while she's here."

"Nacho!" I protested. "I don't need to be looked after! Why are you telling him such things? He doesn't even know me yet," I replied, feeling indignant.

Everyone laughed. "She is a bit of a rebel, you see?" Nacho added, making me even more furious.

"You must be Carmen. Isa told me about you after you met in August," Nacho said.

Carmen shook our hands in greeting. "I own the flat. Well, it belongs to my parents, but I rent the rooms to pay the mortgage. Having my independence outside my parents' house suits me. I'm in my last year of my psychology degree. I can't wait to finish this year and start applying for jobs."

"Would you mind if I slept over in Isabel's room some weekends? I am in a hall of residence and women are not allowed over there, but if we go out at the weekends, it may be convenient to stay over rather than having to get back to my place at night," Nacho said without any hesitation.

I was feeling very uncomfortable about how Nacho, without any private previous discussion, was just arranging things, assuming we were going to share my bed and giving everyone the impression that he had some kind of special rights over me, asking Daniel to protect me and stating that he was my boyfriend. I didn't like it at all and he had just arrived in my flat for the first time. His attitude was arrogant.

"It's up to the individuals to decide who comes to the flat, but the rules are respect and discretion. We all have work to do and anything or anyone loud, rude or interfering will not be welcome," Carmen replied in an assertive way.

"Nacho, let me just get changed and get a jacket; then we can go." I rapidly moved into my room, hoping to leave the flat as soon as possible.

We had an argument on our way to his university. It was difficult not to lose control, letting my rage take over. The fact that we were using public transport forced me to try to be as discreet as possible so as not to attract too much attention.

"What has gone into your mind, Nacho? What makes you think that you can assume so many things are going to happen between us? And what gives you the right to arrange things for me in my own apartment as if you own me? I am really upset about the way you are acting; you don't even discuss things with me." I said this with great indignation.

"Whoa, whoa, whoa!" he replied. "I can see that you are angry. I am not assuming anything; this is what normally happens with young couples. I'm not sure when it will happen, but it is normal to ask these things so we know in advance."

"The timing is wrong and you don't have to take care of me or ask anything for me. Daniel hasn't got to look after me. I am not your possession."

We were in the underground inside the train, nearly crushed by a multitude of people, and the argument broke off until we got to the correct station and got off the train.

"Isa, I'm sorry. I didn't mean to be like this. I understand what you're saying. I have missed you too much over the summer and you seem to be so independent, not needing me at all, and that it is almost scary. Sorry I was trying to control you. Can you forgive me?" Nacho stopped walking and looked straight at me, waiting for an answer, while everyone else who came off the tube went ahead of us.

I looked at him and said, "Yes, it's fine, but please talk to me before you assume things." I realised that during confrontations, as soon as the other person was prepared to back off, not trying to convince me of anything, it was easy for me to calm down immediately.

Nacho stepped forward and kissed me.

The party was gradually getting out of hand. People around us were very drunk, but everyone continued to dance, shout and talk. Nacho seemed to know quite a few students already, mostly from his hall. We spent most of the evening talking about the different things we did over the summer holidays. I told him about all the places I had visited in the United States and the offer I got from Maryland University, although he already knew about it. He told me about news and gossip from students in our old school and different barbecues and parties that he had attended. Nacho's intention was to look for a part-time job during the weekends.

"This is getting too noisy and wild. Shall we go get some fresh air outside the building?" Nacho suggested, holding my hand.

I didn't answer but stood up and walked with him. We headed through the main entrance towards the garden, starting to walk around the building. The silence of the night was deafening and the breeze quite refreshing. As soon as we turned the corner of the building, we found ourselves in a dark spot. Nacho didn't waste any time leaning me against the wall and kissing me again. Our lips opened, allowing our tongues to meet, and we were stroking each other while embracing tightly. The sexual arousal gradually increased. Nacho leant on my body, which felt trapped between the wall and his body and I could feel how his pressure on me was making my breathing become accelerated. His hands started travelling under my blouse, touching and feeling the sides of my body. Nacho's pressure between my legs grew stronger and stronger; I realised that he had an erection. His hands moved forward, slipping under my bra, touching my breasts and stroking my nipples with his thumbs.

"Isabel, you're so beautiful. Please put your hand inside my trousers and touch me," he whispered, panting in my ear and covering me with kisses, trying to fondle my breasts.

Real panic took over me. I wasn't ready for this and I didn't like it at all. His pressure was overwhelming and his light touch incredibly threatening and unpleasant. I didn't wish to touch him; it was too much for me. I pushed him away from me.

"I don't like the way you're touching me, Nacho. I am not ready for this and don't want to commit to any serious relationship," I said, trying to readjust my clothing. "You are just going too fast, not talking to me or giving any warning."

"But what warning do you want? I love you. This should have happened a while ago. I am fed up pretending in front of my friends that things are 'quite active' between us," he said angrily.

"This is not about your friends, Nacho. This is about you and me. I am not a trophy to show off in front of your friends and it hurts me to hear you talking like this. Don't ever touch me again."

"You don't love me enough. You are so focused on your professional success that nothing else matters to you," Nacho said, plainly feeling rejected.

"That's not true. You are putting me under pressure and rushing things, pushing yourself on me. Did you have in mind that this had to happen today so you could tell your friends? I don't want to carry on dating you, and yes, my studies are my priority. I don't have time for this. I am not on a mission to have sex to prove myself. Please don't call me again … and stay away from me." I turned around and started walking outside the premises, looking for a taxi to take home.

I thought of how Ana had tried to warn me about this, and I couldn't stop blaming myself for agreeing to have a boyfriend. This couldn't really happen again until I was ready for it.

Chapter Twenty-Six

DAVID

I became fully engaged in my work and lectures at university. Most of the time I was concentrating on my work, but I slowly started meeting new people and socialising with different groups. Nacho had not contacted me since we stopped going out, and I didn't miss him. What I really missed was having good friends around.

I had also gathered and submitted the necessary paperwork requesting a scholarship in Maryland, but moving to the States was not really on my mind. However, I had frequent news from Ana, who was having a great time over there. It had been confirmed that Ana's dad was returning to Spain in June and he had been promoted in his rank and given the command of the only aircraft carrier that the Spanish Navy had at that moment. It was a great achievement. The ship was based in the shared American naval base of Rota, in Cádiz. Therefore, Ana's family was returning to Cádiz, but Ana was joining my university in September. It was great news.

When I answered the telephone of the flat one day, I heard, "Isabel, is that you?" My heart missed a beat.

"David? Oh my God! I can't believe it! Where are you?" I asked, full of excitement.

"I'm in London. I have a meeting tomorrow, but I have three days off, until Wednesday and I was thinking of coming to Spain to visit you if it's convenient," David replied.

"Of course! It will be fantastic to see you. Please do come. I will arrange some time off and we can visit Madrid together. I haven't had much of a chance to do it yet."

"I have provisionally booked the tickets and will arrive the day after tomorrow at six in the evening. I have also provisionally booked a hotel not far from your address, the Hotel La Moncloa. Is it any good? Shall I give it the okay, then?" he asked, sounding very happy.

"Yes, please do. I don't think I will be able to collect you from the airport, but you can catch the train straight to La Moncloa; it takes about twenty minutes. I will have finished my lectures by the time you get here. Please do call me when you get to the hotel and I will meet you there."

"How is everything otherwise?"

"I'm working hard, but it's early days yet. It's not even Christmas. We will start exams in February. I'm slowly meeting new people, but I miss having good friends around," I answered in full honesty. "How is your job going?"

"I'm still very new to this but learning fast. Same as you, I don't know many people in Miami and have to travel quite a lot to Mexico and Washington, but I never have time to see Martin," David quickly said. "I have to go now, but I'm looking forward to seeing you on Friday, two days' time."

"So am I. Thank you for calling. Bye."

"Bye, Isabel."

The two days passed slowly. I could hardly concentrate on anything and was anxious for the last lecture to finish. I had arranged for a classmate to pass me all the notes from the lectures I was missing and I was looking forward to seeing David again. I wasn't sure what the plan was going to be, but I decided to wait and see what suited best when he arrived. I had been thinking about David's arrival ever since he rang me.

The phone rang. "Hello?"

"Isabel? I've arrived at the hotel. Where and when would you like to meet?"

"I'm coming over now," I answered, trying to remain calm. "It will take me ten minutes and I'll be in the lobby. How was your journey?"

"It was very good, thanks. No delays, which is what matters at the moment. I will see you soon. Bye!" David put the phone down before I was able to say goodbye.

Seeing David again was lovely. We started talking so much in the lobby of the hotel that we didn't realise the time was passing by. We had been there for one hour before deciding that we were actually hungry. I took him to the Plaza Mayor in the centre of Madrid and we moved from one tapas bar to another. The place was packed, as it was Friday and all the students and young people were out. David told me everything he had been doing during the months since I last saw him and I told him about my experience in Madrid, deliberately avoiding talking about Nacho. We made plans as to what to do over the weekend and the first two days of the week before his flight to Miami on Wednesday. The schedule was tight, but we just wanted to enjoy ourselves, talk and relax, at the same time not worrying about having to be anywhere in particular.

On the first day, we went to the Casa del Campo and visited the Museo del Prado, enjoying the Velazquez, Goya, El Greco and Murillo paintings in particular. We only went back home and to the hotel to shower, change and go out again to have something to eat. Time was flying, but it was enjoyable, and David insisted on paying for everything. On the second day, we visited El Palacio Real and went to the Parque del Retiro after lunch. It was late autumn and the tree colours were still beautiful because the temperature had been warm the entire month of October.

"Would you like to rent a rowboat?" David asked me, clearly getting ready for me to say yes.

"On one condition: you do all the rowing," I answered.

"That's fine. We're not in a hurry, are we? I can rest if I need to."

David rented the boat for one hour and we disappeared in the canals of the big lagoon. There was a centre part in the water with a large monument, which was the widest area, but there were also more hidden parts among different trees and branches of weeping willows falling into the water. David stopped rowing.

"I'm having such a good time and I like Spain. Life here is so different than in America."

David talked while I listened, lying down in the front of the boat and enjoying the light of the sun on my face between the leaves of the branches.

I wasn't saying anything and my peace suddenly was broken by a sprinkle of cold water when David splashed one of the oars, calling for my attention.

"Stop it! What are you doing?" I said, immediately sitting up straight and trying to use my right hand to splash some water back on him too.

"You're ignoring me."

"No, I'm not. I heard what you said and was waiting to see if you had finished. I am enjoying your visit very much too. I needed a break and I like talking to you about everything. I was thinking that maybe tomorrow we could spend the day in Toledo. It's a beautiful city just south of Madrid, one hour away by train. It has a very strong Jewish influence, and used to be the capital of Spain when the Arabs were in the south of Spain. It was full of goldsmiths and moneylenders at the time, and you can find swords, knives and many ornaments made out of steel and iron. The architecture is beautiful," I explained, getting completely engaged in my own talking. "Oh, sorry! Am I talking too much?"

"It sounds like an excellent place to visit. Isabel, can I call you more regularly and come to visit you whenever I can?" David asked, sitting face-to-face with me.

"Yes, of course. I'd love to. You are a great friend," I answered, without having any more time to add anything else.

"I know I don't have any right to say this, but I will be waiting for you when you finish your studies. You told me you have a boyfriend and I don't expect anything in return from you. You should carry on with your normal life and meet as many people as possible, but when you finish, if you haven't quite met your perfect match and we're still friends, I'll ask you to come with me. I will also know if I ever have to stop visiting you."

I didn't know what to say and there was a long silence before I spoke again. "I don't really want to commit to anything until my future is more certain. My sister got pregnant at university and has a broken marriage. She is really struggling. You are indeed a special friend to me and I value the time we've spent together. I'm not going out with anyone now – it didn't work out for me – but you're in the States and anything could happen in five years."

"That's right, Isa," he said, holding my hand. "I'm not in a hurry; please just know that I am here for you only if you want me to be."

"There's something else …," I added. "Don't expect me to be like Ana with Martin. I'm not like that."

"You don't have to ever worry about that, Isa. I like the way you are," David said.

Silence fell between us, facing each other in the boat, holding hands but not moving so as not to spoil the moment. I realised I liked David very much; he was a special person. I liked his calmness about everything and his understanding. He was patient and gentle, but it was insane thinking about us in other way than just being friends.

There was a call for boarding the flight to Miami. The time I had had off with David had been a treasure for me. The day out in Toledo had been fantastic and on the last day, we also visited El Valle de los Caídos and La Fábrica de los Tapices, ending up at a nightclub until three in the morning. It was hard to say goodbye after so much laughter together, but I was looking forward to his next visit, although I didn't quite know when it was going to be.

"Try not to take too long to come back again," I said, standing at the security checkpoint. "It was really nice to see you."

"I love Spain and I'm glad I came too. Enjoy as much as you can and I will call you soon. We'll keep in touch."

We both stood looking at each other without talking and then embraced in a tight and meaningful hug, kissing goodbye on the cheeks. David took hold of my hand when he moved apart and kissed my hand too, pressing it against his face.

"Send my regards to Ana and Martin when you see them."

"I will!" he said, letting me go and walking towards the gate carrying his hand luggage.

David turned around once more before I could no longer see him and waved goodbye with a big smile on his face. I also waved and stood there holding the pendant around my neck, which he had given me as a present in Toledo.

Chapter Twenty-Seven

FIVE YEARS LATER

My last year of engineering at university was difficult to combine with the final engineering project required to get a full accreditation and final certificate. Students normally waited to do the project as a final sixth year, but I was combining it with my final year of lectures and theory. I had been talking with the professors well in advance and the faculty board had agreed to take me on earlier, so I was busy. My project consisted of developing a system for horizontal oil extraction. Traditional ways of exploiting oil were based on vertical systems aiming for deep underground pockets. These deposits would eventually run out or become too deep to be accessed, which would inevitably make the oil extraction very expensive. Recent studies had identified substantial lengthy horizontal layers of gas and oil around the planet, but they were quite narrow in depth compared to the traditional deposits. I was aiming to design the mechanical technology to target these horizontal layers.

I was happy with my decision to continue my studies in Madrid, despite getting a full scholarship in Maryland. I had talked it over with my parents, but even having been granted a full scholarship, it was still much more expensive for me to live in the States, not to mention plane tickets to come back to Spain twice a year. The American government prohibited my getting a job while I was there. My studies were free in Madrid, and adding accommodation and maintenance money was still a cheaper option. I had taken a part-time job on Saturdays, working in El Corte Inglés, and this was helping with pocket money. I had even managed to fly to Maryland for ten days last summer to visit David and his parents, and the generous Christmas money that Grandmother Isabel was still giving me each year was a blessing, helping me to manage things.

David and I had been maintaining an on-off relationship based on what we had agreed to five years ago. He had been visiting me two or three times a year, depending on how many times he had to fly to Europe. We had occasionally spoken on the phone and lately exchanged correspondence. It was rather difficult for me to know where he was going to be because he travelled frequently. David was on my mind all the time and I knew by now that I was deeply in love with him. I carried with me an internal happiness which made me very sociable and inclusive with everyone around me. I always joined in and went out with fellow students any time I possibly could.

Since Ana arrived in Madrid, my social life became very busy at university. It was difficult to see her on a regular basis, as she was studying maths in a different building to mine. She and Martin split up in the first year after Ana returned to Spain; Martin never made the effort to come see her and Ana liked being sexually active. She was going out with someone else now, Eduardo.

Things had also moved on at home. Elena was now at secondary school and living with Beatriz in an apartment in Seville. Beatriz was at university studying psychology, and my parents were still living in El Cortijo. Jaime was about to get married in the spring and was still living with grandmother, and Alex was in Rome studying theology, pursuing his career as a priest and hoping to do missionary work. Teresa had remarried and was living in Seville, looking much happier now than she was before, and María was also living in Seville, desperate to have a second baby that for some reason was not coming. Miss Spencer was teaching in a primary school in Seville and living in her own apartment, still very much in contact with us and part of the family. She lived quite close to Elena and Beatriz and saw them regularly. She frequently visited Grandmother Isabel as well.

◯◯◯

Ana's birthday was coming up and she was planning to get a group of her friends together to go out for dinner in Chinchón, which was a small town outside Madrid, and we were going to try a restaurant's specialty, delicious roast suckling pig. The town was also famous for its anisette liqueur and its beautiful bullfighting ring. Ana was planning to party all night long in a selective nightclub that she had chosen, frequently visited by celebrities and footballers in Madrid. Ana was very familiar with the nightlife in Madrid.

We were meeting at nine that evening and travelling in two cars. Eduardo was driving his own car and was bringing four of his friends too; one of them also had a second car. Ana had mentioned that we were meeting three more girls in the nightclub later on; however, the situation reminded me of the night I met David for the first time, when we both went to Martin's party and I didn't know anyone there.

The intercom of my flat had just rung and Ana was waiting for me downstairs. She was with Eduardo in the car; Eduardo's four friends had decided to meet us at the restaurant in Chinchón.

"Happy birthday, Ana!" I said, entering the car.

"Thank you, Isa. You remembered it straight away, not like others ...," she said, meaning Eduardo.

"I have a present for you and have also bought you a birthday card," I said, handing the parcel to her in the front seat.

"Thank you so much, Isa! I love presents! What is it?" she said, not waiting for an answer. Ana ripped the paper open and exclaimed, "It's beautiful, Isa! I love it! You knew I was after this jacket!"

Ana turned around on her seat while Eduardo was still driving and reached my face, kissing me thank you.

"I couldn't resist it when I realised how much you liked it," I replied. "I hope you wear it a lot."

"But I didn't get it because it was too expensive! Thank you. Really, I mean it."

The evening was lively and while we were all waiting for the roast suckling pig to be ready, we were having shots of anisette liqueur. I had never tried it before, although Ana assured me that it was the fashion now when you went out in Madrid. I hadn't even heard of it! The drink was pleasant enough, but it wouldn't have been my choice if I had been able to choose. I was deliberately trying not to drink as fast as the others were, but it was difficult to fall behind, as it seemed that the round of shots came for everyone to drink at the same time, waiting and encouraging the person falling behind to finish the shot as soon as possible before continuing with another round. I lost count of how many shots I had and we were all soon engaged in laughter and intense conversation. I had forgotten the names of Eduardo's friends, but we were all behaving as if we were great friends.

The suckling pig was indeed delicious and came accompanied with an assortment of different vegetables. We ordered Rioja to drink, and although I only had one small glass, it went very well with the meat. I didn't have any more space in my stomach for dessert but felt like having strong coffee after so much alcohol, and thinking about the long night still ahead. Ana was having a great time and couldn't stop laughing at Eduardo's jokes. The more jokes he told us, the greater the laughter; it was contagious.

The time came for us to move on and meet the rest of the group in the nightclub. As soon as I stood up, I realised that I had drunk far too much. Everything moved around me with a slight spinning sensation. I didn't feel bad when sitting, but I was struggling to keep straight with a steady gait when standing up. We all left the restaurant, still laughing and being very loud. Ana was holding on to Eduardo and the other four friends were shoving and pushing each other all the way to the car park. Eduardo opened his car first and three of the friends got inside the back seat of the car at once, still laughing and pushing each other. Ana and Eduardo occupied the front seats, leaving the spare friend and me standing there.

"Oh, there's no space for me in the car," I said.

"I have my car. I'll take you!" he said.

"Thank you. I've forgotten your name." I apologised, feeling awkward, as it was a strange question to ask after nearly four hours in the restaurant together.

"My name's Rafael. You're Isa, right?"

"Yeah," I said. "Let's go!"

I got in the front seat and put my seat belt on. I wished David could be here with me. I missed him so much at times and I had even started thinking about him in a sexual way. It was a strong feeling that was growing inside me, almost a desire. Our relationship had become more personal over the last two years and although we were not formally going out, it was almost impossible not to kiss and hug with great passion at times. I felt free and very much myself next to David. He never demanded anything or took anything for granted. I loved him so much.

"Where are we going, Rafael?" I asked with slurred speech.

"To the night club in Madrid," he said.

"I hope you know the way because I don't know where we are. It's quite dark. Didn't we come on the motorway?" I asked again.

"I am taking a secondary road to avoid the police and will take the opportunity to show you the best view of Madrid from the mountains," he replied.

"I think I'm falling asleep. I'm so tired …"

I was quite drunk and could hardly speak. The movement and vibration of the engine sent me into a stupor which was difficult to fight. I was exhausted and wanted to close my eyes.

As the time passed, I dreamt of David taking my clothes off and kissing me. His body was partially dressed on top of mine and he was making love to me. I loved him so much, but for some reason, I wasn't moving. I couldn't move. I was paralysed. He reached for one of my hands and asked me to touch him. I didn't know what he was talking about, but his kisses where overwhelming me, although I couldn't kiss him back. I felt the hardness of his penis inside me, his pressure and his movement …

"I need to pee. I'll be back," he said, leaving me lying down.

It was so cold, and I was shivering. David was taking too long and I opened my eyes to try to find him. I was inside a car in the middle of the countryside, with a view of the lights of Madrid far in the distance. With horror and panic, I realised that it was Rafael who had just had sex with me. I couldn't remember any details of how it had happened or how he had managed to undress me in the car, but I was horrified and scared.

I finally came to my senses and locked the car as quickly as I could, moving to the driver's seat and switching on the engine. I was scared of Rafael and didn't want him close to me again. I couldn't understand how he had taken such advantage of me. I never thought anything like this could happen to me. I reversed the car, in the stress of the moment not realising that there was a tree behind me, crashing the car against it, but I continued driving forward, looking for the main path, possibly leading me to a main road. I didn't know where I was! I couldn't drive either; I was seriously drunk and still undressed.

"Isabel, open the door!" Rafael said punching my window and running next to the car. "Don't leave me here! I will take you back; I promise I won't do anything else to you."

I stopped the car. Everything was incredibly dark and I didn't know where I was or how to get out of the forest. What would happen if he tried to touch me again? The engine was on, but I still wouldn't open the door. I thought I could eventually find the way out, but I honestly knew I couldn't drive. I had never been this drunk; I couldn't believe how naive and stupid I had been.

"Isabel, please! I won't be able to go back any other way and I'm not fully dressed. I promise to take you back. Please!"

I collected all my underwear and got dressed, moving to the passenger seat. I unlocked the door, but my heart was still beating rapidly, ready to act in case Rafael tried to touch me again or do anything to me. He looked for his trousers, put them on and got inside the car. Neither of us said a single word until we got to the nightclub.

"Where have you been?" Ana asked as soon as she saw us. "We were beginning to get worried, thinking that maybe you had had an accident. You've taken a long time to arrive."

"Someone crashed into the back of my car and we had to exchange documents," Rafael answered, keeping it short and walking towards the bar.

"I'm having such a good time, Isabel. I don't want the night to finish. Come and dance with me. The music is superb!"

"Sorry, Ana. I'm thirsty after the journey. I'll see you later," I told her, not wanting to spoil her evening.

I asked for water and an orange juice at the bar. I was feeling faint and incredibly sad as well as full of disappointment. I was trying to remember the details of what had just happened, figuring out when things had started to go wrong, but I couldn't. I couldn't remember the interval between falling asleep and waking to find Rafael's body on top of me and penetrating me. Did I invite him to do it? In my dream, I was with David. David! What would David think of all this when he found out? My actions were indefensible. He had to know, even if it meant the end of our special friendship.

Ana was all over Eduardo on the dance floor and Rafael was also there, all over one of the other girls I hadn't met yet. The other three guys were sharing a table with the other remaining girls. I was still sitting at the bar torturing myself and feeling stressed out. My agony continued, not being able to remember if Rafael had ejaculated inside me. Everything felt bruised inside me and I was too scared to go to the toilet and find out. I wasn't even on the pill and remembering how I felt Rafael's penis in my hand, I was certain that he wasn't wearing a condom. I couldn't even work out when my last period had been; my head was about to explode.

I finally found the courage to walk to the toilet. My bladder was full and it had become a matter of urgency. I was still staggering as I walked under the influence of alcohol. I looked terrible; my eyeliner had run and I had black splotches all over my face. My hair was undone as if I had just got out of bed and my blouse was buttoned up wrong. I washed my face and hands; the cold water was refreshing and made me more alert. I tried to straighten my hair the best I could, using my fingers and I redid the buttons on my blouse. I noticed that I had some scratches on my abdomen and one over my right breast, and I had a love bite on my neck as well. Despite all my kissing with David, I had never had a love bite before.

I had to use the toilet and realised that there was some blood spotting my underwear, mixed up with loose pubic hair and some dry but jelly-like secretions. I tried to clean myself the best I could, but I was in quite a lot of pain. I was badly bruised. I felt sad and incredibly lonely. I was absolutely terrified and I could only think of one person: David. Had I been raped? I couldn't even tell how I came to have sex in this way. It was incredibly disappointing and I was furious. I couldn't even decide whether I ought to go to the police.

I walked out of the toilet, determined to go home.

I interrupted the snogging. "Ana, I'm going home. It's too late for me and I have drunk too much already. I'll call you tomorrow."

"But what time is it? It's early still. I don't want my birthday party to finish," she replied.

"It's just after three in the morning. I'll get a taxi. You just carry on with your party," I said. I didn't wait for her blessing but just walked towards the entrance.

I wanted to get home as fast as I could to have a shower and clean myself properly. I was really hoping to be able to remember better by the morning what exactly had happened in the car before Rafael got on top of me. It was simply agonising not being able to remember it.

I woke up early in the middle of a nightmare. I was in my bed and was safe, but my head was very sore. I didn't ever want to drink or try anisette liqueur again. I made a strong coffee and took some pills for my headache. I tried to remember again what had actually happened the night before, but I still could not remember my actions between feeling very tired and falling asleep, to waking up in the middle of having sex. I felt that whichever way it had happened, I had been taken advantage of, and I regretted having had so many shots before dinner.

I wanted to talk to Ana, but I knew she was in bed with Eduardo and probably not available until the afternoon. I was shaking and didn't know what to do. I was thinking of the possibility of getting pregnant and how to stop it. I had read in some article that there was a morning-after pill that could be taken in emergencies like missing taking the pill, rape or losing a condom during intercourse. I wasn't sure if it was available in Spain, where girls were not supposed to consent to having sex before marriage. But the thought of having to tell someone horrified me, admitting my own stupidity and facing the macho culture among doctors in which sexual attacks were mostly provoked by seductive women wearing the wrong clothes or doing the wrong things. My doctor might even tell my parents or relatives, as he knew who I was related to and legally my parents were still supporting me despite my being twenty-three years old.

Realistically speaking, what were the chances of my falling pregnant? My last period was two weeks ago, so the chances were high. But were they really high even with one sexual act? I didn't know the answer. Would I keep the baby if I were pregnant? How would it affect my life? The idea of conceiving a baby in this way was not what I had ever planned for and I hated Rafael for acting the way he did.

My torture went on and on over the next few days, and I was becoming psychologically affected and unable to ask for help or to make a decision about telling the doctor. I withdrew and stopped socialising, pushing myself academically even harder. I eventually told Ana what had happened. She was furious with Rafael and blamed herself for not making sure I went in the car with her and Eduardo. Ana knew Rafael had a bit of a reputation for taking advantage of girls but tried to reassure me that she had sometimes lost a condom during intercourse and had never fallen pregnant. She was livid that Rafael had gone so far with me and that he didn't even take any precautions for it.

"When this happens, you need to make sure to wash thoroughly as soon as possible. Isa, you'll be fine. I know the experience was terrible, but you're worrying too much because you have never had intercourse before." She sounded so confident. "But he's a real bastard. Have you thought of going to the police?"

"To tell them what?" I replied, having had time to think seriously about it. "That I can't remember how he actually got inside me because I was so incredibly drunk? I may have even asked him to do it, Ana, or maybe he just went ahead even though I didn't know what I was saying or doing. You know how things are in Spain. I don't want my parents knowing if I can avoid it; they'll never understand."

Two more weeks passed since the incident and I received a call from David.

"Isa? Is that you? Sorry I've taken so long to call you. I'm in Australia."

"Australia? That's far away. Something has happened, David. Do you have time to talk?" I asked, making sure he didn't have to run away soon.

"I have plenty of time. It sounds very serious when you talk like that," he answered.

"It is serious, David."

I told David everything that had happened and exactly how it had occurred as far as I could remember it. I also told him about my fear of being pregnant and how devastated I was feeling. Everything had changed; suddenly I was trying to decide whether I would be capable of having an abortion or not. My world had been turned upside down.

"David, I will understand if you want to end our friendship. You must feel terribly disappointed and I feel so ashamed of myself. I'm very sorry that this has happened."

David hadn't said anything at all and was just listening.

"Isa, it was a terrible experience. It doesn't matter if you tried to seduce him or not. It seems to me that you were totally drunk and incapable and he took advantage of you. You didn't get in the car thinking that you were going to have sex and you didn't ask for the car to be driven to that forest. That guy intentionally did this at some point in the journey. Maybe he didn't know how far he was going to get with you, but he is the one who took advantage of your vulnerable state. There is a very hard lesson for you to learn," David said, keeping quiet for a few seconds.

"David, I was stupid to get into that car," I answered. "And I regret it so much."

"But … I was worried that you were going to say that you had found your perfect match. He's not your perfect match, is he?" he asked, lifting a huge weight from my soul.

"No, David, he definitely is not," I answered with a half smile on my face.

"I still stand a chance, then. Whatever happens, I will be there for you. You are not alone, Isa. I would like you to come to live with me in the States as soon as you finish university. We can live together until you're sure you want to marry me. You could apply for a job in a European company. Maybe BP too … or Shell? You won't be allowed to work in the States until you marry me or live long enough with me. They are quite strict with visas, but looking for a job with a European company will be different." He had clearly been waiting a long time for this moment.

"I will work hard to finish everything, including the project, and I would like very much to do that, David," I answered getting very emotional.

"Isa, I love you. You are so different from everyone else and I am truly in love with you. I had a terrible relationship before I met you and I am not proud of it. I have been waiting for you for a long time." He left a gap for a few seconds. "Listen, Isa, I'll make sure I come back to the States via the London office and from there I will come to Madrid over the weekend to see you. I think it is important that we see each other. I can tell that you are really affected by this."

"David, I love you so much. The sooner I see you, the better. I wish you could be here with me." Tears started rolling down my face as I pronounced these words. The love I was feeling in my heart was so intense that it was actually painful.

"Isabel, you need to trust me. Whatever happens, I am here for you and always will be, even if you decide not to marry me."

"Please don't say that. I love you, David," I said, crying.

"Bye, Isabel. I will be there soon, in one week. I'll call you again soon. Bye."

"Goodbye, David," I said as he hung up the phone.

Chapter Twenty-Eight
THE UNEXPECTED

I had been counting each day and hour of the day during the week, waiting for David to arrive. I didn't feel talking to or meeting people, and I certainly had lost my confidence about parties and returning home by myself, not wanting to drink alcohol when there was nobody there to take care of me. David was the only person who could currently make me feel safe. I had been throwing myself into finishing my project and academic work, determined to pass my remaining exams as soon as possible so I could get my certificate in mechanical engineering. I had two more months ahead of me before going to the States.

David had just rung, telling me he was already in his hotel.

"David, do you mind if I meet you in your room this time?" I asked, hoping to get some privacy when we talked. Neither of us had invited each other to either of our bedrooms in the past.

"Of course not, Isa. I'm in room two-oh-two. I think we need some privacy. I'd like to tell you something that I think is important. I'll be waiting here."

David's sentence kept playing in my mind. I couldn't think what could be so important that he wanted to tell me, but at least it was taking off the pressure as far as what was troubling me now. I walked all the way to the hotel and finally knocked at his door.

"Hello, Isa. Please do come in," he said, opening the door wider.

The moment the door was closed behind us, we embraced and I started crying, not being able to control my emotions.

"It's been a nightmare, David," I managed to say.

"I know, Isa and that's why I'm here. Come and sit on the bed next to me."

"David," I said, looking straight into his eyes, "my period's late and I took a pregnancy test just before you arrived. It's positive." I had a terrible tightness in my chest and my whole body was shivering. My throat was closing up at the same time.

David gave me a tight hug and kissed my head. "Isabel, I know it's not what you were expecting to happen, but things are going to be fine. Look at me. Because it's unexpected, it may seem to you that there isn't any room for this baby in your life, but this child may be a blessing from heaven."

I looked at him in disbelief, as David was talking in a way that I had never expected.

"This baby is an innocent and deserves to be loved and cared for and we can do it together. Think about it. I will support you in whichever way you decide to go ahead with this, but from my point of view, I would like to marry you as soon as possible. If you want a religious wedding, we can do it later on, but we should keep this baby. I will give him my name and take care of him and you. He is your baby, Isa, and he will be a treasure for us. You are an incredibly loving person and people don't need to know anything else about it. Your family will think that he is mine and that will be the end of it."

I didn't know what to say. "I've been so preoccupied questioning whether I was going to be brave enough to have a termination that I haven't actually stopped to think about how I could possibly keep the baby. Everything has been turned around so quickly that having a baby feels impossible. The way the baby was conceived is wrong and that is what my logic is telling me. I suppose there is social pressure too and people will judge me, but I know that I would feel terrible if I had to give up the baby."

"Anybody who really knows you realises the kind of person you are; you don't have to justify anything to anyone. And we will take care of this baby together," David said, pausing. "There's something else, Isa. It's quite possible that I won't be able to have children with you." David waited to see my reaction.

"What makes you say that?" I asked, feeling worried about him.

"I was born with undescended testicles and the doctors realised quite late. I had an operation as a child to correct it, but the doctors told my parents that they were atrophic and quite possibly I was going to be sterile. Apparently, testicles need to be inside the scrotum outside the body because they need a slightly lower temperature to function properly. In my case, they spent a few years getting too hot inside my belly and therefore may not work as they should."

"Oh, David! Why haven't you mentioned it before? Does it bother you?" I asked.

"I didn't want to spoil it, I guess. I didn't want you to feel pity for me and I wanted to make sure that you chose to be with me regardless. I suppose it made me feel insecure in front of you, but I thought you should know before you decide to come live with me. I've recently been to the doctor and my sperm count is very low. It's unlikely that I will be able to have children, but it's not impossible. I think I need a good woman by my side if I ever stand a chance, don't you think?"

"David, I love you so much and you have been carrying all this worry for so long. It wouldn't have made a difference about my feelings for you and I am prepared to explore the possibility with you. You always have this way of making me see things the right way. You value what it is really important. I would love to have children with you if they come, but I also think I should keep my baby. I already love him."

"Our baby, you mean … I think you shouldn't say anything to Ana about the pregnancy because Rafael might find out. We should announce our intention of getting married and moving to the States as soon as possible, and things will follow their own course from then on. We will tell our families that you are pregnant in June, when you finish university. If you agree with me, of course."

"David, I'd like to be able to work and be financially independent as soon as it is possible once the baby is born. I would like to secure my future and the baby's future long term just in case things don't work between us," I said.

"I was counting on that, Isabel, and I know you too well, but you should know that I am not planning to lose you. I have been waiting a long time for you. I am the happiest man in the world!"

"David, there's something else I would like to talk to you about. It's weird how things have developed and how we're fixing our wedding date and I'm already pregnant, but the fact is that we haven't had an intimate relationship yet …"

"Don't worry about it, Isabel. We haven't had the chance to be together properly. It will come and I know next time I see you it will be to marry you. I'm not concerned about when sex will happen, but I know it will one day."

"What I was trying to say is that I am aware of having a kind of blockage to light physical touch, but I am also very drawn to physical pressure. It's difficult to explain. Despite being pregnant, my sexual activity has been limited and my experience has not been good at all so far. In fact, I was a virgin until Rafael. I have sexual fantasies about you and me and dream about being intimate with you, but I know that I can also panic and that this blockage may stop me getting close to you. You should know that before we go ahead and live together."

"I only know the response of your body every time we kiss or I hug you, and I can see tremendous potential. I think you will be an amazing lover because your body almost talks when you're close to me. We need to get to learn each other's bodies and to feel comfortable next to each other. I can tell that you are sometimes incredibly tense, but once you learn to feel safe and relax, rather than feel intimidated, and you're intimately close to my body, desire will grow between us. I know that it will get to the point at which it will be impossible to stop, and we both will be ready for it."

It was difficult to believe how things were changing so quickly in such a short period. I loved David immensely and happiness was growing inside me day by day. I was feeling thrilled about the baby. David had announced to his family that we were getting married in July, and I had also told mine. My parents were resentful about the idea of a civil wedding, as that was too modern for them and not well regarded by their friends. My argument was that I was planning to live with David in Maryland and as it was so imminent, without any time for a wedding in a church, it was morally more correct to be legally married at least. I promised my parents that we would have a religious wedding in the spring. My brothers and sisters were all delighted. Ana was also over the moon.

"So things are finally moving on between you two," she replied. "It's about time, you know. It's been painful watching how madly in love you both are and how you were apart all the time. I don't know how you have managed to cope with it; it would have driven me insane. When and how did he propose, Isa?"

"He was over here last weekend from Australia. He hasn't given me a ring yet and I don't think he had it planned, but he suddenly realised that I am finishing in June and he proposed, hoping to convince me to move to the States to live with him. He only had twenty-four hours to do it."

"That's what I call 'living on the move'. Isa, please tell me that you've slept together," Ana said nosily. "I couldn't bear the agony if you still hadn't."

"I spent the night with him in the hotel, if that makes you happy," I said, without going into any details.

"That was a first, wasn't it?" she asked again, as if trying to reassure herself.

"Yes, Ana. It was a first …"

Epilogue

Fear is defined as an unpleasant emotion caused by the threat of danger, pain or harm.

We can have fear of external or internal things, but the threat of danger, pain or harm is far worse when the source is inside us. Fear can manifest itself in many ways, such as anticipation, anxiety, terror, shame or guilt, but it should not be confused with anxiety. Anxiety is the multi-systemic response associated with fear. I believe that fear is the core emotion and anxiety is the response.

The feeling of fear can be particularly terrifying as a young child, when the different ways of communicating are not yet in place and speech and language are still developing. During childhood, we are fully dependent on the adults around us and it is imperative to feel safe and protected, especially by those taking care of us.

I am a doctor working in the UK and the mother of three boys. My eldest son was diagnosed with Asperger's syndrome when he was eleven years old. For the last five years, I have been reading about the topic and been in contact with different families with children who have social issues, with or without a diagnosis. I have learnt in depth about Asperger's traits and realised that I have lived all my life in and around them. It is because of all these factors that I have been inspired to write this novel, taking the opportunity to reflect on the topic and giving my opinion about it in this epilogue.

Asperger's syndrome (AS) is well described in many books and on autistic societies' websites. It is included in the autistic spectrum disorder, but it is essential to comprehend what the spectrum means and how individuals can vary within that spectrum. Furthermore, there is a dynamic development by which changes can take place, causing Asperger's traits to change in quality or intensity according to the person's age; personality; process of learning; the support at emotional, social and practical levels; and the environmental context of the individual. Isabel, the main character of the story, gives a view of how it feels being within the spectrum as an AS personality. Complex cases can also come with mental health co-morbidity that could mask the diagnosis, as is the case of the character Roberto Grimaldi, Isabel's father.

Children and adults with Asperger's syndrome have normal intellectual capacity but have distinctive traits affecting different areas, such as social interaction, subtle communication skills and restrictive interests. The syndrome can also include a variable degree of motor clumsiness and sensory deficits alterations. The syndrome is not a psychiatric illness but more to do with developmental factors affecting the brain rather than emotional deprivation. Each individual will have his own personal profile that may differ very much from another within the spectrum, although there is a minimum requirement described in the diagnosis. Traits are present from childhood, but, especially in adults, the subjective judgement of the professionals will also count in the diagnosis according to what is considered normal patterns of behaviour since childhood.

Professor Tony Attwood describes it this way on his website, www.tonyattwood.com.au:

> *From clinical experience I consider that children and adults with Asperger's syndrome have a different, not defective, way of thinking.*

The person usually has a strong desire to seek knowledge, truth and perfection with a different set of priorities than would be expected with other people. There is also a different perception of situations and sensory experiences. The overriding priority may be to solve a problem rather than satisfy the social or emotional needs of others.

The person values being creative rather than co-operative.

The person with Asperger's may perceive errors that are not apparent to others, giving considerable attention to detail, rather than noticing the "big picture".

The person is usually renowned for being direct, speaking their mind and being honest and determined and having a strong sense of social justice.

The person may actively seek and enjoy solitude, be a loyal friend and have a distinct sense of humour.

However, the person with Asperger's syndrome can have difficulty with the management and expression of emotions.

Children and adults with Asperger's may have high levels of anxiety, sadness or anger that indicate a secondary mood disorder. There may also be problems expressing the degree of love and affection expected by others. Fortunately, we now have successful psychological treatment programs to help manage and express emotions.

I have tried to describe Isabel as someone being able to reach equilibrium between the majority of her Asperger's traits and her ability to connect with the world around her. Isabel's fear and anxiety, especially during childhood, almost take control of her, straightjacketing her life and preventing her from being in touch with her emotions. She is unable to put words to or process many of the thoughts described in the story, which I have found difficult to write about as an author.

In Professor Tony Attwood's opinion, 10 to 15 per cent of people with Asperger's syndrome can become subclinical, not meaning cured, as it is not an illness, but being able to reach a state of standby in which people are able to work out the neurotypical behaviour and environment around them, with no fear and without anxiety. Obviously, this subclinical state can potentially become apparent again under periods of great stress and anxiety, depending on individual circumstances. People should generally be proud in life, not necessarily about what they achieve but more about what they are able to overcome. It is impossible to change the way you see the world or your own process of thinking, which many people sometimes call the "wiring up" of your brain, but every individual has an internal awareness and a capacity for tuning into the world that should be maximised to the best potential. This is particularly essential and helpful in people with AS.

Isabel's internal fight and psychological storm as a child sustains her in a constant experience of terror, which she gradually manages to work out. The efforts and sacrifices she has to make feel like an ongoing experience which is never finished. It is as though she has to make a conscious effort on a daily basis in order to maintain what she has already achieved, keeping herself socially connected.

Isabel was close to completely switching off from the external world, disconnecting from any reality. She was paralysed with fear and terror, although Isabel never externally behaved as such; instead, she became an invisible and perfect child.

Reading *Unwritten Rules of Social Relationships* by Dr Temple Grandin and Sean Barron was a great inspiration for me. It made me realise that to be able to relate socially to anyone or any given social situation, we all have to acquire two different levels of social skills.

The first level is all about learning social rules for different sets of environments. The more you are exposed to a particular environment, the more you learn about it and what happens around it. Some environments are easier to get to know than others are, and there is an emotional cost to any of them; therefore, the speed of learning will also vary from one to another. For example, it is easier and quicker to learn social rules concerning eating within your own family than the ins and outs of what is expected of you when you are starting a new school. The more you are exposed to that, that you are able to handle, the more confident you become in new challenges. This is a fact than can apply to anybody in life, but the difference with somebody with AS is the degree of uncertainty and the length of time that will take place until you begin to feel comfortable in the new situation and the number of mistakes you need to make before you realise how everything works around you. People with AS have a great amount of stressful observation going on during the period of adaptation, and fear and anxiety are difficult to control at times. They are not good at coping with sudden changes very well.

Once the routine of the situation is learnt, together with your own personal role in it compared to everyone else's, things start getting much easier. Basically, adults and children with AS have to become trained for each situation, but new skills can be developed within a specific environment, such as leadership and communication skills or teamwork, depending on where they find themselves within the spectrum.

The second level of social skills is more complex and is incredibly disconcerting. It is the ability to be able to emotionally relate to people and situations, and by this I mean to have the ability to interpret and infer people's intentions in what they do and say and at the same time also process the meaning of the sequence of events that are happening around them for given social situations.

If people with AS are able to master this second level, it will place them in situations in which they no longer have AS, if this is at all possible. Isabel manages to do this with a great deal of cognitive, analytical and rational thinking and observation, but it is incredibly difficult for someone with AS to consistently maintain this level of social awareness. There are things like external pressures, stress, tiredness, lack of concentration and internal hesitance that can make people feel uncertain in many social situations because they cannot work out what people really mean or because there is a delay in understanding. In my opinion, the "lack of empathy", as it is described in many books about Asperger's syndrome, would apply to a person with AS who is completely oblivious to her or his surroundings, with poor internal awareness too, which can be more common during childhood or in adult cases, such as the one portraying Roberto Grimaldi in this novel. From my point of view, empathy also has a spectrum. This spectrum is dynamic and with training people can also reach a maximum level within their own capacities.

Any awareness about a given situation or people's actions may have different meanings or intentions for somebody with AS. A person with AS can tune to the correct one straight away with maturity and experience, but sometimes uncertainty and a strong feeling of not knowing are what prevail. Isabel can empathise and sympathise with each of the different versions or possibilities when she becomes more grown up, but she may have great difficulty in being sure which one of the meanings is the one to follow. A child with AS can only see one absolute meaning, which in many occasions does not fit in with what was really going on; the feeling of being lost is terrible most of the time.

Being able to infer people's intentions is even more difficult when reading written messages with some degree of emotional content. The lack of speech, tone and corporal language associated with written passages can be incredibly painful when you are desperately trying to interpret what is written with no context around it from which to get some clues. This happens with e-mails and adults sometimes struggle when they are not written in a neutral way.

The way I see the ability to relate emotionally can be explained in the simple imaginary graph that I have created in my mind. It is as follows. The x axis line is time measured in days, and the y axis is ability to emotionally relate to people, which is measured in "ability to trust" (either people or situations). Adults and children with AS learn to move and be in secure zones that they have learnt about. They feel secure if they are far away from the two thresholds of "having to trust" or "no trust". In my opinion, the coming close to these two thresholds is what makes them become incredibly uncertain.

The top threshold of having to trust divides the comfort zone from an area of fully trusting people. Reading the cues of who and when to trust is difficult, and most of the time, they can be too naive, unable to recognise trusting situations and people and not being able to distinguish a situation of alertness from one that is not so much.

On the other hand, finding themselves close to the bottom threshold in which no trust should take place can be equally disconcerting. Again, it is easy to be naive and to trust when you should not, not realising people's rejection or danger fast enough. This is what I have tried to portray in this book.

Wanting to connect with people and situations will constantly put any person around these two thresholds. But for people with AS, it is more difficult to gain these skills. It can be incredibly hard to work them out, sometimes impossible. They will use observation, trial and error and educated guesses, always leaving a space for detecting their own mistakes as soon as they can. The emotional cost around these two thresholds can be enormous and there is always a need for extra time to make up their minds fully about what is really happening around them or to commit themselves to what they truly think about it. There is a deep feeling of not knowing.

Initially, when you are a child, the two threshold lines are close together and the comfort zone is restricted. The personality of the individual wanting to connect and the social skills acquired through life are what will define the expansion of the comfort zone. The better tuned AS people become in order to relate emotionally to people and situations, the wider the two lines will become.

From my point of view, fear is the core emotional trait lying in the background of the autistic spectrum and AS. It is fear that primarily triggers anxiety and repetitive behaviour. There are reasons for this fear due to a sustained and untreatable inability to connect, understand and work out situations and people. It is the not knowing, the inability to reach for their own feelings or to verbalise things and being unable to understand what is expected of them. It concerns not being able to work out a sequence of events or to predict people or situations, the inability to trust themselves around people or situations and the inability to distinguish between situations of alertness and situations where they can trust others. It is the inability to internally process quickly enough the meaning of what happens around them, the inability to understand what people mean or the inability to even be sure to answer yes or no correctly. The paralysing fear can fully control them and internally completely disorganise them to the extent that it becomes easier to disconnect from their surroundings. It can become difficult to find the words because the storm of feelings can tie them in knots.

All this is what triggers the unpredictable anxiety and the need to focus on particular things that become obsessions, which ultimately is just a deep need to find a routine and a structure. They can feel so internally charged up that their speech becomes overly fluent when they are fixating on this particular topic. The need to detail things comes from a deep need to structure thoughts and at the same time a desperate need to get in touch with feelings. Describing situations and objects in great detail is, in my opinion, the best way to try to let others see the emotional impact of a situation or the beauty, interest or attraction of something around the person. It is the only way to allow people to see one's feelings or the reason for his or her feelings, which are often difficult to articulate and impossible to accept or to process. Such people need somebody special around them to be able to see through all this.

The will to connect with surroundings depends on an individual's personality. People with little social skill may desperately try to connect and others with more social skill may not be interested at all. I suppose it depends on the degree of internal balance and ability to cope with the world.

The feeling of physical pressure can be useful for many people within the spectrum, although it can be a threatening experience for others. Fear and anxiety can emotionally overload them, triggering a multi-systemic response in the sympathetic nervous system, leaving individuals in a situation of being hyper-alert and vigilant but unable to fight or flee when they are feeling confined in a space with no way out. The psychological storm and emotional drainage are considerable and the physical tension in their own bodies can reach a quite formidable situation. Any sustained pressure for a long enough period to override the physical tension will help to release the excess of anxiety and sympathetic drive, even if it is only temporary. That moment of letting it go is incredibly healing and reassuring. This reminds me of Dr Temple Grandin's squeezing machine.

About the Author

Sofía Lake moved to the United Kingdom in her twenties and she works as a doctor. She is married and her eldest son has Asperger's traits. Sofía has been reading about this topic over the past few years and has been in contact with families with children with social issues. Learning in depth about Asperger's traits has made Sofía realise that she has been living in and around them all her life. Because of this, she was inspired to write this novel, taking the opportunity to reflect on the topic and giving her opinion about it in the epilogue.

Printed in the United States
By Bookmasters